LIFE

EXPECTANCY

14 DAYS

BY JENNIFER M. CARR

Copyright Jennifer M. Carr © 2011.

The right of Jennifer M Carr to be identified as author
of this work
has been asserted in accordance with sections 77 and
78 of the
Copyright, Designs and Patents Act, 1988.

All rights reserved

No reproduction, copy or transmission of this
publication may be made
without written permission.

No paragraph of this publication may be reproduced,
copied or transmitted without the written permission of
the author, or in accordance with the provisions of the
Copyright Act 1956 (as amended)

Any person who commits any unauthorised act in
relation to this publication may be liable to criminal
prosecution and civil claims for damages

This book is a work of fiction and any names,
characters, places and incidents originate
from the writer's imagination. Any resemblance to

any actual person, living or dead is purely coincidental

4

INTRODUCTION

The beginning of World War II in 1939 was a shock to the British nation, especially after the Prime Minister, Neville Chamberlain had returned from Munich months earlier, after speaking with Hitler, and had declared 'Peace in our Time' and waved the Munich Agreement around as if to confirm his statement.

However, when Hitler ordered his troops into Poland Britain along with other countries declared war on Germany. The whole country was put on a war footing and people were worried about what would happen to them. Children were sent away from big cities to rural towns, and men and women signed up to join the armed forces or the civilian services.

In September the British Expeditionary Force (BEF) were sent to France and were deployed mainly along the Belgian-French border. This period of time was named the Phoney War, because they were not fighting anyone, the Germans had not moved against France, so the BEF were mainly inactive. By Christmas it was generally thought by the British people that the war would soon be over because the general population had not been unduly affected. The government and the hierarchy in the military were the only people who knew exactly what was occurring in Europe.

In the New Year of 1940, provisions were made for a lengthy period of war. Rationing began with the introduction of ration books and the defence of the country was updated by creating the Local Defence Volunteers, later called the Home Guard. They were employed to guard the coastal areas of Britain and other important places such as airfields, factories and explosives stores.

The Germans invaded France on the 10th May 1940 and the British Expeditionary Force along with the French First and Seventh Armies were pushed back. On the 14th May the Germans burst through the Ardennes and advanced rapidly west towards Sedan in France, then they turned towards the English Channel which effectively flanked the Allied forces. The Allies failed to sever the German spearhead which reached the coast on the 20th May, separating the BEF near Armentieres and the French First Army and the Belgian Army, which were further north from most French troops south of the German penetration. After reaching the Channel, the Germans swung north along the coast threatening to capture the ports and trap the

British and French forces before they could be evacuated to Britain. Hitler then ordered his Generals to halt the army for three days. People questioned his decision, not to his face, but they wondered why he did this, because it gave the Allies' time to organise, evacuate and build a defensive line. This occurred at Dunkirk and between 24th May and the 4th June 1940; over 330,000 troops were evacuated from the beaches.

Hitler, realising that now was the time for the invasion of Britain, got his generals to formulate an invasion plan. They devised Operation Sealion, but their plans, along with what Hitler thought, decided that it would be impossible to invade unless the British Royal Air Force was dealt with. So, in summer of 1940 the bombing of key areas of England started. Coastal shipping convoys and shipping centres such as Portsmouth became the main targets. But a month later the Luftwaffe moved its attacks to the RAF airfields and their infrastructure. The Royal Air Force fought this battle with skill and bravery. They were triumphant as they never allowed the Luftwaffe to establish air supremacy. On the 14th September Hitler reviewed the possible invasion date of Britain on either the 27th September or the 8th October. A few days later Hitler decided to postpone Operation Sea Lion indefinitely.

This is all history and is fully documented, but what if it didn't happen like this. What would have happened if the Royal Air Force was defeated and the Royal Navy was kept out of the English Channel by the German U-Boats and destroyers and Hitler did not postpone Operation Sealion? What would have happened if they invaded Britain…

CHAPTER 1

"What the hell is this? What are we doing hanging around outside a Post Office in the middle of god knows where?" said a man who was standing outside a Post Office in Highworth near Swindon in Wiltshire. This man was dressed as a farm worker and he was with four other men, similarly dressed. They were all five Home Guard Auxiliary Officers. They had been given this address and told to make their way to it by a certain time, on a certain day and then told they had to wait. They stood out because they were loitering around the street, looking around and looking very lost, but ironically no one who passed them by, seemed to notice.

"Well these are the co-ordinates that we have been given. Perhaps we should ask in this Post Office, where this training place is?" one of the men asked.

"You go and speak to that old woman in there then," said the original man.

Two of the officers entered the Post office and spoke to a woman standing behind the counter.

"We have orders to come to this address…"

Before he could finish the woman said, in a very off handed way, "I suggest that you do as your orders say and wait... outside."

The men were taken aback by the way they were spoken to by this woman. They left the shop, and as they did the woman picked up the phone and called Coleshill House.

"Five parcels to be picked up," she said and put the phone down and ten minutes later a Bedford 15cwt truck appeared outside the Post office and the Officers were told to get in.

Matt Fletcher was one of these men. In October 1939 he had tried to enrol in the British army when Britain declared war on Germany. At the recruitment office his details were taken down and he attended a medical. He was then told to go away and wait to be informed where to report. Instead of the usual letter from the army to report at a training establishment, which all his friends and colleagues got, he received a letter telling him to continue with his job and they would be writing to him later with instructions. Matt was an agricultural engineer, which involved the science of agricultural, production and processing. It included animal biology, plant biology and mechanical engineering relating to agriculture, and he assumed, and feared, that the government may have made his job a reserved occupation. He had been working in Gloucestershire for the past year, but his family came from Amberley in West Sussex. He was a tall man, 29 years old and was extremely fit, mainly due to his job. He had fair hair and his face had a healthy glow to it, which was probably due to his work being mainly outside. He was very handsome, although he did not appear to know this. He had had a few girlfriends, but he had never met anyone who he thought he could live the rest of his life with, at least not yet. In February 1940, he received a letter telling him to go home to Sussex and start work on his family's farm. He was also informed that he should join the Local Defence Volunteers (the Home Guard) and he would be contacted once he had done this. He had to tell a department in the army of his new location when he had moved to Sussex, where he had re-located to and he had to, then, await his orders. He was also asked to sign the Official Secrets Act which was included in the papers and to return them. He did as he was ordered and began to work for the local council as well as for his family on their farm. He also did as he was instructed and volunteered to join the Home Guard in Amberley.

In May he followed the events of the evacuation of the British Expeditionary Forces from the beaches at Dunkirk and desperately wanted to be involved. He wondered why he was being asked to just sit around and the military were not allowing him to join up. A week after Dunkirk he was approached by a man calling himself Major Frank Taylor who told him that his name had been given to him as a good candidate to become a Home Guard Auxiliary. Matt did not know what an auxiliary did and wanted to know if he was going to fight. It was explained to him at length that since Dunkirk, it was expected that the Germans may invade, and Britain had to be prepared if this happened. Men like Matt, who could live off the land and who knew the countryside, were being sought so that they could fight behind enemy lines if they were invaded. Matt was speechless, he wanted to get involved, but this was full on, and he realised immediately that if he agreed to do this he would be in imminent danger. Matt reflected on what had been told to him and he knew that he had not been told everything, but that did not matter, he agreed to be an Auxiliary and asked when he was going to be trained. He was told that it would happen quickly and that as of now he was given the rank of Captain. That had happened a week earlier and now he was sitting in the back of the truck with four other men, who he could tell from their hands and their faces, all worked on the land.

He could also tell that they came from different parts of the country, because of their accents when they spoke.

The truck arrived at Coleshill House and they got out. They were all shown to individual rooms and told to report in the lounge in 15 minutes to get started. They only had 14 days training and the sooner they started the better. The training for Matt and the others was longer than the Non-Commissioned Officers, who only attended at the weekends. The Officers needed to be taught, not only how to be an Auxiliary, but also how to be officers as well. Coleshill House was a large 17th century house situated in large grounds and because of its isolation it was an ideal place for the Auxiliary units to be trained.

The course started with a lecture and then they all went outside for a practical. Over the next two weeks they were taught how to shoot, use knives, unarmed combat, use explosives, especially high explosives, and sabotage techniques. They had to learn how to use radios, which of course incorporated learning Morse code. Matt's biggest problem was remembering everything that he was taught. Nothing could be written down and the only reference to the course was a 42-page manual about sabotage, which contained information on detonators and explosives and how to combine them. This manual was disguised by having a title on the outside cover calling it 'The Countryman's Diary 1939'.

Apart from the essential elements of sabotage work they were also taught the value of teamwork and how each member of the team should know their role in the team. They were also taught how to avoid detection whilst on patrol and special attention was given to the art of moving silently, although Matt thought that this was obvious if you did not want to be detected.

These Auxiliaries would have to hide in specially built dugouts and bunkers and they had guidelines that told them how they should behave in these areas. One example of this was that smoking would only be allowed for 10 minutes in every hour. The guidelines were common sense and common decency. At the end of the course they had a special lecture about what would happen in case of injury and it also covered the fact that the life expectancy of an Auxiliary was only 14 days. Apart from anything else the food in the hide outs would run out after 14 days, so the men would have to leave the bunkers to get their rations restocked and hence their cause for concern. They were also told that unlike Agents who would be working in France and Germany behind enemy lines who would be given lethal pills, the Auxiliaries would not have them. To cover this, they were told that if it was necessary to kill themselves, they could inject themselves with an overdose of morphine out of their first aid kit. That would do the trick just as well, if, of course, they could get to it in time.

Matt enjoyed the course, although he found it was extremely intensive and he soon realised what Major Taylor forgot to tell him. This assignment which involved being behind enemy lines, was a suicide mission. It was drummed into Matt and the other men that the likelihood of the Germans invading was remote. The navy and the air force would keep them at bay and if they did attempt an invasion, then the army would prevent them from getting a foothold on English land. Matt hoped this was the case and asked one of the lecturers what would happen to the Auxiliaries once it was established that the Germans would not invade. He was told that they would either return to farming, as it was a reserved occupation, or they would be drafted into another unit in the army. This would be decided nearer the time.

In the last couple of days of the course they had to plan and execute a mission. All five men were given a target and a mission that they would have to execute, using the other four Officers. They needed to pass this before they could leave as qualified Auxiliary Officers. Matt's target was a hut in a local wood which hypothetically had a radio belonging to the Germans. He was told that this building was guarded, and the guards would have to be disposed of, and the radio and the code books needed to be retrieved intact. This building needed to be destroyed, because they did not want the Germans to know that they had the code books and the radio.

Matt studied the map of the huts location and he could see that there wasn't a path at the rear of it. It was situated in shrub land and it was ideal for concealment. He wanted to approach it from that direction, which meant that they would have to crawl through the shrubbery to get to it. He arranged for one of the men to deal with the explosives which he had prepared, using a timer detonator. They left the main house at 0100 hours and they arrived by foot at the rear of the hut in the wood at 0230 hours. The reconnaissance at the front of the building revealed that there were two guards on the outside and there was one man inside the hut. Matt and one other Officer dealt with the two guards at the front. They did not hurt them, just tied them up and placed them in the vegetation about 200 yards from the hut. At this distance they would be safe when they blew up the hut. He then knocked on the door of the hut and hid waiting for the third man to come out. This man left the hut looking for the guards and as he turned the corner of the hut, he was grabbed and tied up and placed with the other two guards. Matt entered, leaving lookouts to ensure that there weren't other guards in the vicinity. He managed to remove the radio and the code books, and the explosives were set to explode in 5 minutes which allowed them time to get away from the hut before it blew up. Matt and his men were about quarter of a mile away when the hut exploded. They returned to Coleshill House and handed the radio and code books to his instructor. Matt had passed the final test. The other Officers had other objectives, such as a bridge to blow up, a truck to be hijacked, a kidnapped person to be retrieved and a German to be kidnapped. All the Officers did well on the final test and they all passed the course.

After the course they were told to return to their civilian lives. They would be contacted by someone in charge of the Auxiliaries in their individual areas. Matt did as he was instructed and was approached two days later by Major

Taylor who told him to report to Tottington Manor in Edburton at 10am the following day.

Matt walked down the driveway to the 16th Century farm house called Tottington Manor. It was nestled in the South Downs just outside a small hamlet called Edburton and the views of the Downs were spectacular. Matt could see a herd of cows grazing calmly on the hills and in the distance, he could see the high rolling fields which gave him the feeling of calmness. As he stood there looking at the view, he suddenly heard the noise of aircraft in the distance. The cows, unsure of where the noise was coming from, started to look up and then moved together as if being grouped together would protect them. Matt looked up and saw two planes flying low over the hill and then they disappeared. The noise lingered for a few minutes and then stopped. He saw the cows continue with their previous pastime of grazing and they moved away from each other which seemed to indicate that their perceived danger was over. Matt turned and continued down the driveway and knocked at the door. After a couple of minutes, the door was opened by an elderly woman.

"Major Taylor told me to report here. I'm Captain Fletcher," Matt said.

"Yes Captain, come in," the woman said

"Thank you."

"They are waiting for you in there," indicating a door on the right. "Would you like some coffee?"

"Yes please," Matt said opening the door she had indicated. He found himself in a beautiful lounge. The furniture and décor of the room was stunning. There were many antique pieces of furniture, the curtains were luxurious and fabulously made and there was a very comfortable looking Chesterfield three-piece suite. Sitting in one of the Chesterfield arm chairs was Major Taylor and sitting on the settee was a very distinguished looking man.

"Hello Matt, you found it then, and on time," said Major Taylor. "Let me introduce you to Colonel Armstrong."

"Hello Sir," Matt said.

"Glad you could make it. I have heard some good things about you Captain. How was your time at Coleshill?" Colonel Armstrong asked.

"Good Sir, learnt a lot up there," Matt replied.

"Yes, well let's hope that you won't have to put it into practice, leastways not here in the UK," Colonel Armstrong said.

The woman, who had let Matt in, entered the room with a tray of coffee for everyone. She put the tray on the table and she handed cups round. She then took a cup for herself and she sat on the settee next to the Colonel.

"Let me introduce you to our host, Mrs Mavis Johns. She is the reason for us being here today," said the Colonel.

Matt smiled at Mrs Johns and she smiled back.

"Let me explain, we needed a base for our operations in the South and after looking around we approached Mrs Johns and she agreed that we could use her house and her land, so we have made it the Auxiliary's regional headquarters for Sussex. She has also been privy to everything that we have done and are going to do, so she is an integral part of the Auxiliary Unit. In other words, you can talk freely in front of her. Now we are going to have the coffee and then you, Major Taylor and I are going for a walk," Colonel Armstrong said.

Matt looked puzzled about the walk, but Major Taylor said, "It will all become clear later."

During the coffee they talked about the training course and who would be in Matt's unit. They told him that they had several trained men and he would be meeting them within the next couple of days, but he needed to choose who he wanted. He would need five men, 1 Sergeant, 1 Corporal and 3 Privates. One of his men needed to be an expert in communications and one an expert in weaponry. At the end of that day he would be given some personnel files and he would have to go through them and decide who he wanted to see to assess whether they would be suitable for the team.

When the coffee was finished, Major Taylor, Colonel Armstrong and Matt left the house, leaving Mrs Johns clearing the cups away. They headed a mile down the road towards Edburton. They turned left off the road onto a dirt track that ran up the side of a large field. When they got to the end of this field they turned left again and walked for about another mile. In front of them was a wooded area which they entered. It was July and a very warm day, but when they entered the wood Matt felt chilly. The sun had made them all sweaty but upon entering the wood they lost the direct heat from the sun. They walked for about

200 yards and they stopped. Matt was uncertain what was happening, but he knew that he would be told.

Major Taylor said, "Can you see anything strange about this place Captain?"

Matt looked around, but initially failed to see what the Major and the Colonel were obviously looking at. He was just about to say that it looked normal when he noticed a notch in a tree. He looked up the tree trunk towards the branches but saw nothing, then he looked at the bottom of the trunk and could see that the foliage was not from that tree or the surrounding area. He bent down, and he picked up some leaves and earth that was on the ground and he turned them over in his hands, moved forward a couple of steps and picked up some more undergrowth, which he looked at.

He then stood up, dropped what was in his hands and turned to the other two men and said, "This is wrong. It shouldn't be here. There isn't plant life here that resembles that. (Indicating the undergrowth where he was standing). Also, the notch in the tree is odd. Can't put my finger on it but I would say that it was man made and was made recently."

"Very good Captain. This is something that we shall have to put right in the future. I did not know that the plant life and foliage could be in wrong places; still I have learnt something today. The notch as you say was man made and it indicates that we are close," Colonel Armstrong stated.

"Close to what, Sir?" asked Matt.

CHAPTER 2

"Major, if you will," Colonel Armstrong said.

"Certainly Sir," the Major replied.

Major Taylor stood with his back to the tree facing north (the way the notch was facing) and took 3 paces. He then bent down and felt around on the floor. Suddenly he pulled on something and the ground opened to expose a shaft with a steel ladder attached to the side.

"Good Lord" said Matt looking down into the shaft. It was very dark down the shaft, and he was uncertain how far it went down.

"How far down does it go?" he asked.

"About 12 to 15 feet. Major will you go first," the Colonel asked.

Major Taylor sat down on the side of the shaft and putting his feet onto the rung of the ladder started to make his way down it. Matt followed him, and the Colonel followed Matt. The Colonel closed the entrance hatch and Matt found himself in pitch darkness. He felt his way on the ladder aware that if he was too quick he would tread on the Major but if he was too slow then the Colonel would tread on him. As he arrived at the bottom the Major had lit a torch and he could see that he was in a small room. Once the Colonel arrived the Major opened a concealed panel and he flicked a switch which lit up the whole area. He then turned off the torch, which he returned to the place the major had obtained it from.

He turned to Matt and said, "This is one of the hideouts that the training course talked about. There are a number of these built in the area and if the Germans invade, then they could become your home for a while. They are being built by the Royal Engineers, who will continue to do so until as such time as the Germans come or the invasion is no longer a threat. They are being built all over England, but they are concentrating on Southern England. You and your unit will be only told of ones in your immediate area and only you will know about this place, for security, just in case any of your team is captured. Come on we'll show you the rest of it."

Major Taylor led the way through a door. This led into a very small room which did not appear to have an exit. There was a shelving unit against the wall to the left containing some rusty equipment and looked like an abandoned mine entrance. He reached behind some old lamps and he pulled something, and Matt heard a click. "Help me Captain."

The Major and Matt moved the shelving unit to one side and Matt could see the main bunker accommodation. They entered, and the Colonel turned around and pulled the shelving unit back in place hearing another clicking noise. They were in a domed room. The walls and ceiling were of a continuous sheet of corrugated steel and along the sides were 6 bunks, 3 on each side. At the end of the room was a door but before it, there were 4 wooden armchairs. Matt, initially wondered how on earth they managed to get these chairs down here, but upon examining them, he realised that they were probably made in the bunker. Also, in the area where the chairs were, there were two tables against the wall on either side of the room.

"That table will be for the radio, which is the only equipment that has not been placed in here yet," said the Colonel.

The other table had chairs round it and Matt assumed that they would eat at it. They went through the door into another area, which was very small. Here there was a sink, a stove and a couple of cupboards. The Colonel opened the cupboards and Matt could see that they were crammed full of tins of food.

"Enough food to keep 6 people catered for 14 days," said the Colonel.

"After that time, food will have to be got from outside," said the Major. "There is a water supply coming in so there shouldn't be any shortage of water, but just in case the supply gets cut off, there is a supply of bottled water in there as well."

One of the cupboards also contained equipment such as hurricane lamps, in case the lighting failed, binoculars, shovels and first aid kits.

A door led to a bathroom, a toilet and another sink to wash in, and next to that was another door which led to the armoury. Matt could see that it was already stocked with weapons, explosives, grenades, detonators. In there was gasoline, more first aid kits, ammunition and many other things that Matt knew would be in there but could not see them.

Matt was speechless. He looked around in wonder and when he turned to the Major and the Colonel he managed to say, "Brilliant, absolutely bloody brilliant," and everyone started to laugh.

"It is, isn't it," the Colonel said.

They talked for a while about the logistical workings of such a place and it was agreed that they would only have to stay within the hideouts until the Germans passed over them and then the Auxiliaries would leave the bunker to get intelligence and do their sabotage work, only returning at night to sleep. The longest that they would have to stay concealed in there would be for about 14 days. The bunker was not very big, and one concern Matt had regarded 6 men living in such a small confined space. This was something that the Colonel and the Major were unable to answer except to say that this is why you must get the correct personnel. They will have to get on very well.

Major Taylor said, "Is there any equipment that you would add to what we have in here?"

"Yes. There is something that I believe would be of use. There will be a radio so that we can contact the outside world, but what about a wireless? It would be good to hear the World Service and know that there is still hope, even if it appears hopeless," Matt said.

"That's something we thought about, but we were uncertain if it was necessary. I think that as you have mentioned it, it should be something that we must include. We can incorporate the aerial in with the radio one. What do you think sir?" Major Taylor asked Colonel Armstrong.

After a minute Colonel Armstrong said thoughtfully, "I agree, I think there should be a wireless, just in case the radio packs up or the whole country gets taken, God forbid. I will make sure that all the bunkers are equipped with one. Any other comments Matt?"

"Yes, I presume that the toilets have some sort of sewer connected to it," he asked.

"No," said the Colonel. "They are chemical toilets."

"Good," said Matt, "And what about the cooking? Where does the smoke go?"

"Good question. If you look at the ceiling, you can see a hole, well that is a form of chimney and it has a special filter on it, so no smells permeate outside," the Major said.

Matt thought for a minute and then said, "Is there an emergency exit just in case it is discovered or there is a cave in?"

"Oh yes, come on we will show you," said the Major.

Matt was led past the armoury down through a door into a tunnel. To begin with they could walk up right, but after about a quarter of a mile it became a lot lower, about 4 feet in diameter, forcing everyone to crouch down. They continued until they reached a very small area where they were able to stand upright again, but there appeared to be no exit. Major Taylor picked up a piece of wood which had a hook on the end, reached up with it and pulled a hook that was in the ceiling. A hatch opened, and Major Taylor reached up again with his piece of wood and pulled down a ladder. It was like a ladder that could be used to gain access into attics. Major Taylor then went over to a control panel, picked up a torch and handed it to the Colonel, who turned it on. Major Taylor pulled the switch down and the whole place was thrown into darkness. With the aid of the torch they went up the ladder and at the top Major Taylor opened another hatch and pulled himself into what looked like a cellar of a house. There was food stored in there and a lot of kitchen equipment. Once Matt and the Colonel reached the cellar the hatch was closed, and they went up to a door. The Major knocked three times. It was opened by Mrs Johns and they were led through the kitchen area of her house and into a dining area, where Mrs Johns announced that lunch was ready.

CHAPTER 3

After lunch Matt and Major Taylor went into a room set up as an office and they went through quite a few personnel files. They needed to decide who they wanted for Matt's team. They picked out four definite people, but they could not make their mind up about four others. Matt was going to meet all the people that they had picked out and then decide afterwards who he thought would be suitable. Major Taylor would arrange for them to be at the hall where the Horsham Home Guard met, two days later.

The following day Major Taylor met up with Matt to show him some of the other bunkers that were finished in the area. They met up at the Red Lion Public House on the outskirts of Shoreham-by-Sea at midday and after a pint of beer each, they left and made their way along the A283, Shoreham Road, which is a road that runs between Shoreham-by-Sea and Steyning alongside the Adur River. Major Taylor was driving, and he pulled off the road into a lay-by half way along. They got out and on foot made their way towards a farm called South Downs Farm. Before they got to the farm they veered off north-east along a path towards a wooded area. Once inside the wood Matt looked at the trees trying to see if anything was out of order. He could see that some of the trees had recent marks made on them which he assumed may have been made by the Royal Engineers bringing in equipment to create the bunkers. He looked at the plant life and he looked at the foliage that was on the floor. About 100 yards into the wood Matt stopped and he looked at Major Taylor.

"Here is the place you were looking for," Matt said.

"My god Matt, you are right," Major Taylor replied.

"Yes, the foliage is all wrong; something will have to be done about that. And there are marks on all the trees coming to this place but look over there," indicating a tree about 3 yards from them. "There are no marks at all on that one, so it has to be around here."

"We will have to sort out the foliage and as far as the trees are concerned, I really don't know what we can do about them," Major Taylor said.

"I will think about it, but I think after a couple of months the marks will disappear. I will monitor it," Matt said.

"Yes, you make a wonderful tracker, come on let's get on with this."

Major Taylor stood with this back to a tree with, what Matt thought, was an identical notch that was on the tree in Tottington wood, and he took 4 steps and reached down and pulled on something.

"How come you took 3 steps at Tottington Wood and yet here you took 4 steps," asked Matt.

"Look at the notch Matt," Major Taylor said.

Matt saw that the notch had 4 tiny groove marks.

"Well I never, I didn't have a close look at the one in Tottington Wood. I'll assume that it had 3 tiny grooves," Matt admitted.

"Yes, so if you are given the location of other bunkers, which you will be, you will know exactly where they are from the grooves in the notches and the direction is the way the notches are facing," Major Taylor said.

Matt and Major Taylor entered a bunker that had a similar layout as the one in Tottington Wood and it was kitted out with all the same equipment, (apart from the radio and wireless). Matt was also shown the emergency exit which came up about half a mile away in a small barn on the farm. This was to be the main bunker for Matt and his unit.

That afternoon Major Taylor showed Matt two other bunkers. One was in Coombehead Wood with the emergency exit in Annington Hill Barn. Coombehead Wood is situated on the west of the River Adur and it is nestled in the Downs, whereas Tottington Wood and South Downs Farm are on the East side and the bunker on South Downs Farm is only about 200 yards from the road. The last bunker was close to houses. It was situated in Lancing Ring and the emergency exit came up in a cellar in one of the houses nearby. This bunker would be used as a last resort due to the closeness of the houses.

All the bunkers were kitted out the same and the last two were backup bunkers in case the one on South Downs Farm was discovered.

The following day Matt met up with Major Taylor and he met his potential team at the Local Defence Volunteers hall in Horsham. When he walked in the hall there were eight men lounging around on chairs, but once they saw that the two men entering were Officers they all got up and stood to attention.

"At ease," Major Taylor said. "We need to speak to you all individually and then you will be asked to either stay or leave."

Each man was then asked to come into a side room, set aside for this purpose, and Matt spoke to each one. Three of the four that he had chosen in the paper sift were selected and they were asked to remain but the fourth one was completely unsuitable. He was a loud, arrogant man who was full of his own importance and Matt realised very quickly into the interview that he would never get on with him. He now had to find two others. The other four were interviewed and it was agreed that two would be suitable. Now he had his five men. One of the men had worked in a quarry in Somerset for a year and was really experienced with explosives. Another man had worked at the Royal Small Arms Factory in Enfield for a couple of years before re-joining his parent's farm and then becoming a game keeper on a local estate. He was a real bonus with the kind of knowledge that he had. Finally, one of the men had worked at Marconi when he left school. He had always been interested in radios and electronics but as he came from the country he found it difficult to settle in a town so returned to his roots. But he never lost his interest and apparently had a shed at his home where he tinkered with radios when he wasn't working.

Matt had his communications expert and he had two that had expertise with weaponry and explosives. The others were told to leave, and Major Taylor told them that they would be contacted soon about their assignments. The men chosen were Sid Carpenter, who was a Sergeant, Jack Wilson, who was a Corporal and he had the expertise in firearms, Doug Harris, who was a private and the communications officer, Jake Jolly who was a private, whose expertise was in explosives, and finally Harry Smith who was a private. Once the others had left, Matt then spoke to them explaining that they had been chosen to become a member of his team and that a full briefing of what exactly was required of them would be held the following day. They were going to meet in the Red Lion pub on the outskirts of Shoreham and they would be taken to and shown the bunker where they would be based in South Downs Farm and they would be fully briefed there.

They met up daily and Matt soon realised that he had a good team. They used first names unless another officer was present. Sid was 34 years old, he was the oldest and he was a calming influence on the others. He was able to assert his authority without the men realising that he was doing so. He looked after the others and was respected by everyone. Sid was a farmer before the war. He worked as a farm hand in the Horsham area. He was single although he did tell the others that there was someone special, but she died 5 years ago. He did not go into details, but it was enough for the other men to realise that there was a sadness surrounding him about the incident, but he seemed to be compassionate. Jack was a handsome man and he was 25 years old. From what he said, he had many girlfriends and was knowledgeable about how to get a date and what to do on a date. He was passionate about firearms and he could break down any of the guns in the armoury clean them and put them together without taking a breath. Before the war he had been a gamekeeper. He was a likeable man and the others seemed to like his chatter about his experiences with women. Doug was a serious man who was keen to better himself. He had also been a farm hand after spending a couple of years working for Marconi, but he liked to read and was a quiet, gentle man. He was 26 years old and he handled the radio as if he had been doing it all his life. Jake was the comedian of the group. His surname, Jolly, was very appropriate for him. He was 6'2" tall, but he was very muscular and probably could break a man's neck very easily. He had been a woodcutter in Hampshire before the war and he found it very difficult to sit down quietly and do nothing. Matt realised that he would be the one who would have the most difficulty sitting it out in a bunker for any length of time. He was however very knowledgeable about explosives and their affect from his time working in a quarry. He seemed to know instinctively which the best ones would be to use and how to use them for the appropriate result. Harry was the youngest. He was 22 years old, he had a baby face and looked about 16 years old. He had worked on his father's farm just outside Chichester before the war. He was shy to begin with but after a while he joined in the banter and got on well with everyone. Sid took him under his wing and guided him in the right direction and this made Harry feel part of the team.

After the initial period they all became happy with everyone's company. Matt started by giving out jobs that needed to be done. Apart from setting up a radio and wireless that had been delivered, someone had to itemise the food that was in the store, someone had to check and put in order the armoury, and someone had to sort out the foliage around the entrance. Matt wanted all the foliage gathered up and moved to another area in the wood. More foliage had to be gathered up that was in keeping with the wood and it needed to be spread around the entrance. Matt also wanted the carcasses of some dead animals, put around the entrance. They were to be placed in a diameter of 20 feet from the entrance so that if dogs were used by the Germans they would be distracted by the animal scent and not follow the human scent. Matt arranged with the men that when, or if, the call came for them to go to the bunker they were to bring as much fresh food as they could. This was a problem because of the rationing, but because they all had contacts with farms and farmers they would all try to do this. Matt wanted milk, butter, cheese, bread, meat, vegetables and fruit. Although it wouldn't last long they would, at least, have some fresh food at the beginning.

Matt also wanted an early warning alarm placed on the hatch. If anyone entered the hatch, the people in the bunker would be prepared for them, so Matt devised an alarm placed on the hatch and when someone entered, without deactivating it, a bell would ring in the hideout. The team all knew about the alarm and were able to prevent it going off, but anyone else would set it off. A final thing

Matt did was lay explosives in the bunker with the detonator to it in the escape tunnel, so that if the bunker was discovered they could destroy the bunker, hopefully with the Germans inside. When Major Taylor attended the bunker, Matt showed him what he had done, and he thought they were excellent ideas, especially the alarm and the explosives to destroy it that he suggested that all the bunkers should incorporate this system.

It was now the middle of August and the Battle of Britain had been raging for over a month in the skies above Britain. The news was bad as it was becoming apparent that the Royal Air Force was not winning. The Germans were destroying many allied planes and were hitting the airfields with impunity. Apart from causing serious damage to the aircraft at these airfields, they were also causing injury and fatalities to many ground staff. It was becoming very serious. The Germans were also bombing cities, and civilians were getting hurt and killed.

The government were concerned, and it was now clear that if an invasion occurred then the government should be moved north. The King and Queen had already moved Princess's

Elizabeth and Margaret to Scotland and would be joining them if the Germans set foot on British soil.

Plans had been made in case of an invasion and over the previous 2 months certain things had been put in place. Because of the evacuation at Dunkirk there were many troops with no unit or base, so these were assigned to the newly formed Home Guard and its numbers were boosted by 1.5 million men and they were involved with the anti-invasion preparations. Such things like pill boxes, whether permanent or mobile were built on beaches and airfields, anti-tank barriers were put up on roads and places where they would hold up a German advance. Beaches were blocked with barbed wire. Mine fields were also put in place on and just behind the beaches and these consisted of anti-tank and anti-personnel mines. Other anti-invasion preparations included flooding part of Romney Marsh, as it was believed that this would be the area that part of the German invasion would take place. There were many other things that needed to be done, but because of the German air attacks they were becoming impossible to implement. The navy were trying to keep their ships within the English Channel, but the German Air Force were bombing them relentlessly and this forced the shipping away from the southern coast of England. Ports such as Portsmouth, Dover, Sheerness (on the Thames) and Harwich were targeted, and the ships that were in the ports were forced out to sea to prevent them being damaged or destroyed when the Ports were bombed. In turn they were then being forced out of the channel by German U-boats and destroyers. Although the British Home Fleet could match anything that the German navy could put out to sea, they were plagued by the German air force together with their navy, especially from the U-Boats.

By the end of August, it became apparent that Britain was losing the fight. The government started to move up north where they took over Dunham Massey Hall which is on the outskirts of Manchester. The Royal Family had taken up residence with the Princesses at Balmoral Castle, their Scottish home, which is situated in Aberdeenshire. Both the Government and the Royal Family had planned to go to Canada if the country was invaded and if the invaders got too near to their positions. The army, which had been combined with units of the Home Guard, were moved south and took up positions on or near beaches where they suspected the invasion would occur.

Matt and his team were following the news and would often walk down to the coast either individually or as a group and they would just look out towards the French coast and wonder if the Germans would come. They became aware of the increase in uniformed men in the area and they saw the huge tented cities growing up in the area, which housed the British troops. The government were sending out guidelines to civilians about what they should do if there was an invasion. Apart from the common sense ones about not helping them with information, and being able to identify German uniforms, they were told to stay put and to take shelter in any underground area where they could. The refugees in Europe had hindered the army by trying to move to other areas which caused more deaths than necessary, both to the civilians and the military. Although this was sent out, and the government wanted these guidelines to be adhered to, it was obvious that many families in southern England were sending their women folk and children away. They were going either to Northern England, Scotland or Wales. Although some men also left the area the majority stayed, because that is where their jobs and homes were, and they were still hoping that the invasion would not come.

CHAPTER 4

On 15th September 1940, Major Taylor came to the bunker to meet with Matt. He had some very disturbing news. Reports had come in that German troops were massing in Calais, Boulogne, Dunkirk and Le Havre in France and Ostend in Belgium, and ships were being loaded with equipment, such as tanks along with manpower, which indicated that the invasion was imminent. There had already been an increase in aerial bombardments of the airbases in England and the southern coastal towns from Portsmouth to Dover. The Germans were also targeting the radar stations and had wiped out many of them. The army were sending more personnel to the South Coast as they, as well as Major Taylor, believed the invasion would take place within the next few days. Matt briefed his men with this news and the bunker became a hive of activity. There was a lot of coming and going and each day they had to report to the bunker at 10am to be updated with news. The men also started to bring down fresh food and some extras, like some bottles of beer, a bottle of scotch and brandy, cigarettes and magazines to read. They were also told to bring clothes that would not look out of place on farmers or land workers. They were to have good quality footwear, not army issue, and warm clothing, because they were unsure how long it would take to drive out the German forces, and winter was close.

Two days later the news got even worse. At 0200hours on the 17th September German ships were reported to be leaving the French coast and were heading for England. Around 0600 hours the artillery bombardment from the ships started. The bombardment was from Ramsgate in the east to Portsmouth in the West. This continued for nearly 2 hours. Then German aircraft were seen over Dover and Brighton dropping German Paratroopers and the German ships started to load troops into barges which then headed for the beaches of England.

Matt and his team were ordered to go to their underground bunker and wait. They had a few radio messages from their HQ stating that once the Germans had got a foothold in England, they were to take up permanent residence in the bunker. They could hear the bombardment from the ships and a couple of times the bunker shook quite badly. The team all sat there looking up at the ceiling of the bunker praying that it would hold. The German 16th Army landed on Camber Sands,

Rye, and Winchelsea Beach aiming to head inland towards Hawkhurst and they were to meet up with the paratroopers that had been dropped in the Dover area. They also landed in Bexhill and Pevensey aiming to head inland towards Uckfield. The German 9th Army landed at Cuckmere Haven hoping to follow the River Cuckmere past Alfriston and then on to Ringmer. They also landed on Brighton Beach, where they would meet with the paratroopers and head towards Burgess Hill, and they landed at Shoreham-by-Sea and Lancing Beach where they wanted to follow the River Adur to Horsham and then onto Crawley. Their ultimate aim was to take London. The 6th Army landed at Portsmouth. Their aim was to take over the shipyards. They then planned to head north and north east to meet up with the 9th Army.

The initial landings were hampered by the British Army and the defences that had been put in place, and the Germans were even forced back into the sea at Pevensey and in Brighton, but reinforcements from the ships were sent and they managed to get a foothold in those areas. Matt was now ordered to stay in the bunker and would be informed when they should leave. There was fierce fighting around Dover, Shoreham-by-Sea and in Portsmouth, because these areas had port facilities that the Germans needed, but the Germans managed to force their way inland making the British Forces retreat. The British had stop lines where they could retreat to and one of them was 5 miles from the coast, which was about a mile north of the area of Matt's bunker. Here there was some of the fiercest fighting of the campaign. The Germans and British fought for 5 days at this point and on the 3rd day it seemed that the British were near to forcing the Germans back, but the German air force was bought up and with their help the British suffered great losses. On the 5th day the British were forced to retreat. Matt and his team could hear sounds of the battle that was taking place and there were times when they were very concerned because the artillery was badly shaking the bunker, and they were scared that they may have a cave in. Everyone seemed to be coping well with the confinement except Jake who started to pace around the bunker and looked to the ceiling more times than the others did. Matt knew that it may become an issue but decided to wait and see if Jake could work through it. He made him arrange the meals whilst the bombing was bad, hoping that it would keep his mind off what was happening above them. This appeared to calm him a little and whilst he was working he didn't seemed to be so bothered by the small area that they were ensconced in.

The Germans moved North, and everything quieten down in the bunker. They got into a routine and tried to keep busy, especially Jake. He would occasionally pace the bunker and when this happened, the other men recognise his anxiety and got him to do something. It could be cleaning the kitchen area or doing some exercises with him or even making him check through the armoury or the food store, anything to get his mind off the situation. The radio check was the highlight of the day. It was a chance for the team to find out exactly what was going on with the German advance. The wireless was a little reserved and although they covered the general situation, for obvious reasons, nothing was in detail.

They were aware that the Germans had passed over them as the noise from the battle had ceased. They had been in the bunker over a week but occasionally they still heard noise from above. It seemed to be artillery fire. They waited and listened to the radio and wireless. They were informed that the Germans had been forced back at one point, but they were now advancing towards the next stop line that the British were defending. This stop line was just south of London and if the British were forced to retreat from there they would lose London. It had taken the Germans just over 14 days to get to this point.

Matt and his team stayed in the bunker over 2 weeks. At the end they were becoming desperate. The food was very low, and they were all becoming a little irritable, bearing in mind that the men were all used to working outside. They had to start rationing themselves, but eventually they were forced to radio their HQ and tell them that they were going out to have a look around and to see if they could get some more food. They decided that Jake and Sid would leave first to assess the situation.

On the morning of the 6th October, Jake and Sid mounted the ladder to the hatch. Sid went first, and he tentatively lifted the hatch and looked out. He was surprised that everything around the hatch looked as it had been when they first went down to the bunker. Sid went out first and Jake followed. They closed the hatch and they moved through the wood. They came to the track that led down to the Shoreham Road. Now they could see signs of the battle everywhere. They could see that the railway line from Shoreham to Steyning had been destroyed, possibly by the British when they retreated. The trees in the wood were damaged and there were large craters where bombs had exploded. There were massive craters in the fields of South Downs Farm and one of the barns was no longer there. The Farm itself, however, looked intact. They walked towards the farm and they could see there was some activity. They were uncertain if the people they saw were Germans or farm workers from where they were positioned, so they kept themselves hidden. They edged their way towards the farm buildings using the cover of hedges and when they got closer, to their relief, they saw that the people were farm workers. The owner of the farm was aware that before the invasion, the military were using the wood, but he was not told what for. Sid and Jake were hoping that he would be able to update them with information about what the Germans were doing in the immediate area. Sid and Jake had made it to the outbuildings and they could see that they had been damaged badly. They knew who the owner was as they had seen him before the invasion, but only by sight, so they carefully looked at the men and they saw him. He was busy trying to get some equipment out of one of the barns that had been damaged and they could hear him swearing about the Germans. Sid came out of his hiding place and went up to the man as he was struggling with the machine.

"Mr Bolt, can I give you a hand?" Sid asked.

"Yes you bloody well can, here grab hold of that piece of wood and pull," Mr Bolt replied.

Sid grabbed hold of the wood and did as he was told. The wood became free and that enabled the machine to be pulled out. It was in a bad condition. Jake now appeared and with his muscles they were able to pull out the remainder of the equipment that was lodged under the debris of the barn. When they had all the equipment out Mr Bolt sat on a hay bale. He was exhausted and sweating profusely. He then looked at Sid and Jake.

"Where the hell did you come from?" he asked.

Sid looked at Jake and they nodded at each other.

Sid then said, "The wood!"

"Oh, you mean you were there during the fighting, bloody hell," Mr Bolt exclaimed.

"We were safe. We need information, can you help?" Sid asked.

"What do you want to know?" Mr Bolt asked.

Before Sid could ask, some of the farm workers came over to them, but Mr Bolt shouted at them to 'bugger off and get on with their work' and they all left them.

"Now where was I, yes, there are about 300 Germans in Shoreham town and they have taken over the port, so they are able to bring their ships in and unload equipment and troops. They are using the Shoreham Road through to both the A24 and A23 as a route for equipment coming in from the port. I believe that this equipment is for the Germans fighting the British," Mr Bolt told them.

"Were many British taken prisoners?" Sid asked.

"Good God yes and injured. They are using Shoreham Airport as a holding area for them. There are hundreds of them, and they have set up a make shift hospital there for the injured. The whole of the area has been turned into a prisoner of war camp, there is barbed wire everywhere. I think that they are thinking about moving them back to Germany, but that may be a rumour. There are plenty of them about," Mr Bolt stated.

"Do you get visited by the Germans here?" Sid asked.

"Yes, we have patrols through here regularly. They have told us to get on with farming and once they have established themselves they will come around to see us and tell us what they will want from us, not that I am going to make it bloody easy for them," Mr Bolt said.

"Thanks for that. Mr Bolt I was wondering if you had any food that we could have. We are very short," Sid asked.

"I have some that you can have. The Krauts came around looking for food and they took quite a bit, but they did not find my storage area. I will set up some traps and I will snare some rabbits for you, but in the mean time I will give you some of mine in the store. I also have a good stock of vegetables. How many are there of you?" he asked.

"Can't tell you that, you know it could put you in danger if you knew that, but we would be very grateful for anything you can give us, and we will be round for the rabbits later in the week. Also, we don't have to tell you that you haven't seen us, and you don't know anything about us, do you?" Sid said.

"Of course not, and I will keep my ears and eyes open and if there is any information or news I will let you know, when you come by to pick up the rabbits," Mr Bolt said..

"Thanks so much Mr Bolt…," Sid said, but Mr Bolt interrupted.

"Call me Bill. If you wait here I will get you the food."

Bill left, and the Sid and Jake sat down on the hay bale chatting about what Bill had just told them. Bill came back 10 minutes later with a hessian sack full of food. Sid and Jake thanked him again and left.

Before the invasion, HQ had arranged for dead letter drops, where certain people, who the team did not know, could leave messages that were either too long or to contentious to be delivered over the radio. The radio could be traced when the Germans got better organised, using detector vans, so it was essential that they only used them for short periods of time. These dead letter drops or drop points were near the bunker so whilst Jake took the food back to the bunker, Sid went to a couple of the drops to see if there was anything left. There was only one message which he hid in his boot and then made his way back to the bunker. During their time out of the bunker, they never saw a German.

When Sid arrived back, food was already being cooked in the kitchen and the smell was welcoming. He sat at the table and gave the message to Matt. It was coded, and Matt sat there decoding it. It was a long document and it read:

German equipment, including arms are coming in from the continent daily. They are using the Shoreham Road in your area. The trucks conveying them need to be stopped but need more up to date information before that can be done. Information is needed regarding where in the Port of Shoreham, the weapons and explosives are being kept before they can be despatched. Need Information about Shoreham Airport, believed it is being used as a PoW camp which means that there is a valuable source of manpower there. Need to get in contact with them there. Need info on troop movements and how many in the area. What are they using as their HQ?

There are mobile patrols in the area to locate radios so keep transmissions down to the minimum.

Will be in touch soon.

Matt handed the message over to Sid who read it out to the team. It confirmed what Bill had said, but the men queried how they had so much information about what was occurring in their neighbourhood. Matt stated that there must be others in the area with radios to keep HQ informed. Matt wanted to think about the message and the situation before he issued any orders, so he ate the first fresh meal he had eaten for over a week and after they had cleared up he sat his team round to give them orders.

"Now we have our orders we need to assess and confirm what exactly is happening in the area. We need to find out how many Germans are here and what they are engaged in. We also need to find out more details about Shoreham Port. I will need people in Lancing, Shoreham and the Port and up in Steyning. I suggest that Jack and Doug go to Lancing and to investigate the Airport. Jake and Harry, you will go to Steyning, Bramber and Upper Beeding and whilst you are there see if you can get more food, in fact all of us should try to get more food. Sid, you and I will concentrate on Shoreham and the Port. Now before the invasion you were all given different identities and the relevant papers, so make sure that you have them and make sure that you know the details and the backgrounds relating to them intimately. Have your stories ready in case you are stopped. Do not draw attention to yourselves and if, god forbid, you are captured then hold out for at least 24 hours, it will give us time to move on. Then give up this bunker. Right we will leave here at 0800 hours tomorrow morning and that means that we will arrive in our areas about an hour or so later. We will then rendezvous back here at 1900 hours. Are there any questions?" Matt sat back in the chair and looked at his team.

"I presume that we can wander around with the person we are with," asked Doug.

"Yes, but remember that it may be prudent to look like you are alone if you see any Germans. You could be stopped at control points and if anything goes wrong then only one of you will get caught and that would enable the rest of us to be informed about what is happening," Matt said.

"Ok," said Doug.

"If we get any information it would be better that both of you know what it is so that if one of you gets caught the other will be able to get the information back here," said Sid in a very matter of fact manner.

There were no other questions and the men all moved over to their bunk areas and pulled out their ID papers and rationing cards. They then settled down for an evening of contemplation at their first mission into enemy territory.

CHAPTER 5

Matt and Sid had set off south and were now walking along Brighton Road which was beside the River Adur. Further up Brighton Road they had been able to see across the river and they noted that Shoreham Airport, which was on the west side of the river, was encased in barbed wire and it looked like a tented city. There were hundreds of tents in the area. They could see that around the airport field, towers were being built and German guards were patrolling the perimeter. They could also see many men wandering around, but from this distance they could not make out whether they were captured British troops, although they suspected that they were. They knew that Doug and Jack would get more detailed information, so they continued walking towards Shoreham. They took an alley way between the houses from Brighton Road which was a shortcut to the centre of town where St Mary's Church was located. Whilst going down it they noticed that many properties in the town had been badly damaged during the fighting. There were many burnt out houses and buildings, but upon reaching the Church they noticed that it had miraculously been untouched. As they were walking towards the church they saw a couple of bikes lying in a garden area of a burnt-out house. These bikes appeared undamaged and abandoned. Sid made a comment to Matt regarding how they would be useful and, after looking around to see if anyone owned the bikes, and as no one appeared to, Matt decided to take them, and they rode off on them. When they were walking down Brighton Road they had only seen a couple of vehicles with Germans in them, but now they were in town they saw many more and a lot of the Germans were walking around giving a good impression of tourists. The civilian population, however, had started to appear and from what Matt and Sid could tell they were looking for food. Many of the civilians were also riding bikes so Matt and Sid didn't look out of place. When they arrived at the High Street they were surprised to see a line of British troops being marched down the road. They were heavily guarded and were obviously en route to the Airport. These men looked bedraggled, pretty fed up, weary and some were injured. A few of these men looked at Matt and Sid and after saying something to other prisoners; they started to jeer at them. Matt did not blame them as he would have done the same if he was in the same situation. The guards had to step in and stop them. Matt and Sid rode by quickly as they did not want to attract any more attention to themselves.

They were stopped a couple of times by the Germans, but their stories held out. At this time, it would be impossible for the Germans to check. Matt stated that he lived in Mill Hill, which is the road that goes up on to the Downs and his house had been badly damaged. The Germans wanted to know why he was not in the army and he stated that he had a heart defect and they wouldn't take him. He had paperwork in his ID card that confirmed this. He also told them that he was a clerk and he worked in a bank in Brighton, but of course now he was unemployed. Sid stated that he was a farm worker, which was a reserved occupation and he worked at Manor Farm. He told the Germans that his boss had sent him down to town to find certain food stuff. The Germans had a problem understanding English and of course Matt and Sid were not going to help them.

In town the green grocers had large queues outside, as did the bakers and the butchers. Many shops and businesses were closed. There were not many goods in any of the open shops and, what food that was available in the shops, was heavily rationed. It was difficult to see how many Germans were in town but talking to some of the civilians it was agreed that there were about 300 troops. They did state that there were many more in the Port area, but these troops did not leave the

Port. They also told them that the men at the port may not be troops but could be civilian workers as they did not wear uniforms. They were billeted there, and their main job was to ensure the smooth unloading of equipment and reinforcements for the troops fighting the Allies. They found out that the Senior Officers for the area had set up their HQ at Lancing College; although not much information was known about this other than the top man was called Oberst Baumhauer. The locals agreed that Lancing College gave him and his senior staff the luxury that they craved, and it was central for the area that he was in charge of. This area apparently ran from Worthing in the west, Fishersgate in the East, and Partridge Green in the North.

Matt and Sid needed to assess what was happening at the Port, so after they had wandered around Shoreham, they cycled a couple of miles east to Southwick to watch the comings and goings at the port. They arrived there at midday, and discovering that the Schooner Pub was open, they went in and over a pint they were able to see what was going on. They were told by the barman that much of the equipment was being unloaded at Kingston Wharf, which was about a mile back towards Shoreham and it was then loaded either directly onto trucks or onto trains at Kingston Railway Wharf, to be transported to the Germans lines. Kingston Railway Wharf was a spur off the main line and trains could travel either east towards Brighton and then North towards London or west towards Portsmouth. From where they were, they could see trains passing at irregular intervals and these trains that travelled east had to pass over a bridge just beside Southwick Station. Matt noted that this could be a good place for sabotage. After an hour Sid and Matt travelled to Kingston Railway Wharf and could see it was a hive of activity. There was a pub by this wharf called the Kingston Arms, so Sid and Matt went in. There were a couple of Germans in the bar, so they were very careful what they said. They could see that when the trains left the main line onto the spur they had to go through a tunnel, which had a road over it. This was another good place for sabotage, although it was wide and would need a lot of explosives to destroy it. They would need to speak to Jake about it as a possible target. They watched the Wharf for about another hour and then decided to check further into Shoreham. Just east of Shoreham Station was a large railway goods yard which was heavily guarded. Because of the extra guards Matt and Sid agreed that it warranted extra attention. They found it hard to watch this place as the pubs had closed and there was nowhere to go that would conceal them. They cycled passed slowly and as they did they saw a man, not dressed in uniform, leave the yard. They suspected that he could be a British civilian worker. He was also on a bike and he was given access through the security gate without being bothered by the guards. Matt and Sid agreed that they needed to speak to him, so they followed him. He cycled into Shoreham and then headed north towards Buckingham Park. Just before he got to the park he pulled into a small cottage. As he got off his bike a little girl ran out of the cottage and whooped with joy at seeing the man. The man, balancing his bike against the wall of the house, picked her up and kissed her. He then went into the house carrying the little girl. Matt and Sid watched the house for a while and they decided that this man needed to be approached and spoken to regarding the goods yard, but not yet. As it was 1700 hours they made the decision that they would come down early the following day and speak to this man to discover what he did and more importantly, whether he could be trusted and to assess whether he was a collaborator. Matt and Sid headed back to the bunker. They arrived there a little before 1830 hours and just before they entered the wood they left their bikes in some bushes which they then covered with other branches, so they were hidden. Upon arriving back in the bunker, they discovered that Doug and Jack had returned, but Jake and Harry were not. Sid and Jack went into the kitchen area of the bunker and started getting a meal started. He had nearly finished when Jake and Harry returned. They looked red and flushed as they were carrying a huge bag which was rammed full of food, which even included chocolate, beer and a bottle of whiskey.

After the meal they sat round with some of the beer that Harry had managed to acquire, and they discussed what each team had discovered. Matt and Sid told about their exploits and then Doug and Jack told them that Lancing was quiet. There were a few Germans hanging around in Lancing town, but they had only been stopped once by a patrol. The area was not a problem to them as there was no port and no significant places for them to be concerned about. The airport, however, was what really interested them. They explained that they were unable to approach the place by road, so they took to the fields beside it and were able to assess what was going on there. On the west side of the airport, near to the terminal building, which housed the Germans, was a make shift hospital which seemed to be run by British doctors and nurses. There was an area just north of the hospital tents that housed the women, namely the nurses and any other female captured in uniform. The remainder of the tents housed the male Prisoners of War. It was primitive and the whole area was surrounded by barbed wire. The towers that had been built had spot lights attached and even had machine guns in them and they were manned by the German guards. The Germans had regular patrols both inside and outside the perimeter fence and they were using dogs as a deterrent to prevent the PoWs escaping. Doug and Jack couldn't get too close mainly because of the dogs. At one stage they thought they had been rumbled but fortunately the guards thought the dogs were only trying to chase rabbits. They were able to see that the PoWs were in a bad way. Their moral was deflated, and they wandered around looking defeated. They stayed in the area for nearly 4 hours to see the routine of the guards and they concluded that they were not regular with their patrols. Although these patrols had obviously been told what to do and where to do it, they did not do it with the efficiency that Germans were renown for. They would stop every couple of yards and chat and sometimes have a cigarette. The patrols outside were inconsistent. They would hide up and smoke as well and would take forever to walk from one place to another. Matt nodded and smiled. This was good news. They were probably suffering with what all guards suffered from… boredom.

Jake and Harry told them it was very quiet up in Steyning and Bramber. There were some troops in the area, but they were not interested in stopping men, they were however interested in the women in the area and it was obvious as they only stopped and spoke with them. The area was a rural area and the women were either farmer's daughters or wives and they didn't take too kindly to any advances from the German men, especially as they had invaded their country. Jake and Harry stopped at several farms and as they were British, the farmers assumed they were British soldiers hence the reason they were given a large amount of supplies. The farmers, their wives and daughters were also a valuable source of information. The Germans were planning on using the farms in southern England to supply fresh food to the German troops fighting in England. The farmers had got together and agreed that this was not going to happen, so they had sabotaged their crops, telling the Germans that they were ruined by the fighting and the bombardment from their ships when they landed. Concealed in underground cellars was enough food for the English people to live happily for quite a while and it is this food that was generously given to Jake and Harry. Because of this the Germans would have to provide food for the English people as well as themselves. They did, however, pass Lancing College and they noticed that it was very busy with Officers and troops coming and going. They had been told by the local people that the Germans had removed all the regular staff and bought in their own staff to look after them. Many large Swastika flags were flying outside and the chapel beside the College had been boarded up and there were large padlocks on the doors. Outside the College were a few German vehicles, which they assumed were to take the Officers to and from areas that they needed to visit.

All this information was extremely important, and Matt decided that a message would be left at the dead letter drop covering all this information. He felt that there were priority tasks to be done. The first was to speak to the man who was working at Shoreham railway yard and then to contact the PoWs to inform them what will be required of them. All this was put in the message and Harry was sent out to drop it off.

The following day Matt wanted further information about Shoreham Airport and despatched Jake and Jack back to obtain as much information about the guards and the camp as they could. Matt and Sid were going to contact the worker in the goods yard and Doug would go to Shoreham town to obtain as much information about troop and equipment movements as he could.

The following morning Matt and Sid left at 0700 hours, so they could catch the worker and Jake, Doug and Jack left the bunker later. Harry left even later as the area he was assigned to, Bramber and Steyning, was closer to the bunker. He was ordered, again, to discover anything that would be of interest in this area.

Matt and Sid had walked their bikes along Upper Shoreham Road, and they passed the house, where the man they wanted to talk to, lived. They could see that his bike was leaning against the wall of the cottage, so they assumed that he had not left for work. They reached the park entrance and stopped, looked around, but there was no movement of any kind anywhere. The whole area seemed to be deserted. There were many burnt out houses upon approaching the park, from the bombing, and apart from the cottage they were interested in there were only five houses still standing and appeared liveable. Matt and Sid stood out because of the lack of people around, so they decided that they needed to do something that made them less noticeable. The park, which before the invasion housed many British troops waiting for it to begin, was now littered with the remains of tents and there were many craters where bombs had landed. There was a dilapidated pavilion, but they couldn't see the cottage from there. This was impossible the men thought, as they could see that nothing in the immediate vicinity of the house which would make them invisible if any German appeared, eventually they decided to cross the road and hide in the rubble of a house and wait. Fortunately, they didn't have to wait long. About 10minutes later, Matt and Sid watched a woman walking along the road and go up to the cottage front door. She was greeted by the little girl who led her into the dwelling. A couple of minutes later the man, they wanted to speak to, left the house. He got on his bike and he cycled off. Matt and Sid did the same and as the man was going slowly, they were able to catch up with him.

"Excuse me," Matt said as he cycled beside the man. "Can I have a word with you?"

"What do you want?" asked the man.

"Can we stop cycling first and then I'll tell you," Matt suggested in a friendly manner.

The man pulled over just beside another bombed house. Matt and Sid pulled over and they looked the man up and down.

"Can we speak over there," indicating the burnt-out house.

"We don't want any Germans to get nosey now, do we?" Matt said.

The man looked around and then apprehensively said, "OK."

They all went up an alley between the houses and into one of the rear gardens, where they would get some privacy. They left their bikes in the alleyway. Where they were situated they were happy that it was not overlooked by anyone or anything.

"Now what do you want, and who are you?" the man asked.

"Well Mr... what's your name?" Matt asked pleasantly.

"It's Darcy, George Darcy," the man said.

"Well George we believe you are working at the goods yard and we need some information," Matt said.

"What! You want me to help you?" George exclaimed.

"That's the idea. We need to know what goods are coming and going and when they are being transported out. We need to know how many Germans are in there and what their jobs are, and we want to know how come you are staying in your job and working for the Germans," Matt said.

"I can't tell you that. They will shoot me. I just stayed on at my job once the fighting stopped and the army left the area and well… I needed to feed my daughter, so I decided that this was better than starving. The Germans needed help with the running of the yard, so I offered them my assistance," George said. He looked scared of Matt and Sid.

"Ok so you didn't want to starve, I can understand that, but now you are in a good position to help your countrymen," Matt said.

"You are kidding. That would put me and my daughter at risk," George replied.

"Are you telling me that you would rather work for the Germans than helping your countrymen," Sid asked.

"Yes, I would, and then at least I would be safe," George said.

"Not for long, when the British take back the country what will happen to collaborators like you and more importantly what would happen to your daughter then," Sid asked.

"The Germans have taken the majority of Europe and they have not been defeated by anyone so why do you think it will be different here," George stated defiantly.

Matt was furious and slapped the man across his face. George was a large man and he raised his fists to strike Matt back, but Sid was on him so quickly. He produced his pistol and pointed it at Darcy's stomach and this deterred him not to retaliate. Sid however was incensed by what George had said so he put his gun in his left hand and with his right he punched him in his stomach and the man dropped to his knees. Sid was just about to hit him again when Matt stopped him.

"George I am going to give you an ultimatum. You either help us, or instead of the Germans harming your daughter, we will," Matt said.

Matt hated threatening him with his daughter, and knew that he would never hurt her, but George didn't know this.

"You bastards, hurt a 6 year old. She is a baby," George said.

"Yes," said Matt slowly, "And an easy target. Now I am going to ask you again. Will you help us?"

George looked up at Matt and Sid and said, "Who are you two?"

Matt and Sid did not reply.

"Well as you have asked me so nicely then I suppose I have to. I don't have a choice, do I?" George relented.

"Thank you George, oh and by the way, we have others who know about you and if you inform the Germans about us and we get taken by them, then I can assure you that they will carry out our threat on your daughter. Do I make myself clear?" Matt said.

"Crystal," George said, but he appeared to slump at this.

"Right, so now we are friends, get up and I will tell you exactly what I want to know," Matt said.

For the next 15 minutes they briefed George with all the information that they needed to know, and they arranged a couple of meeting places where he could pass on the information. They wanted him to write down the information and after the initial meeting they wanted him to leave any new information at a dead letter drop. If there was anything that Matt needed to know urgently then George had to put his daughter's bicycle by the front door of his house (he usually took it in at night, but would leave it out by the door if he needed to speak or he had left a message for Matt or his men) and they would know that they were to check the drop point as a matter of urgency. This drop point would be in the house that they were now in. George was able to walk to it at night or could enter it on his way home or to work and leave it without being noticed. Before George left them, Matt warned him again against betrayal and they believed that he was scared enough to do as he was told. When George left, Matt and Sid left via the alley that ran down to the rear of the property to open fields. Before leaving he did tell them that the trains were running an erratic timetable as some lines had not been repaired after the battle during the invasion and the Allies had sabotaged the lines before they retreated. Also, their own bombing had damaged some of the tracks as well. In some places instead of two sets of rails going in opposite directions they were down to one set of rails and this was causing a problem with the regular service. The Germans were trying to repair them, but they had a problem with manpower. He also told them that they had tried to use the captured British soldiers but either because they did not know what they were supposed to be doing or they just did not want to do it and purposely acted ignorant, they made mistakes which could have derailed the trains, so the Germans had to review this and decided that their own troops should repair them. Having heard this Matt began thinking, that this may be an easy way to sabotage the railway.

CHAPTER 6

After the meeting with George, Matt and Sid split up and headed into Shoreham. Darcy had also told them about the station master who had offered his services to the Germans as well. He would be able to help them much better regarding time tables and cargo. Darcy had told them that he left the station at 12.45 for lunch at the Crabtree pub. Matt wanted to meet up with him and see if he would help as well. Sid wanted to go to Southwick to see if the Germans had employed any other British in the port area.

At 1230 hours Matt was positioned near to the station. He wanted to see who came out. There were many Germans coming and going, but they all seemed to be non-commissioned officers. He only saw one officer. At exactly 1245 hours he saw a man in plain clothes, who was in his late 50's or early 60's, leave the station and head towards the Crabtree pub. Matt followed, and he watched as the man entered the pub. Matt followed him in. As he entered he heard the barman say, "Here you are Bert, your usual."

Bert, who was standing at the bar, put some money on the bar, picked up a pint of bitter and went and sat at the table next to a window which enabled him to look out onto the road. Matt went up to the bar and asked for a pint of bitter. The barman pulled a pint for him. After paying, Matt went over to a table near to a blazing fire and took a sip of the beer. He could see Bert, who was absorbed with looking out of the window. The barman had wiped the bar and as there was no one else in the pub, he left the bar, and came into the public area. He went up to Bert.

"How's it going then?" he asked as he sat down opposite Bert.

Bert looked up, "Alright, but those bloody Hun are a real pain in the arse."

"It can't be easy to have to work for them," the barman said.

"Bloody right. They are bleeding well on your back all the time. I can't do anything without them checking and double checking what I am doing. What do they think I am going to do by myself? You don't know how lucky you are, Jo, running this place by yourself. I would quit if I didn't have to put food on the table. Betty has been poorly since they came, and I am worried about her. She can't go out and I have to try and get supplies when and where I can and as for medicines, it is becoming impossible," Bert said.

"I sent Doris to her sisters in Wales when the troops started to appear in the area. Mind you I don't know if she will be safe there. Once the Hun take London they will branch out and take as much of the country as possible and that will include Wales. Still she is safe for the time being," Jo said.

He looked over to Matt and said, "You are new round here."

Matt looked around the bar and saw that there was no one else in the pub. He turned to them and said, "Actually no, I have lived in the area for about 3 years. I worked in Southwick, so I usually drank round there. My place was bombed and so was my business. I am now just finding the joys of Shoreham."

"Sorry mate, anyone in the house?" Jo asked.

Matt decided to get the sympathy vote and said, "Yes my wife died. I was in the garden at the time and survived. I'm lucky, aren't I?"

"Sorry mate…"

They all sat in silence for a moment or two when Matt said to Bert, "I am sorry, but I couldn't help overhearing what you said before. How the hell can you stand working for those bastards, I mean they are Germans. I just couldn't do it. I would rather die of hunger than well… you know."

Bert looked at his drink and then straight into Matt's eyes.

"It's like this. I hate it, I mean really hate it, but I must. My wife has MS, multiple sclerosis, and she needs regular food. She is housebound, although I use to try to take her out before the Hun came, but now it is impossible. She is bad. I would even say that she may be on her last legs. I need medication for her and these I can sometimes get through the Hun but believe me I would rather shoot the both of us than do this, but I can't. It is really difficult," Bert said.

"When do you leave to go home to her? I mean is it a full day or do they allow you time to be with her," Matt asked.

Bert laughed, "Not on your bleeding life. I work 9 hours, I start at 8 so I leave at 5. They don't even pay me for a lunch hour."

"Have you got far to go home?" Matt asked.

"No, just live 5 minutes from here in Ravens Road," Bert said.

"That's good, you can get home quickly then," Matt said.

"Yes."

Matt had heard enough. He would speak to him on his way home and he was pretty sure that he would be useful to him. Matt drank his drink and then made his excuses and left.

He spent the remainder of the day around Shoreham and even entered the church. He wasn't a particularly religious person but felt drawn in. He sat in a pew and looked around. This church was quite beautiful. He looked up at the stain glass windows and wondered to himself how these windows had not been damaged during the bombing. The architecture was amazing. He realised that it was extremely old. He was the only one in there. He sat there for about 5 minutes when he heard the door behind him open. A vicar walked down the aisle passed him. He went to the altar, placed a challis that he had in his hand on it and then walked back down the aisle. As he approached where Matt was sitting he stopped, looked Matt up and down and sat down in the pew in front of Matt.

He turned around and said, "Sorry to disturb you, but I don't know you, do I?"

"No father, this is the first time I have come in here. It is a beautiful church," Matt said.

"Yes it is," said the vicar.

The priest looked at Matt, "What do you want my son?"

"What do you mean?" Matt asked.

"Well it's like this. You are obviously British, and you are of an age where you should be in the army, but here you are sitting in my church dressed as a work hand but speaking in a very articulate way. Did you escape from the airport?" the vicar asked.

Matt wanted to laugh, but this may be a good contact, "No father. I have a heart defect and couldn't join up."

"Oh," said the priest, who kept looking Matt up and down. "If you say so, but you look fit enough to me."

"Not much would get passed you now, would it?" Matt said.

The vicar turned to Matt and said, "I don't think so, but do you need help?"

"Not yet, but I may in the future. Tell me do you get many Germans in here," Matt asked.

"No, although I believe that they want to come. I have only been able to hold a couple of services since they have invaded. The first service there was none, and the next one there were about five. I have, however, spoken to the Oberst Baumhauer, the officer in charge of the area. He wanted my help to keep the civilian population in order, as he put it. I told him that I would do what I could. He wasn't very specific," said the vicar.

"What was the man like?" Matt asked.

"He was a very short man and therefore seemed to have a booming voice to compensate. Why is it short men speak so loudly? Anyway, he was officious, and I think a bit arrogant. I think that he could be cruel. It's his eyes. They didn't seem to have any depth," the vicar said.

"Did he come in alone or was he with any of his officers?" asked Matt.

"There were two of them. He did the talking and he didn't introduce me to the other officer, but he looked a real bully. He was tall and very large. He strutted around the church whilst we talked. Luckily there wasn't anyone here at that time," the vicar said.

"Do you know if he is coming back?" asked Matt.

"Wait a minute, are you interrogating me?" asked the vicar.

"No father I was just interested," Matt said.

"No this is more. Are you here for another reason?" the vicar said looking at Matt in the eyes.

Matt looked at the priest and wondered if he could trust him. He didn't want to put the priest in an awkward position, but this man could be valuable to him.

"Ok, now I am certain. You need information, don't you?" the vicar seemed to come to some sort of decision.

"If I said yes would you be prepared to keep your eyes and ears open?" Matt said tentatively.

"It would be dangerous for me and my parishioners, but I will let you know if I hear anything. Now if I am to help you, you must tell me who and what you are?" the vicar said.

Matt stood up and said, "That would definitely make it dangerous for you, Father."

"Would it? I wonder…," said the vicar.

"I think so," said Matt.

"Perhaps we could be of mutual help to each other," said the Vicar. Matt was unsure what he meant by that.

"What do you mean?" asked Matt.

The priest now stood up and walked to the end of the pew. He indicated for Matt to stay where he was. He walked to the back of the church and he looked around. He then indicated for Matt to follow him. Matt followed him into a side room. This room was very dusty. It had a table in the middle which contained prayer and song books and a book case which had even more prayer and song books in it.

The priest turned to Matt and said, "I do hope that I can trust you. I am not usually wrong about people."

Matt was puzzled and was thinking the same thing. The priest closed the door and he went over to a book case and he pulled a couple of books out and reached in. Matt heard a click and part of the book case opened. The priest returned the books and opened the bookcase fully. He indicated that

Matt should enter. Matt followed. The door was closed, and Matt was led down some stone steps. He entered a cellar and once his eyes got use to the darkness he could see that there were people in there. There were women, children and two very old men.

Matt turned to the priest and said, "What's all this?"

"These people are Jewish. We know what is happening in Europe. The Germans are rounding up the Jews and taking them away or killing them. We believe that they are also putting them into camps, but what's happening in those camps is unknown. It is not going to happen here, so I went around to all the Jews in the area that stayed, and I have bought them here."

"My god. How many are here?" Matt asked.

"There are 10 here and I have another 15 or so hidden around the town," he said.

"Wow, this is heavy. Why are you telling me and what do you want of me?" Matt wanted to know.

"Help of course, like you wanted me to do. I don't know you, but I think I am a good judge of character and I think that you are more than just a farm hand or labourer. Look, come with me and we can sit down and discuss what we both want," said the vicar.

"Alright."

Matt was just about to turn and leave the same way he had come in, but the Priest turned in the other direction and indicated for Matt to follow. They passed all the people in the cellar and he entered what Matt assumed to be an alcove in the wall. The priest touched something, and the back of the alcove sprung open. The priest pushed the wall open wider and entered. Matt followed. They walked down a tunnel, after the priest closed the door, and after a few minutes they arrived at a door, this time with a proper handle. The priest opened the door and Matt found himself in a study.

"Where are we?" Matt asked.

"This is my study at the vicarage. Sit down and I will get us some tea," he said.

"He left the room and whilst he was away Matt looked around. There was nothing strange about this room. In fact, it was the exactly what he would expect to find in a vicarage. Matt sat in an arm chair near to a fire that was turning into embers. Matt got hold of the poker which was on a stand with other fire implements beside the fire and prodded it to see if he could get it started again. There was a log beside the fire, so he put it on and gave it another prod. The smouldered remains might start up again, but Matt was uncertain.

The priest returned with a tray of cups, teapot, sugar and milk.

"Sorry but couldn't find any biscuits. Bea must have hidden them, and she is out at the moment," he said.

Matt frowned, and the priest continued, "Bea is my housekeeper."

"Oh," Matt replied.

The priest put the tray down on a table that was in front of the fire and he started to pour tea into the cups, followed by milk. Matt indicated that he didn't want sugar when he was offered it. The priest handed a cup to Matt and they both sipped the tea in silence. The priest then purposely put the cup back on the tray and looked straight at Matt and said, "Right then, shall we start with names. I'm Father Andrew Fairweather and you are?"

Matt said, "My name is Paul Taylor, how do you do?"

Matt was using his alias that was on his ID and ration card that he was carrying.

"Now Father Andrew, I need to know how you knew you could trust me. Did I stand out or did I do something that made you suspicious of me?" Matt needed to know because this could have been fatal if the Germans suspected that he was more than a farm worker or a bombed out civilian.

"Paul you questioned me like I was being grilled by the Police, so I thought you were either a Police Officer or something more and as the British Police were moved north with the troops I thought that you must be something more. I could see that you were honest about needing information and I believed that I could trust you because of the look on your face when we were talking about the

Oberst Baumhauer and his henchman. I suppose it was a hunch and I think that hunch is going to pay off," Father Andrew said with a smile on his face.

"Father you took a huge risk trusting me. I could have been a Nazi spy," said Matt.

"I know, but I need help and I am at a loss as to who will help locally. I know that you may have been just a farm hand, but I thought, just for a moment, that some divine intervention may have occurred. I realise that you have to take some risks in life and with you it was probably the biggest risk I have ever taken, and I just knew you were nothing to do with the Germans," he said.

Matt sat there thinking about what he had said. He had never been referred to as 'divine intervention' before.

"If I am to help perhaps we can start with information about how many other people know about those people in your cellar?" Matt asked.

"Not many, just my curate and my housekeeper, Bea, know about the people in the cellar and that they are Jews, but there are other people who are looking after the remaining 15. They have been told that they are wanted by the Germans, not that they are Jewish. Everyone who knows can be fully trusted; I can assure you of that," Father Andrew stated.

"Perhaps," said Matt, "but I would suggest that you do not tell anyone else about them. When food becomes really short, and it will, they will sell their own mother to get hold of some, so I suggest that we keep this information to ourselves."

"I take your point Paul," Father Andrew said.

"Now, what help do you need. I can't promise that I can help, but we will see," Matt asked.

"These people need to be moved north," Father Andrew said seriously.

"What, past the Germans lines, you are joking," Matt said, although he was not making light of what the Father had said.

"No, but we need to get them to safety," Father Andrew said.

"It will be impossible, sorry Father. They should have left when they could, but now they are here we have to do something that will allow them to go about their lives as normal Christian, British citizens," Matt stated. He was thinking hard, "Yes, do you know anyone who could provide them with false ID and ration cards with good British names on them?"

"My goodness, no. How would I know anyone who would do that?" said Father Andrew.

Matt sat for a moment in silence thinking and then he said, "Look I will tell you my plan and I may be able to help, but I cannot promise. Father, I think that you need to give them new names, and backgrounds making sure that they are not connected in any way to anyone or anything that is Jewish and make them into Christians. Whilst they are in your cellar they could be taught about Christianity by you and your curate and they could be taught Christian customs and even start to attend church services. It will be difficult for them but a necessity if they are to survive. I would suspect that the younger ones will be alright with this, but it may be a problem for the older ones."

Father Andrew thought about this and then said, "What about the ones that are not living in the church?"

"You will have to go to them to teach them," said Matt. "It is a lot of work for you, but you could save 25 people."

Father Andrew sat back in his chair and looked at the fire, which had just started to flicker with flames, he then sat forward and said, "Yes I could do it, but I will need false papers for them."

"This is where I may be able to help there. I cannot promise, but I will speak to a contact of mine," Matt said.

"See I wasn't wrong about you," said Father Andrew who had a bit of a smug look on his face.

Matt did not reply to that comment except to reaffirm his previous comment. "Perhaps, but do not tell anyone else about them. If the Germans catch them or find out about you helping them, your dog collar will not help you. By the way did they come to you for help?"

"No, when Oberst Baumhauer spoke to me, he was asking about Jews in the area. I pleaded ignorance and said that as far as I was concerned they had all moved north before the Germans had landed. I suspected that they were in danger and also after all the things that I have heard, all be it that they are rumours, I went to all the Jewish people I knew and apart from two they all agreed to be helped."

"Who are the two that refused help?"

"It was an elderly couple who refused to leave their home, so they are stayed put, but I have warned them to be careful. They told me that they had a son in the area and he would make sure that they would be safe," said Father Andrew.

"Do they know where the others are?" asked Matt.

"No, I arranged to meet them in an abandoned house. I then arranged for some to go to other homes and informed the rest to come to the church either individually or in pairs, which they did," he said.

"Good, you must always cover your back. Now is there anything else I can help you with?" asked Matt.

"Well there is something," Father Andrew asked tentatively. "It's a question of food. We are getting a bit short, with all the rationing. Do you know of anywhere we can get some extra rations?"

"Father, I suggest that you visit some of the farms in your parish and I will do the same a bit further afield," Matt said.

Matt looked at his watch it was 1620 hours and he wanted to speak to Bert on his way home.

"Now I have to go as I need to meet someone, I will be in touch and I would be grateful if you could keep your eyes and ears open about what the Germans are up to. Any information about them would be great. I would suggest you tell your guests what we have suggested," Matt said as he stood up.

"Yes, I will and thank you. Paul, I don't know what you are up to but please take care and I will pray for you," said Father Andrew earnestly.

"Thanks" Matt then left the vicarage. He made his way to the church picked up his bike and cycled to the bottom of Ravens Road where he waited for Bert to pass.

CHAPTER 7

In the bunker all the men were discussing what they had discovered. Sid had gone back to the port but was unable to discover anyone who was working there that could help them. He had been able to see troops landing, and they were immediately being loaded onto trucks and left heading west along the coast road towards Shoreham. Doug stated that he had seen the trucks and they turned north at the River Adur heading north. Sid also saw some of the equipment, such as mortars, weapons and crates that looked like they contained armaments and food, ready to be transported, and he suspected that they would be going to the front line. These were left on the quay side and were being placed into containers. Sid had also seen some of the other containers being loaded onto trains, but it appeared to him that they were having trouble getting these trains moving. He continued to tell the group what George Darcy had told Matt and him about the rail tracks that had been damaged, so this could be the reason for the delays. Matt then told them that he had managed to speak to Bert who was willing to help and confirmed what George had said. He was going to give them information about the timing of the trains so if they were going to sabotage any of them they needed to be important ones. Bert also told Matt that George was extremely friendly with the Germans and to be careful of him. He may lead them into a trap. Matt made a point of telling this to his men and because of this, anyone picking up a message from George at the drop point in the burnt out house should be extremely careful. In the meantime, someone, other than Matt or Sid would approach George again and reiterate the threat to his daughter. This was to prove that there were others who would follow up on the threat. Doug volunteered to do this, and Harry volunteered to give Doug backup in case of trouble.

Jack and Jake then told them about the airport. Apparently, from their position in the scrub land to the west of the airport they were able to talk to some of the inmates. They found out that the Germans were short of guards and they had not built all the lookout towers round the airport so there were some areas that were not very well guarded. Jack and Jake had found just such an area, although every so often a guard did walk along that part of the fence. They were told that the Allies OC, (officer in command), was Colonel Grant whose regiment was the Coldstream Guards.

He had been injured in the fighting and was constantly in the hospital area because of his wound, but he was trying to help organise the camp. His second OC is a Major Russell, who was trying to carry out his orders, but because of the size of the camp, and the amount of PoWs, he has a huge job on his hands. They were told that everyone was pretty fed up and moral was really low, so Jake told them that the British were fighting back and had made some advances and for the prisoners to pass it round the camp. It may not have been quite true, but it would give the PoWs hope. "We need to speak with Grant or Russell. I need a way in," Matt said thoughtfully.

Matt then told them about Father Andrew, but he did not tell them about the Jews in his cellar. He told his men that Father Andrew was trying to help the elderly and disabled in the area and he needed extra food, so when the men were out could they try to get some extra rations. The bunker's store was full so for the time being anything extra would be given to Father Andrew.

Troop movements were also discussed as well as their deployment and it was commented upon by Doug that they only had 2 guards on the Adur Bridge, which was surprising considering it was the main road to the west and it had a railway bridge running beside the road. They then discussed prospective targets to be sabotaged and the Adur Bridge was on the top of the list. They decided that after sending the daily message by radio to H.Q. they would make plans to start creating havoc in Shoreham and the surrounding areas. They agreed that the following night they would deal with the bridge and plans were put forward in order to achieve this goal. Matt left his men to formulate the plans whilst he wrote his message out to HQ, which incorporated asking them for 25 new identity cards and ration cards and coding it so that Doug could send it. Doug usually did the coding, but occasionally Matt would do it telling Doug that he wanted to keep his hand in. Whilst they were doing this they were listening to the wireless, which was initially playing music, but suddenly there was a breaking news announcement. The Germans had advanced and were marching into London. The news announcer was telling Londoners to stay put and find a place underground to stay until the fighting was over. They were also told not to leave, as it could put them in danger. Matt and his team stopped what they were doing and listened to the announcement and when it had finished Matt could see that all the men looked physically shocked, so he turned round to them and said, "This is really bad news, so our job is now vital to stop this advance and to give more advantage to our chaps who are fighting. I would like to see not just one plan for the Adur Bridge and the railway bridge beside it, I want a plan to hit the bridge in Southwick at the same time. This will stop cargo and their equipment from going east as well, so how about it?"

"Will we have enough men to do this?" asked Doug.

"Well Sid, Jack and Harry will do the Southwick Railway Bridge and Doug, Jake and I will do the Adur Bridge. If we do it together it will give those bastards a real kick up their backside. They are getting just a bit too cocky," Matt said.

Everyone was now laughing at Matt, but they were in complete agreement with him. After about an hour they had come up with a plan. When Sid had been watching the port, he had noticed that a couple of trucks were unloading people, who were dressed in civilian clothing. He really didn't pay too much attention to the people, but Matt suspected that they could either be Jews or intellectuals, who could cause problems for the Germans. Anyway, Sid's point was that the trucks were parked in a parking area away from the port. He stated that he could only see one guard which made them an easy target for the team, and if they stole a truck and blew it up under the bridge in Southwick it would probably bring the bridge down. Jake would put together a bomb in a bag and they would leave it in the cab of the truck and using a timer detonator, they could get away before it went off. The plan for the Adur Bridge was to use a canoe. All along the River Adur and other rivers in the south, before the invasion, the Royal Engineers built into the river banks areas that boats (canoes) could be kept. They were concealed from the river users and the other bank using hinged flaps. The fact that these were hinged was important in the River Adur as it was tidal and as the river went down the flap went down but as the river raised the flap went up. They were positioned about every 500 yards on both banks and they contained two canoes each. Matt and his team knew where these sheds (this is what the team called them) were. This also gave the team access to the other side of the river at night when they may need to cause trouble for the Germans. Matt, Jake and Doug would make their way down to the bridges using four canoes, one of which would be towed. They would attach one of the canoes with explosives in, beside the middle pier which supported the Adur Bridge and another canoe also containing explosives to the centre pier of the railway bridge. Jake stated that it should bring the centre section down and with a bit of luck the river may help with the remainder of the bridge.

The following day Jake and Jack, with Sid and Matt helping, were busy putting the bombs together, whilst Doug and Harry went into Shoreham to deal with George and also to scout around. They were also tasked to check on the car park where the trucks were kept. It was agreed that they would hit the bridges at 0230hours. At 1400 hours they had completed their tasks and Doug and Harry had come back confirming the information about the car park only having one guard. They had met up with George and he was warned about informing the Germans about them. They, along with Sid, Jake and Jack, decided that they would rest for the remainder of the day as they would be up for the majority of the night. Matt decided that he wanted to check some of the dead letter drop points before he put his feet up. He could feel his adrenalin running through his body already and needed to do something to calm down.

He left the bunker and checked a couple of the drops points but found nothing. He decided that he would check one final one which was near to Bramber and then head back. This drop point was beside a bridle path. One side of the path was a wooded area and on the other side was a high hedge behind which was an area with large shrubs. Matt was behind a tree in the wooded area and was just about to approach the drop point when he heard a noise. He stayed put and saw a lovely grey horse approaching. Sitting astride the horse was the most beautiful woman he had ever seen. When she reached the drop point, much to Matt's surprise she dismounted the horse. Matt could now see the woman in detail. She had auburn hair, which was extremely long, and it fell loosely down her back. She was very slim and tall, about 5' 7", maybe a little more. She was wearing riding clothing, riding britches, and a warm jumper with a jacket over it, which wasn't done up. She was absolutely stunning. The woman reached down the horse's leg to check it, but whilst she was doing this she seemed to be looking behind her at the same time. She then dropped the horse's leg and reached up under the saddle and pulled out a package. It was a fairly large package. She then bent down and placed the package into the drop point. Because of the size she had to cover it with foliage. Once she finished she stood back and looked at it, probably checking that it was hidden. She then started to walk off holding the reins of the horse. Matt was still behind the tree about 20 yards away from her. Suddenly Matt and the woman heard someone shouting. The shouting was coming from down the bridle path. The woman turned, and she started to look scared. Matt then heard someone shouting "Fraulein…, halt."

The woman stood her ground and waited, "Fraulein. Halt. Where are you going?"

The woman replied, "Riding. I am exercising my horse, why is there a problem?"

The German soldier went up to her and in very bad English said, "Nothing wrong. Just wanted to speak to you."

The woman just stood there saying nothing. The soldier stepped very close to the woman and touched her on the arm. The woman stepped back pulling her arm away from the man. The German said, "You no like Germans."

"It's not like that. You touched me. You shouldn't have done that. It's not right," she said.

The soldier took hold of her arm with his right hand and then touched her breast with his left hand. The woman pulled away again and this time dropped the horse's reins. This angered the German and he slapped the woman.

"You do as I want," he demanded.

The woman shouted, "No."

The horse, as if sensing trouble, trotted of up the bridle path. The soldier then punched the woman in the face and she dropped to the ground. The soldier was on her in a flash. The woman appeared to be unconscious. The soldier bent over and pulled her jumper up exposing her breasts. He then started to undo his trousers and pull them down. He got on top of her. Matt was furious and got his knife out of his boot. He carefully and quietly left his hiding place and cautiously made his way to the soldier and the woman. The soldier was too busy to care about anything other than to rape the woman. He was squeezing her breasts roughly and was moving down to her britches. Matt put his hand over the soldier's mouth and pulled his head back and at the same time he cut his throat. The soldier died very quickly. Matt pulled him off the woman and making sure the woman was alright. He pulled the soldier through the hedge and dumped his body out of sight from the path. As he was doing this the woman came too. She started to scream. Matt went up to her and said, "Don't scream, you are safe now."

The woman was sobbing and was adjusting her clothing to conceal her breasts. Matt helped the woman up, but she was weak and staggered. Matt decided that he would have to help this woman home. Bruising was already coming out on the woman's face and there was blood on her clothing from when Matt cut the soldiers throat. He took off his coat and he put it on the woman.

He then said, "Come on now. We need to get you home."

"Where's Madison?" The woman asked through the sobs.

Matt looked puzzled and woman said, "My horse."

"She ran off. I think we should get you home first and then we can see if we can find… Madison… later," Matt replied. "Where do you live?"

"Not far, left at the end of the path and then right at the end. I have stables there," she said.

"Ok come on then," Matt said.

He helped her along. Occasionally she would stumble and had to lean on Matt, but they arrived at a large house 10 minutes later. Beside the house Matt could see a stable block and in the yard was Madison. She had come home by herself.

"Go inside, I'll shut the gate, so Madison can't get out and then once you are ok you can put her in her stall," said Matt, who was concerned about this woman.

After he shut the gate to the yard he went to the house and entered. He found himself in the kitchen and the woman was just standing in the middle of the room.

"Bloody Germans, why did they have to come? I have had to get rid of nearly all my horses and now this," she said.

She then sat in a chair at the kitchen table and started to really sob. Matt went over to a sink and put a tea towel under the cold-water tap. After wringing it out, went over to the woman and placed it on her face.

"You are safe now and your face will be fine in a day or two. You are just shaken up by what happened. Keep that cloth on your face for a while and it will ease it," Matt said in a quiet voice.

He then looked at the women and said, "Look you are in one piece and you should be more careful. A beautiful woman will attract attention and you are beautiful. You should try and make yourself less attractive."

The woman who had been sobbing stopped and really looked at Matt for the first time and then to Matt's surprise she suddenly started to laugh.

"Oh, I'm so sorry. I am so selfish. There are soldiers dying to try and liberate us and all I can do is wallow in my self-pitying. I didn't thank you, but what did you do with that bastard?" she asked.

"Let's just say he won't hurt you again. I killed him," Matt said.

"Oh, you mean… you actually killed him," the woman asked. She was stunned by this statement.

"Yes."

"Well he deserved it. I have seen him around, you know, and he always seemed to be staring at me. I thought then that he was dangerous," she stated.

"Let me make you some tea. It is good for shock," Matt said.

"Thank you. I wouldn't say no. My face is hurting a bit," the woman agreed.

"I'm not surprised. You have a real shiner coming up. Keep that cloth on it," Matt told her.

Matt was really warming to this woman. Apart from being stunning she had a lovely character as well.

"What's your name?" the woman asked. Matt was unsure what to tell her, so he told her his alias, "Paul, Paul Taylor and you?"

"Eleanor Frobisher. Nice to meet you. Where the hell did you come from?" she asked.

"I was walking through the woods, looking for wild life," Matt lied.

"Well you certainly found some. Why aren't you in the army?" she asked.

"I have a defective valve in my heart, so they wouldn't take me," he lied.

"Sorry I didn't mean to be nosey, it's just you seemed to be able to kill without worrying. You talk about it like it was normal for you, so I wondered…," Eleanor did not finish the sentence. The woman was thinking for a moment and then continued "Wait a minute you aren't… well I mean you weren't waiting in the woods for me, or what I had?"

"I don't know what you are talking about," Matt said.

This was becoming awkward. He knew she was a courier, but it would be dangerous for her, as well as for him, for her to know what Matt did.

"You don't know Mrs Johns then?" she asked.

"Mrs Who!" Matt asked.

"Look I know that this is dangerous and if you are what I think you are then your secret is safe with me," she said as she looked at Matt.

Matt said nothing but turned and finished making the tea.

"For someone who is in shock you are asking a lot of questions and surmising a lot. I think we should change the subject," Matt told her.

Matt handed her a cup of tea with lots of sugar in it and after the first sip he could see that the colour was returning to her face. He also had a cup of tea himself and he sat down at the table opposite Eleanor.

"Yes, I agree. Paul, what will happen when they find the body?" she asked.

"They won't find it. When I leave here I will bury him and they will think that he has deserted," he told her.

"Good, so I don't have to worry," she said.

"No, you are safe, but I would suggest that you do as I say and stop looking so bloody gorgeous," Matt said.

Eleanor was laughing, "Stop teasing."

"I'm not. Put a scarf over your hair and don't wear makeup," he said.

"I don't wear makeup," Eleanor said.

"Well wear baggy clothes and put on a pair of old glasses, anything but do something," he begged.

"I will try," she told him.

"Good," said Matt. "Now after I have drunk this, I must go."

"Oh," said Eleanor. "Will I see you again?"

"I hope so, but I don't know when. I'll pop in if I can," he said.

"I'd like to see you again. Come around for dinner one evening," she said.

"Look Eleanor, I would love to, but I cannot promise or arrange a date. I have work to do and I cannot commit myself until England is in the hands of the English again. I also do not want to put you in danger, so I will come around, but I cannot say when," he said.

"Alright I understand. But you must be careful."

Although Matt had not told her that he was an auxiliary, Eleanor instinctively knew, and she knew that he would be in constant danger. She also liked Matt and although they had just met she felt that this was going to be more than just a one-off meeting, well… she hoped it would be more.

"And you," Matt said.

He finished his tea and he said his farewells. He knew that he would visit again and soon, but he didn't want to commit himself at the moment.

CHAPTER 8

Matt returned to the bunker and told his men what had happened. He took one of the spades and returned to the bridle path with Jake and they buried the German in the shrubby area. They then picked up the package and returned. Much to everyone's surprise it contained the blue prints of Shoreham Airport. There was also a message stating that the items Matt requested would be provided but they needed photographs of all the people concerned. Doug had decoded this message and although he wondered what it was concerning he didn't mention it to the others. Matt made a note of this and decided that he could trust him with other confidential matters if, and when, they arose again. The men would be leaving around midnight, so they settled down for the evening listening to the wireless. Every so often Jake and Jack would check the explosives to make sure they were correctly made. Matt realised that it was nerves that was making them do this. About 9.30pm there was another news announcement on the radio. It stated that the German High Command had installed the Duke of Windsor and his wife, Wallace Simpson as King and Queen of England. They had been bought to London during the day and were now living in Buckingham Palace. The announcer stated that Winston Churchill will be making a statement in 5 minutes. The men in the unit were furious about this news and they waited impatiently for the statement from the Prime Minister.

"Hearing the news today about the Duke of Windsor and his wife taking the title, which they do not deserve, of King and Queen of England, is repulsive and offensive to the British people. Hitler may have thought that this would quieten the people of this good land, but I can assure you that he does not know them, as I or our King George and Queen Elizabeth, do. We shall take back this great nation and when we do I will personally make it my quest in life to get the Duke and his Duchess charged with treason. I do hope that the good people of this country will not be forced to bow and scrape to these two imposters. I urge you, British people, not to attend anywhere they go or if you are in the vicinity of them then turn your back on them or walk away from them. The invaders of this country believe that they have the upper hand, but I can assure you that they don't. We are being supported in our fight for our good land by the Canadians, Australians, New Zealanders and Indians. They are coming over in

their masses and are fighting side by side with our boys, so if you are unlucky enough to have Germans camped out on your doorsteps in your town then do not despair we will boot these arrogant, bullish people into the Channel and they may have acted in haste, but they certainly will repent at leisure. Make sure that you keep your British grit and I promise you we shall be victorious."

All the men in the bunker cheered and the conversation turned to the Duke and Duchess of Windsor which was not very complimentary to them. This banter continued for a while but soon quietened down when they realised that they had a job to do in a couple of hours' time. During the excitement about Winston's speech, when it had finished someone knocked the dial on the radio whilst trying to turn it off. Suddenly the wireless broadcasted again and instead of the British announcer, Lord Haw-Haw was speaking. He was talking about how the British people should welcome the new King and Queen and how the cowardly ex-British government were leaving all the good people in Southern England to fend for themselves and how they should thank the Germans for being such good people to them. He continued incessantly about how good the Germans were and spouting anti British government messages. The men in the bunker initially laughed at him, but as he continued they started to get very angry. It turned out that the Germans had bought him over to London and he was broadcasting from there. Still the men would show the Germans tonight exactly what they thought of them.

Sid, Jack and Harry left at midnight with their equipment. They had decided that they would take the bikes (they had managed to acquire a couple more) but keep to the side roads so if they saw any German patrols they could hide in burnt out buildings or in fields till the patrols went by. They arrived without any problems in Southwick by 0045hours. They hid the bikes about a mile away from the bridge and they walked down to the car park and waited. As they were early they watched what the guard was doing. Jack suddenly became excited about something and Sid said in a whisper "What is wrong with you?"

"Look over there," he was pointing at the far end of the car park. Sid looked but could not see what had got Jack so excited.

"What?"

"Look by the shed. There are a couple of gas bottles, acetylene and oxygen, the ones they use in welding," he said.

Sid said, "So?"

"Well we can use them. I can attach some plastic explosive to them and using a detonator attached to the timer they will explode as well and that will make sure that the bridge will come down," he said.

"Oh," said Sid. "But I thought that the explosives we have, will do the job."

"Yes, it will, but the gas bottles will ensure that the job will be done and with a much better result," Jack said.

"Ok, do we have some spare plastic explosives with us?" Harry asked.

"Yes. I put some in," Jack said.

"So how long will it take you to prepare it, bearing in mind that we are trying to be as quick as possible in the truck when we take it," Sid asked concerned.

"A couple of minutes. I can do it in the back of the truck when you are driving it to the bridge," Jack said.

"Ok then," Sid said.

They stayed hiding till 0200 hours when they made their move. They knew the guard's route round the car park and Sid and Harry grabbed him. Harry put his hand over the guard's mouth and held onto him whilst Sid stabbed him in the back. Harry kept hold of him until they were sure that he was dead. They did not want any noise. They then put his body in the back of the truck. They took the truck nearest to the entrance. Jack had got hold of one of the gas tanks and was pulling it over to the truck. Once Harry had helped put the guard's body in the truck, he went over and got the other gas cylinder. Once they were all in the truck, Sid tried to get it started and as there were no keys they had to pull some wires out of the dashboard and put them together to get it going. Jack started to prepare all the explosives and was ready by the time they arrived at the bridge. Sid parked as flush to the wall of the bridge as he could, they set the timer on the explosives and they all jumped out and left the area. Sid looked at his watch, it was 0225 hours.

Meanwhile Matt, Doug and Jake left at 0100 hours as they only had a 10 minute walk down to the river and it would only take them about a half to three quarters of an hour to paddle down to the bridges. When they got to the river they got the two canoes out of the nearest shed and paddled down to the next shed where they got the other two out. They packed two of the canoes with explosives and with Matt and Doug in one canoe and Jake in the other, they towed the other two canoes as planned. They kept fairly close to the bank as the tide in the centre of the river made the current there fairly strong. They arrived at the bridge at 0157 hours. They tied the canoes, with the explosives, up to the middle piers of the two bridges. Explosives with a timer were also connected to the two outer piers of both bridges. They finished planting the explosives by 0210 hours and they hastily paddled back up the river arriving back at the shed at 0225 hours. They quickly put the canoes away and then lay on the bank sweating from the exertion of rapid paddling.

At 0230 hours the explosion from the Adur Bridge and the railway bridge could be heard by Matt and his men who were lying on the bank. They could not see the result of their work as there was a bend in the river, but they could see the sky light up like a massive firework display. The men cheered, and they hurriedly got up and ran back to the bunker and waited for the team from Southwick.

In Southwick the men had got back to their bikes when they heard the explosion from their endeavours. Again, they were unable to see the bridge collapse but they, like the other group, could see the sky light up with huge flames which was pretty spectacular. They hurried back to the bunker arriving an hour later. The men were all excited and because of this were unable to go to bed and sleep so they celebrated their first mission with some beers.

The following morning, they all made their way down to Shoreham. They went down individually so as not to arouse suspicion. They passed the Adur Bridge and the railway bridge and saw that the centre section of both had collapsed into the river and there were a number of German soldiers standing round staring at it. They then made their way to Southwick and this was even more spectacular. The bridge had completely collapsed and the tracks on either side of the bridge were completely destroyed. This was going to take some repairing. Matt who was with Sid made their way back to Shoreham as he wanted to see Father Andrew. They were about to turn off the coast road to go into Shoreham Town when they saw a German check point. They were stopping everyone passing and they were pulling out individuals who were standing beside the wall at the checkpoint. Matt was looking at these people and was surprised and then concerned that Harry had been picked out. Doug was walking towards them with a worried look on his face. Matt and Sid turned off the main road into a side street but stopped around the corner and waited. Doug had seen them turn off and went to meet them.

"What happened?" asked Matt.

"Harry approached the checkpoint ahead of me and we thought it was just an ordinary check but suddenly they started to pull out the people you saw along with Harry. I went up to the checkpoint thinking they would stop me, but they let me through. They have even pulled out some women. All together there are 10 of them. I don't know what they are going to do," Doug said.

"We have to do something," said Sid who was normally very sensible.

"What?" asked Matt?

"I don't know but we have to get him away from them," Sid said.

Sid was really fond of Harry and the way he was reacting showed this.

"Sid. Stop it. We will just have to wait and see what happens, but there is nothing we can do at the moment. Let's see where they take them," Matt said. "Sid, find a position where you can see what happens to them and let me know. I am going to the church and will meet you outside the town hall in half an hour. Doug, go and find the others and warn them. Tell them what has happened and tell them to be careful."

Sid and Doug left, and Matt made his way to the church.

At the church Matt entered the vestibule of the church and he could hear a heated conversation taking place.

"...these are ordinary people going about their lives. You can't kill them. I don't know who sabotaged those bridges."

"Well father, if you don't know or purport not to know then perhaps you should join these people," said a man who had an accented British voice.

Matt realised that Father Andrew was talking to a German. Matt retreated to a recently dug grave and knelt beside it. If the Germans came out all they will see is the back of him kneeling over a grave? He waited listening intently when suddenly he heard a voice not far behind him say, "It will take place at noon unless the people responsible come forward."

Then there was silence.

Matt waited a minute then turned around to see that the Germans had left the church grounds. He got up and entered the church. Father Andrew was sitting in a pew, bent over, praying. Matt didn't like to interrupt him but felt that he needed to know what that German had told him.

"Father," Matt said tentatively.

Father Andrew looked up. He looked like he had aged 20 years.

He said, "Oh it's you Paul. What can I do for you?"

Matt looked at Father Andrew and was concerned about him. He then said, "Father, are you alright?"

"Bloody hell, what am I going to do?" Father Andrew said.

"What has happened?" Matt asked.

"Those bloody Germans. They want to know who the saboteurs are, and I don't know and even if I did, I wouldn't let on, but they have got 10 people and if the saboteurs do not give themselves up then they are going to kill them. What am I to do?" he said.

Matt was silent for a minute and very worried. Although Father Andrew did not know for certain it was Matt, he was intelligent enough to guess that it was him or he was involved in it.

Matt then said, "Father, this is war and people are ordered to do some things that can cause reprisals. Father, people get killed in war, soldiers and civilians. You know this because if you didn't then the people in your cellar wouldn't be there. You have saved 25 people. I know that they are rounding up the Jews in the area and they are being shipped back to Germany. They have been seen. Now stop it, those people will need you, so come on"

"You are right Paul, but I still can't help feeling helpless. I can't help those people," Father Andrew said.

"No, but I may have some good news which means you can help those other people. I may be able to get them all ration and ID cards. All I need is a photograph of each of them," Matt said.

"My goodness, thank you, I will arrange it. I will give you the film when it is done," Father Andrew said with a smile on his face, which was short lived when he recalled the 10 people that were going to be killed.

"Another thing, I have food for you as well. We will have to arrange where to meet so I can get it to you," Matt said.

Father Andrew thought for a moment and then said, "Yes, what about St Nicolas Church."

"Ok, 6pm tomorrow night, and that means you will be back by curfew. Look it is approaching midday. Where did they say those people were going to be?" Matt asked

"Um, yes at the Adur Bridge. I need to be there, will you come with me?" asked Father Andrew.

"I think that we should make our own way there. We don't really want to be seen together," said Matt.

"Alright, I'll leave in a minute, but you go, now," Father Andrew said. He appeared to have gained his composure and had to find the strength to deal with the forthcoming execution of his parishioners.

Matt put his hand on Father Andrews shoulder and left.

Outside in the graveyard he met up with Sid, who was looking unusually flustered. "They have moved them to near the Adur Bridge. They are all just standing there, but there are a large number of soldiers. They seem to be waiting for someone. Also, there is a large crowd forming," he said.

"Come on let's get over there," Matt ordered.

"Is there anything we can do Matt," Sid asked, but now he was thinking, and he knew the answer, even before he asked it.

"I don't think so, but let's wait and see," said Matt.

"My God, I expected for me to get hurt, but not the others. I really don't know if I can do this anymore," said Sid.

Matt turned to Sid and said, "Sid you are my right-hand man, and the other men need your strength, knowledge and expertise. For Harry's sake we all knew that this could happen, well it has happened, but Harry is not dead yet and it may be possible that they are just threatening the locals. Sid come on you need to be there for him."

"I suppose so," Sid said. He was extremely concerned about this situation and he looked dreadful, but they headed to the Bridge.

When Matt and Sid arrived at the bridge they could see a large number of people hanging around. Doug, Jake and Jack were in the crowd.

The 10 men and women including Harry were standing in front of the entrance to the bridge and behind them it could be seen that the bridge was demolished. In front of them, apart from the soldiers was a very short man in a German uniform. He was strutting up and down and he looked extremely angry. Matt assumed this was Oberst Baumhauer, and near to him was a very large man. Oberst Baumhauer called him Oberleutnant Schafer, and he was standing very still looking at the 10 people lined up. Matt could see that Harry was looking out to the crowd and when he saw Sid, his face lit up. Sid shook his head as if indicating that there was nothing that could be done to help him. Harry smiled. Sid was nearly at his wits end and Matt thought that he would have to watch Sid if anything happened, in case he did anything stupid that could put him or the others in danger.

Father Andrew arrived and went straight up to the 10 men and women. The soldiers pushed him away and he went up to Oberst Baumhauer to protest. Oberleutnant Schafer walked over to the priest and pushed him away. Father Andrew walked away and from a distance started to pray. He turned to the crowd and instructed them to say the Lords Prayer with him and the English people all said it in unison. At exactly midday, Oberst

Baumhauer stood in front of the 10 people and facing the crowd said in extremely good English, "You are defeated. It is only a matter of time before we control all of your country. I am your master and you will do as I say or there will be consequences. Now last night there were a couple of incidents. This, (indicating the bridge), was one of them and it will not be tolerated. I want to know who was responsible."

He looked around the crowd, but there was complete silence. Matt was looking at Harry and he was shaking his head. Sid was looking directly at Harry and Matt was now really worried. He was worried that Sid was going to say something, and he was worried about Harry.

Oberst Baumhauer looked around the crowd and then continued, "I will give you 5 minutes for someone to come forward and tell me who did these acts. If by that time no one comes forward, then these people will be shot."

The crowd gasped. Matt felt physically sick and could feel his head spin on hearing this, but he was also aware of his Sergeant and he put his hand round Sid's shoulders, partly to stop him doing anything and partly to give him support. Doug could see that Sid was visibly distressed and he made his way over to Sid and Matt.

He stood beside Sid and whispered, "Harry knew the risks. He is telling you, not to do anything, look at him."

Sid was looking directly at Harry, in fact he had not taken his eyes of him and Harry was still shaking his head.

"He needs you here for support, regardless of what they do to him. Come on show him you are his Sergeant and act appropriately," Doug said.

Sid looked at Doug, and Matt thought he was going to hit him, but instead a small smile went across this face. He then looked at Harry and again the smile appeared. Matt could see that Doug was trying to pull him out of this mood and from what Matt could see he had done it. Matt still held on to him. The five minutes passed by very quickly. Oberst Baumhauer shouted a command and 10 soldiers stepped forward and marched over to face the 10 civilians. Oberst Baumhauer shouted another command and all the soldiers raised their rifles and took aim. He shouted yet another command and they fired. All 10 slumped to the ground and blood could be seen on the front of all of them. A couple of them were still moving so Oberleutnant Schafer walked over to them, removed a pistol from his holster, and he fired a shot into the head of each person. Sid was nearly physically sick. His whole body went rigid and Matt and Doug had to pull him away. Matt knew exactly what Sid was feeling but was unable to show it. He could feel himself shaking with anger, and sadness, and he could feel his eyes were welling up with tears, although he strained not to cry. He looked at Jake, Jack and Doug and could see that they had tears in their eyes and they all appeared to be very pale. He could sense their anger and rage. They were all feeling the same and they were all fighting the urge to do something. The whole team left the scene and made their way back to the bunker. On the way Sid released himself from Matt and Doug's hold and he ran down to the river. Doug told Matt that he would follow him and deal with him. Matt, Jake and Jack continued on the way to the bunker. When they arrived, they all sat in the chairs, not saying anything. All of them were badly shaken about what had happened. Matt needed to say something but could not think of the right words. They sat in silence. About an hour later Doug and Sid arrived back. They didn't say anything. Sid sat on Harry's bunk and started to cry. Still no one said anything. They sat in silence for about another half an hour. Matt got up, went over to a cupboard and pulled out the bottle of scotch. He put 6 glasses on the table and poured the scotch out.

The men, including Sid, came over to the table and before Matt handed round the glasses he said, "I know how shocked we all are about what has just happened. Harry was a good soldier and he will be missed. He was brave and a valuable member of this unit, but he knew, like we all do, that this was a suicide mission. Anyone of us could be killed at any time. You must remember what they said on the courses, that the life expectancy of Auxiliaries was 14 days; well we have been here for longer than that so in reality we are all on borrowed time. Now we have seen what could happen, we must make sure that it does not happen again, so from now on we make sure that we have succeeded in our mission at the time of whatever sabotage we do, and we stay away the following day. I trust that the civilian population will also do the same. Now I want us to raise our glasses," (he handed round the drinks, leaving one on the table), "to a brave soldier and colleague, our friend Harry." They all drank their drink and the 6th glass was put on a shelf.

Sid sat at the table and said, "I was really fond of Harry and I am sorry for being an emotional idiot, but I think I would have felt the same about any of you. I have had time to think about this and Harry would have wanted us to go on. So, because of this I think we should plan another job quickly. Those bastards looked really pissed off about the bridges, so I suggest that we hit the bridge between Steyning and Bramber. This means that the Officers will not be able to get to Shoreham Town and the port." Lancing College where they have based themselves was on the west side of the river and Shoreham and the port are on the east. This would make life very difficult for the Germans. Matt liked Sid's thoughts.

"We can do the same as before with the canoes," said Sid. Matt and the others agreed, so that afternoon, they put together the explosives. Matt decided that he needed to warn people in the area to stay in the following morning, so he went to Eleanor and told her about Harry and then to ask her to warn as many people as she could, and they in turn, to warn the people they know not to go out the following morning. Having seen Eleanor again he realised how much he liked her.

That night at 0230 hours they blew up that bridge. They all waited about a mile down the river to check they had done the job properly and seeing it crumble into the river they returned to the bunker.

There was no celebration that night. They went to their bunks exhausted but they all had problems sleeping.

CHAPTER 9

All along the coast the Auxiliaries were busy sabotaging railway lines and ambushing provisions, equipment and troops being transported by trucks, essentially cutting routes for supplies and replacement men up to London and the German's front line. This was having a devastating effect on the Germans and the reprisals were hard on the civilian population. There were many firing squads, killing of civilians and some were arrested and tortured for information. This, however, did not deter the Auxiliaries. They continued with their efforts. These reprisals really irritated the civilians, but their anger was aimed at the Germans not the Auxiliaries. In some areas resistance groups were being created and they were fighting the Germans but in an unorganised way. Auxiliaries were ordered to identify resistance groups in their area and to assist and even to train them. They could be useful to the Auxiliaries.

A week had gone by since Harry had been killed and although initially everyone, especially Sid, were sad about their comrade's death they had eventually got over the grieving and had now become an even tighter group of men. Matt was very busy with information coming in and acts of sabotage. They had managed, successfully, to destroy a convoy of trucks that was travelling up to the front and contained vital supplies, which included equipment parts, and they had managed to ambush trucks with troops in and kill them. George Darcy and Bert along with a couple of other people who were working for the Germans had managed to supply the team with useful information. The munitions that had been delivered by ship were being stored where George Darcy was working. They were there so that they could be transported to the front line by train, but because of the work of Matt and his men, they were now considering transporting them by truck. This was a slower way of doing it and until the Germans agreed what to do, these munitions would have to stay in the goods yard. George also stated that they had put extra guards in the goods yard, especially at night, but he was able to mark out on a plan where the munitions were and the guards patrol routes.

Due to the acts of sabotage that were occurring the Germans were in a quandary about deploying extra troops in these areas in order to capture those responsible, or at least to try and stop any other acts of sabotage. These extra troops that they would have to use were destined for the front line and London. Apparently, the high command decided that the current troops in these areas would have to cope, as the front was under severe pressure. The Allies were forcing the Germans to retreat in some places. From the wireless, the auxiliary units were able to hear reports that the Germans were taking some serious losses, which had been noticed by both the Auxiliaries and civilians. They had seen lorry loads of injured and dead being loaded on to ships in the harbour to be transported back to Germany. In the port they had also set up a makeshift hospital which was full. The wireless also reported that the RAF had managed to increase their number of pilots and had a delivery from Canada, and even America, of new aircraft. They were now able to bomb airfields such as Croydon which was hindering the backup for the Germans on the front line and British aircraft were seen in the skies heading for the English Channel. The BBC World Service, which was transmitting on the wirelesses, was reporting that it wouldn't be much longer before London was retaken and then the army would push the Germans back to the coast and then right into the English Channel. Matt realised that the Germans in the area had started to become very nervy, so perhaps this information was correct, but he was realistic, he knew that it would take many months for the Germans to be kicked off the British Isles. The radio and the dead letter drop messages were also extremely encouraging. It was now imperative that contact was made with the troops that were imprisoned in Shoreham airfield. If the Germans did retreat the Allies wanted them to leave the British shores or to be captured and certainly not to stay in any of the channel port areas where they could be supplied. A force at the rear of the German lines, to secure ports and the seaside towns would be needed, and the men at the PoW camps would be essential. All the camps along the coast needed to be armed and ready to be deployed.

Matt got out the blue prints of the airport and laid them on the table. He and Sid, who although was still very sad about Harry's death, seemed to be back to his normal self, were studying these blue prints. For about half an hour they were coming up with various plans to enter the camp, but all of them were very risky and they decided that it would be too dangerous for them. They continued looking at the blue prints when Matt saw something that may be a very easy way in.

Matt asked, "What's that?" pointing at an area that was on the north east side of the airport.

Sid looking at where Matt was pointing said, "It looks like an outlet into the river."

"Yes, but look how long it is. It travels from the river, across the fields beside the river, and appears to go under the whole of the airfield and even comes out on the other side. It must be a couple of miles long."

"My god, you know what this is. It is a drainage tunnel, so that the runways do not get flooded when it rains."

"I think you're right, we need to find where the outlet comes out into the river and then we need to excavate it," Matt said.

Matt tasked Jack and Jake the unenviable task of scouting around the river bank searching for the entrance. It took them two days of playing 'hide and seek' with German patrols, but they eventually found it. It was about 2 miles upriver from the Adur Bridge. There was a grill on the entrance which was held in place with a rusty padlock and it was hidden from the river by undergrowth which had grown around it. That night Matt, Sid, Jake and Jack went down to the river with a pair of bolt cutters and some extra padlocks. Doug stayed behind as he had some urgent messages to send.

They crossed the river using the canoes and Jake and Jack pointed out the entrance. They managed to cut the padlock off and because they could now put on their padlock they would have a key which enabled them to enter whenever they wanted. Once they had got access, Matt and Jack went in and Sid and Jake stood guard outside. The tunnel was big enough for a man to crawl through. They crawled for a long time, well over half an hour. They had a flash light to help them. It was pretty dirty in the tunnel and, as it had been raining, it had areas of stagnant water. They eventually came to the first of a number of outlets into the camp. They could see that on all the outlets there were grills and they were padlocked from the outside. The bolt cutters were able to fit through the grill and could just reach the padlock, so they tried to cut it. Initially they were unable to this, but eventually and with some clever manoeuvring of the bolt cutters, they managed. They were conscious that at midnight any noise that they made would be heard in the camp, so they had to keep as quiet as they could. Matt, who had bought with him a tin of grease, greased the hinges to stop them squeaking. He tentatively lifted the grill and was able to look out. This exit was in the middle of an area beside the fence and Matt could see immediately that if he used this exit he would be seen by the guards in the towers. He closed this grill and they padlocked the grill on the inside. He and Jack moved on down the tunnel till they got to a second exit grill. They again struggled to cut the padlock on this one, but eventually managed to do it. Matt then greased the hinge again and he carefully and slowly opened the grill. As he poked his head out he could see that it was beside a tent and fortunately the tent hid the grill from the guard towers. Matt and Jack got out of the tunnel and they lay on the ground beside it. They attached the broken lock on the grill, so it looked intact. They waited to see if they had attracted any attention. The quiet was eerie. Matt did not know where to go, so he decided that he would have to go into one of the tents and get the men in there to help, so they untied laces on the tent door nearest them. They saw that it was occupied with 10 men. It was very cramped, and they knew that if they woke anyone, everyone would be awoken which could cause a commotion. Suddenly a man lifted his head and said in a calm whisper, "Can I help you?"

Matt saw that no one else had woken.

"Yes, we need to speak to Colonel Grant," Matt said.

The man sat up and put on his shoes and overcoat without waking anyone else and he crawled out of the tent. They went around to the side of the tent and in a whisper, he said, "Come on I'll show you. Where the hell did you come from? I haven't seen you around."

"I'll tell the Colonel," Matt replied in a whisper.

They followed this man who was walking bent over and occasionally crawling. Eventually they arrived at a tent about 10 away from his. He opened the front flap of the tent and went inside. They could see that it was also crowded but from the insignias on the uniforms he could see that the men were all officers. The man went over to someone who was snoring. He gently shook his shoulders and the man awoke silently. The man sat up and said quietly, "What do you want Smith?"

"I have some visitors for you sir," Smith said.

"What are you talking about man?"

"Excuse me," Matt said in a whisper, "But I don't have much time. I need to speak to you, orders from Winston Churchill. I'm a Captain in the Auxiliaries, my name to you will be Matt."

"My god, about time." He sat up and the whole tent seemed to wake up as well, but amazingly no one made a sound. The Colonel ordered Smith to stand guard outside the tent and Smith left and the whole tent seemed to move in unison to sit up and listen to Matt.

In very quiet voices Matt said, "I have come here to tell you the news from the front and for you to begin getting organised. Firstly, London has been taken and the front runs from Felixstowe in the East to Bristol in the West. The good news is that the Allies are now holding their positions and are even pushing the Hun back in places. It is a slow process, but they are definitely pushing them back."

There was a murmur of approval in the tent.

"The Allies have been reinforced by Canadians, Australians, New Zealanders and Indians. Also, there are a number of Yanks that have come over via Canada. The RAF have been able to recoup their losses, both in aircraft, pilots and ground crew and are now bombing certain strategic areas. The news is good, and it is believed that it won't be long before they take London back. I don't know when they will push those bastards back across the Channel, but I believe that we could be liberated between 6 months and a year."

Matt hesitated to allow that news to sink in. He then continued, "Anyway, I need to tell you the reason I am here. I am one of the Auxiliaries that were left behind enemy lines and we will need fighting men ready and equipped when the Allies get closer so that we can hit them from the rear, take the port and the surrounding towns so the Hun do not make a last stand here."

"Are you telling me that you have been here since the Germans arrived?" asked Colonel Grant.

"Yes sir," replied Matt.

"You must be the ones that have been sabotaging them. We have heard about it from the guards, who I must say are not very happy about it," Colonel Grant said.

"Yes sir," Matt said.

"Good show. Right then so what do you need from us," asked Colonel Grant.

"We know that moral is fairly low here, so we need you to get them prepared. Give them hope and also we need them fit and ready to fight when the time comes," Matt said.

"That is not a problem; we will start a fitness program. The Germans are a disciplined lot and would like to see us doing this. We will also put the news you have given us around the camp, that should cheer the men up and give them an incentive to start wanting to fight back," said the Colonel.

"Good, now I need 10 men which will include either 2 officers or an officer and a Sergeant who will help remove a munitions dump in a goods yard. These men must be able to handle themselves. I need them to be able to handle explosives and also won't mind being stuck in a hole for weeks on end before and after the action. I don't want anyone who will cause trouble. I need fighting men and men who can kill. Just as a matter of interest, how many of you are here and are you counted by the Germans?" asked Matt.

"There are over 3,000 men and you are joking about counting us, there are so many of us and what with the deaths they can't keep tabs on us all. They take the word of the officers that everyone is present and correct. I can get the men you want together, but how are they going to get out?" the Colonel asked.

"We will let them know when we come to collect them. I would ask that the 10 men are put in Smith's tent on the night we arrange," Matt said.

"That will be done. Now you said that we are going to be needed to fight, but what with?" asked the Colonel.

"This is where it is going to be interesting," Matt said laughing. "We, along with your men, are going to raid the port's goods yard and remove their arsenal of weapons. We will then bring them here and you are going to hide them. Can this be done? Can you find an appropriate hiding place?"

"Well… um… that may be difficult, but it could be done. The Germans have asked if we could help build some huts for us to live in. I do believe they are thinking of making this a permanent PoW camp now. It was suggested to me that we could be moved to a camp in Germany, but I believe that has now changed, thank God. I refused to build them. You know anything to make their life more difficult for them. I think I may have a change of mind," the Colonel said with a smile. "Anyway, when my men build these huts I will make sure that they will all have hidden cellars. It should be easy. We will say that the large holes are the foundations. I think our captors won't want to be too involved with us whilst we are busy. They will only want to account for the tools that we use. We will be able to store the weapons there when they are completed, but how are you going to get them in here?"

"Colonel, again let us worry about that, all we need you do to is to get your men fit and raise their moral and arrange a storage place for the munitions," said Matt.

"Yes Captain, I will do that," confirmed the Colonel

"Sorry about this but I really need to go now. I will be back in a couple of days to pick up the men, shall we say the day after tomorrow. I should be here between midnight and 0100 hours," Matt said.

"Yes, and thank you Captain. Good luck and keep safe," he said.

"Can Smith take us back to his tent now?" asked Matt.

"Of course, Goodbye."

Matt and Jack left with Smith leading the way. Once back at the tent, Smith went inside, and Matt and Jack climbed back through the grill, padlocking it from the inside as well.

CHAPTER 10

The following day the bunker was a hive of activity. They had many plans to make and arrangements to sort out in order to accommodate the 10 men from the camp. The two other bunkers which would house the men, needed to be checked and stocked up with fresh food. Plans of the attack had to be formulated and further intelligence gathering from George and Bert needed to be done. They had to pick up all the messages from the drop points and they needed to inform HQ of their plans via a radio message, which all needed to be coded. The following day Matt decided that his team needed some R & R (rest and relaxation). They hadn't had any time off since the Germans had landed and they needed to be de-stressed. He also wanted them fresh for the missions ahead. He informed the men that they could do what they wanted but if they went out then they were tell someone where they were going, just in case of trouble. Sid decided to stay in the bunker as he wanted to write some letters, Jack and Jake were going to go to the Red Lion pub for a drink and perhaps some lunch. Doug, who had some family in Partridge Green wanted to visit them. Matt agreed to all those requests and the following day when all, but Sid had left, Matt decided to visit Eleanor. He told Sid, who grinned, so at 11.30 Matt left and made his way to her stables.

On his way to the stables he noticed that there was a lot German activity in the area. He was surprised to find a radio detector van parked up. This was about a street away from the stables. He hurried on his way, making a mental note to inform Doug on his return to the bunker and to ensure that the messages that they now sent out on the radio were kept to a minimum time.

Upon reaching Eleanor's house he went up to the front door and knocked. He waited for a couple of minutes but as there was no reply, he went around to the stables. As he went through the gate he saw Eleanor struggling with a bale of hay. He rushed up and he started to help her. Eleanor looked up and said, "Oh wonderful, it's you Paul, how are you?"

"Great, let me do this, where do you want it?" he said.

"No leave it there," she said.

"Oh, I thought you were moving it," Matt enquired.

"Well yes, but it can wait," she said.

As they were talking Matt saw some movement in the road outside the stables. He looked closely and then saw the Germans detector van outside and soldiers were being employed knocking on people's houses.

"Look the Germans have got their detector vans out. They are knocking on people's doors," Matt mentioned.

Eleanor's face suddenly had a look of panic on it.

She pulled Matt into the barn and said, "You can't be found here, come, I need to hide you, quickly."

She pulled him into her office which was just off the stables and she fiddled with a peg on the wall. It turned, and a door opened.

"Go in there and I will get you out when they have gone, and please be quiet," she said.

Matt entered and found himself in a very small room. On a small table at the end of the room he saw a radio. It was exactly the same as the unit had in his bunker. Now he knew that apart from delivering messages, she was also receiving them. This room looked like it was purposely built, and he suspected that it was constructed before the Germans came. He sat in the chair and he listened. Suddenly a light next to the radio came on and then went off. Again, it came on but stayed on a little longer and then turned off. He then heard talking outside. He couldn't hear what was being said, just a murmur.

Outside Eleanor appeared to be struggling with the bale of hay when one of the Germans approached her. He said, "Fraulein, may I help you?"

"No thank you," Eleanor said.

"Look it is heavy, here it is better that I do it," said a voice in broken English.

The German, who was a massive man, lifted the bale by himself and Eleanor indicated that he should put it in one of the stalls, which he did.

They returned to the barn door where another German soldier was standing, and he then asked Eleanor, "How long have you been in the barn?"

"My goodness, I suppose for about 3 hours. I was grooming my 2 horses and feeding them and sorting out the hay. I was going to go for a ride in a while, why?" she asked.

"Someone in the area is using a prohibited radio. So, do you know who it is?" asked the German.

His English was not very good and had a problem pronouncing some of the words.

"Good grief, no. Why would I? Anyway, how on earth do you know that someone is using one?" asked Eleanor.

"We have a van that can tell if someone in the area is using one," the German said.

"That's clever," exclaimed Eleanor. "Well it's not me. I am far too busy trying to exist with you over here. I am trying to not only feed myself, but to feed 2 horses, and I am trying to earn a living, but it is impossible and now you are coming here saying that I have a radio."

Eleanor started to ramble on and appeared to be getting upset.

"Fraulein, we are not saying you have the radio, we are trying to find out who has one," said the German.

"Well I don't know," she said.

"Good, but I need to look at your papers and then we shall leave."

"Oh, yes, just a minute, they are in the office. I will get them."

Eleanor left the soldiers standing in the doorway and entered the office. She got her ID and rations cards and took them back to the soldiers. They looked at them and they said that they were in order, but they needed to look in the stables and her house. Eleanor told them to help themselves, which they did and after half an hour they left. Eleanor stood at the door watching the comings and goings of the soldiers. They had been to all the houses in the road and when they had finished the soldiers got back into their truck and with the detector van they left. One of the neighbours was standing at the gate to their garden shouted over to Eleanor, "Are you alright Nellie?"

"Yes, thank you Cora, I'm fine now," Eleanor shouted back.

Eleanor went into the office and turned the peg. She let Matt out of the room.

"That was close. Thank goodness you came first," she said.

"What do you mean?" Matt asked.

"Well when you arrived at the house, the light came on to indicate I had a visitor and I had to leave the radio before I had finished the message. It was a really long message and I was probably transmitting longer than I should. But your visiting meant that I couldn't finish the message and the detector van couldn't plot the exact position of the radio, so thank you," she said.

"Oh Eleanor, you must be careful. I thought that you were only a courier. I didn't realise that you were also communicating to Command by radio," Matt declared.

"I don't use the radio very often. Usually I get packages delivered or left at certain drop points for me to pass on, but sometimes I have to use it. I will be more careful in future," she said.

"This is twice you have nearly come unstuck. Perhaps you shouldn't do it anymore," Matt said. He was now concerned about her safety.

"What are you trying to do, stop me doing my bit for the country? When I was approached and trained, I was told of the dangers and I was fully aware of what I was getting into, so I suggest that you accept it or else just go and let me get on with it." Eleanor was really angry, and Matt now realised that he was out of line saying what he had said.

"Eleanor, I was just worried. You could have been caught and you could be in the hands of the Hun now. Don't be angry. I was just concerned. You really need to be careful," he said.

"Alright Paul. What are you doing here, anyway?" she asked.

"First of all, my name is Matt, not Paul. That is my cover name and as you are one of us then you should know my real name," Matt said trying to make amends for his earlier comment although he had decided to tell Eleanor his real name when he was walking to her house. "And I have a day off, so I thought I would like to spend part of it with you."

"Oh, yes I would like that too... Matt... and as we are on proper name terms, then can you call me Nellie. Everyone calls me that," she said.

Matt and Nellie laughed. They went into the house and Nellie made them lunch. They then spent a restful and relaxing afternoon chatting. Nellie told Matt how she was recruited into being a courier. It turned out that Mrs Johns was an old friend of her mother; they went to school together. Nellie's father died in the First World War and her mother died 2 years ago. Mrs Johns, who Nellie knows as Martha, is her godmother. She was approached about 6 months before the invasion and she was trained in radio communications and Morse code at Coleshill House, where Matt was trained. The longer Matt was with Nellie the more he liked her. Even though she had taken his advice on dressing down, she was wearing a pair of baggy work trousers that had a bib which covered her slim figure, a sloppy-jo jumper and her hair had been put up in a scarf which was tied at the front, she still looked beautiful. Matt stayed with her all afternoon, but he needed to leave before curfew which started at 2000 hours. He left at 1830 hours after giving Nellie a kiss, and made his way joyfully back to the bunker, arriving at 1925 hours.

All the men had arrived back in the bunker. Sid had written to his mother, although he knew he wouldn't be able to post it and had spent the remainder of the day in his bunk reading. Jack and Jake had had a few pints in the pub and a good meal, using their ration cards. They then returned to the bunker to spend the afternoon sleeping or reading. Doug was really happy as he was able to see his Aunt and Uncle and he had been given a huge lunch. They were all able to relax which pleased Matt. This coming evening was going to be busy, getting the 10 men out and housed in the other bunkers.

The whole team left the bunker at 2330 hours and as the entrance to the drainage tunnel was a 10 minute walk away, they went down to the river together. They were constantly on the lookout for any German patrol. They had to hide when they crossed the road by the river as a troop convoy of trucks went by. Matt did say under his breath that the next mission was to stop these large convoys. They crossed the river and upon arriving at the locked gate and undoing it Matt and Jack entered while Sid, Doug and Jake waited in the shrubbery next to the gate. It took Matt and Jack, again, half an hour of crawling to reach the outlet grill. They undid the lock on it and they carefully opened it. They could see immediately that there was no one about and the camp was silent. They got out of the tunnel and they lay beside it for a moment to ensure that they had not disturbed the camp. They edged their way to the entrance of Smith's tent and opened it. Inside there were 10 men all sitting to attention! Colonel Grant was also in there. It was very crowded. It was a 10-man tent and now with all the men, the Colonel, Matt and Jack there was no room left.

The Colonel went up to Matt and shaking his hand said, "Captain, good to see you. As you can see these men are the fittest and best qualified for the mission. Let me introduce you to Major Jackson and Sergeant Green. They will be the people in charge."

Two men carefully got up and reached over the other men and shook Matt's hand.

The Colonel then said, "I have done what you said, and I passed round the information about our troops pushing those bastards back and I have informed them that we may be needed to kick their arses when the time comes. The moral in the camp has improved 100 percent. I have started a fitness regime and they are all throwing themselves into it. The Hun keep looking suspiciously at all of us, but they probably think that we have accepted how it is and are making the best of a bad situation. I also informed the Commandant of the camp that we will build the huts, so they are now in the process of being built with the added room, the cellar. We have got all the lads who were labourers, carpenters, plumbers and electricians in Civvie Street and we have briefed them fully about what is required of them. We reckon that we can complete a hut in two weeks. But we are starting four at a time which means that we will have four cellars ready in a week or two, although it will take at least a month to complete the initial buildings. I must admit I am really thankful for you coming in personally, to give us hope and to make us useful."

"That is all good news, but the Germans retreat may take months although I suppose that will enable your men to be ready as, and when, they will be needed. One thing that is bothering me is the women in your camp. We don't want reprisals or any harm to them, so I think that if we are going to go into action we must keep the women safe. Think about that Colonel and the next time I see you perhaps either you or I will have some sort of plan for them. How many women are there?" Matt stated.

"Yes, the women. I have thought about them, but I must admit I was so excited by what you are planning that I never thought they may be in danger. I will give it some thought. There are nearly 250 women here," he said.

"Ok we will think about that. Now we must get going," Matt said.

Matt then addressed the men. He had to speak in a whisper, but he needed to brief them about the escape route.

"Men, I am Captain Matt Fletcher and from now on I am your Officer in Charge. You need to be divided into two groups of five with the officer in charge of one and the Sergeant in charge of the other. When we reach our destinations, I will inform you of the mission and what will be required of you. Now the first group move to the front of the tent. We will direct you down the tunnel and when you reach the end you will be met by other members of my team. You will then wait very quietly in the undergrowth until all of you are out. If we are disturbed by Germans, then run for it. If this happens then make your way to either St Nicolas church on the outskirts of Shoreham or to South Downs Farm. The farmer there will hide you till we can get to you. Now as quiet as you can be, follow Jack," Matt ordered.

Jack got on his stomach and crawled round to the grill that led to the drainage tunnel. The men did exactly the same. The first five left and just to be safe they waited a few minutes to make sure that the Germans had not heard anything. Matt was just about to leave the tent with the next five men when Colonel Grant said, "Good luck Captain. I will look forward to hearing from you soon."

"Thank you, Colonel. I will be in touch," Matt said as he left.

By 0230 hours all the men were laying in the shrubbery beside the gate and the river. Matt locked the padlock on the entrance gate and he turned to Sid who confirmed that all was quiet. Sid and Jack were tasked to take a group to the bunker in Coombehead Wood and Jake and Doug would take the other group to the bunker in

Lancing Ring. Matt was going to go to both bunkers to brief them properly about the plans to take the munitions from the goods yard. Sid's group was with Major Jackson and four men and Jake's group had Sergeant Green and the remaining four men. They were a solemn crowd, but then having been locked up in a PoW camp with little food and low moral it wasn't surprising. They all left and went across country so that they wouldn't be seen by any patrols. Even though they went across country they still had a few roads to cross. The majority were minor but there was one which was very busy, but they managed to cross them without any incident. Matt went with Sid's group first to Coombehead Wood. The men were so surprised with their new quarters and they were really impressed with the larder and the food supplies. Major Jackson's first job once he had got his bearings in the bunker was to get two of his men to make a meal for them, but Matt had to interrupt him and his orders. He needed to brief them because he wanted to get to Lancing Ring and do the same there.

"Men this will be your new home for a while," Matt said. "I would like you to stay confined in here until we set out on our mission. I know that being cooped up is not ideal, but I cannot afford for any of you to get in the hands of the Germans, also they are completely oblivious to the fact that we are able to remove you from the camp and we would like it to stay that way. I know what it is like being stuck down here for a length of time, so I will plan the mission within the week. Now there is enough food to last you, but if you need anything special then you must let us know when we visit you. The room over there," indicating the door to the arsenal of weapons, "Contains weapons that you will need for the operation, so I suggest that over the next couple of days you go through them and decide which weapons you will take with you. The target will be a goods yard in Shoreham. There is a container which holds munitions for the Germans front. They are having trouble shipping it to the front line because we have taken out the railway access, so it is believed that they are being taken by road in small consignments. I have been informed that there is a large shipment of arms coming in to the port in 2 to 3 days, so I suggest that we hit the goods yard in 3 or 4 days. I will come to both you and the other men nearer the time with comprehensive plans. Now please settle in and please try to keep sane."

Major Jackson then said, "We will be fine here, and we will check out all the weapons that are here. As far as our sanity is concerned we are better off here than in that bloody camp. We will be ready for action, won't we lads."

The other four men cheered and the Major continued, "Thank you for getting us out and we won't let you down."

The men all muttered in agreement.

Matt then left and headed for Lancing Ring. There was ice on the ground, as it was the beginning of December, and he found the terrain hard going. He entered the bunker at Lancing Ring and he repeated what he had said to the other men. When he arrived here he found the men sitting around the table already eating a sumptuous meal and he left them eating whilst he talked to them. These men were chattier with Matt and all of them were telling him that they won't let him down and kept thanking him for getting them out of the camp.

Matt eventually got back to his bunker at 0515 hours and after a cup of tea he fell into his bunk and slept.

CHAPTER 11

The men in the bunkers spent their time checking the weapons and the explosives. They also made use of the food supplies, and they cooked meals that would give them stamina. They hadn't had much food in the camp and needed the extra to build them up. Meanwhile Matt went into Shoreham to speak with George on his way home from work. He confirmed with Matt that a supply ship was due in within the next two days which would have a huge shipment of weapons. He also confirmed that they would be stored in the secure container in the goods yard and that it would be heavily guarded. Matt told George that he needed to know how many guards would be on at night and he wanted to know how to access the yard. George said that the yard backed on to the railway and access could be obtained from the tracks. There was a wire fence and even a gate which he believed was locked, but he would draw a plan of the yard, so they will know exactly where to find the container and where the gate is located. There were many containers in the yard, but only one contained the weapons. He also told Matt that there was an area that held parts for the tanks and they would be going up to the front possibly with the weapons. Matt made a mental note that they needed to be destroyed. George would leave the plan showing where the weapons and tank parts containers are situated and the number of guards in the yard, the following day at the drop point. Matt needed him to provide paperwork for him to enter the front gates of the yard with trucks. George agreed to provide such paperwork and he would leave that and any other information that he could think of at the drop point either the next day with the plans or the following day.

Matt left George and made his way to the church. He needed to speak with Father Andrew. He entered and saw that there were several people sitting in the pews. Matt sat in a pew at the back of the church and waited. Father Andrew was in front of the altar. He turned and went up to a woman sitting in one of the front pews; he talked for a moment and then moved on to a man sitting a little back from the woman. They spoke for about 5 minutes and then turned and walked up the aisle. He saw Matt and he nodded for him to follow him. Matt got up. Father Andrew left the church, followed by Matt. He saw him walk through the graveyard and cross the road and enter the vicarage. Matt followed and entered through the vicarage door which Father Andrew had left open. Matt knew that Father Andrew would be in his study, so he entered the room, closing the door behind him. Sitting in his chair by the fire was Father Andrew.

"Come in Paul. Sit down," Father Andrew said. "How are you?"

"I'm good and you?" Matt asked.

"Yes, busy but fine. Now what have you got for me?" he asked.

Matt sat down and reached inside his jacket. He pulled out a package and gave it to the priest. Father Andrew opened the package looked at the contents which consisted of ration cards and ID cards. He got up went up to a safe, that was behind his desk, opened it, put the package in and then returned to his chair.

"Thank you, Paul. You have just saved 25 people. The couple I told you about who refused to come to the church have disappeared. I suspect that the Germans have taken them. We are now the saviours of the Jewish people in the cellar," Father Andrew said.

"Good, have you been training them in Christianity?" Matt asked.

"Oh yes. Didn't you see the people in the church, well they are from the cellar?" he said.

"My God Father, you are premature in allowing them out. What would have happened if the Germans had come instead of me?" Paul declared.

"I had lookouts outside the church. They would have informed me in plenty of time to get the people back in the cellar. Now we can officially put these people back in the community. I see that there were also clothing vouchers as well," he said.

"Yes, the people I know were able to provide all the relevant papers. But please tell your new flock to hide their old papers. Tell them to put them in a tin and bury them somewhere. They mustn't be caught with both sets of papers," Matt ordered.

"That is all in hand, we have taken their old papers and they are already hidden. We need to get these people back to living normal lives. We are putting them in houses where the previous residents were either killed or moved away before the invasion.

Nearly half are moved already. When we get our country back they can then go back to their normal lives. You really should be proud of yourself for what you have done," said Father Andrew.

"Father we have done what is right and just. Now I need to know if you have any information that I can use," Matt said.

"Oberleutnant Schafer came in the church yesterday and wanted to know if I knew where the saboteurs were. I told him I didn't know who they were. He threatened me a bit, you know he is becoming rather persistent and his threats are becoming more severe. Anyway, when he realised that he wasn't getting anywhere with those threats he tried the gentle approached. I just pleaded ignorant," said Father Andrew. He then said, "He did say that they needed the area to be peaceful as they had some important people coming to the port. He told me that my King and Queen of England were going to visit the area in a week's time. They were to visit the camp to make sure that the PoWs were being treated well and they wanted to visit Shoreham Town. He wanted to inform me that they really wanted to visit the church, as it was such a historic monument. I told him my King and Queen were in Scotland so who was he talking about. He, of course, was referring to Edward and that Wallace woman, so I had to tell him that they wouldn't get a very good reception from the towns people and this made him angry. He repeated that they were our King and Queen and I repeated that our King and Queen were in Scotland and would return when he and his army left. Until then we would not accept anyone else in their place. He tried to remain calm, but I could see that he was getting upset so I continued and told him that the PoWs wouldn't honour them either and he would have a problem on their hands if they visited a place like that," Father Andrew said.

"Good grief I am surprised you are still alive after telling him that," Matt said.

"Well, he told me that they were coming and that there would be people here to welcome them whether we liked it or not. I have passed this information to my congregation who have all refused to be present when they come and as it was an order from Winston Churchill in his broadcast not to go any place where the phoney King and Queen are, they feel obliged that they must obey, don't they. So, I suspect that there will be no one here to greet them," said Father Andrew.

"Be careful Father," Matt said.

"I will."

Matt thought about this for a moment and said, "Did they say exactly when they were coming."

Father Andrews replied, "Not exactly, only a week's time. He did say that he would give me full details nearer the time."

"Good. Let me know as soon as you know. Leave a message where you pick up the food," said Matt.

"Alright Paul."

"One other thing, how many people will your cellar in the church hold?" Matt was thinking about the women from the camp.

"Um… Well I suppose at a push about 100, why?"

"Do you know of any other place that could provide shelter for another 150 people?" Matt asked.

Father Andrews thought about this for a moment and then said, "I will have to think. St Nicolas Church also has a crypt, but it is smaller and then there is the old school house which was abandoned. It is in The Street, but I think that it may have been taken over by the Germans as a mess for the officers or something. I'm not quite sure, but I will try and find anywhere that could help. Why do you need to know this?"

"I can't tell you Father, but can you have a think about it. I may need to conceal about 250 people, not yet though," Matt said.

"Good Lord. Yes, I will think about it," Father Andrew said with a thoughtful look on his face.

"Thank you. I must go now. I need to get back before curfew and I need to see someone else first," Matt said.

"Thanks again Paul. I'll see you soon."

Matt got up and left.

He made his way to Ravens Road, where Bert lived. It was 1830 hours and he needed to speak to him quickly and then head back to the bunker before curfew started at 2000 hours. He knocked on Bert's front door who answered it very quickly.

"Oh, it's you, what are you doing here?" Bert said looking up and down the road.

"Can I come in, just for a minute?" Matt asked.

"Oh yes… yes come in quickly. I don't want anyone to see you here," Bert said opening his front door wider.

"Are you alright?" Matt asked. Bert looked a bit worried.

"I'm ok, but the wife is bad. I really need a doctor, but he won't come out," Bert said.

"What is wrong with her?" Matt asked.

"It's her MS. She has been bad since the invasion. Stress bought it on and I think that she is now going into a coma. It is worse than it's ever been," he said.

Matt followed Bert through the hall way and in the back room he could see, from the hall that it had been converted into a bedroom. In the room Matt saw an elderly woman lying on the bed. She was asleep or, so he thought just by looking at her.

"Is there anything I can do Bert?" asked Matt.

"I don't think so. I will wait till morning and the doctor will come out then, but I know that there is nothing that can be done. He hasn't got any drugs and he cannot get hold of them," said Bert.

"Oh, Bert I am so sorry. Look, shall I go?" he asked.

"No. What are you here for?" Bert wanted to know.

"I need to know if you can access the goods yard from the railway track," Matt asked.

"Come in the kitchen."

They entered the kitchen which was large with a table in the middle, where they sat down.

Bert said, "Right, yes there is a gate that the staff at the station used to get into the yard. It is padlocked and access to it is now forbidden. You must go in the front where the Germans check all the comings and goings. The gate is about 50yards from the end of the station platform on the south side and you can get access to the track via the station car park. There is only a thin wire fence there that can easily be cut. Before the invasion, kids would often get onto the platform that way without buying a ticket, so if kids can do it, then you can."

"Thanks Bert. What about Germans, how many are there at the station at night?" asked Matt.

"There are only about five and from what I hear they do not patrol the station, they usually sleep. Lazy Buggers," said Bert.

"Good. If there are any changes in what they do, then can you let me know?" asked Matt.

"Of course. Oh, by the way have you heard about Edward and his whore coming down here?" Bert asked.

"Actually, I have just heard, why?" Matt replied.

"Well the Germans are really excited about them coming down. They are talking about it and it appears that the troops will be out in force when they come. I don't know when exactly they are coming but I think it will be soon," said Bert. "They are going to visit the troops in the port and then go on to the airfield to visit our boys. I don't think that it will go down well there."

"I agree with you. I need more details about that, so can you keep your ears and eyes open and I'll get back to you in a day or so," Matt said.

As they were talking there was a knock at the front door. Bert looked worried.

"Who the hell is that?" he said more to himself than to Matt.

He got up and then turned to Matt and said, "You had better leave by the back door."

"Yes, I will. I'll be back the day after tomorrow. Hope your wife is… well you know," Matt said not really knowing what to say.

"Thank you, bye."

Bert then left the kitchen and Matt headed for the back door. Before he left he heard Bert talking in the hall.

"Doctor, what are you doing here? I thought you weren't coming tonight," Bert was saying.

"I decided to come," said the doctor.

Matt then left before he heard the rest of the conversation.

Matt made his way back to the bunker, arriving just after curfew. With the information he had, he needed to get a plan sorted out. The shipment of munitions would be here in a couple of days and they needed to hit it immediately it arrived as they didn't want it to be sent up to the front. There was the added information about the Duke and Duchess of Windsor coming to the area. He needed to do something that would take the gloss off that visit. He and his men sat down to organise something. He wanted to inform the men in the camp about this development and he didn't want them to feel disheartened about this situation. Colonel Grant should be forewarned. He tasked Jack to enter the camp and let him know the following night.

CHAPTER 12

Matt and his unit spent the next two days drawing up plans for the raid on the goods yard and one thing that they needed urgently, was a couple of trucks to transport the munitions. The day before the raid, the unit went down to the car park in between Southwick and Shoreham to see if they could get hold of the trucks from there. They saw that they had increased the guards to three and these guards did roving patrols of the parking area. Matt's men split up, Jake and Sid went to the rear of the car park and moved on one of the guards. He was standing beside a wall at the rear of the park smoking a cigarette. He was looking away from Jake and Sid and this enabled them to quietly creep up behind him. Jake had a large Bowie type knife in his hand and Sid had a silenced pistol ready. Jake reached over the guard's head and he put his hand over his mouth, pulled his head backwards, and making sure that he didn't make a sound; he then cut his throat. He kept hold of him until he felt his body go limp. The mission on the goods yard also required that some of the men wear German uniforms, so they removed this guard's uniform and then disposed of the body under some rubble that was lying by the wall. The other two guards were chatting near the front of the car park, so Matt, Jack and Doug waited. Eventually the guards separated and one of them headed towards them. Matt and Jack stayed together, and Doug followed the other guard. Matt and Jack were positioned in the shadows of a lorry. The guard walked right past them without seeing them and Jack came up behind the guard and with a hand over his mouth pulled his head back and pushed the knife into his back in an upward motion. It went into the guards' heart. He could feel the guard collapse in his grip but held on to him for a moment to ensure that he had died and that he wouldn't cry out. They also removed his uniform. That left the last guard. Doug had seen him enter a small hut by the entrance of the car park. He indicated to Jake and Sid, who had come over to join him, where he had gone and all three of them made their way to the hut. It had a window and they could see that he was boiling a kettle and making some hot drinks. When he had finished, he came to the door, opened it and softly whistled. Of course, there was no response to his whistle, so he stepped out of the hut and Jake, with a gun fitted with a silencer in his hand stepped forward. "Don't move," Jake said.

The guard stood still and then said "Nicht schießen, was wollen Sie?" (Don't shoot, what do you want?)

"I don't speak German and I never will. Raise your arms. Move," said Jake indicating that he wanted him to move towards the back of the hut.

The German lifted his arms up and moved where Jake wanted him to go. When he got to the back of the hut Jake shot the guard in the head and then removed his uniform.

Matt arrived and said, "Good, now find the trucks with the most fuel, just in case."

All of them, quickly and silently, went to the trucks in the car park and found two that not only had a full tank of fuel but also had keys in the ignition. They got into the trucks with Sid driving one and Jake driving the other. They were aware that there were road blocks, so they headed up through the back streets eventually arriving at Buckingham Park. They then drove north up The Drive and onto the Downs. They knew that Buckingham Barn had been empty since the invasion, so they drove the trucks into the barn and locked the doors. The barn was some way from any residential area and they had to cross a few fields to get to it. The barn could not be seen from any road as it was positioned in a dip. Matt felt it was safe for the trucks to be kept there ready for them to be used on the night of their mission. The reprisals for the three dead soldiers were bad. They rounded up another 10 civilians and they escorted them to the local Police Station, which the Germans had taken over, and here they were placed in cells and they were all systematically tortured. None of these people would have survived the torture but before they died they were paraded in front of the other civilians, showing their tortured faces to their towns' folk and they were then killed by firing squad. The people of Shoreham and Southwick were so angry with the Germans that upon hearing that the Duke and Duchess of Windsor, or the imposter King and Queen as they were now calling them, were visiting, they all decided that they would not come out for them or if they were forced to do so, they would turn their backs on them regardless of the consequences. What could the Germans do if the whole town did this; they couldn't shoot all the town's people.

The Germans were a bit smug about the visit and Matt did not like this attitude at all. He had been up to the other bunkers and had briefed all the men about the mission and he was glad to see that their spirits were high. They all seemed to be relishing the idea of action after such a long time of inaction. They also wanted to 'kick the Germans arse's', as one of the men said, for having the audacity of thinking that the British people would just lie down and allow them to take their country. Jack had gone to the camp and told the Colonel about the visit. Colonel Grant was initially shocked that they had the nerve to allow such a visit, but once he realised that this would happen he then said that he would make appropriate plans on how they would greet them and from what he said it wouldn't be a pleasant greeting. The bridge over the River Adur and the railway bridge had been partially repaired. The railway track was now capable of taking a train, but only one train at a time and the road would only allow one car or truck to cross at a time. Matt felt that it would be prudent to perhaps destroy it again, perhaps on the day that Edward and Wallace came to visit. The Germans had increased patrols on the bridge, but they didn't patrol the river. It appeared that they did not have any craft suitable for river travel, leastways not yet.

A day later George left a message at the drop point stating that the shipment had arrived and was stowed away in the container. He also left the appropriate paperwork for the men to enter the goods yard. Matt decided that they would attack the goods yard that night. He arranged with the men in the bunkers to be in Buckingham Barn at 2200 hours. Jake and Jack had got all the explosives ready in the afternoon. These explosives had been placed in 4 back packs and they would be strategically placed so that they would destroy all the other containers and goods stored in the yard. The uniforms from the dead guards were cleaned and mended for use, and they had obtained other uniforms over the previous weeks, so they needed to be cleaned as well. Major Jackson, who was called Johnny, spoke excellent German and would be driving one of the trucks and wearing one of the uniforms. He would speak to the guard on the gate and hopefully there wouldn't be any trouble. One of his men, a private called Alan Butcher, also spoke passable German so he would also be in uniform and he would drive the second truck. Matt would be with Johnny in the front of the first truck and he would be wearing a uniform. Doug would be accompanying Alan in the front of the other lorry. Jake, Jack and Sid, with three other men from the camp, would enter the goods yard via the gate by the railway track. The rest of the men would be in the back of the truck and if the guard wanted to know who they were then Johnny would explain that they were the labour force from the port. These men would be dressed as dock labourers in black trousers and jumpers. This was the uniform the German dock labourers were wearing. They had a supply of clothes in the bunkers and all the camp men had changed out of their uniforms into them. Everyone had weapons, which included Lee Enfield rifles and knives. The rifles were hidden in the back of the truck and the knives were secreted about their persons. In the back of the truck they also had some grenades in case anything kicked off. They arranged that the trucks would enter the goods yard at 0100 hours and at the same time entry would be gained at the rear gate. Apparently according to George, this was the time that the Germans started to have a meal break, so the yard would only have half the guards on patrol.

Jake, Jack and Sid with the other three men left the barn at 2230 hours so they could arrive at the station on time. They needed to be careful that they weren't seen. They also had to go on foot, so it would take them about an hour to an hour and a half to get to the station. It took them longer because there were a number of German patrols in the area and at times they had to use the destroyed buildings and back alleys for cover, so they wouldn't be seen. This all took time, but they arrived at the car park at 0025 hours. They hid behind some bushes by the side of the station car park and they watched for any Germans on the station. None appeared, so it seemed that Bert was correct about them sleeping on night shifts.

Matt and the remainder of the men waited until 0030 hours before leaving the barn. They travelled over the Downs without any lights on, which was a little bit hairy. The ground was very hard and at one stage they nearly landed in a ditch. They eventually got to The Drive and then drove through the back streets to the sea front road. They needed to approach the goods yard from the east which indicated that they had come from the Southwick area or the port. They arrived at the gates to the goods yard at 0055 hours.

Upon approaching the gate, a guard unlocked the gate and went up to Johnny's window.

"What are you doing at this time of night?" asked the guard in German.

Johnny replied in German. "I know it's bloody late. They just got me out of my bed. Got to collect this lot and take it to the front." (Handing him the paperwork for the munitions and both he and Matt prayed that it was all correct). "I won't be back till tonight, but our boys are in dire need of it."

Johnny watched the guard as he looked at the paper.

The guard then said, "I wondered when that lot would be going. I suppose it is better to move it at night. Right you will find the container on the right of the yard. How are you going to move it?"

"I have some men in the back of the truck. They were working at the port, so they were ordered to help with the loading the crates from the container," Johnny said.

"Good," the guard went around to the rear of the truck and lifted the tarpaulin which covered the back of the truck. He waved at the men and he then went back to the window.

"Ok then, is it just the 2 trucks?"

"Yes. We shouldn't be too long. These men know their job and when we are finished we will be escorted to the front. The escort is waiting for us, so we need to hurry," Johnny said.

The guard moved to the gate and opened it wider to allow the trucks to enter. Once the trucks were through he closed the gate and locked it.

Johnny drove into the yard, followed by Alan in his truck. They both reversed so the back of the trucks were next to the door of the container. Johnny and Matt got out of the truck and they went over to the container and opened it. It was packed full of guns, grenades, ammunition, mortars and explosives.

Johnny then went around to the rear of his truck and said loudly in German, "Come on lads the sooner we do this the sooner you lot will be able to go back to bed."

The men were out of the truck and loading the trucks immediately. Matt looked around the yard and could see two Germans wandering around. They appeared to be very bored. He watched them go behind a container and was saw smoke coming from where they were. He presumed that they were having a cigarette. He then looked around and could see movement over the far side of the yard. He presumed that it was Jake and his group. Matt went to the container and helped load up the trucks.

Jake, Jack, Sid and the other three men had managed to cross the railway track and had forced the lock on the goods yard gate. The gate's hinges looked a little rusty, so they used oil to lubricate them and then carefully opened the gate. There was a little squeak, but it was barely loud enough for anyone to hear. They entered and pulled the gate closed. They needed this to be used as their exit. They kept to the shadows, Jake, Jack and one of the camp men, Dave Briggs, who was extremely knowledgeable about explosives, due to his training in the army, started to deposit the prepared explosives around the compound. Sid and the other two men stood beside them to protect them if they were discovered. All of these explosives had timers attached, but they needed to be set. They calculated that it would take about 45 minutes to load up the trucks and then leave the yard, so the timers were set for 55 minutes. Quietly they managed to put all the explosives in place and where they couldn't be seen by anyone walking past. It had taken them 20 minutes. They then headed back to the gate. They did not leave immediately because they wanted to make sure that the trucks got out as well, so they concealed themselves by the gate and waited. From where they were positioned they could see that the loading of the trucks was going well.

Matt and the men had been hard at work for about 40 minutes and had loaded one truck completely and nearly three quarters of the second truck. The container was still half full, so it would be impossible to remove all the munitions. They suspected this would happen, so they came prepared to destroy the remaining contents of the container. Two of the men in the container had removed a box containing rifles when the pile of other boxes started to fall. They fell on one of the men who were carrying the box and as it hit him, he shouted out a swear word in English. He was trapped by the box and it became obvious to all the men that he was badly injured. One of the guards, who were hanging around near the container, heard the scream from the injured man and was unsure what exactly had happened. Johnny who had seen the incident went up to the guard and said in German, "We've had an accident. One of the men is hurt."

"Did he speak in English?" asked the German

"Don't be silly. You just heard a scream," Johnny said.

"No… he spoke English." As the Guard spoke he raised his rifle. "Who are you?"

"Don't be silly, we are Germans, it was a scream you heard," Johnny repeated.

The guard was uncertain, and he lowered the rifle. Inside the container some of the men were taking the box off the injured man and as they did the injured man screamed out in English again. The guard with Johnny, hearing the English spoken again, raised his rifle, but he was too slow because Johnny pulled out his pistol and he shot the guard. Unfortunately, the pistol did not have a silencer and it echoed around the yard. It bought the other guards that were patrolling the yard, towards the container. It was now obvious to the guards that something was wrong, and they had their rifles raised. Matt shouted out a warning to the other men. All, except the man who was injured, came to Matt's side with their rifles and they started shooting. The two guards went down. Matt told two men to get the injured man and put him in the truck and to set the explosives for 5 minutes and to get ready to leave. Jake and his men saw what had happened and were ready to act. They saw the two guards shot and then they saw Germans appear from a building near the entrance. They also saw a few Germans appear from the back of the yard. In all there must have been about 20 Germans. They were slightly outnumbered, but because they were uncertain what had happened, they were unclear who had done what and as some of Matt's men were wearing German uniforms they thought that they had been attacked from outside the yard. As the Germans ran across the compound Matt and his men opened fire and Sid and Jake threw a grenade into them. The grenade killed 2 guards and injured 3 of them and Matt and his men shot another 5 of the Germans but the others veered towards containers and they took cover by them and they started to return fire. The fire fight continued. Matt and his men had taken cover in the container and behind the trucks. They put down covering fire while the injured man was put into the truck. They continued to fire at the containers where the Germans were. Matt could see that a couple of his men had been injured and he shouted at his men to continue firing. Jake could see that some of the Germans were trying to get behind the munitions container and attack Matt and his men from the rear, so he threw another grenade at the Germans to stop them. Fortunately, the grenade caused one of the containers to explode. It must have had explosives or some sort of inflammable substance inside it. This container blocked the way of the Germans trying to attack Matt from the rear, so the uninjured ones returned and tried to see where the grenade had come from, but Jake and his men were well concealed. The time was getting on and they had 5 minutes before the explosives, that Jake and his group had placed in the yard, would explode, so Jake and his men decided to leave. They got to the gate and could see that the five Germans at the station had woken up and were standing on the platform looking at the yard. These men had their rifles aimed at the goods yard. They were in a dilemma about whether they should go to the yard and help. Jack and David went through the gate and immediately opened fire on the five Germans standing on the platform. They hit two of them and the other three immediately returned fire. Jake, Sid and the other men came through the gate firing. The Germans returned fire and they hit one of the men and Jack. Jack fell to the floor and the other injured man fell on top of him. Sid continued firing trying to cover the injured men. Jake, who was still at the gate and was about 50 yards from the Germans, reached in his pocket and removed a grenade and threw it. It was an amazing throw and landed at the feet of the Germans. It exploded wiping them out. He then bent down and picked Jack up. He carried him through the car park and up an alley with the others carrying the other injured man, who was called Will. When they stopped and checked the extent of the injuries they found that Jack had been shot in the thigh and his injury was not life threatening. Will, however, was not so lucky. He had been hit in the stomach and he was in agony. They pulled out a first aid kit that they carried, and they gave both men a shot of morphine to dull the pain. They then proceeded to head back, carrying the injured, to Buckingham Barn.

Back in the yard Matt, realising that the explosives would be detonating soon, called for his men to retreat to the trucks, but during this fire fight, a couple of his men had been shot. The men managed to get all the injured into the trucks and Matt ordered Johnny and Alan to leave and the men in the back of the truck to continue firing. As they approached the gate, they saw that the guard had been joined by another one and they were firing at them. Matt tried to fire back through the side window of the cab. Johnny and Matt kept their heads down but were able to just see out of the window. One of the guards was standing his ground and firing. Johnny pressed his foot onto the accelerator and kept the truck in a straight line. The windscreen was shot out, but apart from a few cuts from the glass, Johnny and Matt were unhurt. Matt continued firing now through the broken front window. They ran over the guard who was standing his ground and firing at them, whilst the other jumped out of the way. Matt fired through his side window at this guard and he believed that he hit him. Johnny accelerated and hit the locked gate which took it off its hinges and they left the yard at speed. The trucks had to turn left on to the coast road and because of the speed they were doing, they took the turning on two wheels. Johnny and Alan had trouble keeping control of the trucks, but they managed, and they sped off. They then made the journey to Buckingham Barn peacefully. As they were travelling along the coast road they heard a couple of loud explosions from the yard and Matt heard a cheer go up in the back of the truck. Matt and Johnny could see the sky light up and the sight of that sky was magnificent. There had obviously been some other incendiaries in the yard and they continued to explode for a quite a while afterwards. The trucks kept to the back streets and they did not turn their lights on. Within 15 minutes they were up on the Downs crossing the fields in the dark. They managed to get the trucks in the barn without seeing another German.

Once in the barn they assessed their condition and they discovered that they had 4 injured men from bullet wounds and the man who had been crushed by the crate in the container. This man had a broken leg and although 3 of the men were only slightly injured and would recover very quickly there was one man who had been shot in the top part of his chest. This was serious, and he could die if he didn't get medical help. For now all they could do was give him morphine for the pain and hope he could wait till medical help could be arranged. They waited for over an hour for the other team of men. They were uncertain if they had got away. During the fighting they had heard firing coming from the area around the station and the explosion from the grenade, but they did not know what had happened. Matt had put look outs on the Downs to make sure that the Germans were not about and to keep an eye open for the other group.

The second group took nearly two hours to get back to the barn and Will, the injured man was not looking good. It was now 0430 hours and the sun would be up soon, so it would be impossible to move them. Matt decided that a doctor was needed urgently and the only place to get one from was the hospital at the PoW camp, so he ordered Sid and Jake to go to the camp immediately and see if Colonel Grant could assist with this request. Sid and Jake left for the camp and the rest of the men remained at the barn. They would go to the bunkers the following night. Sid and Jake had been gone for nearly 3 hours and it was getting crucial as medical treatment for the two worse men was urgently needed. Ken, the man who had been shot in his chest and was breathing badly which indicated that he had been hit in the lung, and Will were in excruciating pain. Matt knew that they could not give him any more morphine and he felt that they were both hanging on by a thread.

The wait for Sid and Jake was unbearable. Matt and all the men were worried about Will and Ken.

Suddenly Sid and Jake came in with another man and a woman. They were introduced to Matt as Doctor Arthur Lawson and a nurse called Trudy Mann. They were immediately shown to Will and Ken and the doctor examined them both. He had a problem because they both needed certain medication and an operation. They both needed a saline drip and even a blood transfusion, especially Ken. The doctor noted Ken's blood group. It was the common blood group, O and a couple of the men in the barn had the same group so using some tubes that he had bought with him he set up a transfusion, but instead of putting the blood in a bottle, it went directly from man to man. Will's problem was not that he been shot in the lungs, it was his tubes going to the lungs. He needed medication and both Will and Ken needed serious painkillers as well as surgery. Although the other men were injured they were not as serious. Jack had a bullet wound to his thigh, but it had gone right through and the doctor would need to clean it up and stitch the entry and exit wounds. He would live but need to rest up for a couple of days. Another man had been shot in the hip area. The bullet was still in him so that needed to be removed. The doctor was uncertain whether the bullet had hit any bones because they did not have X-rays, but he would heal and then he could get treatment for it later. The other 2 who were injured had minor injuries. There was an arm wound but that could be cleaned and bandaged, and it would heal and there was an injury to the side of the other man. Again, it was a scratch although he may be bruised, and it would be painful for a couple of days, but the wound would be cleaned and bandaged and would heal quickly. The man with the broken leg had to have his leg put in a splint. It wasn't a bad break, but he would need to keep the splint on for about 6 weeks. The doctor kept apologising about the lack of medication and how little he could do for the injured men. Trudy, who was a trained nurse, looked after the minor injuries. Matt couldn't see the men in pain just because they needed some pain killers and as they needed operations, the need for medication was vital, so he decided to go into town and see if Father Andrew could help. He asked Doctor Lawson if he could make a list of drugs that he needed, which he gave to Matt, who then headed into town.

CHAPTER 13

When Matt arrived in the town it was swarming with Germans and they were stopping everyone. Matt got stopped a couple of times, but his story was firm and was allowed to pass. Surprisingly they did not search him, but this could be due to them stopping everybody who passed and there were many people queuing to get through the check points. Matt eventually reached the vicarage and knocked at the door. A woman answered it. Matt asked for Father Andrew and she went off leaving Matt on the doorstep. Suddenly Father Andrew was in the hall and ushering Matt into his study. Seeing the look on Matt's face he realised that Matt's visit was urgent. He also saw that Matt was very pale and looked very tired. He told Bea, his housekeeper, to rustle up some coffee and something for his guest to eat. Matt sat in the chair by the fire and he suddenly felt very exhausted. Father Andrew closed the door and came over to Matt.

"Are you alright Paul? If you don't mind me saying, you look dreadful," he said.

"I'm alright, but I have a problem and I need help. I don't know if you can help me?" Matt replied.

"Tell me what you want," demanded Father Andrew.

Father Andrew sat in the chair opposite to Matt.

"Well I suppose you must have heard about the raid on the goods yard last night," Matt said.

"Yes, that took some doing. It was brilliant, the whole yard has gone. The Germans lost quite a few men and they realise now that it was done by a professional group, not just some vigilante group. They are not even rounding up any civilians this time. They are furious, anyway what about that raid?" Father Andrew stopped talking and then looking at Matt said, "You… it was you, wasn't it?"

"Father, I didn't want you to know about any of this directly. You may have suspected things about me, but you weren't sure and that is how I wanted it to be," Matt said. He continued, "But I have a problem now and I need help. You see I have two very badly injured men. They are in terrible pain and need an operation urgently. We need certain drugs for them and even then, we don't know if they will make it or not, but I don't know where I can get these drugs from. I was wondering if you knew anyone who may have these drugs."

"How do you know what drugs these men need? Are you a doctor?" Father Andrew asked.

"No, we have a doctor, but he hasn't got access to any medication. Look Father, I really don't have time. These men could die anytime. Can you help me?" he asked.

"Drugs are very short at the moment, but I do know someone who may be able to help. He will be very expensive," Father Andrew told Matt.

"I thought about that. I have £300, will that be enough?" he asked.

"I think so, but I really don't know. I will see what he wants and perhaps I can barter for the drugs. Have you got it with you?" asked Father Andrew.

"Yes."

Matt took his jacket off and he started to rip the lining. He removed the money which he had put in there before the invasion. He then replaced his jacket and handed over the money. Father Andrew put it in his trousers pocket.

Before they could continue there was a knock on the study's door. Father Andrew said, "Come in."

It was Bea with a tray of coffee and a plate of bacon sandwiches. She put the tray on the desk and asked, "Anything else Father?"

"No thank you Bea. I will be going out in a minute, but my guest will be staying in here till I get bac," Father Andrew told her.

Addressing Matt, Bea said, "Is there anything that you need Sir?"

"No thank you," Matt said.

Bea then left the room leaving the door slightly ajar. Matt got up, closed the door and went over to the desk, took a cup of coffee from the tray and one of the sandwiches.

"They are all for you," indicating the sandwiches. "I've had my breakfast. I am going now, and I should be back within the hour. Make yourself comfortable."

"Thank you Father and be very careful."

"I will, bye," and he left.

Matt ate the sandwiches and drank the coffee. He prodded the fire till it burst into flame and then he sat in the chair and immediately fell asleep. He awoke to a noise. He didn't move, and he didn't open his eyes. He was aware of someone standing over him. He was unarmed, and he was vulnerable. He felt someone reach into his jacket. Very slowly he opened his eyes and at the same time grabbed the arm of the person who was searching his jacket. He saw Bea standing over him. Matt jumped up and Bea screamed.

"What are you doing?" Matt demanded.

"Nothing I was just checking that you were alright," she said.

"I'm fine, but what were you really doing?" he asked more seriously.

He still had hold of Bea's wrist. She was a woman in her mid 50's. She had grey hair and looked like a typical housekeeper wearing a bib type apron and very sturdy shoes. She was trying to pull away from Matt.

"Alright, alright. I look out for Father Andrew and when he left, well he looked worried. I wanted to know who you were, and I wanted to check you didn't have some hold over him. I didn't want him to be put in danger," she said.

Matt watched Bea's face as she was speaking. She looked sincere, but he had a nagging feeling, he had to make sure.

"What about the people in the cellar? He was in danger with them there too. Did you search all those people as well? I helped him out then and I am sure that when he comes back he will confirm that I am a good friend and that he is in no danger from me," Matt said sternly.

"Oh… you know about our… um… guests then," Bea asked.

"Yes of course I do," Matt said.

"So you are a friend then?" she asked.

"Yes, I am, but I am now wondering if you are trustworthy. Do you think I should speak to Father Andrew about you?" Matt asked.

"Look Mr ... um... well I am sure that you are safe, and I only had the interests of Father Andrew at heart. I think that perhaps I was a bit hasty," she said.

Matt was uneasy, but said, "Bea isn't it?" Bea nodded. "I have a nagging feeling about you and I don't like that feeling. I am a friend of Father Andrew's and if anything happens to him, anything at all, I will be the person trying to find out who is to blame. I will be coming to you first and if you think the Germans are bad then I can assure you that they are milk maids compared to me, so I would suggest that you do keep your Father very safe and keep your nose out of his affairs unless he asks you to help him. Now do I make myself clear?"

"There is no need to threaten me," Bea said indignantly.

"I didn't threaten you; I made a promise to you. That's different. Now I suggest you get on with your duties and leave me alone," Matt said.

Bea went to leave the room; her face was red and she looked like she had been slapped in the face.

"Bea," Matt said. Bea looked round. "Don't forget the tray."

"Oh yes," she said.

She re-entered the room, picked up the tray and left, closing the door firmly behind her. Matt was uneasy about her, but he could hear her moving around the house. Matt sat there for a moment but the gut feeling that he had about Bea, was unbearable. The house suddenly became very quiet. He couldn't hear Bea moving around and he knew deep inside him that there was something wrong with that woman, but he couldn't say what. Matt got up and opened the door to the study. He turned left and went down the hallway to the kitchen. He entered the kitchen, it was empty, but the back door to the garden was open. Matt carefully went out into the garden and stood quietly by the fence. He could hear a conversation taking place in the ally next to the garden.

"…he is in the study now. I think he is dangerous. He has threatened me," Bea was saying.

"Do nothing Frau Brown, I will deal with it. Did you hear what he was saying to the priest?" the man asked.

"No, the door was shut, and they stopped talking when I entered. I tried to leave it open when I went in with the coffee, but it was closed immediately by someone. I know he has come here before, but I don't recognise him. He is not from this town," Bea said almost in a whisper.

"Well that is interesting. How long is he going to be here?" the man asked.

Matt had heard enough, so he immediately went back into the house and headed for the front door. Outside he turned towards the ally where Bea was talking to the German. He looked around the corner and he saw Bea go back into the vicarage garden via a gate and the German was walking away in the opposite direction to Matt. Matt followed the German and, just as he was about to turn the corner into the next ally, he caught him up.

"Excuse me, have you seen a cat. Mine has disappeared," Matt asked innocently.

The German looked round and was just about to answer Matt when Matt hit him in the throat and then in the stomach. He hit him with such force that he knocked him through a fence into another back garden. Matt followed him into the garden and could see that the hit to the windpipe had rendered the German unable to get his breath and he was gasping for oxygen. Matt removed a knife from his boot. As he did so he then stamped on the Germans windpipe again and then calmly stabbed him in the throat. He could see immediately that he had killed him. Matt wiped the knife on the German's clothes and he replaced it in his boot. He then wiped the sweat from his face and he retraced his steps to the vicarage. He was concerned about Bea. What had she reported to the Germans, how much did they know. He needed to find out, but he also needed to inform Father Andrew immediately. He could be in imminent danger, in fact so could Matt. He went to the front of the vicarage but did not go inside. Instead he went to the graveyard where had a direct view of the vicarage front door and all the approaches to it. He waited for Father Andrew to return. He kept a look out for anyone watching the place, and to his relief he couldn't see anyone.

About 15 minutes later he saw Father Andrew walking down the road. Matt left the graveyard and walked up to him and said as he was passing, "Don't go into your house, don't acknowledge me, go to the church instead."

Matt continued walking and headed for the church.

Father Andrew walked passed as if nothing was said to him. He got to the entrance to his house where he seemed to change his mind and headed over to the church. He entered and at the vestibule Matt pulled him into a recess and said in a whisper, "Your housekeeper is a German informant."

"No," was all Father Andrew could say. He was literally speechless.

"I caught her going through my pockets when I was asleep, and she then went out to the alley beside your garden and spoke to a German about me and you. You are not safe. She needs to be spoken to immediately," Matt said.

"My God, I have known that woman for 20 years. I thought… Are you sure… Of course, you are.

Oh dear, what shall I do now?" Father Andrew said. He was stunned by what he had just heard.

Father Andrew could not speak. This news of betrayal had taken the wind completely out of his sails. Suddenly he seemed to pull himself together and said, "What about the German?"

"I have dealt with him, but he may have told someone that he was dealing with Bea, so we need to get you and Bea away urgently, and I need to speak to her. I need to know what she has told them," Matt stated.

"Of course. By the way I have your medicines. They cost £100," Father Andrew said.

"Great. Now I need you to bring Bea up to the Downs. Do you have a car?" Matt asked.

"Yes, but I don't use it much. Can't get the petrol. I have some but not a lot," Father Andrew said.

"Good. Now I need you to drive to the end of The Drive, where it joins the Downs. Get out of the car and walk onto the Downs. Do you know where that is?" Matt asked.

"Yes."

"Just make sure that Bea is with you. I will make my way there now and I should be with you in less than an hour. You leave in 30 minutes, no later," said Matt.

"Alright. I'll see you then. Oh yes here are the medicines and your money," said Father Andrew as he handed over a package and money which Matt put in the lining of his coat and they both left. He hoped that Father Andrew would be safe.

He could see that there were still many Germans in the area, but they had stopped pulling people over. Matt managed to get to The Drive with no trouble although he did cover a lot of the way through alleys and back gardens. When he reached the end of The Drive he could see a Riley Adelphi 6 car parked and he could see a man and a woman just ahead of the vehicle walking onto the fields of the Downs. He went up to them. It was Father Andrew and Bea. Together they all continued walking across the field in silence. Bea kept looking at Father Andrew and then at Matt and eventually she stopped and said, "Where are we going? I thought we were going to see someone who was ill?"

Father Andrew turned to Bea and said in a very calm but serious way, "Bea, we are not here to see anyone. We know you are a German informant, but what we don't know is why and what exactly you have told them, so Bea we are going to have a talk."

"Father that is… it just isn't true," Bea said.

"Bea, don't lie, you were seen and heard talking to that German in the alley, so come on. We are going somewhere quiet," he said.

He took hold of Bea's arm and followed Matt across the Downs. They walked for a while and Bea started to struggle, but Father Andrew kept a firm hold of her. When they arrived at the barn Matt told Father Andrew to take Bea to a dip in the ground just behind the barn and wait. This area was completely hidden from everyone even the barn. Matt went to the barn and gave the medicines to Doctor Lawson and he told Sid that he needed some help to deal with a German informant, so he and Jake accompanied Matt to the dip where Father Andrew and Bea were.

Matt went up to Father Andrew and said, "Father you may not like what we will have to do, so do you want to wait in the barn? We have some injured men in there, which may need some spiritual help."

"I don't know, perhaps I should stay here. I would like to know what she has to say and why she did it," he said.

"Suit yourself, but don't try to stop us. This is for your safety as well as mine," Matt said.

"I am aware of that, but I need to know about the safety of my other parishioners," Father Andrew said with a concerned look on his face.

"You can talk to her when we know that she will talk to us and tell the truth. I will call you out then," Matt said. Matt did not want the Father present during this interrogation as he was uncertain how violent they would be with her.

"Ok… Paul I have known her for 20 years. I thought I could trust her. What would make a person betray someone she says she loves? I just don't understand it," he said.

"I intend to find out. Look we may have to be harsh with her but once she starts talking and I am convinced she is telling the truth I will call you out and you can speak to her, now go to the barn," Matt kept saying.

Father Andrew walked away looking like he had lost a battle. He was distraught and felt so betrayed.

Once Father Andrew had gone into the barn Matt turned to Bea.

"I warned you, but you didn't heed my warning, now did you. First, I will ask you some questions and if I do not like your answers I will be forced to do things to you that are very nasty. Now let's start," Matt said in a matter of fact way. a

Sid had gone around the back of her and Jake was standing in front of her.

"Who was that German you were talking to?"

"I wasn't talking to any Germ...,"

Jake punched her in the stomach, forcing Bea to bend over, but Sid made her stand up and stopped her from falling to the ground.

"I will ask again, who was that German you were talking to?" Matt repeated.

"Obergruppenfuhrer Weber. He threatened me. He said that he would arrest Father Andrew if I didn't do what he said," she said.

"He is Gestapo then?" said Matt.

"I think so, I don't know," Bea said.

"How long have you been giving him information?" Matt asked.

"A month or so," she replied.

"What have you told him?" Matt asked.

"Nothing really," she said.

Jake punched her again in the stomach, this time Sid let her fall.

"Stand up. What have you told him?" Matt repeated.

Bea stood clutching her stomach. She faced Matt and defiantly spat towards him. She missed but Sid took hold of her arm and placed it round her back and Jake hit her again, only this time in the face. She swayed backwards but was forced to stay standing by Sid who was holding her arm. This time with her arm at such an angle, when Jake hit her, the stagger back broke the arm. She screamed. Sid released her, and she fell to the floor.

Matt then said, "We will keep this up all day and after your arm there is the other arm then the fingers, oh yes and the nails, then the legs. Bea we will get all the information out of you. You can do it the hard way, or we can do it the easy way. I can tell you now that we are not pleasant English boys. We are actually trained to inflict as much pain on someone as possible without them dying, so it really is your choice."

This time when Matt asked a question Bea answered it without hesitation. It took Matt over an hour of interrogating her before he was satisfied that what she was telling them was the truth, but what she was saying had disturbed him. He left Bea with Jake and Sid and returned to the barn.

He called Father Andrew out and they sat on a bale of hay beside the barn and told him what she had said, "Father the news isn't good. She has completely betrayed you, the Jewish people and the people who were helping you out. She gave the Germans the names and address of the Jewish couple that stayed in their home and who disappeared. She also told them about your cellar and how the Jews were going to mingle with Christians. They were going to raid one of your services and question everyone there about Christianity, anyone who gave a wrong answer would be arrested and that included people that are real Christians. They told her that they would be able to identify the Jews. She told them that you were getting new identity and ration cards for them. She also told him about me, but she had very little information about me which was fortunate. When she saw me asleep she decided to try and find out who exactly I was and then tell Obergruppenfuhrer Weber. She listened to your private conversations by listening at the door because usually you did not close the door properly, so it was easy for her. She also told them that you had access to food but didn't know who provided it. Oh yes and she gave the German all the names and addresses of the people who kept the Jewish people for you. They are in danger, but I do not know what to do about them. The only addresses she didn't give were the ones where the Jews moved to when they left the cellar. Apparently, she didn't only speak to that Obergruppenfuhrer, she has spoken to other Germans, so they are fully aware that she is an informant, so when she goes missing, which she will, they will be bringing you in for questioning and we all know what that means, so Father you are in dreadful danger. If you go back to the church, you will be arrested especially when they find the dead Obergruppenfuhrer. You will have to stay with us."

"I can't, my flock need me," Father Andrew said. He was in shock and couldn't think straight.

"Not if you're dead or arrested Father," Matt said seriously. He had to make sure that Father Andrew was aware of what could happen to him

"Damn, what has she done?" Father put his head in his hands. "Did she say why she did it?"

"Apparently, she said she was protecting you," Matt told him.

"What…," then turned to Matt and said, "Can I speak to her?"

"Of course."

Father Andrew got up and walked over to the area of land where Bea was. He could see Bea sitting on the ground. She was holding her arm.

He walked up to her and standing over her he said, "I just can't believe it, why Bea, why?"

"Oh father, they forced me," she said.

"What do you mean they forced you? Did they have a hold over you?" he asked.

"No, it wasn't like that," Bea said. She was looking at the ground as she spoke. She was unable to look at the Priest.

"Tell me, what it was like then?" Father Andrew said.

"Well they put it to me that they were going to arrest you if I didn't tell them what was going on, and I couldn't see you getting arrested," she said.

"But they had nothing on us then," Father Andrew said.

"They said they did," she said.

"They were bluffing, you silly woman. Don't you see, they saw you as a weak link and they played on that? Why didn't you come and tell me?" he asked.

"They knew something," she said.

"What?"

"I don't know," she replied.

Father Andrew looked at Bea and said, "Well they know something now. All those people are in danger because of you."

"I'm sorry Father, forgive me," she asked.

Father Andrew knew that he should forgive her, but he kept thinking of all the people that she had put in danger and after taking a long look at Bea he turned his back on her and walked away, back to the barn.

Bea was crying, and she said, "Father," but Father Andrew ignored her.

Then she shouted, "Father, I'm sorry," but again Father Andrew kept walking.

He had tears in his eyes, not for her but for the people that she had put in mortal danger. He kept thinking as he walked and hearing Bea shout that there were people in the barn that needed him, and he would not think about Bea again.

Matt watched him enter the barn and he said to Sid, "She needs to be disposed of now and she cannot be found."

"Don't worry Matt, I'll deal with it," Sid replied.

"Thanks Sid."

Sid went up to Bea and shot her in the head. He then went into the barn retrieved a spade and went outside and started to dig a grave.

Matt entered the barn and could see the Doctor and the nurse were working on Will and Ken. They were both hanging in there and with the medicines, the prognosis had just improved.

CHAPTER 14

The doctor and Trudy operated on Will and Ken. It was too soon to know if the operations were a success. It was decided that Will and Ken and the man with the broken leg should stay in the barn as it was too dangerous to move them. Father Andrew eventually agreed that it would be too dangerous for him to return to the vicarage and his parish, but he wanted to warn as many of the people who had helped him and who had been put in danger by Bea. Matt agreed that he should try and warn them, but he wanted Jake and Doug to go with him and he had to listen to them especially if they suspected any danger. They would use Father Andrew's car, so they could reach these people quickly and then afterwards they were ordered to burn the car and Father Andrews would join Matt and his men on the Downs. He agreed and left with Jake and Doug.

After all the excitement of what they had done and the after effects, Matt was physically and mentally drained. He went outside the barn and although it was December and extremely cold, the sun was shining. Sid joined him. They talked for a while about what had happened with Father Andrew and they then discussed the injured. Whilst they were talking they were joined by Doctor Lawson who had finished the operations and patching up the other injured men. He told Matt that he would have to return to the camp as soon as possible as he would be missed if he was gone too long. Sid was aware of this and said that he would be returned that night as it was safer in the dark. Suddenly they heard a noise coming from the East. All three of them looked up and saw a plane in the sky. "My god it's a Fieseler Storch. A German scout plane," said Sid. "Quick, get in the barn."

Matt, Sid and the doctor immediately ran into the barn. The plane was circling the Downs to the south east of them and was now heading in their direction. It passed over the barn, but continued on its way north west. It appeared to Sid that it was following a grid pattern and every so often would double back on its course.

"They are looking for something," Sid said.

Matt was looking at the plane through the slats in the barn and he said, "They are looking for us. We need to move out of here. It is too obvious."

Sid nodded in agreement. It was coming up to night and Matt told the doctor that before he returned to the camp, he needed to help to move these men to another location. The doctor said that it was too dangerous for Ken and Will to be moved, but Matt stated that it was too dangerous for them to stay here. It was getting too cold and they couldn't light a fire. The doctor reluctantly agreed. They all watched the Storch fly around for about half an hour and then disappear. Matt put lookouts onto the Downs just in case the Germans decided to send troops out. He suspected that if the troops were going to come they would do it in day light and not at night, so he made the doctor prepare the injured and place them in the trucks ready to leave. Sid was concerned about where they were going to go. Matt had already had a place in mind, and although it would be a very dark and dismal place, they could light a fire and he felt that they would be a lot safer there.

He took Sid and Johnny outside and said to them "Look the only place that I can think of that may be safe is the Cement Works on the A283. It closed when the Germans came. The owners and many of the workers went north in front of the army. It hasn't been used since. It is a cavernous place and the actual workings are hidden from the road and the air, so we can light fires and the injured can stay there till they have recovered enough to get them somewhere else. We can also put the trucks in there. When I last looked the entrance had a thick metal door which can be locked from the inside. There is also an emergency exit so if the Germans do find it we can get out. What do you think?"

"I came with you to look it over before the invasion and I agree it would be a safe place, but anyone entering or leaving would be seen from the road," Sid said.

"Yes, so after we are all inside, we will then only use the emergency exit which is at the rear," Matt said, after thinking about the problem.

"Yes, that would work," said Sid.

"Is it far from here?" Johnny asked.

"No. We will cross the Downs and we will leave them just this side of Bramber. Once we reach the road, we need to travel about half a mile down the A283 and we are there," Matt said.

"I think if we are all in agreement. It will be dark in half an hour and once Jake, Doug and Father Andrew returns we'll leave immediately."

Everyone agreed. They went inside to inform everyone to get ready. They also agreed that Sid, Johnny and a couple of Johnny's men would leave now, on foot, and have the Cement Works secured and the doors open so that the trucks could drive straight in and not hang about.

Jake, Doug and Father Andrew did not return until nearly 2200 hours, and everyone was getting concerned by the lateness. It appeared that the German troops had been around to some of the addresses before Father Andrew, Jake and Doug had got there and they had taken several people into custody, but there were a number that had not had visits and they were warned to leave immediately. At one of the homes the Germans arrived just as they were telling the occupants of the house what had happened, so Jake, Doug and Father Andrew had to leave, hurriedly, by the back entrance. They had a lucky escape, but it meant them leaving the car, so they could get away on foot. When they arrived at the barn Jake, Doug and Father Andrew were told that there was a change of plan and they were leaving the barn immediately and they hastily got into the back of one of the trucks ready for departure.

The trucks were heavy, with the armaments and the people, but they managed as the ground was hard. They couldn't put on the truck headlights, so they had to take it very slowly and getting off the Downs was trickiest part. They had to go down a very steep hill and in places there was ice which caused the trucks to slip and slide some of the way. Eventually they arrived at the road and turned left. There was nothing on the road and when they arrived at the Cement Works the doors were immediately opened and they drove in. The doors were shut and bolted behind them, so no one else would enter, but Matt put a lookout at the door just in case there was any interest being showed by the Germans. They drove the trucks through the Cement Works and parked up in a huge storage area. The place was extremely dusty and dirty. It had a fine layer of cement on everything. Trudy and a couple of the men cleaned up an area so that the Will and Ken, along with the other injured men, would be able to be removed from the trucks. A fire was lit, and it started to warm up very slowly. Ken was bad, and the doctor said that he didn't think that he would last the night. It was 0120 hours and Matt told Jake to get the Doctor and Trudy back to the camp. Trudy heard this comment and marched up to Matt and said, "I am not leaving here. I came here to look after the injured and they need me. I will not just up and leave. The doctor can go, he will be missed, but I am one of many women in the camp and I do not stand out, so I can stay."

Matt was about to argue with her but looking at her face and the expression she had on it, he thought better of it.

He did say though, "You will have no privacy and it will be bloody uncomfortable here. There are no proper latrines and the water system is old and I suspect it will get pretty smelly."

"Where do you think I have been for the last few months, the Ritz?" she asked.

"Alright. You can stay, but you must obey orders, and do as you are told. I know that you are here for the wounded, but I am here for all the men, and you as well, and I may have to give the order to leave and abandon the injured. You will obey me. Do you understand?" Matt said firmly.

"Yes, I do. I can take orders and I understand that that could happen," she said with a smile on her face. She knew that she had won this argument.

"Good, well get back to work Trudy and thank you. The men really appreciate what you are doing for the wounded," Matt said.

Trudy's face reddened at this and turned back to the man she was dealing with before. "Jake, take the Doctor back. Doctor Lawson thank you for what you have done," Matt said.

Doctor Lawson shook Matt's hand and wished him well and left with Jake.

Matt and Sid walked round the Cement Works and at the end of the tour they realised that this was a place where they could put the women from the PoW camp, to keep them safe from reprisals, if, or when the fighting started again.

When he returned to the storage area, he found Trudy standing beside Ken. She was shaking her head and when she turned towards Matt he could see she had tears in her eyes.

"What's the matter Trudy?" Matt asked.

"Ken has died," she said. She wiped her eyes, bend down and put his coat over his face.

Matt did not know what to say, but Father Andrew heard and went over to Ken and started to pray over his body.

It was a very sombre time. Matt knew that he had work to do and had to concentrate on that. The injured were in good hands now and he needed the rest of the men to help him focus on the job ahead. They needed to get food to the Cement Works and they needed clothing and blankets. This was a priority. They also needed to plan what they were going to do about the visit from Edward and Wallace. That was going to take place in a couple of days. He also needed them to help with ambushing some trucks that were en route to the front. In other words, he needed to keep the pressure on the Germans.

He decided that everyone needed to get some sleep, so at 0400 hours he told all the uninjured men in Sergeant Green's group to return to their bunker in Lancing Ring. Johnny's group only had one other who was uninjured, so they were told to stay at the Cement Works to look after Trudy and the injured men. Father Andrew was going to stay at the Cement Works as well. Matt, Sid, Jake, and Doug would return to their bunker. They needed some sleep and then they needed to send a message about what had happened, and it was felt essential to leave some messages at the drop point as well as checking on some of the other drop points.

Matt was just leaving when Father Andrew approached him.

"Paul, can I have a word with you?"

"Of course, what do you want? By the way my real name is Matt," Matt said.

"Yes, I wondered about that, anyway I was wondering if I could get in the camp. I don't think they have any clergy there and it would be a good for the men," said Father Andrew.

"I'll have to think about that. I don't think you would be safe there. There are Germans there and I am uncertain whether the Gestapo go in and look at or interrogate the inmates. If they do and you are there, they may recognise you, also I should think that Oberst Baumhauer may visit occasionally, and he would definitely recognise you. I think for the time being you are safer here," Matt said.

Father Andrew was uncertain about this and tried to continue with this request, so Matt told him he would think about it. He then left the Cement Works.

CHAPTER 15

After Matt and his men had slept they were kept very busy. One disturbing thing had come to light from Jake when he returned from the camp, having taken Doctor Lawson back and after speaking with Colonel Grant. He had some terrible news. Apparently, Colonel Grant had been taken to the commandant's office earlier in the day. He was concerned because he thought that they may have discovered that some of the men had left the camp, but he was wrong. He was told that Edward and Wallace would be visiting the camp in 4 days and that he required all the men in the camp to welcome them in an appropriate manner. They needed to cheer and wave at the couple. Colonel Grant told the commandant that they would do no such thing. The real King and Queen were George and Elizabeth and he and his troops would not accept someone who had been put in that position by the Germans. The Commandant was furious and threatened Colonel Grant with serious reprisals if he refused, to which Colonel Grant informed him about the Geneva Convention and how to treat prisoners of war. This infuriated him even more and he told Colonel

Grant that he would have a firing squad in the women's compound and if there were any bad behaviour. They would shoot three women for each infringement of this behaviour. Colonel Grant was horrified. He told him that when the Allies retook this area he would personally make sure that the commandant would be tried for war crimes, this infuriated him even further and he shouted at the Colonel that the visit would go ahead along with the killing of the women if they decided not to comply. He then told Colonel Grant to leave.

Matt was very disturbed about this, so he made the decision that the women should be removed from the camp as a priority. He immediately wrote a message to his command telling them that he needed ID cards and ration cards to enable some of the women to be moved to rural areas to be taken in by British civilians and work for them. Some of the women were land girls so they could work the land again and some worked in communications, so they would be useful as couriers or to do anything, but it was essential for all of them to be moved. It would be impossible to feed that amount of people. The message was sent as a priority. Initially he would move them to the Cement Works and then, as the ID papers were obtained, they could be moved on. So that day

Jake returned to the camp to inform Colonel Grant what was planned. Colonel Grant needed to have the women available that night. It was a big operation but a necessary one. Doug and Sid went down to the river and made a raft attached to ropes on both sides of the river so that they get many women cross the river quickly. They concealed the raft and returned to the bunker. Doug was sent to the Lancing Ring bunker and after informing them about the women it was arranged for them to come to the river that night at 2200 hours to help get the women to safety. That night at 2200 hours Matt, Sid and Jake were sitting in Colonel Grant's tent.

"It has been a huge operation to get the women out of their compound, but we have managed. We have put a few men in their dressed as women. They are walking around with their heads down and if the situation wasn't so serious, it would be funny. Once the women are all safely out they will return to the men's compound. When the Germans discover that the women have gone there will be a real hoo-ha. I have spoken to the men and they are happy with the arrangements. I have told them that there may be reprisals but they all agree that the women's safety is more important. This way the Hun won't be able to make us do their bidding and the women will be safe. Right I have all the women in the tents near to Smith's tent," Colonel Grant said.

"Good," said Matt. "It will take a few hours to evacuate all of them, so we need them to understand that they mustn't make a noise, we can't afford the Germans to hear them."

"I have told them that already," said Colonel Grant.

"Right, now before I go, this is going to cause problems with getting the weapons into the camp," Matt said.

"I… um… don't think so. We have found an alternative method," Colonel Grant said smiling.

"Brilliant, let's get the women going and whilst this is happening we can discuss that," Matt said.

Matt left the tent with Sid and Jake. Jake would lead the first women through and Sid would make sure that the camp end was run efficiently. The evacuation started. The women were completely silent during the exodus. They entered the tunnel which wasn't very pleasant without any complaints and they moved to the end of the tunnel. They were then transported over the river in batches of 15 on the raft with men both sides of the river pulling on the ropes. It went brilliantly. Whilst this was happening the Colonel and Matt discussed the movement of arms into the camp.

"On the north side of the camp, near the huts that we are building, we noticed that the two towers do not cover the whole of that area. They do put guards up there periodically. We are timing the guard's movements and it appears that they go along the wire there every half an hour. The wire is loose there and can be lifted. At night we can bring the arms in under the wire there and as it only a few yards to the huts and our cellars. It shouldn't be too difficult," said Colonel Grant. He was quite smug that he had discovered this.

"We mustn't be caught doing this. It would be a disaster. We have gone through so much to get them. We have even lost a life doing it," Matt said,

"I agree. I will get my officers on to it, but I think that we should get them in here after the visit from Edward and Wallace," Colonel Grant said.

"Yes, right I will be in touch once the visit has been completed," Matt said.

"Good,"

"Now I must see to this evacuation," said Matt.

Matt then went over to Sid to confirm it was all proceeding well. Sid was pleased although they had to bring it to a halt for 15 minutes when a guard got too close for comfort, but it was now going very well. They had nearly half the women out.

It took nearly 3 hours for all the women to leave the camp, but the problem they had was the river crossing. When they were out of the tunnel they were told to lie in the undergrowth on the river bank and wait their turn to be taken across the river. Although the river crossing was relatively safe a passing German patrol on the road may well see them, so lookouts were placed, so that the raft could be stopped if one passed. This happened a couple of times and nerves were getting a bit rattled. Once they were across the river they were taken in batches across the road and on to the Cement Works. Father Andrew and Trudy had been called in to help here. At 0500 hours the last of the women crossed the river and road.

When all the women were safely in the Cement Works, Matt and all the men made their way there too. When he entered a big cheer went up. Matt and the men were kissed, hugged and cheered as they walked through the women. He felt that he needed to inform them all what was going to happen to them now, so he stood up on a platform where the loading of cement would have taken place and after the room quietened down he said, "Welcome to the Cement Works. I am afraid it's not much and will be very uncomfortable for you. I am sorry about that, but I suspect that you will be safer here than in that camp."

There was a lot of mumbling, but as Matt continued they fell silent.

"Now you will all have to stay inside here now until we get you ID and ration cards. We are then going to move you out to rural areas where you can fit in with the populace there. Some of you will work the land and others will do whatever you feel you can do, but I can tell you now that you will all be looked after. Now we will be bringing supplies to you as soon as we can. There is a water supply although it is a bit dilapidated and I am afraid it is also temperamental. There is some food, but you will have to ration yourselves and we will get more to you as and when we can get hold of it. As you can see you can light a fire which is fortunate as I am unable to get any blankets to you, leastways not yet. I am working on it. You may have to huddle up as it is getting very cold now. I know that you will have loads of questions, but I am sure that Father Andrew," Matt pointed him out, "and Trudy, who I think you know, will be able to answer them for you," as he was speaking a woman put her hand up.

"Yes," Matt said.

"I just wanted to say thank you on behalf of all of us. Colonel Grant told us that we were going to be shot or held as a kind of ransom, so I think that we all owe you our lives, but what will happen to the men when they find out we are gone?" she asked.

"All the men in the camp, without exception, agreed that you all should leave. They are all aware that there will be repercussions and they are all prepared to die for your safety. I know that it is hard to bear but being British means that we have our values and we value our women. By the way, there will be a lot more patrols in the area, so none of you are to leave until we say. Do you all understand that?" he said.

The women all murmured their understanding.

"Now we have to go. We will be back, so try and keep warm and good luck," Matt finished.

Matt and all the men left. He needed to get things moving. He had given Father Andrew a camera and lots of films. He needed him to photograph all the women for the ID cards and as Matt left he saw and heard him organising the women.

After Matt had rested he went to the drop point by the bridle way as he needed to know if control had agreed with his demands. He also wanted to know it there was any access to clothing and blankets for the women. He had seen that some of their clothes were in a bad way. Sid came with him and upon reaching the drop point they could see, further up the bridle way that a horse was grazing on a grassy area. This horse seemed to hear them approach, even though they had crawled through the undergrowth, and moved away suddenly from where it had been grazing. Matt recognised the horse as Madison and he became worried for Nellie. If Madison was here, then so should Nellie. He wondered if she had been thrown, but this horse would have made its way back to the stables, not stayed in the area. Matt whispered his concerns to Sid and they were now both worried.

Matt and Sid looked up and down the path from where they were laying but could see nothing. Matt decided to go up to the drop point and see if there was a message, so he furtively moved to the spot. There was a message and he picked it up, opened it and saw that it was not in code. It read:

Am in the shrubbery opposite.

Come and find me.

N

Matt showed Sid the message and they both went over the hedge on the other side of the path and started to look around for Nellie. They had been looking for about a minute when suddenly 2 people stood up.

"Thank God you've come. We have been here nearly all night." It was Nellie and she had a man with her. Matt immediately pulled out a pistol from his coat and Sid did the same.

"Are you alright?" Matt asked.

"Of course, now you are here," Nellie said.

Matt looked at the person she was with and asked, "Who's that with you?"

Nellie and the man came forward. "Sorry Matt, let me explain. This is Major Finch, he works for the auxiliaries and he has come to help you."

"Has he got papers?" Matt asked cautiously.

"Yes, yes, I have, here," he put his hand in his jacket.

"Careful. Do it slowly please," Matt said.

"Sorry yes."

He pulled out some papers and handed them to Matt. They were orders from Colonel Armstrong to meet up with Matt and his team and assist regarding the women from the camp and afterwards join the unit.

"Thank god for that," Matt said. "We are really worried about them. We need to feed them, cloth them and keep them warm. I hope you have come to help with that."

"I have, and I have supplies being brought in urgently. It has been logistically a problem at such short notice, that is why I have been drafted in and hopefully we will get these supplies within the next couple of day. I have asked Miss Frobisher to help as well so you can get on with other things and I can deal with the women. Oh, by the way, HQ and especially Colonel Armstrong are really impressed with what you have achieved. They thought that you would all be dead by now, but you seem to be invincible. They were sorry about Private Smith, but for the rest of you to last this long is remarkable. The other units have been badly depleted. We are trying to get more men into those areas to support them, but you have done wonders. You know that you have been promoted," said Major Finch.

Matt had been feeling uncomfortable with this man talking the way he did. Nellie could see how he was, so interjected, "Oh really Major, what rank is he now?"

"Why a Major of course. It is a field promotion," he said.

"Wow did you hear that a Major in three months. At this rate you will be a General before the end of the war," Nellie laughed, as did Sid. Matt thought that this was astonishing, but he was level headed enough to realise that talking like this in a shrubbery was not good sense.

"Right, well as a Major I am ordering us to move from here and let's get somewhere safer," he said.

Major Finch wanted to get to the women and he wanted Nellie to go with them. Matt did not agree. He didn't want Nellie to know their location because it would put her in danger and said this, much to Nellie's annoyance. He told her that she should go home now, and he would be in touch as soon as possible. He was sure that Major Finch would have messages for her to be sent and passed on. Although Nellie disagreed, she did as she was told and made her way back to the bridle path, got hold of Madison and rode home,

There was one question that he wanted to ask Major Finch, however, "Did you come here on that horse as well?"

"No, I walked beside it, as if I was leading her," Major Finch said.

"I just wondered. I was trying to imagine both of you riding that horse," Matt said with a bit of giggle.

They led Major Finch through the wooded area and then over the Downs. They got to the Cement Works forty five minutes later and they entered through the back entrance. Matt was surprised at how organised the women had got in such a short time. The whole place seemed to be clean as well. He suspected that it was probably down to Father Andrew and Trudy. They welcomed Matt and Major Finch who wanted to be called Dave with a lovely cup of tea and biscuits which someone had made over the open fire. Matt was really impressed considering the little amount of food that they had. He left Dave with Father Andrew whilst he went and spoke to Trudy. He wanted to know how the injured men were, especially Jack. He wanted him back and wanted to know when he would be fit again. Trudy said that Will was doing well but he was still very ill. The man with the broken leg, Sean, was fine. He was walking around on a make shift crutch. Jack was doing well and should be fit in a week. Jack had heard what she was saying and started to complain that he was alright now and could go back to work immediately. Trudy interrupted his complaining and told him that he would not be fit until the stitches were removed. Trudy was not going to be undermined by any of her patients. She had the last word and Matt respected that. Trudy had also employed a few of the other women, who were obviously nurses, to help look after the wounded.

Understanding that the women would get bored being in this place he thought he could get them to check the contents of the trucks. They needed to know exactly what they had got, and they needed to give the women some weapons just in case of an emergency. He told Father Andrew and Dave that he would appreciate if they would do this.

Matt and Sid did not stay long. They told Dave that they would be back the following day and they left.

CHAPTER 16

When Nellie left Matt, she rode home. She was angry with Matt for refusing to allow her to accompany the Major and help him. She put Madison in his stall and was unsaddling him, when her neighbour, Cora, came into the yard. She entered the stable block and went over to Nellie

"Saw you come back. Have a good ride?" she asked.

"Oh, hello Cora. Yes, I love the fresh air on my face, although it is now getting a bit cold," Nellie said.

"Yes. I wouldn't be surprised if it snows soon, it is getting really cold," Cora said.

"Yes," said Nellie.

"Do you fancy a cuppa and some gossip? I have just made some cakes," Cora asked.

"Love to Cora, can you give me 5 minutes to settle Madison and I'll be over," she said.

Cora left, and Nellie busied herself making Madison comfortable. She popped into her office and went into her room with the radio. She kept all her courier's papers there that needed to be delivered and she needed to sort them out, because she didn't just do the one drop area by the bridle path, she covered a couple of others which usually contained packages to be picked up and then she would have to pass them on to Matt's unit. She'd had to leave them quickly when the Major arrived. She now slid them into her safe which was under the table in the radio room. She locked it, left the stables and went over to Cora's house. She used the back door which took her straight into Cora's kitchen. Cora was a lovely lady although some would call her a bit of a busy body. Nellie loved her as she had been a very good friend of her mother. Cora looked out for Nellie and was always there for a shoulder to cry on when things went wrong and would help at a moment's notice. Nellie, however, did worry that she did say things to other people about her, but there was nothing really that Nellie was ashamed of, so it really did not matter. On entering the kitchen Nellie could smell cakes cooking. It felt so homely and it reminded her of her mother when she was alive.

She would always be cooking something delicious.

"It smells glorious, what are you cooking?" Nellie asked.

Nellie sat on a chair at a table situated in the middle of the kitchen. Cora turned around and said, "It's a Victoria sponge. I used some eggs that Frank gave me, and I had some spare flour." Frank owned the farm at the end of the lane.

She placed a cup of coffee and a plate, with a piece of cake on it, in front of Nellie and did the same for herself. She then sat down opposite Nellie.

"You are looking thin. Are you eating properly?" she asked. She always worried whether Nellie was eating correctly.

"Yes Cora. I am fine. How's Howard?" asked Nellie.

Howard was Cora's husband. He'd had a heart attack a year ago and had to take it easy, which Cora made him do, much to his annoyance.

"He is really good. This new diet with food being rationed is actually very healthy. He has lost weight and he is so much fitter," said Cora

They spent the next half an hour gossiping about people they knew. Nellie was just about to leave when Cora said, "Have you got a new man?"

Nellie shook her head and Cora continued, "Well I saw him come to the yard this morning."

"Oh, him, no, he was someone who wanted to know about keeping a horse. I just took him out with me to show him some finer points about horses and Madison is such a fine example," she said.

"No not him. The man I saw came into your yard after you had left," Cora said.

Nellie was puzzled; it couldn't have been Matt as she knew that he hadn't come around this morning.

"I don't know who you are talking about Cora," Nellie said.

Cora thought for a moment and then said, "It was about 10 minutes after you left, a man went into the yard. He didn't go to the house, he went straight into the stable block and was in there for about 15 to 20 minutes and then left. I thought I recognised him, so I assumed it was through you and the horses, but perhaps not. I cannot think where I have seen him before. Howard saw him as well so perhaps he may have recognised him."

Nellie was really concerned and asked Cora, "Can you ask Howard. I need to know. It may be important."

Nellie was frowning and wondering why someone spent that amount of time in her stables. What could he have done in there? Cora saw the expression on Nellie's face and immediately went into the lounge where Howard was sitting reading.

He came into the kitchen with Cora and after saying hello to Nellie he said, "I think that man was with the Germans when they came around with that detector van. He didn't go into any of the houses or your yard then. He just hung around the van. He wasn't in uniform, but I think he is definitely something to do with the Germans, possibly the Gestapo."

Nellie asked, "Could you see what he was doing in the yard?"

"He seemed to be looking at the roof over your office, but I could have been mistaken. He went to the end of the building, by your office and kept looking up for something. He then disappeared into the stables and was there for ages. When he came out he went back to the area outside your office. Something obviously fascinated him," said Howard. "I was going to get Cora to go over and see if we could help him, but he just went. I didn't see any vehicles outside. When he left he walked down towards Frank's place. Is everything alright Nellie?"

Nellie was now worried. She then said, "I'm not quite sure but it could be trouble."

"Is there anything that we can do?" asked Howard.

"No, I don't think so."

Nellie got up and was about to leave when she seemed to come to a decision.

"Cora, I think that I need to go away for a while, will you look after the boys for me?" The boys were her horses.

"Of course dear, how long will you be away and where are you going?" Cora asked.

"Don't ask her that," Howard said, noticing the look on Nellie's worried face.

"You be as long as you want, love," said Howard. "And don't worry about the boys, we will look after them."

"Thank you so much. I must go now," and she left Cora and Howard.

Nellie hurriedly went over to the stable and went into her office. She looked around to see if anything had been disturbed. She went into her radio room but was unable to see if anything had been touched. She went to the safe and removed everything which included all the packages and code books that were in there. She put them into a back pack. She put on her warm fleecy jumper, her riding coat, gloves, scarf and hat and she left the stables by the back door. She went through her paddock and over a fence to a small path that led to the bridle path. She knew that this was the only place that she would be able to meet up with Matt again, and she really needed his help. She needed to find somewhere safe. Nellie was unaware that as she went through the back door of the stable a truck with 6 Germans pulled up at the front gates of the stables. They entered the stable and started to pull the place to bits. They checked the horse's stalls, much to the disgust of the two horses and they eventually turned their attentions to the office and although they had been told that there was something wrong with the building they were unable to find the radio room. The man who had come in earlier entered the office and standing in the middle of the room turned in every direction. He could sense that there was something wrong with the room but couldn't put his finger on it. He went over to the wall, which should be an outside wall and he put his hand on it. It should have felt cold to the touch, but it wasn't, it was warm. He looked at the wall and he turned to the German troops and said "Ziehen Sie diese Wand herunter" (pull that wall down). The troops did as they were told, and they discovered that the wall was a false wall and behind it they found the radio and the safe. They forced the safe open to find it was empty. Fortunately, Nellie had taken all the code books along with the packages, so although they had the radio they did not have anything else. The Germans then searched the house but found nothing. The man in charge ordered the troops to go around to the neighbours and questioned them but none of the neighbours knew anything, in fact they were surprised that the Germans were suspicious of her. When they went to Cora's house, she told them that Miss Frobisher had left the previous day and they didn't know where or for how long. She told them that she was looking after the horses for her. They wanted to know if this was unusual to which she replied that it wasn't. She always helped Miss Frobisher with the horses since her mother had died. The Germans believed her, and they left. When the Germans left Nellie's house Cora went over there to find out what they had done. The office was a shamble, and she saw that a wall was missing. All that was left in the radio room were the desk and lights. Cora smiled and then went over to the horses and after patting each one, and after giving them each a treat and making sure that they were comfortable, she left.

The following day Matt visited the Cement Works and Dave had some messages that needed to be sent. Matt took them, and he went directly to the drop point by the bridle path. He made the usual checks and he went over to the drop place. There was another note there and it said the same as the one the previous day. He thought for a minute that he had left it there, but he knew that he had destroyed it. He went over the hedge and into the shrubs on the other side of the bridle path. He whispered Nellie's name. There was a rustle of some bushes just to the left of him which made him look in that direction. He saw Nellie huddled in the undergrowth. She had her eyes open and was staring at him. She was frozen and could barely speak because her teeth were chattering so much. Her lips were blue and although she had gloves on, her fingers had also turned blue. Matt put his arms around her, started to rub her all over to try and warm her up.

"What has happened?" he asked.

Matt was really concerned and needed her to tell him what had happened. Nellie managed, through chattering teeth, to tell Matt briefly what Cora had told her and how she had just cleared out the radio room and ran. She knew that she had been compromised. This happened the preceding day and she had been in this shrubbery ever since, which meant that she had been there overnight. The temperature overnight had fallen to minus 2 and she was freezing cold. Matt decided to take her immediately to the Cement Works as she needed to warm up and she needed to be cared for. The walk to the Cement Works should have taken about 45 minutes but it took him over an hour and a half to get there. Nellie was walking at a snail's pace as the cold had got into her legs and this caused her to stumble a lot. Matt was nearly carrying her when they eventually arrived. Upon entry Trudy and the nursing staff took her from Matt and efficiently warmed her up and cared for her. Matt waited until Trudy finished and then sat with her until she could speak properly. About an hour later and, after having some warm soup and drinks, she felt more like herself. She did have a splitting headache but was told that was due to her body going from freezing cold to hot, but it would go. She then told Matt the full story and she told him that she probably will not be able to return to the stable, so she could continue from here. Matt was shocked that after what she had been through she still wanted to help, and he said this to her. She said in a matter of fact way, "We all have a job to do. I can rest when the Allies get here."

Matt shrugged and when he looked down at her, he realised how much he liked her, not because she was so beautiful, but because she had something else, bravery, determination, courage, in fact, real grit. He bent over her and he gave her a kiss on the lips. He didn't mean to, but he couldn't resist. She responded. It was a long lingering kiss and afterwards she looked up into his eyes and said, "I think I'm hooked."

"Hooked?" Matt asked.

"Well you know. I think I have a crush on you," she laughed.

"Oh that. Well good because I have definitely got a crush on you," Matt replied.

Within the next hour Nellie was up on her feet and walking round. When she saw all the women in the storage place she laughed, "Well Matt you certainly have a harem here."

"Pardon me. Some of them would have been killed if we hadn't got them out," he said seriously.

"I know I was only joking. Lighten up," she said still laughing.

Dave, who had been watching Matt and Nellie, went over to them.

"How are you Miss Frobisher?" said Dave politely.

"Got a bit of a headache but I'll live, thank you for asking," Nellie said.

"That is fortunate," Dave said.

"What do you mean?" asked Matt.

"Well we now have our own radio operator. All we need is a radio," he said.

"Yes, Matt can you get a radio?" asked Nellie.

"No, I can't, and you are not transmitting from here. They found you at your home and I do not want them to find this place. There is too much at risk here. We can't put these women in danger because you want to keep your job going. No I can't, and I will not get you one," Matt said firmly.

"I can go onto the Downs and transmit. They would have a hell of a job finding me up there," Nellie said.

"Look Nellie, they must have your name now. They certainly have your description and I think if they suspect that a radio is being used on the Downs and they catch you up there, they will put two and two together and come up with four. Don't you? Look I know you feel redundant, but I can assure you, that once we have sorted things out and got you a new id, you will be required again, but until then you need to take a well-earned rest," Matt said. He was determined that Nellie should not be put in danger again.

"I must admit, your unit and all your couriers have seemed to last longer than other auxiliary units, so perhaps you are right Matt," said Dave.

Nellie looked defeated and tried to think of something to say, but couldn't, so she stayed silent. Dave however said, "I need to get a package dropped off and some messages passed. How do we do that now?"

"Give it to me. I have other drop points and there are other couriers," he said.

Dave handed over the package and a message. He also wanted another message to be sent urgently by radio. He gave that to Matt as well. Matt told Dave that after the next couple of days he would show him where the drop points are, and he can do the drops himself. Dave was grateful.

Matt did not want to leave Nellie but knew that he had to, as he had things to do.

The visit of Edward and Wallace was going to take place the following day and Matt and his men wanted to take out the bridge before they went across it. Jake had prepared the explosives and they were going to explode them via a detonator box. It meant that a wire had to be taken from the explosives to the box, but the consequences of which was the person operating the box would have to be near the bridge. It was felt that as the majority of German troops would be on the east side of the river because Edward and Wallace would first be visiting the port and church, which were on that side, before going over the bridge to the camp which was on the west side of the river, then the operator of the detonator box should be on the west side. There was a lot of natural vegetation which would give the operator cover after the explosion and during the confusion he would make his get away by going up the river bank using the natural vegetation as cover and cross the river using a canoe from one of the sheds when it quietened down. Jake and Sid both volunteered to deal with the detonator. Matt decided that it was probably better to have two men, just in case there was trouble. Matt and Doug, along with some of the men from Sergeant Green's group, were going to put the explosives in place. They were going to place the explosives at night and Jake and Sid would then hide themselves until they were ready to blow the bridge up. There was one problem with this plan. Due to the river being tidal they couldn't put the explosives on the middle pier just under the water line, which they would do in a non-tidal river. When the river dropped at low tide the explosives would be seen. They would have to put the explosives on the ledge just under the road and the railway track and then thread the wire along the underside of the bridges and then onto the bank, making sure it was hidden. They would use something like plasticine to hold the wire in place, so it would not interfere with the detonation and then put grease and dirt over the wire to hide it.

At midnight Matt, Sid, Jake and Doug were all by the river edge by one of the sheds. They were waiting for the other men who had gone to another canoe shed further up the river to get the canoes that they would be using. Matt's men had got their canoes out and Jake had put the explosives and detonator box in one of the canoes in preparation for the off. The other men arrived just after midnight and they all set off towards the bridge. They hugged the bank, so they were almost invisible to anyone on either side of the river. When they got in sight of the bridge they were surprised that instead of being lit up, it was in complete darkness. They could see that there were guards at each end of it but none of them were looking towards the river. Quietly they went up to the centre pier and as it was high tide they could reach the ledge where they were going to put the explosives. Jake and a couple of men passed the explosives to Sid and Matt who put them in place and then very carefully they threaded the wire under the two bridges and down the side to the bank. They were very careful not to pull the wires out of the explosives. Once the wire was on the bank, Jake and Sid left their canoe and they got onto the bank. They quietly crept to an area which would conceal them, unwinding the wire as they went. This was the most dangerous part of the plan as there were Germans about 10 yards from them as they crawled. Eventually, about 50 yards from the bridge they arrived at a suitable place. They lay down and concealed themselves. Jake immediately connected the wire to the detonator box and now all they had to do was to push a plunger down which would detonate the explosives. Matt was happy that Jake and Sid were well concealed and that the explosives had been placed and hidden, he now ordered the rest of the men to return up the river. They had to tow the empty canoe behind them, but again they kept to the bank and arrived at the sheds without any incident. They arrived back at 0230 hours because the current was much stronger returning than when they left. Matt was aware that it was freezing cold and he was worried about Jake and Sid. They were wearing frogmen wet suits under normal clothes to try and keep warm. They also had a flask of hot tea, but Matt was still concerned for them. All the men returned to their bunkers and although Matt tried to get some sleep, he couldn't. The following day he became restless. In the morning he went to a couple of the drop points but eventually he did what he wanted to do when he first got up, he went down to the river and sat there waiting for something to happen. He believed that Edward and Wallace would be arriving in Shoreham at lunch time and he also believed that they planned to visit the camp at 1400 hours. Matt looked at his watch. It read 1130 hours, so he had to wait about 2 ½ hours before Jake would detonate the explosives. After about an hour he was joined by Doug who sat down beside him. They were in such a position that they were hidden by large bushes and this undergrowth looked like a hide, a place where it looked like a part of the natural environment. It even had a kind of roof, so they would be kept dry if it rained. Doug had bought some sandwiches and a flask of coffee.

Matt didn't feel like eating but he forced himself to do so. He was thankful for the coffee as the cold was seeping through his body. He thought about Jake and Sid having to lay in the cold all night. Doug turned to Matt and said, "Look at the sky?"

Matt looked up but saw nothing. "What?"

"The clouds, they look ominous. I wouldn't be surprised if it snowed. It certainly is cold enough," Doug said.

"Oh," Matt said looking back up at the sky. He saw what Doug was looking at.

"My god we don't want it to do that," Matt said.

"No, we don't, but I hate to break it to you, I think that it is already starting," Doug replied.

Matt looked across the river and could see that something was falling. It was very wet snow and luckily it was not settling, leastways not yet.

They both sat there in silence and literally watched the clock move. Time went by very slowly. Eventually it got to 1345 hours and now they paid attention to the sky line. They knew that they may not hear the explosion as they were about 4 miles away, but they should be able to see the smoke from the explosion. Matt and Doug kept watching the skyline and then suddenly at 1355 hours they saw the smoke. They also heard a noise. It sounded like a muffled bang.

"They've done it, now they have to get away. Blast this snow," Matt said, who was staring down the river knowing that it was too early to see the men.

"Yes. It should take them a couple of hours to get up here. Let's go to the Cement Works and warm up and then come back at 1600 hours Matt," said Doug.

Matt wanted to stay, but he was frozen, and he realised that when Jake and Sid got here they may need help, so reluctantly he agreed. At 1600 hours he and Doug returned, and they sat in the undergrowth and waited.

Once Jake and Sid had set off the explosives they immediately left their hiding place and ran up the side of the river. They ran crouched over and the natural vegetation partly gave them the cover that they needed to get away. They were very stiff from lying on the cold ground for such a long time, but because of the wet suits and the clothing they were in remarkably good shape. Suddenly there was a blast from a German machine gun which was set up on the east bank. They dived for cover and fortunately they were unharmed. They continued to run again. They were only couple of yards before they came to the bend in the river and they would be out of range from the machine gun and, at this point, they would not be seen from the bridge. The gun was fired again. Sid dived for cover, but Jake was a little late in his dive and he got hit twice. He had a wound on the side of his head and in the shoulder area. Jake was a large man and very strong, but the bullets, along with being so cold, took its toll. Sid crawled over to Jake and started to pull at him. He was very heavy. Jake came to his senses and stopped Sid pulling him. He managed to get up and with Sid's help they rounded the bend. Sid could see that Jake would not make it much further, he was losing blood and he could see hear that the Germans had sent out dogs to search for them. Sid's quick thinking probably saved them both. About 15 yards from them was one of the canoe sheds so he manhandled Jake up to the shed and he managed to get him inside. He also made sure that there wasn't any blood in the area that the Germans could follow. He laid Jake in one of the canoes and he laid in one himself. He knew that they couldn't be seen by anyone on the bank, but he worried that the dogs may find them. In theory they were lying on the river and he was hoping that the dogs will indicate that they went into the river. Both Jake and Sid were lying silently in the canoes when they heard the Germans with their dogs nearby. They heard the dogs approach the shed and even enter the river, but the cold stopped them venturing in too far. The Germans assumed wrongly that they had gone into the river and tried to cross it. They did not find the shed. Once the Germans left, Sid managed to look at Jake's wounds using a torch. The head wound was a scratch, but the shoulder wound was serious. All the men carried some form of first aid with them and in the kit was morphine, so Sid injected Jake with it and he bandaged the wound as best he could. Now they had to wait. They would have to stay until nightfall. Sid looked at his watch, it was 1515 hours. Because they were lying on top of the water it was extremely cold and both Sid and Jake were now starting to feel it badly. If they were able to see each other properly they would see that their lips were turning blue. They lay there all afternoon. About an hour after they had been in the shed they heard a boat pass and realised that the Germans had put a boat on the river. At about 1730 hours Sid risked looking out. Jake had been sleeping due to the morphine. He could hear something and was unsure what it was.

Sid looked out and could see a boat with a spot light on top just north of them. He watched them for a moment and then he realised that the river was at low tide and this boat was not a flat keeled boat. He thought to himself that if they weren't careful they would go aground. Sid got back in the shed and listened. The boat went past, Sid looked out again. It was now about 20 yards to the south of them. Suddenly it did exactly what Sid hoped it would, it grounded. The forward propulsion forced the keel further into the mud and eventually it was stuck solid. Sid laughed quietly to himself. It was now time to move. It was snowing quite heavily, but the weather would conceal them when they moved the canoes out on the river. The German boat was stuck so even if they did see them they couldn't do anything. He knew that the boat probably had a radio and they could radio their position, but by the time any backup arrived hopefully Sid would be able to have moved up stream from the position the Germans gave out. Anyway, Sid's decision was made. He pulled the canoe with Jake in out of the shed and he got in and started to paddle up the river. He could feel that he was weak but because it was low tide, the current wasn't very strong. He could see that with every stroke of the paddle he was getting further and further away from the German boat. The snow was now falling hard and it was laying. He needed this snow so said a prayer that it wouldn't stop. He knew that he had to paddle for about 3 to 4 miles, so he tried not to think about it and just got on and did it. He kept to the bank but at some stage he needed to cross the river and that meant going into the centre where the current was much stronger.

Matt and Doug had sat in the bushes for two hours and it was now 1800 hours. Jake and Sid should have been back at the latest an hour ago, but there was no sign of them. It was snowing badly now, and they had seen a German boat go by with a spot light aimed at far bank. Matt and Doug ducked down in case they swivelled the light round to their side of the river. The boat passed and still there was no Jake and Sid. About an hour after they saw the boat going up the river again, it returned still searching the west bank of the river. Matt and Doug waited for it to go past.

"Something must have gone wrong," Doug said.

"'I don't know. If they had been captured, why are they still looking up and down the river? No, I think they got away. We'll give them some more time. If they can get back they will," Matt said.

Although it was now minus 3 degrees and still snowing Matt did not feel it. His concerns for the safety of his men out did any concern for his own welfare. They sat there for another hour and both were peering through the snow, which was now falling very heavily.

Suddenly Doug shouted, "Look over there," pointing at the far bank about 30 yards south of them. They saw a black shape appear and move towards the shed which was almost opposite them. It was a canoe and they could see two heads.

"It's them," shouted Matt standing. "It's them."

They could see that there was a problem. Only one of them was paddling and the man in the back was leaning over. Sid pulled up to the shed and was too exhausted to paddle another inch. He was frozen to the bone and his strength had just given up. Matt and Doug were down at the water's edge shouting at Sid. Sid looked up and saw them. He shook the paddle at them trying to indicate that he could not go any further. Matt and Doug knew instinctively what he was trying to tell them, and they shouted that they were coming. They had to go the nearest shed which was about 200 yards north of them, but they ran all the way. They pulled a canoe out, got in and paddled as quickly as they could to Sid and Jake. When they got to them they hauled Sid into their canoe and Matt went into his canoe, and Matt and Doug paddled them back across the river. At the shed they hauled Sid and Jake up onto the bank and put the canoes away. They ascertained that Sid could walk unaided, and Matt and Doug carried Jake to the Cement Works. They delivered them to Trudy and the nurses, who immediately started working on Jake and getting Sid warmed up. Matt told Johnny and Father Andrew that because of the snow there were foot prints coming into the Cement Works that needed to be erased. Johnny, with Father Andrews, went out and dealt with it. They returned 20 minutes later saying that the snow had turned into rain and the footmarks were gone.

Trudy and the nurses had some concerned about the injury to Jake. The bullet had gone through, but he would need some antibiotics to prevent any infection. They had some from the medication that Matt and Father Andrew had previously got, but they were uncertain if there was enough. Jake would also need his wounds stitched up, which they could do. They did not know if any bones in his shoulder had been damaged. They would bandage him up and hope that he would be alright. Matt knew that it was all Trudy could do, but Jake was a strong man and if anyone would pull through he would.

Sid was frozen and was being warmed up slowly by the fire. He had been given some hot soup and the strength was slowly returning. Matt sat down beside him. "How are you feeling Sid," he asked.

"Getting there, God it was cold out there," Sid said quietly.

"That was marvellous of you to get Jake away, how on earth did you do it?" Matt asked.

Sid then told him exactly what had happened.

"My god Sid, you were both very lucky. That boat sticking in the mud was a bit handy," said Matt.

"Yes, this river being tidal is a real bonus, but the Hun will sort their equipment out soon, so we shouldn't get complacent." Sid was always the most practical and sensible of all the men.

"I want you to rest up now and get your strength back. You did an outstanding job today and I will pass it on to HQ. I wouldn't be surprised if there wasn't a medal in it for you and Jake," Matt said.

"Shut up boss." Sid was suitably embarrassed now and turned to the fire and continued eating his soup.

CHAPTER 17

Sid recovered very quickly from the mission, but Jake would have to stay at the Cement Works for a couple of weeks. He was in a very weak state with the injury and the cold. Matt was concerned because his unit now consisted of Doug and Sid, so he decided to recruit Johnny Jackson and one of his men Corporal Philip Crumpton, who was known to them now at Pip. He wanted one other which would make his strength up to 6, so he spoke to Johnny about it and he suggested another man from Sergeant Green's group, Private Steve Crane. Pip was reasonably knowledgeable about explosives. He was not up to Jake's standard, but he knew enough to be of an advantage to him. Steve was an older soldier, he was 35 years old and he seemed to be a solid and reliable person, but time would tell. Sid and Doug showed them around their bunker and they then took them, as well as Dave, out to show them to where the drop points were. Whilst this was happening Matt needed to go into town to speak to Bert. He also wanted to know if George had left any messages and find out exactly what the Germans reactions were to the destruction of the goods yard and the ruining of Edward and Wallace's visit to the area. He also needed to see Colonel Grant. He had not seen him since the women left and he wanted to know what the repercussions had been. He planned on going there during the night.

He arrived in town at 1630 hours and discovered that George's drop point had a couple of messages. He concealed them about his person and headed down to Ravens Road to speak to Bert. He arrived at his house at 1700 hours and was surprised to see it was a hive of activity. He stood at the gate when a woman approached and said, "Sad isn't it?"

"Yes," said Matt, thinking that it must be something to do with the previous days visit and his men's actions.

"Come on in. Bert needs all his friends now," said the woman.

The woman led the way into the house and Matt followed. There were many people in the front room, even some Germans. Matt was curious and slightly worried as he had George's messages on him. Why had Bert got Germans in his home? Matt walked through to the kitchen where he found Bert speaking with Jo, the licensee from the Crabtree Pub.

Bert turned to Matt and said, "Thanks for coming. The old girl would have been pleased with such a turn out."

Matt realised that Bert's wife had died, and this must have been her wake.

"I'm sorry Bert. Are you alright?" Matt asked.

"Yes, I'm great! Sorry, just a bit upset. She passed away 2 days ago, and it shouldn't have happened. It's the bloody Germans fault. I couldn't get the medication for her," he said. Matt could see that Bert was angry.

"Don't know what to say. Who are the Germans in the front room?" Matt asked quietly.

"They work at the station with me. They wanted to come for support, but I wish they hadn't," Bert said.

A German entered the kitchen and said to Bert in a heavy accent "Have to go. Sorry about your wife. See you tomorrow, yes?"

Bert looked at the German and muttered something. The German nodded and left.

"Thank God they have gone," said Jo.

"Bert can I have a word in private. I'll only keep you a minute and then I will go," Matt asked.

"Look, have a drink first. Jo has kindly bought some along." He poured Matt a glass of beer, which he took and toasted Bert's wife as he drank the beer.

Matt and Bert excused themselves from Jo and went outside to the garden.

"Sorry Bert I wouldn't have come around today if I had known," Matt said sincerely.

"That's alright, son. If you want to know about the goods yard, well it was completely demolished, and you managed to kill 15 of those buggers. It was a brilliant job. You also managed to kill two on the station and injured the others. What else do you want to know?" said Bert.

"Yesterday, how did the visit go?" asked Matt.

"Oh yes, I forgot about that, well the visit to the port was a great success, but the only people there to welcome them were the Germans, so of course it was going to be a success, but the church visit was a debacle. There was no vicar, only the curate, no towns folk and only the Commander of the area, Oberst whatshisname and his henchmen. Did you know that the Vicar and his house keeper have gone missing? There was a rumour that the Germans have taken them? For the funeral I had to use Father Dennis, the vicar from Saint Nicolas's church," Bert said.

"Bert, I know about that and just for your information, Father Andrew is safe and will return once the Germans have gone," Matt said.

"I'm glad. Nice man, anyway what else… Oh yes. Them bogus royalty had the shock of their life when the bridge blew up. I liked that, was that you?" Bert asked.

Matt did not reply, just smiled.

"Of course it was, anyway them royalty were hurried away and the Oberst thingy was furious, but he has stopped killing the town folk, although he did bring in a couple of them to find out what they knew. Of course, they knew nothing and were eventually released. There is another rumour, that there was a mass break out from the Airport. Is that right?" Bert asked smiling.

Again, Matt smiled.

"You know of course, that the commandant at the airport has been replaced and he has been shipped back to Germany. They have now got some real bastard over there, but I don't know any more about that. One thing though and I suspect you don't know, but about an hour after the bridge went up they were expecting some important stuff, not quite sure what, by train from Portsmouth and of course they couldn't get it through so that is now stranded near to Worthing. The whole transport system has come to a standstill, so if it was you, then well done. I shall be going to work tomorrow, and I will keep my eyes and ears open and I will let you know if there is anything of interest occurring," Bert said.

Matt was happy, as his work and that of his men has really messed up the Germans, not only the transport, but the visit.

"Thanks Bert. I will now leave and again I am truly sorry about your wife," Matt said.

"Thanks but promise me you will not stop what you are doing. The town's people are behind you," he said.

"I promise," Matt said.

Matt then left and returned to the bunker. He passed on the information to them and they decided to have a couple of drinks of whisky not only to celebrate but also to welcome their new colleagues.

Johnny wanted to return to the camp with Matt so at 2300 hours they left and made their way to the camp. They arrived at 0010 hours and because Matt was with Johnny who knew the camp well, they were able to go directly to Colonel Grant's tent. When they arrived in the tent they noticed that there were very few officers in there and Colonel Grant was not there. An officer who Johnny introduced as Lieutenant Charles Lewis invited Matt and Johnny to sit down and he explained where everyone was.

"After the women went, the Commandant called the Colonel into his office. The Commandant was furious, no not just furious, he was livid. He told the Colonel that he wanted to know where the women were and how they had disappeared from the camp. The Colonel said that he didn't know where they were, which was true, and he told them that he did not know how they got out of the camp, a white lie. The Commandant got some of his officers to hit the Colonel about a bit but of course he said nothing. The Colonel returned here and all the senior officers that is Captain and above were then pulled in, one by one, and roughed up a bit, but no one said anything. The whole camp was searched but they couldn't find the escape route. Over the next day there was a lot of coming and goings from other German officers and we had the Commander of the area in here quite a bit. Then of course yesterday that bridge exploded. There was such a cheer from the men. You should have seen them; you would have thought that we had won the war. Well the visit did not go ahead but the repercussions were bad. The Commandant was removed immediately, and it is rumoured that he has been returned to Germany and we have a real bastard in charge of us. Ten of our men have been put in front of a firing squad and shot. The senior staff, Captains and above, were all taken, and they are in solitary confinement and will be for a month, but we think that they are also being beaten up daily. The Colonel is not a fit man and I hope that he will be able to cope, anyway I have been left in charge," said Lieutenant Lewis.

"My God, I am sorry," Matt said.

Lieutenant Lewis smiled and said, "Don't be, the men's moral is very high. They were furious about the men who were killed but it has made them all the stronger to fight when the time comes. If Colonel Grant is killed, well I hate to think what they will do when the time comes, but I can assure you it will be nasty. They are building the huts by the way and if a German comes around to check them, well the language is dreadful, and the German leaves very quickly."

"Yes, about the huts, are the cellars ready?" Matt asked.

"Absolutely. There are 4 ready to be filled, and they have started digging 3 more. These should be ready in about 2 weeks," Lieutenant Lewis replied.

"Good. The last time I spoke to the Colonel, he said that there was a possible route in via the fence on the north side of the camp," Matt enquired.

"Yes. I thought after everything that had happened, the Germans would have sorted that out, but they haven't. It was arranged that a rope pulley system would be put in place and all that is needed is for you to attach the crates to the rope and they can be pulled through. The fence has been dealt with and it can be lifted and returned without any sign that it has been touched," Lieutenant Lewis said.

"Good. I think that we should wait for everything to quieten down again and perhaps we can try in a couple of weeks. Then you will have 7 cellars and I think that will take all the arms that we have got," Matt said.

"I agree with you," Lieutenant Lewis replied.

"I will send someone to confirm this in about 2 weeks. I may stop missions for the time being so that no one else will get hurt," Matt said.

"Don't you dare Sir, we want you and your men to do as much damage and sabotage as possible," he exclaimed.

"We may need some more of your men in the camp to help us out, would that be possible?" Matt asked.

"We were hoping you would, we already have men clamouring to be chosen, so anytime. Just let us know how many and when," he said. He was excited about this and informing the men that some of them would be required to help.

"You are still not being counted, then," Matt asked.

"Well we are, but they are unable to ever come to the same figure. We make sure that they don't. We have people who run along the ranks and get counted twice and even three times."

Matt was laughing imagining this.

"So, as I say, they are, but they really have no idea how many of us are here," said Lieutenant Lewis who was laughing at Matt laughing.
"This new Commandant, who is he?" asked Matt.
"His name is Mencken and we think that he is Gestapo, but we are uncertain. He very rarely wears his uniform and when he does it is one that we haven't seen before." Matt thought about this.
"I've not heard of him. Perhaps he was bought to this area from another area?"
"Perhaps, anyway he is in for a shock when the Allies get closer," Lieutenant Lewis said.
"Well I must leave now, so keep rebelling and I will be in touch," Matt said.

"Look, how do we get in touch with you just in case we need to pass on something to you?" Lieutenant Lewis asked. "At the moment we must rely on you coming in, but we may have to tell you something urgently."

"Yes, point taken. Um …," Matt thought about this.

"Perhaps I can help," Johnny said. "We can't use the north side because we don't want to draw attention to that area and the rest of the wire is under surveillance, apart from an area in the east of the camp. There is a big boulder which I think must have been an anti-tank measure, well just beside it is another smaller boulder and the fence goes right over it. You can leave a message under that boulder or place a large stone beside it and we will know that you want to speak to us and we will come in."

"Yes, that is a good idea," said Matt.

"OK I know the boulders you are talking about and I will arrange for a smaller stone to be placed next to it, if necessary," Lieutenant Lewis said

"OK then," said Matt

"One final thing before you go, are the women alright?" Lieutenant Lewis asked.

"Yes, we are looking after them well. They will get their ID's soon and then we are moving them to other locations where they can have a more normal life," Matt said.

Matt looked at Lieutenant Lewis and realised that this was more than a general enquiry.

"Lieutenant is there someone particular that you want to know about?" asked Matt.

"Yes, actually. Can you give her a note?" he asked.

"Of course. If anyone in here wants to write to anyone then we will take their letters," Matt said.

"Thank you," said Lieutenant Lewis.

He reached under his blankets and he produced a letter, "It's for Emma, Emma Rogers, she is a nurse."

"I will find her," said Matt.

Matt, Johnny and Lieutenant Lewis left the tent and went to the grill. As they were moving about they noticed that there were more guards on the perimeter fence and Matt whispered this to the Captain.

He said, "Yes that is since the women have gone."

They arrived at the grill where the Captain said good bye and Matt and Johnny left.

CHAPTER 18

The next couple of weeks were quiet. Christmas came and went and although the women in the Cement Works tried to make it festive it was a sad time for them. They were worried about their families and sweethearts and although they tried to be jolly they found it very hard. Matt had not told them about the people who had died in the camp or about the officers being in solitary confinement. He had delivered the note to Emma, a nurse who worked closely with Trudy. She was overjoyed about receiving a letter and once the other women found out some of them asked if Matt or Johnny could deliver a note to someone special in the camp. Matt and his men became postmen for a couple of days to keep them happy and because it was Christmas. One of the women sent a letter but did not get a reply and Lieutenant Lewis told him that the man she wrote to was one of the men that were killed, so Matt had to break the news gently to her but being careful not to say how, exactly, it had happened or that others had been killed as well. A couple of the women were writing to officers, and it was explained to them that they were well, but they couldn't reply. They would, however, be able to reply in about 3 to 4 weeks.

No other explanation was given and although they were curious they did not ask why. Once the Christmas period was over he told the women and Lieutenant Lewis that they had to stop the daily delivery of letters, but he would take them once every two weeks. All the people concerned were happy with this.

The injured men were all doing nicely. Jack was back with the unit and although Matt had 6 men, he decided that more was better than less, so he kept Steve, but now he had 7 men. It was a bit tight having all the men in the bunker, but they managed, which was mainly because they all got on so well. They set up a bunk in the area where the tables were. Jake, however, was fighting an infection in his shoulder, but Trudy was certain that he would pull through. Although Jake was unwell he still managed to chat up the nurses and Trudy had to have words with him about it. She was not complaining, it was because the nurses were arguing over who should nurse him. Will was slowly recovering but still needed round the clock nursing. He was remarkable though; whenever Matt saw him he always had a smile and never complained. He was also popular with the nurses, but not in the same way as Jake was.

Dave had managed to get over 100 ID's, ration cards and clothing coupons, so within the next couple of weeks these women would be leaving the Cement Works for homes further up the country. They were all being given background information, so they would have a firm story just in case they were stopped by the Germans. This was really exciting for some of them and they would sit around rehearsing their stories. It was also very good news for Matt, as food was becoming a real problem with so many people to feed. He and his men were foraging for food when they should be planning or executing missions, obtaining information or nurturing informants. HQ had arranged for a supply drop on the Downs, which consisted of food, but also, clothing and blankets. This was an exciting night, especially for the women. Dave had to employ some of the women to help with it and for some of these women it was the first time they had been out of the Cement Works since they had arrived. It was not a problem as they could get up onto the Downs via the rear of the Cement Works, which meant they did not have to use any roads and they had good cover if they saw any Germans in the area. As it happened there were none. It was a bit of a climb at the rear of the Cement Works, but the women managed, and they used a couple of the trucks to transport the supplies back. These trucks obviously used the roads to get onto the Downs.

When they returned and looked through the provisions they even found chocolate, and lots of tinned food. Someone at HQ must have been a woman as makeup had been sent. The women danced around seeing what had been sent and were very happy with everything.

Dave had also managed to get Nellie a new id and this enabled her to get out to her drop points and pick up messages. She persisted goading Matt about getting her a radio, but he kept refusing. Doug was very busy because he had to send, not only his normal messages, but ones for Dave and for Nellie. Matt was aware of Doug's problem and had even seen the detector van on the road by South Downs Farm. Doug did keep his messages down to 20 minutes, but the Germans knew that there was a radio operating in the area. It was eventually agreed that when he had to send two or three messages a day, Doug would send one from their bunker then go to Lancing Ring and send one from there and then go onto Coombehead Wood bunker and send one from there. It was time consuming, but it was safer. Matt thought about putting Nellie in Coombehead Wood bunker and then she could continue with her job, but for the time being Dave didn't want this. It was convenient for him to have her close so that she was able to drop off messages and pick up packages in the area, especially as there were more ID's to be picked up and messages to be left. One day when Nellie was out and about she went to the area she used to live. She decided to go and see Cora and find out how the horses were. She knew this was dangerous but if she was careful she thought it would be alright. She approached Cora's house by the back and quietly let herself in the kitchen. She closed the door silently and immediately saw Cora standing in her usual place, over the stove.

"Hello," she said.

Cora jumped, turned around and when she saw Nellie she ran over to her and hugged her.

"My dear, are you well? We were so worried," said Cora.

"I'm really well. Sorry I had to go but I was in danger," she said.

"I know. About 5 minutes after you last left here, you had a visit from the Germans. That man we saw was one of them. They ripped your place up a bit," Cora said.

"Well I won't be coming back for a while. I suppose not until the Germans go," Nellie told her.

"We thought that. Oh, it's so good to see you, but isn't this dangerous?" Cora asked.

"I suppose it is, but I just had to see you and I needed to know that the boys were well," Nellie said enquiringly.

"Howard has taken over looking after them. It has given him something to do. He occasionally takes Madison out for a ride. They are well fed and loved but are missing you," Cora said.

"Thank Howard for me, won't you," Nellie said.

"Of course, I will. He is over there now. In fact, I don't seem to see that much of him lately. He is always over at the stables," Cora laughed.

"When this bloody war is over I will have you over for a huge meal to thank you," Nellie said.

"I will hold you to that," Cora said with a tear in her eye. She really loved Nellie and treated her like a daughter.

"I can't stay. But I will try and get back again soon," Nellie said.

"Keep safe and here," Cora went to her larder and she put a ham, some cakes and biscuits in a bag and gave them to her.

"You are looking thin," Cora declared

"Thanks, bye Cora," and she left.

Matt wanted to keep up the pressure on the Germans, so he did a couple of missions on trucks. He and his team blew up a convoy of trucks with equipment heading for the front. It was going through Southwick at the time. This was information given to them from Bert, and they also hit a couple trucks going up the A281, again information from Bert. These trucks had soldiers heading for the front. They blew up the trucks and killed the men on board. They managed both without incident or injury to any of their men.

One thing that had resulted from the Goods Yard in Shoreham being destroyed, they now had a mole in the port. George had been moved over to the Port, where he could continue with his job and he hadn't been suspected of helping with the raid. He had come up with information that arms were coming in and being transported immediately to the front, but not through Shoreham. They were being transported by a freighter to Lancing, where the Germans had built a temporary pier, so they could moor up and unload and they were then being taken by truck to the front from there. Matt had to laugh because now he knew, it would be easier to attack and confiscate these arms than in the Goods yards. He decided to let the Germans get away with this for a while and then he would hit them when they are lulled into a false sense of security.

It was two weeks since he had spoken with Lieutenant Lewis about getting the arms shipment into the camp. He decided that he needed to get them into the camp urgently, because if he took any more arms then he needed room to store them. Although the Cement Works was a good place to store them, he was aware that to put more trucks in there would start to cause a problem to the people living there. He entered the camp one night with Sid and he went to the officer's tent. The tent was fuller, but Colonel Grant was still not there. It turned out that the officers had been released early from solitary confinement, but Colonel Grant had been beaten so badly that he had been taken to the hospital upon release and he was in a bad way. Matt was angry, but not as angry as the other officers. He looked around the tent and could see cuts and bruises on the faces of some of them. It was obvious to him that they had been beaten as well. It was probably because these men were younger than the Colonel that they fared better.

Lieutenant Lewis told him that the three other cellars are now ready, and it was agreed that they would bring the arms in the following night. The officers said that they would have the pulley system in place, and men to pull the crates through. They would also have men ready to stow the arms away immediately. Matt said that he would be there at 0130 hours, but he would have to park the truck quite a way from the fence, so he may have to struggle getting the crates to the fence area. It was suggested that some men from the camp would be able to help if they could leave with him. Matt thought for a moment. He had 6 of his men, 7 including him, and he had 3 from Sergeant Green's group. He realised that perhaps he could do with about 3 more, just to be on the safe side. He agreed. One of the officers left the tent and got the extra 3 men together and when he left he found these men in Smith's tent next to the grill. The men were led through by Sid, and Matt followed them at the rear.

The following night was a hive of activity at the Cement Works. Some of the arms were going to be kept there for security of the building, but the majority were going into the camp. The trucks were packed up with the help of Father Andrew and Trudy who had the inventory of the arms and ammunition. At 0030 hours they left, and they made their way to the north side of the camp. It took them nearly half an hour because they had to go the long way around to it, via the Upper Beeding Bridge. They had to kill the two sentries, so they could pass. This meant that the trucks could not return to the east side of the river and they would have to dump them before they could return to the Cement Works.

They parked the trucks in some trees about 500 yards from the perimeter fence. They were well hidden both from the camp and the road. Matt and Johnny went up to the scrub land about 15 yards from the fence. Here they were hidden from the camp. At 0125 hours they crawled to the fence.

The men in the camp saw them and they crawled to meet them. They handed Matt and Johnny the rope which they took back to the shrubs where they were hidden. They then fastened the rope round a tree stump, so they now had a continuous rope going in and out of the camp. He saw two of the men from the camp pull the wire up about 3 feet, which was big enough to allow the crates to go under. Matt's men had bought up the first couple of crates and Johnny and Sid fastened one to the rope and they pulled on one side of the rope and the men in the camp pulled on the other side of the it. The crate went through the wire superbly, and silently, and was released from the rope pulley within 45 seconds. They continued for about 15 minutes, but they had to stop as a guard was seen nearby. They waited about 10 minutes until they were sure that the guard had gone, and they continued. It took them approximately three quarters of an hour to get all the arms through and they were back in the Cement Works at 0300 hours. The whole process was a great success. Matt was relieved that the arms were now safely hidden in the camp.

Another great success was the movement of the women to their new homes. Over the last couple of weeks five women were moved out daily to their new locations. It was rather hard on the women as they had to walk to these locations and some of them were over 5 miles away. They also had to find the places. They were given detailed maps and although they were told to try and keep off the roads as much as they could, although sometimes they had to go on the road. But without exception they all got there without any incidents. In 2 weeks they managed to re-locate 70 women. Dave had now managed to get another 75 ID's and ration cards so within another couple of weeks they would have moved well over half of the women. All the nurses were going to remain, as they may be needed when the fighting started and some of the women who were telecommunications officers also stayed as it was realised that they may be helpful again when the fighting started, so that still left nearly 70 women in the Cement Works. Some of the local farmers were approached and after explaining that it was for the women from the camp and an explanation about why they had to be removed from the camp, they provided nearly all the fresh food for them without complaining. They even took some of the women from Dave to work on their land. The women left in the Cement Works were extremely good at rationing themselves and they had nominated women to do the cooking and when Matt and his men arrived there, they were always surprised at what they were cooking with so little ingredients.

Matt and his men daily monitored the wireless broadcasts from the World Service and this had kept them up to date with what was happening on the front. Over Christmas it had been quiet, but since then, it was now the middle of January, it seemed that the Allies had got the bit between their teeth because they were making some significant advances and were now on the outskirts of London and were on the verge of re-taking it. The World Service also talked about troops that had been left behind enemy lines and about the wonderful job they were doing. It also commented that many had been killed but there were still people out there doing a marvellous job. This caused a cheer in the bunker from the men. They also talked at length about Edward and Wallace and they had heard that the reception they were getting from the British people was wonderful. They either wouldn't turn up to events organised by the Germans for them or if they were forced to go they refused to cheer, clap and certainly wouldn't speak to them. The wireless also recorded messages from King George and from Winston Churchill. It really cheered everyone up who had heard them. Another thing the wireless did was to pass messages to relatives who were caught behind the German's lines. They were messages for ordinary people, from wives, husbands, daughters, sons, mothers and fathers. It was heart wrenching at times especially when people wanted to tell of a birth or a death of someone in the family. The broadcasts also thanked the many nations that were helping British troops with equipment or manpower and the troops on the front line were becoming multinational. One fighting force that the Germans feared were the Ghurkhas. They had been shipped over to England and were now fighting alongside the British. The Ghurkhas were fierce fighting men and no German wanted to be on the end of the justice that they dished out. Occasionally they would change the channel on the radio and listen to William Joyce or as he was commonly called Lord Haw-Haw. He would praise the Germans in the care of the British in Southern England and he would continually criticise the BBC World Service for telling lies. He reported the reverse of what the BBC World Service said. The men in the bunker would boo and swear at him and afterwards they would feel so much better having let off a bit of steam at his expense.

A week later, Matt and the men were listening to wireless and heard that North London had been taken. There had been some fierce fighting especially in the West End. Many historical buildings had been damaged or destroyed but they had successfully pushed the Germans over the

River Thames to South London. Edward and Wallace had been hurriedly moved south but their whereabouts were unknown. The broadcasts told how Croydon Airport was being mercilessly bombed and no flights were able to fly in or out of there. Much of this information was verified by messages from Matt's HQ. Matt realised that he had to inform everyone in the Cement Works and in the camp, so he tasked Johnny and Pip to go to the camp and inform them and he and Sid went to the Cement Works.

When Matt told the women, Father Andrew and Nellie about it, there was a lot of patting on backs, kissing and hugging, (by the women), and much excitement and merriment. Matt did put a damper on the excitement by saying that although the troops were making fantastic progress he felt that it would still take possibly 6 months, or even longer, to re-take the whole of Southern England. Everyone told him to lighten up and enjoy this moment.

The information passed through the camp quickly and they couldn't contain their excitement. The guards did not understand why they were so happy, until one of them asked one of the prisoners directly. Of course, the man told him, and the guard looked puzzled. He was unaware of this and he made some enquiries and this information was confirmed. The guards became very solemn. Apparently, the new Commandant was furious that the PoWs knew this and wanted to know how they had found this information out. He suspected that they had a radio and the whole camp was searched, but of course nothing was found. Matt visited the camp a week after they had been informed of the Allies' progress because HQ wanted him to formulate plans for when the Allies were closer to them. It was essential that they hit the Germans lines from the rear and took possession of the port.

Around this time Matt became aware of two people who were collaborating with the Germans. This was a worry to Matt as there were people in town who knew of his and his unit's existence and if there was careless talk then these collaborators could pass information to the Germans.

One of these collaborators was believed to be the owner of a Night Club in Rope Tackle. It was positioned beside the river and was called the Waterside Club. Matt knew that it was frequented by many Germans and that some of the local women went there as well. The owner was called Henry Stubbs. He wasn't a local man. He came down from London about 15 years earlier and took over the existing club.

Matt decided to speak with Henry so, with Sid, they went down to the club one night to see if they could make contact with him.

They entered the club and went up to the bar. They sat having a pint of bitter and watched the people in the place. There were many Germans and they seemed to be really interested in any English girl that was in the place. Matt and Sid could not see any girl available, they all appeared to be with someone, whether it was German or not, did not seem to bother them. They watched a man, who they assumed was Henry, approaching some of the Germans. He was making sure that they had everything that they wanted. Matt and Sid stayed for about an hour and decided that they would hang around outside and see if they could speak with Henry when he left to go home. They positioned themselves beside a wall which backed onto the river. It was a good place as they could see both the back and front of the club and as they were in the shadows they couldn't be seen by anyone coming or leaving the club. They stayed until 3am when they saw that people were starting to leave. They had to be careful as there was a curfew and if any German saw them then they would be asked some awkward questions, or they could even be taken in by them. They saw the club being closed up and eventually at just before 4am they saw Henry standing at the back door. He locked the door and headed over to a car.

There was no one else around so as he was unlocking the car Matt and Sid went up to him.

"Hello, it's Henry, isn't it?" Matt said.

"Yes, do I know you?" Henry said looking at Matt and then at Sid.

"No, you don't, but we hope that we are going to be good friends," said Matt.

Henry looked at Matt closely and then said, "Look I don't carry anything valuable on me if that's what you are after."

"No Henry that is not what we are after. We just want to speak to you. Perhaps we should go into your club and then we can sit down for that talk," Matt suggested.

Henry was alarmed at this and was just about to complain when he saw Sid remove something from his coat. It was a pistol.

"Oh… alright," said Henry.

They all went back into the club and once inside they sat at a table and Matt said, "Glad you are being reasonable about this. Now to start. We hear that you have been collaborating with the Germans. Giving them information and… well helping them as much as you can."

"Where the hell did you hear that? I haven't. I would like to know where the resistance is, and I would give them snippets of information that I hear in the club from time to time. The problem is that the resistance is invisible, and I don't know who they are," said Henry.

"Are you telling us that you haven't been giving information to the Germans?" asked Matt.

"No of course not. I hate them. I must open the club up and unfortunately, they use it, but I listen, and I hear things. Are you the resistance?" Henry got up and he went behind the bar and produced a bottle of scotch and 3 glasses. He bought them to the table and poured it out.

Matt and Sid watched him, and then Henry said, "Right I hope you believe me. I want to help, and I can listen out. I get some of the senior officers in here and once they have a drink they get talkative."

He then put a glass full of scotch in front of Matt and Sid.

"Henry, information is valuable. If you can provide it then you will be helping certain people out, but if you are playing with us, you will find a bullet in you. We may be the ones sitting opposite you now, but I can assure you that if the Germans capture us and the information came from you then you will be killed. Am I making myself clear?" Matt said.

"Look how can I prove myself to you?" He reached in his jacket and produced a wallet. From the wallet he pulled out a photograph, it was of him with a younger man.

"This is a picture of my son. He was in the British Expeditionary Force and was killed at Dunkirk. That is my reason to help you," Henry said.

"Ok Henry, I will give you the benefit of the doubt. Come up with information for me and prove that you are a patriot," said Matt.

Henry then told them about a couple of troop movements and about plans for what the Germans wanted to do in this area. He then spoke about someone he was concerned about. A very prominent business man was being softened up by the Germans and he often attended the club where all his drinks are bought for him by them. The name that Henry gave was Tobias Crawford. This was the name of the other collaborator that Matt already had information about. Henry told Matt that he should be very careful with this man. He had the ear of the Germans and he was dangerous.

When Matt and Sid left they were happy that Henry was onside with them and over the next few weeks he came up with some valuable information concerning the commander of the area and the commandant of the camp.

Matt organised surveillance on Tobias Crawford and it was reported to him that he spent much of his time with German senior officers. He was seen going into Lancing College on many occasions and he was often wined and dined by them. He lived in one of the big houses on Mill Hill and he had offices in town. His business was export and import which caused Matt real concern as he assumed that the Germans were homing in on

Tobias's contacts in other countries. This could account for his popularity.

Matt decided that he needed to speak to him and if he was collaborating then he needed to be dealt with. Matt's whole unit of seven men went to Tobias's home in Mill Hill. Two of his men were position out the front, watching for anyone who was approaching the property, especially Germans, as he was often picked up from the premises by them. The remainder of the men approached it from the rear crossing a couple of fields to get into the rear garden. They could see someone in the conservatory, so they carefully and silently approached the rear French doors which they believed took them into a lounge. Fortunately, these doors weren't locked, so they entered. They found themselves in a lounge. It was furnished rather lavishly with antiques, but the room looked awful. Nothing seemed to match, but it did appear to show that Tobias was wealthy. They carefully made their way into the kitchen, but no one was there. They then heard a noise coming from the conservatory. Whoever was there was singing to themselves. Matt and his men made their way into the conservatory where they saw a grossly overweight man sitting, drinking a cup of tea.

"Tobias Crawford?" Matt asked.

"Yes, who the hell are you? And what are you doing in my house, get out," Tobias shouted.

Matt was armed with a sten gun which he pointed at Tobias.

"We are here to speak to you, now I suggest that you stay exactly where you are and do not make any sudden moves," Matt said.

Tobias looked from the gun to Matt's face and said, "Now son, we aren't going to use that, are we?"

"Tobias Crawford, we aren't if you answer my questions. If you don't then we may use it," Matt said sarcastically.

Matt sat on a chair opposite him. After staring at him for a moment he said, "It has come to our notice that you are being friendly with the Germans. This has been verified by certain individuals and from our surveillance. We want to know what you are telling them. This is important, we need to know."

"You need to know nothing. That is my business. I will speak to whoever I want," Tobias said defiantly.

"Well Tobias it is our business. You see, we are here working on behalf of Winston Churchill and King George. You do remember them. We want to know what you are doing with the Germans," Matt said.

"We are a beaten nation. I am just befriending the Germans because I know when I am on to a good thing. Now if you don't mind I would like to finish my tea and then leave for the office," said Tobias as he picked up his cup from a table.

Tobias seemed to dismiss Matt and his men, but Sid who was beside him grabbed hold of Tobias and dragged him out of his seat and he fell to the floor along with his cup of tea.

Matt stood over him and said, "You may be finished with us, but I can assure you that we haven't finished with you. Now get your fat arse up off the floor and we are going to search your house."

Tobias was in shock with the treatment that Matt had dished out and was only able to say, "Search my house, you can't"

Matt looked at his men and nodded. They all left the conservatory leaving Matt alone with Tobias.

"I am going to give you some advice," said Matt. "During the time my men are gone I suggest that you talk otherwise my men will not be happy."

Tobias was struggling to get back in his chair. "What do you want to know?" he asked.

"Let's start with what do the Germans want from you and your business?" asked Matt.

"They don't really want anything from the business, just some contact names," he said.

"Well in that case I need you to write them down," said Matt.

"I can't remember their names. I just get my secretary to give them all the details," he explained.

"What else do they want?"

"They want me to take over the running of the area when they take the country. They want me to act as the head of a group of people who are friendly towards them, and I have agreed. So, what are you going to do about this?" he said defiantly.

At that moment a couple of his men came in and nodded indicating that they have found nothing.

Matt waited for all his men to return and said, "Tobias, will you supply me with those names and the names of the other people who are collaborating with the Germans?"

"No, I will not," he said.

"In that case you will be killed," Matt said in a matter of fact way.

"You wouldn't dare. I am an important man in this area and my death will cause you nothing but trouble," Tobias said not believing that they would kill him.

Matt looked at him and realised that this man would not say anything as he appeared to be waiting for something to happen. Matt then concluded that Tobias was waiting for the Germans to arrive. He was dressed as if he was going out. Matt turned to the men to leave and as Matt turned to Tobias he raised his gun and shot him in the head. Tobias wouldn't be helping anyone now.

The men left the same way they entered and just as they were crossing the field at the back of the house a German patrol entered the house where they found Tobias dead on the floor of his conservatory. These Germans did not see Matt or his men in the fields.

There were other reports of collaborators and although they were a serious concern to the Unit they decided that unless they were a real danger to the men then they would leave them and deal with them after the Germans were kicked out of Britain. Matt's job was to hinder the Germans and that is what he wanted to concentrate on.

January had turned into February and the Allies had now taken the majority of South London. Colonel Grant was now out of hospital and Matt could see that he had aged considerably with the treatment that he had received. He was, however, still an imposing man and he was not going to let the Germans think they had mentally hurt him.
"Matt the news is so good, I agree we should make plans for the future," said Colonel Grant.
"It is brilliant news, but we need to deal with what you and your men should do when the time comes. First though, how many men have you got in your hospital?"
"About 25, why?" asked the Colonel.
"Because they are your weak link, a bit like the women. They can be used against you," said Matt.

"I see what you mean, but we can't get them out," said the Colonel.

"I know, so I would suggest that once everything starts to kick off you make sure that they have armed guards in the hospital to protect them," Matt said.

"That will be done," agreed the Colonel.

"Now, when the Germans line is about 10 to 15 miles from here we need to do 2 things. We need to ensure that this place is secure. You need to take it and hold it. Then we need to take the port. Although we need the Hun to go, it would be beneficial for the future to incarcerate as many of the buggers as possible. If we can do that then liberating Europe may not be so difficult," Matt said.

"I agree. We can secure the camp at a moment's notice, and then I will ensure that you will have as many men with officers as you need. We are still training hard and they are now very fit. Fit enough to put up a good fight," the Colonel said proudly.

Further details were discussed, and Matt left happy that plans were in place when they would be needed. When he got back to the bunker he informed HQ, via the radio, with brief details of the plans and he was then informed that HQ had other objectives that needed to be put in place, but these would be sent via courier.

This was an exciting time for all the men. Father Andrew who had been getting pretty fed up stuck in the Cement Works wanted to be useful and approached Matt about it. Matt could not think of what he could do, that would keep him safe, but Father Andrew had other thoughts. He was concerned with the civilian population when the German army returned. Matt had not thought about them, so he asked him what he had in mind.

"Matt, I have put a lot of thought into this and I hope you agree. The locals were all at serious risk when the Germans invaded, and many lost their lives, so I thought we could put them somewhere safe when they return."

"It sounds good, but where?" Matt asked.

"Well the PoWs will, I presume, be fighting alongside you and your men, and I presume that the camp will be in our hands, so couldn't we move the civilians in there and put some sort of large Red Cross in the area so that the Allies will not bomb it." Matt thought about what Father Andrew had said and then said, "It is an idea, but how will we manage such a huge task? It will take manpower to do it. Father we really will not have the manpower at that time to do it."

"I thought about that as well. I, of course, will help with this and I have spoken to Trudy and the nurses and they will be happy to assist me. That way we can all go out and inform the civilians. They can make their own way to the camp and be greeted by British troops, the PoWs," said Father Andrew.

"In theory that is good, but we will not have secured the town at that stage, so the nurses and you will be at risk. Also, for security reasons we couldn't inform the civilians that this was planned until the actual time we would have to evacuate them. They may panic and again put you and the nurses in danger," Matt said.

"I know, but the nurses and I are prepared to take the risk," he said.

"But perhaps I am not prepared for you to take this risk," said Matt.

As Father Andrew and Matt were talking, the nurses had started to congregate behind them as if they knew exactly what they were talking about.

Trudy moved forward and stood beside Father Andrew and said, "Matt, Sir, we are aware that you want to keep us safe and we are all very grateful to you and your men, but now everyone has to stand up and be counted. We are in complete agreement with Father Andrew about helping the civilians. They will get killed if we don't do something for them. We can look after ourselves. Most us can shoot and handle firearms and we have been teaching the others here how to since we have been here. I suspect that you are going to secure the camp, but you are going to need to hold it and that will take up manpower that really is needed elsewhere. Well we could do that, and we can get the civilians into the camp. We are not just useless women," Trudy said in a very serious way. She was one of those people who you did not mess with, but this time Matt was going to try.

"Trudy, I understand that you want to do something, but don't you think that you are going to be very busy with the wounded when the time comes. I would rather that you were employed in this way and not running around with guns. I think that you will all be taken back to the camp and it will become a field hospital, but running around the town collecting civilians…, well I am not sure."

Trudy crossed her arms and then said, "Are you refusing us? Are you telling me that we cannot do anything dangerous because… what… we are women."

All the women were starting to murmur, and Matt could see that it was going to get nasty.

"We are just as capable as you and the men to shoot and… well… even kill. I can tell you that when the time does come, I will not sit here and wait for the wounded. I will be moving civilians into the camp where it will be relatively safe, whether you like it or not. How about it ladies are you with me?" Trudy shouted to the other women. The women cheered and nodded their agreement.

"I think Matt, you are outnumbered, and we are going to help those civilians. We will not let our duty to the wounded be hindered, but until there are these duties for us to perform, we will assist the civilians. You can inform Colonel Grant about these plans and that when we return we can look after the camp and his men will be free to do what they must. We will go out with Father Andrew when it looks like the town is in danger," said Trudy.

Matt was at a loss as to what to say. He didn't agree with this, but he knew when it was time to back off. He was just about to say this when Dave stepped in and said, "Matt, I have had the pleasure of being with these wonderful women for nearly 2 months. They are a force to be reckoned with. That being the case I would be prepared to direct operations along with Father Andrew. I will be responsible for them and by the way I think you are underestimating them. I am sure that they will kill any German that gets in their way and I am sure that they will do exactly what is asked of them. They would never compromise their duties to the injured and once all the civilians are in the camp I think that they could secure the camp admirably. I would be on hand to ensure that it is done."

"Dave I can't believe that you have taken their side. I will have to think about this and I will pass it on to HQ. They, I think, should have the final decision," Matt said to Dave and the women standing in front of him.

Trudy looked at the other nurses with a smug look on her face and she then turned to Matt and said, "We will do our duty and we will move the civilians."

Matt looked at her and all the nurses and realised then that he had lost.

CHAPTER 19

It was important that the arms which were being unloaded in Lancing were dealt with so Matt along with his team and the other men that were holed up in Lancing Ring agreed on a plan to take them. The trucks would be heading north to get to the A24, which then took them up to the Germans front line. They decided that the trucks would be attacked about two miles from the landing site on a stretch of road which had fields on both sides.

The fields had large hedges which the men could hide behind and this stretch of road was straight, so they could see them coming and see any security that was looking after them. They had already watched a previous assignment go through and it consisted of 3 trucks carrying the munitions and 2 further trucks one in the front and one at the rear carrying a few troops. They also had jeep type vehicle, called a Kubelwagen, with a machine gun fitted to it, bringing up the rear.

Matt and his men would block the road using a couple of cut down trees and they also had another couple of trees, which had ropes attached, that could be pulled across the road behind the convoy.

It essentially blocked the trucks in. They had measured the road precisely and had explosives placed in strategic places to take out the accompanying trucks and Matt would have a machine gun set up so that if any troops got out they would be mowed down. The Kubelwagen would be the problem, mainly because it carried the machine gun. They felt that it would be necessary to take that out first so once the convoy had stopped, the machine gun would open up on the Kubelwagen and then they would blow up the 2 accompanying trucks.

At 0100 hours they were all in place waiting for the trucks to come along. It was estimated that the trucks would arrive at this part of the road at approximately 0210 hours and the men were ready to move the blockade in place. At 0205 hours they could see the lights from the trucks coming up the road, so the blockade and the explosives were put in place. The trucks arrived and when the first truck saw the blockade it tried to reverse, but the drivers of trucks behind, who hadn't seen the blockade did not understand what was happening. During this confusion the rear blockade was pulled across the road and the men on the machine gun opened fire on the Kubelwagen. The explosives were set off and Matt's men opened fire on the Germans who had survived the explosion. The men in the trucks with the munitions got out with their hands above their heads. Matt couldn't take prisoners so ordered them to be killed. The whole operation took 5 minutes. They removed the blockade and they drove the 3 trucks with the arms in, to the Cement Works. The whole operation went like clockwork. No one was injured apart from the Germans. It was a great success and Matt knew that this would cause the Germans to rethink their plans to get the munitions to the front.

The drop points were checked regularly and after Sid had gone into town and checked George Darcy's drop point it revealed that George needed to speak to Matt urgently as he had some very interesting information. Matt went down to town at 1600 hours and waited for George to pass on his way home. Matt followed him on his bike and when he got parallel with George, he indicated for him to follow him. They passed George's house and they went into Buckingham Park. The park had a dilapidated pavilion which they went into.
"Paul, I have some information that you should know about urgently," said George.
"I got your message, what is it?" Matt asked.
"There has been a lot of chatter by the Germans over the last week about their troops losing against the Allies. They are aware that they may have to retreat over the channel and they are very happy

about it. They don't like being here. By the way there are many wounded coming down to the port to be transported back to Germany, so I believe the rumours that they are losing are true. But more importantly they are talking about Edward and his wife, that Wallace woman. They are going to get them out of the country within the week. They will be coming down on Friday next and they will be on a boat on Saturday morning heading for France."

"That's really interesting. Do you know where they are coming from and which route they would take?" Matt asked.

"I heard some officers talking the other day and they were saying something about them staying at the South Lodge Hotel in Horsham, which would indicate that, they would be travelling down via the A281. I would suspect however that they will have a lot of security," George said.

"Perhaps. This is good news. Is there anything else?" Matt asked.

"Oh yes, plans are being made for the retreat. I have not been able to see them, but I will try to, and if I can, I will copy them. Although I think I am trusted I must be very careful. If I get anything I will drop them off at the usual place," George said.

"Good, thanks"

"Paul… um… I am worried. If they do retreat back here, then the fighting will be bad won't it?" said George.

"Probably, why?" asked Matt.

"It's my daughter. Is there anywhere I can put her to keep her safe. I have already lost her mother and I can't lose her as well," he said.

"I see, well George, I think I can find somewhere safe for her when the time comes. Have a bag packed and ready to go at a moment's notice," Matt said.

"Thank you, Paul. I need to go now," he said.

George left, and Matt stood there for a while thinking about this development. Whilst he was down in town he decided to look in on Bert. He made his way to Ravens Road and he knocked at Bert's front door. There was no reply, so he went to the bottom of the road and waited. He waited for half an hour but still there was no sign of him. Matt decided that he needed to know if there was a problem, so he went to the Crabtree Pub to speak to Jo. He entered and discovered it was completely empty of customers. Jo was standing behind the bar.

"Hello Jo, how's business?" Matt asked and then ordered a pint.

"Bloody awful. Still a couple of locals will be here soon, but the curfew is dreadful for business," he said pouring the pint.

"Seen Bert lately," asked Matt.

"He hasn't been in for a couple of days which was strange. He hasn't been his old self since his wife died. That was a bit of a shock for him, you know. He really loved her. Still I suspect he will be in tomorrow," Jo said.

"I went around the house and he wasn't there," Matt said. He was trying to sound casual, but he was starting to get worried.

"That's odd. He's usually at home at this time. I know he finds going to an empty home difficult, but he's usually there. I don't know. Look if he comes in tomorrow I will tell him you were asking after him," Jo said.

Matt and Jo continued chatting mainly about the Germans till Matt had finished his drink and he left. He decided that he would try Bert's place one more time and if he still wasn't about he would leave.

The house in Ravens Road was still in darkness and there was no reply to the knocking. Matt was just about to leave when he thought that he would just go to the rear entrance to the garden and see if the back door was locked. He just wanted to check the house out.

He tried the back door and found it open, so Matt entered. He went through the kitchen which looked in order and then into the back room which had been Bert's wife's bedroom when she was ill. The room was exactly as Matt remembered it. He then went into the front room. He looked around and was about to leave the room when he heard a noise coming from behind a settee. Matt went to where he heard the sound and to his surprise he found Bert lying there. He was covered in blood. His face had been severely beaten and from the look of his body he was suffering from broken bones. Matt could see his arm was broken. When he tried to move him, he accidently touched his rib cage and Bert screamed in pain, so Matt suspected that he had broken ribs. Bert also felt very cold and it looked like he had been there for quite a while, as the blood was drying. Matt wanted to make Bert comfortable, so he ran into the back bedroom and removed a pillow and a blanket from the bed and he returned to Bert and covered him with the blanket to keep him warm and put the pillow gently under his head. Bert was barely conscious, but Matt thought he'd try to find out what had happened, so he asked him. Bert said only one word, "Germans." Matt realised that he needed to get Bert some help, but how and where. He told Bert that he had to leave him for a while to arrange help but he would be back. He didn't know if Bert heard him or if he did, did he understand him. Matt went into the kitchen and stood there for a minute. He hadn't got any transport to move Bert, so it was essential that he got some. He could steal one, but vehicles that the locals owned did not have petrol, so it would be a fruitless exercise. He did wonder if Bert's friend,

Jo, the barman at the Crabtree Pub, may know of someone who could help him. He left the house immediately and he returned to the Crabtree Pub. When he entered he saw that a couple of the locals were in the bar. He went up to the bar and before Jo could say anything Matt said, "A pint please," and then in a whisper, "Need to speak to you privately. Bert's been hurt."

Jo pulled a pint for Matt and when he gave it to him he said in a whisper, "Through that door," indicating a door that had a sign on it saying 'Toilets'. Matt picked up the pint and went through the door. Instead of finding himself in a toilet or a passageway leading to a toilet he found himself in the snug bar. No one was in there. He took his pint to the bar and he sat on a stool.

Jo appeared and said, "What's happened. Is Bert alright?"

"No, he has been severely beaten up and is in serious need of medical help," Matt said.

"Shit, who did it?" Jo asked.

"He only said one word and that was 'Germans'," said Matt.

"The bastards did that to him?" Jo looked worried.

"I don't know, but I suspect that they did. Look Jo we need to get him help. I can assist with that, but I need transport and someone to help me get him in the vehicle. Can you help me?" Matt looked at Jo and wondered if he was the right man to be asking. Jo looked at Matt but did not say anything. Matt was concerned now, not only about Bert, but with Jo's reaction.

Then Jo said, "Who are you?"

"I am Bert's friend and I am probably the only person that can help him and keep him safe," Matt said in a very matter of fact way. He also put his hand into his trouser pocket and he had hold of his knife, just in case of trouble.

"You aren't from the Germans and testing me, are you?" Jo asked, and Matt thought what a daft question. If he was he wouldn't let on, but because he said this it put Matt's mind at rest. Jo was only worried that the Germans would know that he had helped Bert.

"Jo, I am not from the Germans and if I was I wouldn't tell you, but you know there are times in life when you have to feel that something is right. Gut feeling, I suppose you would call it. I am nothing to do with the Germans, quite the opposite. Now can you help Bert or not?" Matt asked again.

Jo looked at Matt and then Matt saw his face soften and he nodded, "I will trust you. I can get hold of a vehicle and it is full of petrol. Where do you want it?"

"Thank God" said Matt. "Bert is on the floor at his house. Can you bring it there and can you help me carry him out to the car? I have some morphine which I will give him, and he should be able to be moved"

"Ok. I will be about 15 minutes. It isn't my car and I need to pay someone to let me use it," Jo said.

"How much?" asked Matt.

"About 20," Jo said.

Matt reached inside his coat and he produced £40 and handed it over to Jo. "That should cover all expenses. What will you do about the bar?"

"Oh no worries there. One of the locals will cover for me and lock up," he said.

Matt was happy with the arrangements and he left to return to Ravens Road. When he got there, he gave Bert a shot of morphine and this seemed to ease the awful pain that he was in. He put a splint on his arm using some wooden spoons he found in the kitchen and he tore up a sheet to fasten them in place. When he finished he sat with Bert who was now unconscious and could see that his breathing was laboured. He was worried that Bert would die. Jo arrived a little later than the 15 minutes, explaining that he had to do some bartering to get the car, but it was outside. Matt and Jo carried Bert out to the car and they laid him on the back seat. Jo was just about to get in the driver's seat when Matt stopped and said, "I think you should leave now. You don't want to get involved in any of this."

"Why not, I have run my quiet and safe pub since the invasion and I have wanted to do something useful. This is the most excitement I have had since the invasion when all I did, then, was hide in a cellar and hope that the pub would still be standing when it had finished. Now I believe that there is more to life that just running the bar, and seeing Bert like this, I am angry, and I need to be more involved. Please let me help." Matt needed to get going and he couldn't argue with him in the road. A German patrol could appear at any time, so he agreed, but he drove, and Jo got in the back to help Bert if he needed any. Matt drove off and although he saw a couple of German patrols it was still early, so they didn't get stopped. He drove Bert directly to the Cement Works and once inside Trudy and her nurses looked after Bert.

Matt told Trudy that he needed to speak to Bert when he came around, but Trudy told Matt that he would have to wait. She confirmed that he had broken ribs and she also suspected that his ankle, as well as his right arm was broken. She noted that the fingers on his right arm were all broken and that he had a couple of nails removed. She told Matt that Bert had been tortured. Matt and Jo stayed close to Bert whilst he was cleaned up and it became apparent that he would need certain medication to stop infection. Father Andrew, who knew a source that would provide these medicines gave the information to Matt and Jo and once morning arrived Jo was given enough money to get them. He took the car and within 2 hours he had returned with them. Trudy started to administer the pain killers and the antibiotics and within an hour Bert was conscious. Matt sat with him and waited until he felt up to talking.

"I said the wrong thing," said Bert.

"What did you say?" Matt asked.

"It was coming up to lunch time and a couple of those bastards were talking. They were talking about Edward and Wallace. I recognised the names, but I didn't know what they were saying. Suddenly they turned on me and said in English, 'They are a good King and Queen,' and I said they are bloody imposters and if Winston had his way they would be hung for traitors. I don't know why I said it, but since Betty died, well, I really couldn't care. They then said that they would win, and Britain would be theirs and well… I had to say something, so I said yea, like the goods yard; it really looks like you are winning. With that they hit me and then before I knew it I was down the nick being beaten to within an inch of my life. I thought well this is it. They kept telling me that I knew who the saboteurs were and that I was going to tell them, well I just laughed in their face and they then started to kick me and when that didn't work they broke my fingers and removed my nails, god it was bloody agony. I still refused to talk so they broke my arm and then more. I must have lost consciousness at times because they kept waking me by throwing buckets of water over my face. I didn't talk Paul. I must have been there for

3 days and I think they realised that I didn't know anything, but suddenly they dragged me to a car and drove me home and left me where you found me. There leaving comment was 'You don't work for us anymore,' as if I would return."

Matt was horrified about the brutality Bert had endured and he was angry. This was unacceptable and now he would make sure that they would pay. It would soon be time to deal with these people, but now was not the time to get angry. In the meantime, he would kidnap the Duke and Duchess of Windsor and make sure that they are held so that justice could be done to them. That may help Matt's feelings, but he didn't think so. Jo decided that he wouldn't stay but he told Matt that occasionally Germans came into his bar and he would listen to them and if there was anything interesting then he would pass it on. He told Matt that he could keep the car it may be useful to them. Matt asked, "What about the owner?" and Jo replied, "I paid him enough for it, it is yours now and if anything is said I have enough to hold over him, so he won't disagree."

CHAPTER 20

George came up with the exact information about Edward and Wallace's actual movement and the timing of their arrival at the port. They were going to be travelling down on Friday arriving at the port at 1600 hours. They were then due to leave for France on the 10 o'clock boat, the following morning. The route from Horsham was to follow the A281 through to Henfield, then the A2037 to Upper Beeding and then to follow the Adur River along the A283 into Shoreham. Matt decided that the place to ambush them was on the A2037. It was extremely rural, and they would be able to hide till Edward and Wallace's entourage of vehicles arrived. Matt also decided that more man power was going to be needed because he felt that the Germans were going to put up a real fight to keep them safe. This he organised with Colonel Grant and he got 5 extra men to help. Matt had a plan and needed a woman to help with this, but it meant that the woman would be put in severe danger. He asked the women in the Cement Works if anyone would help and was immediately inundated with offers. Nellie, who had been standing back, very casually went up to Matt and said, "I am the most logical person for this. I know the area like the back of my hand and I will be able to get away quickly and unseen if necessary. These other women do not have the knowledge that I have." Although Matt wanted to disagree he realised that Nellie was the logical choice, so he agreed.

Friday came and Matt and the men blocked the road at 1530 hours with a mock accident using the car and a truck. The whole road was impassable. Nellie was then made up to look like she had been involved in the accident. Her face, arms and legs had blood over them, (actually it was cochineal, which is a red food dye, which had been added to water). She was then laid half in and half out of the car. She looked dead to Matt. The rest of the men hid behind the hedges about 30 yards along the road. They also did what they had done with the ammunition truck's and they had some trees ready to be pulled across the road to block it so that no vehicles could reverse. They set this up just round a bend, so the convoy of vehicles would be on the accident immediately they went around the bend. They had a lookout on the other side of the bend who would tell them when the convoy was in sight. They waited for about 5 minutes and the lookout indicated that the vehicles were coming. Everyone prepared themselves for action. They had 2 machine guns, one for the front vehicles and one for the rear vehicles. All the men were under strict instructions that they were not to hurt Edward or Wallace. They were to be captured unharmed.

The vehicles arrived at the accident. There were 5 vehicles in all, but they were all cars. The men in the front vehicle got out of their car and walked over to Nellie. Before they got to her the machine gun opened fire and at the same time the tree was placed in position behind the fifth car. The men in the rear car saw what was happening and tried to reverse before the road was completely blocked but failed and their vehicle hit the tree and couldn't go any further. They then got out of their car with guns firing. The machine gun killed all of them. The people in the other cars were now firing from their windows and Matt's men were returning fire. The people in the middle vehicle did nothing. They could see Edward and Wallace, a driver and one other man in it and they were all just sitting there watching what was happening. Nellie had got up and gone over a hedge and she waited to see what would happen. Matt could see that a couple of his men had been injured and it was getting to the point when something needed to be done. He ordered that the explosives should be put under the cars where the firing was coming from. They had already prepared some, using bamboo canes, which are used in gardening. There were 5 canes tied together and the last cane was stuffed with explosives. The wire to a detonator box was put through the other canes. From their cover all they had to do was slide the bamboo canes under the car and then detonate the explosives. One at a time the cars exploded killing all the occupants. The only car left was the one with Edward and Wallace in. Matt shouted to the driver and the other occupant of the vehicle that he did not want to harm the Duke and Duchess, but he would, so they were to open their doors and throw out any guns from it. Matt waited and initially thought that they wouldn't do it but very slowly the front doors opened, and 2 guns were thrown out. Matt told them to get out of the car, and they did. He now addressed his comments to Edward and Wallace and told them to get out of the car. They would be unharmed if they did as they were told. The back door of the car opened and very slowly they got out of the vehicle. Matt and his men ran forward, and the driver and the other man were taken away and shot. Edward and Wallace were unceremoniously searched. Edward had a small calibre pistol which they removed, but Wallace was unarmed.

"How dare you," said Edward in a very pompous manner.

"How dare YOU, sir," said Matt. "Impersonating our King and Queen."

"What is going to happen to us?" asked Wallace in her American drawl.

"Don't talk. You will be told once you are safely incarcerated, so Winston Churchill and the government can deal with you when the time comes, now get back in the car," Matt ordered.

Sid and Johnny got into the driving and passenger seats and two men sat in the back and once the others had cleared the road they drove off. Matt and the rest of the men helped his injured men back to the Cement Works where they got medical help from Trudy and the nurses. One of Matt's team, Steve was badly injured with a wound in his chest area, the rest were relatively minor. Once Matt was happy that the injured were being treated he instructed Doug to inform HQ immediately that they now held Edward and Wallace. Trudy approached Matt and she said to him, "Matt, Steve is really bad. I don't think that he is going to make it."

Matt looked over to Steve and could see nurses putting bandages on his chest wound. "He's a fighter, he'll make it," Matt said.

"No Matt I don't think he will. Look at him. His breathing is laboured he has lost so much blood," Trudy said.

"Shall we get a doctor over from the camp?" Matt asked.

"Matt, I don't know," she said.

As they were talking the nurse who was looking after Steve stood up and then bent over and covered his face with the blanket. Both Matt and Trudy saw this.

"Sorry. It was just too severe a wound," said Trudy.

Matt walked over to where Steve was lying, and he pulled the blanket back. He looked at him and he could feel a lump in his throat. Father Andrew, who had seen what had occurred approached Matt and placed his hand on his shoulder.

"He is with God now. Matt I am sorry, but you have things to deal with. I suggest you get on and do them." Matt looked at him and nodded.

Father Andrew pulled the blanket up over Steve's face and then he knelt beside him and prayed. Matt then headed off on foot with Jack to where they were going to keep Edward and Wallace.

When they were planning the operation to kidnap Edward and Wallace, the biggest dilemma was where they would keep them. Initially they thought they could be kept in the Cement Works, but they didn't want the women in there to be pressured by having the most hated people in Britain in there with them, so eventually they decided that they would be kept in one of the bunkers. As Lancing Ring was being used constantly by Sergeant Green and his men it was felt that the bunker at Coombehead Wood would be better. They then got a couple of men to adapt it in to a detention place for them. They literally split the place in two. The bunker was small, but now it was a minute space. They put up a partition wall, so that the guards and Edward and Wallace would have some privacy. They had also deliberated on who should look after them. They wanted a woman to be on hand there as well, so they asked Trudy to nominate two appropriate people. There would also be four male guards. They would have a rota of 2 days about, with 1 woman and 2 men with them at all times. Sergeant Green was put in charge of this. It would be very cramped in the bunker but then what did anyone expect.

Sid and Johnny arrived at the road below Coombehead Wood within 10 minutes. They had arranged a hiding place for the car in a burnt-out barn. They then made the royal couple trek through the farmland and into the wood. Since they left the vehicle they had been blindfolded and occasionally they stumbled. Wallace found this extremely hard, mainly because she was wearing a pair of high heels. Once into the wood they found the hatch and they helped Edward to get down the ladder into the bunker. Wallace had a temper tantrum about climbing down the ladder blindfolded, but she was told that if she refused she would be thrown down the 12 foot hole. She agreed to co-operate. Once inside they were introduced to Sergeant Green and the first guards. None of the people in the bunker gave their correct names. This was for security. They were then shown where they would be kept, and both objected, not only about their treatment, but also about the bunker and the lack of space. Sid told them to shut up and be thankful that they weren't killed. If he had his way they would have been. That shut them up for a while. They were told that they would have to do their own cooking and cleaning and would have to ration themselves with the food, as it was in short supply. They were told that if they ate all their food at once they would not get any further supplies for a week, so they would get hungry. They were introduced to their warders and they were told that if they tried to escape they would be shot. Edward tried to reason with Sid who refused to talk back to him saying that his senior officer would be here soon and to address all his questions to him. Wallace had sat on one of the bunks and looked as if she was going to cry. Edward went over to her, put his arm around her and they both sat in silence. When Matt arrived an hour later, he was surprised to find the whole place was in silence. No one was speaking. He went up to Edward and said, "I am an officer from the Auxiliary Home Guard and you are here on the express wishes of our Prime Minister Winston Churchill. You will be kept here until the Germans leave our shores when you will be delivered to London to stand trial for treason. Do you understand?"

"How dare you speak to me in that tone," Edward said.

Matt looked at him and was astonished that he could think that he was so important.

He continued, "I am your King and you will address me in a correct manner."

"You are what… You are an imposter, my King is George. You abdicated if I remember correctly for this woman." Matt was pointing at Wallace, "And then you have the audacity to pally up with the enemy of our nation, Hitler. You are a disgrace and because of that you will be treated as a common criminal, which is exactly what you both are."

"We had to do it. It is not as clear cut as you think… um… I was coerced, and I was threatened with my life," Edward stuttered.

"It's a shame they didn't kill you. Now you will be hung by your people," said Matt. He really didn't want to listen to this, but felt he needed to reiterate the rules, which he knew that Sid would have told them.

"So, as you are alive and as we want a public trial you will be kept alive. You will do as you are told, or you will suffer. You will not be allowed to commit suicide and you will not be allowed to die. You have been told the rules of this place, so I suggest that you get on with them. Your life in here can be really uncomfortable, but you can make it bearable. I suggest you do the latter. Now

I will come down now and again, but I will hear if you are causing trouble then we will separate you. We are giving you the chance to stay together but if you do anything that causes a problem, Wallace will be taken somewhere else and I can assure you it will not be a very pleasant place for her. Now have we got that clear?" Matt said.

Edward was in complete shock. He had never been spoken to or treated like this before and he did not like it. The fact that they are threatening to remove Wallace was like a slap in the face and again he was unable to respond to such treatment. He sat down on the bunk next to Wallace and he looked at Matt. Suddenly he stood up and said in a very royal way, "Who am I speaking to, your name man?"

"You will not be told any names. We are all using other names, not our real ones. And I suggest that you do not put on any airs and graces in here. My men will not stand for it. We have given you the courtesy of allowing one of your warders to be a woman, but if you give her a hard time she will be removed and replaced by a man. Now I am going," Matt said.

Matt turned his back on Edward and Wallace which further irritated Edward.

"Don't you turn your back on me like I am some flunky…"

Matt turned quickly and interrupting him saying, "That is exactly what you are. You are nobody.

Do you understand? NOBODY. Don't push me. I lost a good man today and I may do something I will regret."

Matt then turned again and before anything else was said, he left, with Sid, Johnny, and Jack following. The men and woman staying had been briefed previously and they were left with them. Matt did wonder how they would all cope, cooped up in such a small space, but he would receive reports from them and he would visit in about a week.

The repercussions of the taking of Edward and Wallace were horrendous. As it happened between Upper Beeding and Small Dole, the Germans pulled in over 50 residents. They were brutally tortured to try and find out who had done this, but of course no one knew, so were unable to say anything.

When Oberst Baumhauer heard the news about the kidnapping he had been sitting in his office in Lancing College reading some reports. He had been told by one of his Officers, who quickly retreated from his office. Oberst Baumhauer started to shout and he wanted all his senior officers in front of him now to answer why this had happened. He wanted these damn terrorists, and he wanted them now. Why can they get away with all these atrocities and his troops were powerless against them? He wanted something done, hence the reason for the brutality to the civilian population. He knew that they wouldn't know anything, but he was hoping that they would be angry about what was happening to them and take it out on the next British person who came around wanting food or help. How wrong he was, all it did was make them angry with the Germans. The local British civilians loved the idea that their imposter King and Queen were kidnapped, and the rumour was circulated that they would be tried for treason when the country was back in the British hands. The Germans were furious with this, particularly Oberst Baumhauer. He was also really concerned about his position as the Allies were now pushing the German front line back. He had heard that they had retreated to Surrey and North Kent. This was disturbing. It was now mid-March and instead of the army retreating they should have taken the majority of England. He kept asking himself why The Fuhrer had got it so wrong. These damn British people were a persistent lot. He had already started to planning to leave if he felt that the Allies would push the German army to within 20 miles of his area. He wasn't going to be caught. This kidnapping was like the icing on the cake. He was furious, and he wanted his Officers to feel his wrath.

All Oberst Baumhauer's officers that were running his area, which included the Commandant to the camp, were in his office within half an hour.

Initially Oberst Baumhauer ranted and raved about the kidnapping and his officers sat around listening to him. He then continued ranting about the German army being pushed back, but eventually he did calm down and demanded that they came up with ideas on how to catch the perpetrators of the kidnapping. The officers told him that they had already pulled in many people and interrogated them, but none of them knew who these people were. Oberst Baumhauer seethed about this and told them that they already knew that they were not local people, but trained professionals that were probably put there before the invasion and of course the local people would not know anything about them. One of the officers said that they had interrogated someone a little while ago who had worked at the station and they were convinced that he knew something or was even involved in the raid on the goods yard before Christmas, but because of his denial under considerable pressure they released him. They would pick him up again and continue interrogating him. Oberst Baumhauer was still not satisfied, but as he sat there listening to his officers, he suddenly hit the desk and stood up. "Right, these terrorists must stand out. They are men and they should be of an age which would take them into the army. Think about it, they probably have been stopped many times, but they had reasonable stories. I want all men who are aged between 18 and 40 bought in."

One of the officers said, "But we have a problem, the farm workers in this area were all in a reserved occupation here and therefore would not have been called up for the army. We are living in a mainly rural area so there are many who fall in that category. We would be pulling in the workers and then the production of food would be hindered."

"I don't care. I want all those men questioned and all their stories checked up on. Am I making myself clear?"

All the officers nodded in agreement.

"One other thing, we have an informant at one of the farms and he has suspected that the terrorists may be working from the Downs. He told us a couple of months back that he has seen movement around a place called Buckingham Barn and he thinks that they may have a hideout up there."

"Well what have you done about it?"

"Nothing really, we put up scout planes, but they have come back having seen nothing. The area is vast and therefore it would be impossible for troops to search the area." The Officer exclaimed.

"I want troops up on those Downs and I want those people found. Do it. They must have a bolt hole somewhere and I want it found. The Downs is the logical place for them to be. I want all the buildings up there searched and I want all the farms up there searched thoroughly including their outbuildings. I also want your informant in to find out if he has any further information."

"Yes sir. I will get right on to it," said the Officer. "One of the men who was with Edward during the attack was still alive when they were found, and he stated that they had taken the car, so where is it. I want it found," Oberst Baumhauer ordered and then he added. "There was a woman involved in this attack, Commandant, do you think it could be one of the women that disappeared from the camp," asked Oberst Baumhauer.

Hauptmann Mencken stood and said "I do not know. All attempts to obtain information about those women have proved fruitless. I am at a loss about where they are. They could be anywhere and yes that woman in the attack could be one of them. I just don't know for sure."

"Have you found out how they escaped?"

"Not yet. We have searched the camp time and time again, but we cannot find their escape route. We also believe that men are disappearing as well. My predecessor did not have up to date records of all the men in the camp, so I cannot tell you if they are all there," Hauptmann Mencken replied.

"Have you got up to date ones now?" asked Oberst Baumhauer.

"It is something that I will be doing soon," said Hauptmann Mencken.

Oberst Baumhauer hit the desk again. "Well damn well do it, as a matter of urgency."

"Yes Sir."

"You were bought in to replace the previous commandant because it was thought you would get to grips with the problem. Well I suggest that you do it immediately," Oberst Baumhauer demanded.

"Yes Sir," Hauptmann Mencken repeated and sat down.

"I want results and I want them soon. You are all dismissed."

The officers all left and Oberst Baumhauer got up and started to pace his office.

CHAPTER 21

Matt and his team continued in their duties of collecting information from locals and picking up messages from drop points over the next couple of days. HQ was excited about the kidnapping of Edward and Wallace when they were informed. This information must have been passed to the government in the North of England and they in turn passed it to the BBC World Service, because within 24 hours of informing HQ, it was on the wireless so everyone in the country knew about it.

Jack had been tasked to go into town and check the drop point for information from George the previous day but had not returned and the men in the bunker especially Matt were becoming concerned. Usually they sent two men together, but this time Jack said that he wanted to go by himself and it was suspected that he was going to meet a lady friend he had met, so no one objected, but now he had gone for over 24 hours everyone was worried. Matt decided that he needed to know what was happening, so he sent Sid and Pip to investigate. They left the bunker to go into town and within 20 minutes Sid had returned, without Pip.

"Matt, I think there is a problem. Bill Bolt is in the wood outside and he wants to talk to you," Sid said.

"What is the problem?" asked Matt as he was putting his coat on.

"He was rambling on about his men from his farm, but he was in a bit of a state, so I told him I would get you and Pip stayed to calm him down," Sid told him.

Matt and Sid left, and they found Pip with Bill on the edge of the wood. He apparently had calmed down.

"Are you in charge?" Bill asked Matt.

"Yes, Mr Bolt, what is the problem?" he asked.

"Well there are two things really, but the first is that all my men have been taken away by the Germans," he said.

"What do you mean all your men?" asked Matt, not really understanding what had happened.

"They came in trucks last night and they loaded all my men, except the old ones. I have 2 men plus me, left to run the farm. What am I to do and why take all the younger men? I also hear from other farms that they have done the same with them. They also have road blocks set up and any man passing who is young is taken in by them," said Bill.

"Are you telling me that all young men have been rounded up by the Germans?" asked Matt.

"Yes, that is exactly what I am telling you."

"Bloody hell, they must be desperate," said Sid, who had been listening to the conversation. Matt was thinking about this development. The Germans must have taken in hundreds of men. What are they doing?

"Mr Bolt…," Matt started.

"Call me Bill"

"Bill… I suspect that they are trying to locate the saboteurs and the kidnappers, and they are bringing in any man who is young enough to be working for the British army to ascertain whether they know any information and to check up on their backgrounds. We have a man missing so I can only assume that he has been taken by them as well. Bill your farm has been given as a background for my men, so my man may say that he works for you. If they come to check you must say that he works for you," Matt said.

"That's not a problem. I don't keep records of my farm hands. They are casual labourers, but what are we going to do about them?" he asked.

"I don't think there is anything that we can do. Just wait, I believe that they will be released once they find out that they have no information," Matt said.

"I hope so," said Bill who sat on a cut tree trunk.

"Where do you think they are going to keep all those men?" asked Sid. "The local Police Station won't take them."

"I don't know," said Matt.

"I heard they had been taken to the school in Pond Road. All the local kids have been given a few days off, not that there are many of them going there these days," said Bill.

"Well there you are. They will be back in a couple of days," said Matt. He was really worried about Jack and he hoped that he would keep calm during this situation.

"Of course, you lot will have to be very careful now. They will log everyone in the area and if you are not on that list then they will want to know why," said Bill.

"I hadn't thought about that," said Matt. "As you say, we will have to be extra careful now. Right Bill is that it."

"No, actually there is one other thing."

"Fire away," said Matt wondering what other problem he had.

"I have had suspicions about a man who works for me. He came to me just before the invasion from a farm in Cowfold. He was a good worker, so I didn't think too much about what he was doing to begin with, but over time I started to get suspicious of him. He went missing yesterday, before the trucks came and that's why I am mentioning him now," Bill said.

"Who is he and what has he been saying to make you suspicious?" asked Matt.

"His name is Mike Wilkinson. To start with he was asking about him," indicating Sid.

"How did he know about me?" asked Sid.

"Do you remember the first time you came to the farm. You helped me pull out some equipment," Bill said.

"Yes, of course I do, why?" asked Sid.

"You appeared from nowhere and then disappeared again. Well Mike noticed, and he asked me who you were and what you wanted? I told him to mind his own business, but he kept on and started to ask the other farm hands," Bill said.

"Is that all?" asked Matt.

"No, when all the other things happened, the goods yard, the trucks being ambushed, the bridges being blown up, he started to ask everyone if they knew who was doing it. Of course, no one knew, and he then started to ask me. Again, I told him that he should mind his business and that anyone doing these acts had my blessing. He stopped asking me then, but he still pesters the other farm hands. He also started to question them about Buckingham Barn. Apparently, he was up on the Downs one night, quite a while ago, shooting rabbits, when he saw a big lorry up there. He hid but the lorry was in the distance. He believed that it had come from the direction of the old Barn and he has since been up on the Downs and he has seen people up there. I don't know if there was any truth in what he saw, but all the farm hands have said that they haven't seen anything when they were up there. Also, he has started going missing. He is allocated a field where he should be working and when I go and check up on things he isn't there. I have spoken to him about this and he denies that he isn't there. He says that he may have gone for a smoke or to the toilet, but he states that he was there. One day when I checked, and he wasn't where he should be I hung around for 4 hours and he still hadn't turned up," Bill said.

"That's interesting. Do you think he is informing the Germans?" Matt asked.

Bill thought for a moment and then said, "Possibly."

"Ok leave that with me. We will deal with him when he returns," Matt said.

"Thank you. I couldn't bear having someone like that working for me. He should be ashamed of himself. What will you do?" asked Bill.

"Well… we will have to confirm what you have said and then we could always give him false information, or we could kill him," Matt said.

"Um, that's a bit drastic," said Bill.

"He could put you, your farm and your workers as well as us in danger if we don't do something," said Sid in a matter of fact way.

"You could be right," considered Bill.

"We won't do anything for now. Let's wait and see where it leads to," Matt said.

Bill rose from the tree truck and said, "I've been gone long enough, and I have so much to do. If I hear anything more I will let you know."

"Thanks Bill. Let us know when this Mike comes back, and I will put someone on to him," said Matt.

"Ok, bye,"

Bill walked away and left Matt, Sid and Pip standing there all in deep thought. They made their way back to the bunker where Matt sat on one of the bunks and thought about what he had just heard from Bill.

"Sid, we need to know if this information is true. I need someone on the Downs to keep watch to see if there is any troop movement up there especially around Buckingham Barn. If there is then we could say that information was passed to them, whether it was this Mike person or not, he would have to be assessed," Matt said. He thought for a while and then said, "I also want someone out on the edge of the woods. If the Germans have Jack then I need to make sure that he hasn't talked, not that I think he would. But if there are any troop movement in this vicinity then we will have to leave. I also need to inform the people at the Cement Works to be prepared to leave, just in case. Jack may give this bunker away, but he wouldn't give anything else away."

Sid immediately deployed Pip to go to the Cement Works and Jake to stand guard in the wood area near the bunker. Sid and Doug went up to the Downs to set up an observation post to see if there were any movements up there. They were far enough away from Buckingham Barn to remain hidden and leave without being seen if there were any troop movements, but able to see all the surrounding areas with the aid of binoculars.

Matt and Johnny remained in the bunker.

"Matt, do you think this is going to cause us a problem?" Johnny asked.

"I do, Johnny. Jack is a good member of the team and I know that he would hold out under interrogation for as long as he can, but if he does talk then we will have to move. We then have a logistical problem. The other bunkers are being used now, so we would have to go to the Cement Works and because we are always coming and going it would put them in danger. I am hoping that he will be able to mingle in with the others. There may be too many of them to find out anything of interest. They will take all the names, and we must find out some of them so that we can use them. I will contact Bill and he can give me details of his workers, so we can get ID's made in those names. That way we can still get around," Matt said.

"That's good, but what about this informant?" Johnny asked.

"I don't know yet," said Matt. "I suppose if we can verify that he is passing information to the Germans then we can do something."

Johnny was thoughtful and then said, "You know if Jack does come back and as he would be known to all the men as a farm labourer, perhaps we can put him on Bill's work force and he could keep watch over him."

"We could do that, but let's see if he returns," Matt said.

Matt and Johnny then sat in silence with their own thoughts.

Jack was sitting on the floor of the school assembly hall surrounded by about 250 other men. The Germans were standing guard at the doors. There was a lot of joviality from the men and they thought the whole exercise was hilarious. They caused the Germans problems when they all decided that they wanted to go to the toilet at the same time. The Germans were at a loss about to how to deal with them. The officers said that details had to be taken and the men were all handed a piece of paper to write down their names and where they lived and worked. The men refused to do it. They said that they wanted food and drink first and then they would think about it. They were threatened but they all stood fast on the food and so the Germans had to cater to their demands. The officers then started to bring each

man in individually to be interrogated. After a dozen of interviews, the Germans realised that this was a futile exercise, but because they were ordered to do it by Oberst Baumhauer they continued. It seemed to take forever and after 2 days of continuous interviewing they had come to an end. They had nothing at all. Jack watched the proceedings and he had made some friends with the men around him. One of these men interested him. Before the invasion he had worked at the power station in Southwick and because it had been taken over by the Germans he had become redundant. He was chatting to a group of men. This group included Jack. During the discussion they were having about how they would deal with these 'bloody upstarts' (meaning the Germans), this man said, "You know with all the sabotage that has been done, I am surprised that they hadn't hit the power station. It would be so easy to do."
Jack replied, "How's that then?"
"Well there is a tunnel that goes from the power station, under the port area, and comes up in Southwick. I don't think the Germans know anything about it, because the entrance is not guarded. It has all the cables in this tunnel. If they blow up the tunnel they would cut the power lines which will kill all the power in the area and the tunnel will be flooded so the Germans wouldn't be able to repair it. Easy really."

Jack was listening keenly to what he was saying. Another man sitting close said "That's a good one, but what about closing Southwick port altogether. That could also be done easily."

Another man in the group said, "Oh yes and how could they do that?"

"All they would have to do is blow up the lock gates at the entrance of the port. That would take months to rebuild them," said the man.

"Yes of course that would be great," another man said.

"I would think it would be better to try and blow up their communications system back to Germany," said another man.

"And how would you propose to do that?" one man asked.

"I don't know, but they must have some sort of large antennae to allow for them to transmit, surely it would be easy to find out where that was," he said.

The group of men were coming up with other areas of sabotage and Jack was listening intently to them.

The men who were sitting around him were all a similar age and he asked one of them, "Do you go shooting often?"

"All the time. We must live and as food is so short I go up onto the Downs and shoot rabbits and sometimes I see the odd deer. I haven't shot one yet, but you never know," one of the men said.

"Wouldn't you like to help the saboteurs, I know I would if I could," said Jack.

"Oh yes. I would be there, in a shot if I could," and the other men all agreed with him. This gave Jack an idea. When, or if he was released he would speak with Matt about his idea, but for the time being he had to concentrate on this predicament. Jack's turn to be interviewed eventually happened. He went into the room, which he assumed had been a classroom and he was told to sit in a chair. He gave his name and address (South Downs Farm) and he told them that he worked on the farm as a farm hand. He was asked if he knew who the saboteurs were in the area to which he replied he didn't. He was asked if he thought anyone that he worked with was suspicious and he said that he didn't. They asked for a bit of history regarding his work which he gave, but they would find it impossible to check up on, as he told them that he had worked in the Midlands for a while and then in Nottinghamshire but came down to Sussex about 4 years ago to be near his girlfriend. After 15 minutes he was sent back into the hall where he was told to wait.

The 2 days spent in the hall with all the men together made it smell disgusting and it was a real mess. This was done purposely as they wanted to make it impossible for the Germans to keep them there. The German Officers reported to Oberst Baumhauer that nothing was discovered, and he ordered them to release all of them. They were not, however, given a lift back to their farms. When all the men left, and the majority went to the local pub and had a drink and a good laugh at the Germans expense and then made their way back to their homes or work places.

Jack's return to the bunker which heralded a celebration by the men. They were all very relieved that he had been released with no injury. Sitting in an arm chair in the bunker he told them all what had happened. He also related the conversations that the men were having about other sabotage areas and Matt was particularly interested in the power station. Jack had managed to discover, from the man who spoke of it, his address, so he thought that he may be worth a visit. Then Jack spoke of the idea that he had when he was sitting with those men.
"You know those men are all doing a brilliant job, but I think that we could use them when the Germans retreat. If we arm them they would be willing to fight beside us. I know that they are untrained, but if you had heard them talk you would have realised that they were so willing to be useful and if they stayed put and had to go into hiding I feel it would be a waste of manpower. The older men may have fought in the last war and would have experience with weapons," Jack said.

Matt like this idea, but how could it be organised. He would have to think about it.

Matt had spoken with Bill again, when the men had returned. He found that Mike Wilkinson had returned with them and had told Bill that he had been rounded up in the street. The funny thing was, that none of his other workers remember seeing Mike in the hall. So, having confirmed with Bill that it was agreeable with him to put Jack on his work force to keep an eye on him, this was done the following day. Jack was informed about this and after Jack had a day relaxing, he became a farm hand working at South Downs Farm.

The Cement Works were told to stand down as the danger was over, but the look outs on the Downs continued. A day after the men were released from the school Pip, who was the nominated look out that day, saw a lot of activity in the area around Buckingham Barn. Then he saw about 100 Germans spread out and start to search the Downs. They were heading for Truleigh hill and the South Downs Way. They would have to cover about 4 miles to get there. Pip decided that it would be prudent to return to the bunker to report it. Matt and Johnny were of a similar opinion that perhaps the information about Mike was correct. They would however wait for Jack's report before they acted.

Bill had put Jack to work in the field adjacent to where Mike was working. At first nothing happened then one day about a week after he had started working, he saw a stranger in old work clothes walking across the fields towards Mike. Mike saw him and immediately started to walk towards a hedgerow. Once he got there he waited, and the stranger approached him. They talked for about 10 minutes and the stranger then left. Jack decided that he would follow the stranger. He went back across the field then followed the hedgerow down to the road. Jack thought that he would turn left towards Shoreham, but instead he turned right towards Steyning. He walked up beside the River Adur, passing the Cement Works and then at the bridge between Steyning and Upper Beeding he crossed, and he retraced his steps on the East side of the river. Eventually he arrived at Lancing College which he entered. Jack hid in some shrubbery across the road from Lancing College and watched who was entering and leaving. After about an hour he saw the same man re-appear only this time dressed in the uniform of a German Major. This was the proof that they needed. Jack returned to the bunker. He told Matt and Johnny what he had seen, and they now realised that they needed to do something.

Matt put a lot of thought into what they should do. At first, he wanted to pass false information to the

Germans, but he felt that this could be dangerous for his co-workers, so he decided that they should speak to him. They would have to find a nice quite place to do this, so they spoke to Bill to see if there was any outbuilding on his farm that they could use. On the very outskirts of his farm was an old cottage that used to be lived in by one of his workers, but it had fallen into disrepair. He told them that he could get Mike to go to the cottage to do some repairs on the place. He would say that he wanted to employ a couple of other hands as he was so short at the moment and he needed a place for them to stay. Matt agreed with this so the next day Bill told Mike and Jack, who was still allegedly working on the farm, to do just that.

Matt, Sid, Johnny and Pip were already at the old cottage when Mike and Jack turned up.

"Where the bloody hell do we start? This place is in a right old state. Look the roof is nearly falling in and there are no windows. I think Bill is having a laugh. I wouldn't live in here," said Mike.

"No Mike, neither would I," said Jack who was purposely a few paces behind.

Mike entered what was left of the front door and found himself in a front room. There were 4 other men in there and he was very surprised to see them.

"What are you doing here?" he demanded to know. "You are trespassing."

Sid had produced a gun and said, "Come in Mike and take a seat."

Mike turned to leave, but Jack had his gun out and pointed it at him.

"Do as you are told Mike and then perhaps nothing will happen to you," Jack said and pointed to an old seat in the room.

"You. You are one of them?" said Mike.

"You could say that. Now sit down," Jack ordered.

Pip went over to Mike and searched him, "He's clean."

"Sit," shouted Matt.

Mike sat on the old chair.

"What do you want with me?" he asked.

"Now let's think. Could it be that you are giving information to the Germans or could it be that you are just a crummy worker? Now shut up and listen," said Matt. "We know what you are up to and our concern is not for you but for your co-workers…,"

Mike interrupted, "I haven't done anything. I haven't put any of the workers in danger. I never would. I don't know what you are talking about."

"I told you to shut up and I suggest that you do that. We know what you have been up to and we know that you are informing, so all we have to discover is what you have been saying," Matt said.

Matt turned to Jack and Johnny and said, "You two go and keep watch, we don't want to be disturbed."

Jack and Johnny left.

"Now let's get to business," said Matt. Sid kicked the chair away from Mike and he fell to the floor. He stood up and Sid immediately hit him in the stomach. Mike wasn't a tall man, but he was stocky and certainly muscular, so he reacted which caused Pip who was standing behind him to hit him in his kidneys. This made Mike fall to the floor. He tried to get up, but Sid put his foot on him and told him to stay down.

"Right, now we have got your attention," said Matt. "I want to know who that man you were talking to in the fields yesterday was?"

"I wasn't talking to anyone," he said.

Sid pulled him up roughly from the floor and hit him again in the stomach.

"Wrong answer son," said Sid.

"Do I have to ask everything twice, who was he?" said Matt.

"I don't know what you are talking about," Mike shouted.

This went on for a little while and eventually Matt realised that he would take more to break this man. He removed his gun from his pocket in his coat and he removed a silencer from the other pocket. Very slowly he attached the silencer to the pistol. He then aimed at Mike's leg and said, "I am getting very annoyed and fed up, so I will move this along a bit. I will start at the thigh," moving is gun to the thigh area. "Then I will move down to the shin. I will then do the same on the other leg. If I do not get a result from that I will then aim for the hand and elbow on both arms. So, I will ask you again, who were you talking to?"

The man was either very brave or very stupid because he stayed silent. Matt shot him in the thigh of his right leg. The man screamed and held on to his leg. After a moment he shouted, "Screw you". Matt shot him in the knee of that leg and knew that this shot would prevent him from walking properly again. The scream had now turned into sobs and he must have been in excruciating pain. Matt asked the same question and this time between the sobs he said, "Major Scholz."

"He is German then?" asked Matt.

"Yes, yes."

"What did he want?" asked Matt.

"The usual, information," Mike said. He was crying, and it was difficult to hear what he was saying.

"What did you tell him?" Matt asked.

"Nothing, I know nothing, so how can I tell him anything?" Matt aimed at the other leg.

"Alright, alright. I'll tell you. I told him the saboteurs were on the Downs. I saw them when I was shooting for rabbits, up there one night. It was quite a while ago. I saw a truck leave a barn and head across the Downs with no lights on. I went into the barn and found medical dressings, blood and bits of food. They must have been using that place, so I told the Germans," he cried.

"What else have you told them?" Matt wanted to know.

"I told them that the local vicar was helping the Jews and they must have dealt with him, because he has gone missing," he said.

"And?"

"When I saw the Major last I told him where Edward and Wallace are hiding," he admitted.

Matt looked at Sid and said, "And where exactly are they hiding Mike?"

"Well I am not quite certain if it is true, but there is a rumour going around that they are under the Germans noses in the PoWs camp. They are being hid in the new buildings that are being built there. Apparently, they have a false wall and that is where they are being kept," he said.

"Who told you that?" asked Matt.

"I was in a bar a couple of days ago and someone spoke of it. Mind you he was a bit drunk at the time and the other people in the pub all laughed at him," Mike said.

A little smile crossed Matt's face, but then realised that this man knew nothing really apart from the Jewish people and Father Andrew, so Matt asked,

"Mike, why are you informing the Germans of this?"

Mike was still crying, but his time it was not the pain of his leg that was causing it. Matt waited for him to stop crying to ask him again.

"I moved down here when I heard that the invasion was imminent because I have some elderly parents living close by. I called on them a couple of times and they seemed alright and coping, but then a vicar came to call and told them that they were in danger and offered a way to help them. They told me about this visit and asked me what they should do. I told them to stay put and they would be alright. When I went around the next time no one was there. I was just leaving the house when a man in plain clothes approached me. He told me that my parents were the enemy of the Germans and that they had been taken away to be transported to Germany. I was worried," Mike said. He now had tears running down his face although he was not making any noise.

"Just a minute Mike, are you Jewish?" Sid asked.

"Yes."

"But your name isn't Jewish?"

"No, you are right. I changed it a couple of years ago. It was easier to get a job with the name Mike Wilkinson that Moeshe Auerbach. I wasn't taken seriously so it got changed," he said.

"Alright, continue with your story."

"Anyway, the man said that my parents were being held in England ready to be transported to a camp in Germany in a couple of days, but that could change if I agreed to help them. I told him that I didn't know anything, so he told me that I would be taken in as well and transported with them to Germany and you know what that means. I would have to go in one of their camps. I would have managed but my parents are too old to cope. They would die. I agreed to help them. I knew that the information I could provide wouldn't be that important, so I didn't think it would be a problem. They only came by a couple of times over the last few months and then suddenly they were on my case all the time. I had to find things out and they kept threatening me. I asked around about the people doing the sabotage to the bridges and things, but these people were well hidden, and I suppose only a few people knew exactly who they were, so I couldn't tell them anything. Suddenly I was pulled in and they really frightened me, so when I heard about Edward and Wallace in the pub I thought I may be out of trouble with them. When I told them they were really excited," he said.

"Oh Mike, you have been so silly. Your parents are almost certainly already in Germany and I hate to say it, but they are probably dead by now. I am sorry, but that is the truth. You see there have been quite a few ships that have already left with

British Jews on board. Oh, and just for your information the vicar of the church is safe. We got to him before any harm was done to him," Matt said.

"See what I mean I haven't done any harm really," he said.

"No but you are not safe. You would get people in trouble and if it wasn't for our intervention then the vicar would have been arrested and possibly killed and that is not acceptable. We could do one of two things with you; we could kill you now and that would be the end of it or we could give you information that sounds good but is incorrect. That could put you in danger. The dilemma I have is that you now know us and have seen our faces, which makes you able to tell the Germans who we are…"

Mike interrupted Matt saying, "Quite right. I will tell them who you are, if there is a slight chance that it may save my parents. I don't care what you say; I must believe that they are still safe. You have to understand that family must come first."

"I believe you would," Matt said sadly.

Matt and Sid went outside, leaving Pip with Mike. Outside they discussed the situation with Johnny and Jack, and after a lengthy discussion, it was felt that as he had seen all their faces he was too much of a liability, so he would have to be disposed of. Sid and Jack agreed to deal with it. Matt didn't like it as he was only looking out for his family.

He blamed the Germans for using people like Mike, but he realised that there was more at stake.

Matt went in and said that he was sorry about his parents but to inform on the British was not acceptable in any way. He would have to be killed. Mike seemed to accept it and, in a way, welcomed it. He must have been living under such a strain for the last few months, but suddenly he completely broke down and sobbed saying, "My parents, oh my parents."

Matt said, "Mike get it through your head, they are dead already and you could have done nothing to saved them."

Matt left him with Sid and Jack. He wanted to go over to the camp because he wanted to know if there were any repercussions to the information that Mike had given. He would wait until night and Johnny said that he would come over with him.

Sid and Jack shot Mike in the head and they buried him behind the cottage. They then told Bill Bolt that Mike had left the area and would not be returning.

CHAPTER 22

Oberst Baumhauer was livid. He had just received reports from Hauptmann Mencken and a couple of other officers which were disturbing. Hauptmann Mencken stated that after nearly demolishing two of the buildings in the camp that the prisoners had built, they discovered nothing. All the buildings were measured inside and outside, but there are no secret rooms and had concluded that the information from the informant was untrue. Another report from another officer stated that the station worker who they suspected had information had disappeared and the neighbours had not seen him for a while. Major Scholz then reported that his informant, the Jew, had also disappeared and enquiries at his place of work revealed that he had left the day before and it was believed that he had gone back up to Cowfold to work. They had no other information about him. Oberst Baumhauer called Oberleutnant Schafer into his office. "Have you read these reports, Schafer?"

"Ja"

"Well this is not good. Informants or possible informants are disappearing. It seems that those damn terrorists know exactly what is happening inside our walls. Do you think we have a mole in our ranks?" he asked.

"Who knows? I do know that our officers were chosen for this assignment in England because they spoke English. Perhaps they have more of an affinity with these British people than we realised," said Oberleutnant Schafer.

"I want a check done on all of our officers to make sure they are not betraying us and as all our efforts are hindered by these terrorists, I want something done that will really hurt the British. Do you understand?" he ordered.

Oberst Baumhauer had dealt with civilian populations in Belgium before coming to England and he was always accompanied by Oberleutnant Schafer, who did his dirty work when it was required. He did not have to tell him exactly what should be done. He just gave Schafer the authority to do what he felt was required, which was usually ruthless and vicious.

Schafer just nodded his head and left the office. Oberst Baumhauer sat down behind his desk, put the reports in one of the trays on his desk and sat back with a smirk over his face.

Lily, George Darcy's daughter, was playing in the front garden of the cottage. Her baby sitter, Evie, was preparing lunch for her and was in the kitchen. Lily was a quiet girl and very pretty. She was the apple of her father's eye. She was playing with a ball, throwing it up in the air and catching it. She threw it up against the wall of the cottage and it rebounded out of the garden onto the road. Lily looked around and decided that she would go and get it. She opened the gate and went out onto the road. The ball had rolled across the road to the gutter on the other side of it. She crossed the road and was just picking it up when a German appeared and said, "Hello little girl." Lily was too shy to speak and just stood up with the ball in her hands.

"Come here I need to speak to you," the German said.

Lily did not move.

The German moved towards Lily and when he got close he said, "I need you to come with me." He then reached out and held Lily's arm and made her move towards a vehicle that was parked just along from her home.

Lily was so scared that she was shaking but bravely said, "I live there. I must tell Evie."

The German said that he would tell her, but she must come with him now. She was then lifted into the back of the car and they drove off.

Outside the school in Pond Road a crowd had massed. There were 10 children lined up, being guarded by some Germans and opposite were some parents who were shouting abuse at the Germans. One of the mothers had pushed forward and was approaching one of the children. A German stepped forward to prevent her access to her child and when she started to hit him he punched her in the stomach and then slapped her across her face. She fell to the floor. Other adults went to her and helped her back on her feet and they moved her away from the Germans. In the line of children was the pretty Lily, who was sobbing and saying between the sobs that she had to go home. The other children, who were aged between 5 years and 12 years, all stood quietly, but then the majority had their mother or father in the crowd. Lily's sobs were loud, and it was making a bad situation worse as the Germans kept saying to Lily to shut up. This only made it worse and she sobbed even louder. Suddenly one of the Germans stepped up to Lily and struck her hard around the face. This forced the little girl to be flung backwards and land hard on the ground. The crowd gasped. Lily had stopped crying and when the crowd looked at her she was laying on the floor with her head at an awkward angle. The crowd surged forward and were striking out at the troops standing in front of the children. The Germans did not know what to do and some of them raised their rifles and fired in the air. The noise made the crowd stop what they were doing but seeing their own children in the line caused them to surge forward again. The firing brought a couple of officers, who were passing nearby.

They saw Lily lying on the floor and the line of children and the parents trying to get to them.

One of the Officers stepped forward and shouted in a booming voice, "Everybody stop." The parents looked over to him and the Germans, seeing that he was an officer, stood to attention.

"What the hell is going on here?" he said in English.

Everyone, including all the parents in the crowd, started to speak at once. He silenced them all and he went up to the German who seemed to be in charge and said in German, "What is happening here, why are the children lined up and what is up with that little girl"

"We were ordered to round up 10 children and threaten to harm them, so the locals would give up the terrorists. Those," indicating the crowd, "are the parents, well some of them."

"And the little girl on the floor is she alright?"

"She kept crying and she got hit. I don't know if she alright, the crowd just kept coming afterwards," he said.

The Officer went up to Lily and he turned her over and discovered she was dead

"She is dead, what have you done?" the Officer asked.

"Dead, no she was only hit," said the German.

"Who did it?" the Officer demanded to know.

A large German was pointed out and the officer continued, "Well it looks like he broke her neck. I would suggest that you release the other children, pretty quickly, or you will have a riot on your hands. At the moment only a few people are here, but if they hear about this, the whole town will be here and then I would hate to think what could happen. Also, I would suggest that you get that little girl to the mortuary. Are her parents in the crowd?"

"I don't know. Shall I ask?" the German asked.

"Release the other children and disperse the crowd and then we will deal with the little girl and see who comes forward," the Officer said.

The German did as he was told and within 5 minutes the whole area was cleared of people. Lily's body was removed to the mortuary.

George Darcy was working in one of the offices when a German entered and told him that there was a woman at the gate who wanted to see him urgently. George asked if he had got the right man and the German told him yes.

George left the office and was at the front gate in minutes to find Evie there in a real state. She told him that Lily had been playing in the front garden and when she called her in for lunch she did not answer. When she went outside she discovered that Lily had disappeared. Evie had searched the whole area but couldn't find her and was worried. George looked very anxious and said that he would come home immediately. George and Evie searched the area; the park, the burnt-out houses and the roads leading from the cottage. George told Evie to stay at the cottage in case she returned and decided to search further afield. He eventually landed up in the churchyard where he sat down on one of the seats, pondering exactly what he should do. He decided that he would go to the Police Station and tell the Germans that his precious daughter had gone missing. As he sat there, two women passed, and he heard them talking about an incident at the school involving a group of children and the Germans. He only managed to hear part of the conversation, but enough to get him concerned. He went up to the women and asked them to tell him exactly what had happened. As they related the story he started to get fear for his daughter. Then they told him about the little girl that was hit because she was crying too much and that the hit had killed her, George nearly collapsed. The women went up to him and helped him back to the seat. They continued with their story and at the end he was now convinced that the little girl was Lily. He started to cry, and the women did not know what to do. After a while he came to his senses and the women who were with him offered to take him home. He declined; instead he left the women and made his way to the Police Station. He was now relatively calm, leastways on the outside, but inside him he was churned up. He asked the

German at the Police Station where the body of the little girl killed by the Germans was. The Germans looked uncomfortable especially when he said that he thought that the girl may be his daughter. The Germans called for their Officer who asked for a description of his daughter, which he gave and the look on the Officers face said it all. This Officer was the one at the incident. He told George that the little girl was at the mortuary which was in the High Street and he would take him there. They immediately made their way to the mortuary. They entered, and George was shown into a room. The Officer went off to the find the mortician. A couple of minutes later the Officer returned and he took George into another room. In the middle of this room was a table. On the table was the small body of a child under a sheet. George went over to the table and lifted the sheet. It was his Lily. He gently lifted her and cradled her. He cried. His body heaved with tears of grief falling down his face. He stayed with her for an hour and then he left. The Officer wanted to take him home, but George refused. He wanted to be alone, but first he needed to tell Evie.

George stayed at home and arranged Lily's funeral. He stood at Lily's grave, which was next to her mothers, and he knew that he had to do something, but what? He stood there for a long time. All the other people who had come to the funeral had left, apart from Evie, who was standing well back from George. He appeared to suddenly come to a decision and he said in a whisper, "Lily you will be avenged, and I will be with you soon. Be good until then."

He then turned and walked away.

Evie caught up with him and said, "Are you alright Mr Darcy?"

"Yes Evie, I am great. I will be returning to work tomorrow, oh yes and I will not need your services anymore," George said in a very strong voice.

"Oh Mr Darcy, are you sure," asked Evie. "You have had such a shock. I really don't mind helping you until you have recovered from Lily."

George turned to Evie and said, "Evie, I am fine. I will return to work tomorrow and I will be able to look after myself from now on. You are no longer required. You were employed to look after Lily and now she has gone… well… there is no job anymore."

Evie looked at George and thought how calm he looked, but she knew that inside Lily's death was eating him away. George left Evie standing in the graveyard and instead of going home he headed to where he left messages for Matt. He wrote something on a piece of paper and left it at the drop point. He then went to the pub and got very drunk. The following day he returned to work and all the Germans who worked with him were very surprised that he had come in and mostly surprised that he had not changed in his attitude to them, considering it was one of them that had killed his daughter.

Matt had spent the last couple of days planning a mission on the power station. He had tasked Jack with contacting the man who had told him about the tunnel and was waiting for his report. He had also visited the camp with Johnny and had heard that although the Germans had partially destroyed a couple of the huts they had built they had not discovered the 'cellars' with the arms in them. The huts were now in the process of being rebuilt. Matt had more munitions to move into the camp and he discussed this with Colonel Grant. He believed this should wait as the guards were being particularly vigilant now, so it was decided that they would move them in a couple of weeks, although no fixed day was set. Colonel Grant also told Matt of another development at the camp. The guards were taking names and details of all the detainees. Matt thought that this may be a problem if more men were needed on the outside, but Colonel Grant said that it wouldn't be, because there are 4 guards taking the details and men are going to all four and giving false names and of course when the count is done, the numbers were never correct. In other words, the prisoners were giving the Germans a real run around, one way or another. Matt also visited the Cement Works. He wanted to find out how the injured men were. He wanted to know if Jake was operational. He discovered that although the care he had received from Trudy was exceptional, he had a problem with the movement of his shoulder. Trudy and the nurses were doing physiotherapy on it and it was getting better slowly. He wanted to return to the bunker, but it was full, so he was told to stay put and if they needed him to help with explosives he could do it from there. As for going on missions it was agreed that he would wait until his shoulder was stronger. Matt hadn't been able to see Nellie for a while, so whilst he was there he asked her if she wanted to go for a walk so they could talk. Nellie readily agreed, and they spent the remainder of the day on the Downs. The Germans had searched the Downs earlier and of course had come up with nothing, so they were relatively safe to walk about up there now. The time they spent up there was brilliant although the weather was not particularly good. It was cold, foggy and there was a drizzle of rain falling, but neither of them seemed to notice.

"You know my darling, when this is all over I am going to treat you to a slap-up meal in a restaurant, a show and then afterwards… you never know what may happen," said Matt, who was definitely falling in love with her.

"I would love that… all of it," said Nellie giggling. They had stopped walking and Matt bent over her and kissed her. Nellie responded.

"I really miss you when I don't see you," Nellie said.

"I know what you mean," Matt agreed.

"I worry, you know. You could be killed, and I sometimes wonder what I would do if that happened," said Nellie.

"Sorry, but I have a job to do. I worry about you as well. You are still at risk even though you have another id. I do hope you are being careful?" Matt looked into Nellie's eyes.

"I know, let's not worry about each other. Let's do what we should do and live each day as it comes," Nellie said.

"It's a deal," Matt replied.

Matt realised that he would ask Nellie to marry him. He wouldn't do it now, but the moment the Germans left he would. They continued with the walk with the occasional stolen kiss and agreed that they should do this again and soon.

When Matt returned to the bunker he discovered that Jack had returned, and he was please to discover that Jack's information from his informant was spot on. The man had shown Jack the tunnel entrance and they had even managed to enter it to see what the security was like. There was none. It appeared that the Germans were unaware of it. Matt was really pleased and decided that this would be hit next.

Sid and Pip returned from the drop points and handed the message that George had left. It was very short and said:
Pavilion
2000 hours tomorrow
G
Matt looked at the message and was surprised at the shortness of it and wondered what was wrong. Matt had a gut feeling that there was a problem which was the reason why the message being so abrupt.

Usually Matt would see George alone, but decided that he would take Sid with him.

The following night they were standing in the pavilion at 1950 hours waiting for George to arrive. At exactly 2000 hours George arrived. As soon as George arrived Matt realised that there was something wrong. George then told them about Lily and Matt and Sid were horrified.

"You see I now need to do something and I have a plan, but I need your help with it. I know that you will approve," George finished.

"I am so sorry George. Your lovely little girl," said Matt who recalled seeing her for the first time, running out to meet George.

"Thank you, but if I recall you threatened me with hurting her," said George. He was talking in a monotone voice. He was angry, but with whom, them or the Germans.

"I'm sorry about that, but you know we would never have hurt her. She was a child and we value our children," said Sid.

"Yes, well maybe, but the threat was there. Look I am not condemning you, but I need to get back at the Germans for murdering her. I want them to be sorry," George said.

"Ok George, what are you planning?" said Matt who was still uncertain whether he blamed him or not.

George then outlined his plan and ended up saying, "So I need enough explosives to do it"

Matt thought about the plan and the only problem that he could see was how would George escape? He asked him.

"That is all in hand and I will be able to escape. I will let you know nearer the time," George said.

Matt and Sid discussed it for a minute and then told George that he could have the explosives which they will leave in the pavilion suitably packed up in 3 backpacks. He would have to be instructed how to connect them to the detonator box so one of Matt's men will come down and show him what he had to do. They wanted to know when he was planning to do this, and he told them that he would do it on Friday next. That will allow him to get the explosives into the port and get access to a boat.

Matt returned to the bunker and Jack and Pip got to work on the explosives. He also decided that the tunnel should be destroyed at the same time because once George's mission happened the Germans may close the port area and that meant that access to the tunnel may not be as easy. It was agreed that next Friday was the day to blow up the tunnel as well.

George's insides were in turmoil. He felt like his heart had been broken into a thousand pieces. At night he would go home and cry. He had a bottle of scotch which he had bought off one of the Germans at the port. One night he drank the whole bottle, but he did not get drunk. He did however sleep for the first time since he had seen Lily in the morgue. Jack had delivered the explosives and the detonator and gave George instructions on how to connect it up and of course how to explode them. Jack had been instructed to question George on his escape route, but all George would say was that it was in hand and he had an escape route. Jack didn't press this. He could see that George was determined and he knew that because his plan seemed perfect he would no doubt have his escape planned just as well.

Over the week George smuggled the explosives and the detonator box into the port and kept them in his locker. Friday arrived, and he was ready. He went into work as normal and for the first part of the morning he did his job as normal. None of the Germans could see anything different about him. He asked the German in charge of him if he could use one of the motor boats to take a crate over to the other side of the port. This was not an unusual request, so he agreed and told him to use the Officers boat which was beside 'B' Quay. George went to his locker, took the explosives in the back packs and the detonator which was in another back pack to a small crate, placed them inside and fastened the lid in place and then carried it to the boat. He started the boat up and headed out in the port. He stopped in the middle of the entrance to the port and he went over to the crate. He connected the explosives to the detonator box and he then waited. A large freighter was due to leave the port within the next 10 minutes. He could see movement along one of the quays. The freighter was leaving its mooring place. He watched the freighter move out towards the entrance to the port which meant passing the little boat with George in. He waited and at just the right time, as the ship was approaching the entrance George started his boat and he aimed it towards the middle of the hull of the large ship. The ship was now within 5 yards of the entrance when George's boat rammed it and at the same time George hit the detonator. The freighter literally jumped out of the water and a huge hole appeared on the waterline of the ship. It immediately started to take on water and the ship very quickly began to list to one side. Very slowly it started to sink. The crew tried to alter course but fortunately the explosion had taken out the steering and once it started to go under, it went down very quickly. The crew abandoned their posts and were seen jumping overboard. The ship sank blocking the entrance to the port. George was successful. George, however, did not have an escape plan. He was killed outright, as he had always intended, and afterwards everyone said that it was a mercy as he had nothing to live for, losing his wife and his little Lily.

Matt, Jack, Sid and Johnny made their way to the tunnel entrance in Southwick at about the same time as George had got into his boat on B Quay. They entered the tunnel and walked about 30 yards into it. They set the explosives with a timer detonator and they left. They hung around the area to discover the extent of the damage that it would do. Almost at the same time the ship exploded, there was another huge explosion in the tunnel leading from the power plant. Because of the explosion in the port, the Germans did not realise that this was another bomb. Cutting the power lines caused an area from Lancing to parts of Brighton and north to Henfield to be plunged into darkness. The tunnel which was situated under the port was flooded and it would be impossible for the Germans to repair it quickly.

They would be lucky to find out exactly what the problem was.

Apart from George's death, that day was a great success. Now the Germans wouldn't be able to get supplies into the port and they did not have any electricity to help with salvage operations of the sunken ship, so the port was put out of action. Ships would have to be diverted to other ports on the south coast and that meant that they had longer routes to the front line. German senior officers were furious with this and the blame fell wholly on George. It was reported that he was so distraught over the death of his child that he wanted revenge on the Germans, so planned and executed this act of sabotage. The German that hit Lily was arrested and efficiently dealt with, he was executed. They also put the sabotage of the power station down to George so that the German High Command could easily write off the incidents as a result of an unfortunate accident, the culprit of which having been dealt with.

The Germans had to bring some experts in from Germany to resolve the problem of the power. They managed to get power back on within the week, but they had to drape huge wires across the port which would prevent any large vessels from entering.

CHAPTER 23

News from the front was encouraging. The Germans initially had held the line in Surrey and north Kent and had made a couple of advances to the outskirts of London, but because of the lack of support, due to the work of the resistance groups and Auxiliaries in southern England, they were forced to retreat again and again. It took the Allies 3 weeks to push the Germans back to north Sussex, half way down Kent and to the outskirts of Portsmouth in Hampshire. The front line was just north of Canterbury, through Maidstone, about 5 miles north of Tunbridge Wells, in Kent, about 10 miles north of Crawley in Sussex and in Hampshire about 15 miles north of Portsmouth. The Germans were suffering from losing many of their troops due to either injury, death or being captured and they were not efficiently being reinforced with men or equipment. It was now becoming dire for the Germans and the moral of their troops was falling daily. The RAF was now flying sorties regularly over Sussex to the coast and their planes were attacking German shipping in the English Channel. The Germans were having a problem dealing with them as they were mainly doing hit and run attacks on the ships and locating the British aircraft was difficult for them. The Royal Navy had also re-formed and was now advancing on the English Channel as well. They were still having a serious problem with the German U-boats but they had efficient radar and sonar systems which were locating them in time to be able to drop depth charges on them. One or two of the British ships were disabled because of the U-boats, but more U-boats were being destroyed now. The German High Command were troubled about the situation and they now feared that there would be an attack on them from Russia and were having to send more men and equipment east, to that area. Hitler was furious about the situation in England and was on the verge of informing his Generals that he wanted his armies to retreat from England, but he was aware that getting his army back to main land Europe would be difficult. He did order all his fighter aircraft based in France, Belgium and Holland to support his ships in the English Channel, but the RAF were managing to repel these attacks and were more on the offensive than on the defensive now.

All this good news was reported on the BBC World Service and sometimes Matt and the men would go up onto the Downs as they could hear the guns in the far distance. It was good news, but now Matt knew that the real fighting for his men was just about to start. HQ had sent out messages to all the Auxiliaries and resistance groups that they now had to get organise. Once the Germans were 10 miles from their position, strategic places which had already been named, such as the port in Matt's case, needed to be taken and the retreat had to be stopped. Matt had informed Colonel Grant and they felt it was imperative to get more arms into the camp. This was done using the same method as before and again without being discovered. HQ had also informed Matt that when the time came the women should help with the civilian population, so Matt was countermanded. Of course, when he told Father Andrew and the women there was a big cheer and Dave was ordered to take command of them. Matt also told them that it would be soon, so they had to be prepared. His men were busy as well. Jack's idea of using the able-bodied men in the area was now highlighted as a priority and it was arranged that a meeting should take place to get these men to help. The only place that Matt could think of that would accommodate all the men concerned in secret was Buckingham Barn, but when they spoke to Bill he offered a large barn on his farm. Bill had been concerned that Mike had informed the Germans about Buckingham Farm and they could still have a look out on the Downs. Over the next week Matt's men went around to each farm, public house, and club in the area to get the men to agree to such a meeting. As it turned out it was word of mouth from colleagues and friends that got the men to the meeting. Look-outs were put out round the farm and because the meeting was arranged at 2100 hours there was a problem with the curfew and Matt thought that this may deter many of the men from coming, but amazingly about 200 men attended. Matt, Jack and Johnny stood up on a platform area, made of straw bales, in the Barn and after a couple of minutes there was silence.

"Men, you have been called together because of what is happening with our army and because of what my colleague here," indicating Jack, "had heard when you were all guests of the Germans a month or so back. Whilst you were kept in the school my colleague heard you talking about wanting to help in getting rid of the Hun when the retreat came and to fight them in this neighbourhood, well that is why I am here now to ask if you are still willing to help. I suspect that you have all been listening to the wireless about the advances that the Allies have made and at present are in north Sussex. I suspect that it will take another month or so before they are on our doorstep, which means that we now have to get organised. We plan on taking the port and holding it, so that they cannot retreat by sea from this area. If we hold the Germans here then the German High Command will lose a fighting force from Europe, so when the time comes to fight in Europe there will be less Germans to kill. We now need to know if you are willing to fight," Matt asked.

There were a lot of cheers in the barn and the men were excited about the prospect of fighting and even killing the Germans for all the atrocities that they have done during their time over here.

One man stood up and said, "That is all very well, and in principle we agree but what do we fight with, pitch forks! Some of us have shotguns, but not all of us and we will be fighting an organised and well-equipped force."

"Of course not, we have supplies of weapons which have been taken from the Hun and we would arm you with those and we will show you how to use them. We have other people who are going to be taking up arms in this area. We have over 3000 men already, so you would not be alone. We just want to make sure that you are ready when the time comes. We also want to inform you about the women, children, older people and any other civilians. We will try to get them to a safe place. That is being planned as we speak, but we need as many fighters as we can. Can I rely on you then?" Matt asked in a rallying cry.

A louder cheer went up and Matt, Johnny and Jack looked at each other and smiled.

"Right, that being the case, we need a system to inform you that it is starting. Can anyone think how that can be done?" Matt asked.

A man put his hand up and said, "The farms in the area have a cascade system that allows all the farms to be contacted if there is information that is vital that we should know about, perhaps we could do that. You know one farm ringing 2 farms and then those 2 farms each ring 2 other farms and so on. This way the farm workers can be informed within a day. I don't know about the other people here."

Another man put his hand up, Matt acknowledged him, "Well we all know each other here and well we meet up, usually in the pub or at work. We can use word of mouth so as long as one of us is told the others would be informed."

"Good in that case can we use you as the first contact?" said Matt.

"Yes, why not," he said.

"Give your name and how to contact you to my colleague," indicating Johnny. "Now I would like to arrange another meeting nearer the time, but because of security we cannot tell you when or where, so we will test our contact arrangements and let you know where and when it will occur then. At the next meeting you will probably be given weapons, so I suggest that you think about where you are going to keep them. One other thing, when you are fighting you may run out of ammunition, please remember that you are using German arms and you will have to get more ammunition of them, preferably when they are dead. British ammunition is not compatible with the German arms. There is much to think about other than just aiming and firing a weapon. I presume that you are all able to use a rifle," Matt said.

There was a murmur saying yes, but Matt could see a couple of men who looked worried. Addressing those men, he said, "Some of you look worried, what are your problems?"

A man stood and said, "I have never used a gun in my life. I know the end you point and that a gun has a trigger, but I know nothing about shooting or for that matter fighting."

"We had thought about that. You men will become medics. We will have a mobile hospital manned by medics, so you can join them if you like. That way you are helping and not hindering," Matt said.

This seemed to stop the worried looks on the faces of some of the men.

Matt then continued, "I have nothing else to say but if there are any questions then this is the time."

There were a couple of questions, but they were ones of concern about the local population and the time span. Matt answered the questions as best he could and then they all left. Matt, Johnny and Jack were pleased with the meeting and went back to the bunker happy.

During this time Matt had a serious problem with Edward and Wallace. He received weekly reports on how they were behaving, and he tried to visit the bunker at least once a week. The men and women looking after them hated them and it was apparent that Edward and Wallace hated them as well. He had to get Sergeant Green to change the men regularly and he had asked for more volunteers from the women to assist. They were a good bunch of women and although they didn't really want to help, they nevertheless, offered their assistance. One incident was particularly disturbing which made Matt pay an early visit to them. The incident involved one of his men putting a loaded pistol to Edward's head and threatening to shoot him. Apparently, Edward had been goading this man relentlessly for weeks and his man did not like the treatment of the women volunteers by Wallace. She was trying to treat them like her personal maids. This man had stated that their treatment by Edward and Wallace was contemptible and loathsome and he wasn't prepared to be treated like that anymore. Sergeant Green immediately removed the man from these duties and Matt went over to see if he could improve the situation.

Once in the bunker Matt immediately felt the tension between the men looking after the Royal couple and the Royal couple. He was with Sergeant Green and he was astounded at the mess in the place. Edward and Wallace had been in the bunker for over a month and the place was disgusting. He wanted to know why. Sergeant Green explained in front of them, "When they get up in the morning they expect drinks and breakfast bought to them, and when they are refused they start to moan about the treatment they are getting. They do eventually get up and then demand this and that continually all day. They do not get off their fat arses to feed themselves, wash themselves or their clothes and when there is a comment they then say that it is not what they do. They are so reliant on others to do these things they do not know how to do it. As for cooking, it is impossible; they use every pan and plate in the place and will not wash up after them. They expect to be waited on hand and foot. I have not heard a nice word come out of either of their mouths. One or two of our women felt sorry for them and agreed to do some work for them and they are treated like 'lackies', not someone who is trying to help them. I am sorry Sir, but this has to stop. I would rather kill them that continue the way we are."

Matt was horrified with what Sergeant Green had said, especially the part of killing them. Sergeant Green was the most laid back, calm and pleasant man he had ever had the pleasure of knowing and for him to say this it must be bad. Matt turned to

Edward, who was sitting in a chair and was sneering at him.

"Get your arse out of that chair," Matt shouted.

Edward looked at him as if he had just slapped him in the face.

"What did you say?" Edward said.

Matt did not repeat what he had said, he grabbed hold of Edward and he pulled him out of the chair and threw him on to the floor. Edward got up and was about to sit in the chair again when Matt picked the chair up and threw it against the wall. The chair smashed. Edward was now standing.

"What have you got to say?" Matt demanded.

"The man held a gun to my head and when this ordeal is over I will make my protests at the highest level," he said in an aloof manner.

"You pompous idiot," said Matt. "You were lucky that I had given the order that you were not to be harmed, you would probably be dead now and when this ordeal, as you call it, is over you will be in jail awaiting trial for treason and then you will probably hang. So now we are straight about our situation I am going to lay down some rules for you and your woman to adhere to."

"We will not be hung. Wallace is American, and they will make sure that we will be looked after," Edward said in the same manner as before.

"Just for your information, the Americans are furious that you sided with the Germans and I think you are under an illusion that you will be spared. I should have recorded Winston's speech because he is furious with you. When I reported that I have you, he made a broadcast about what he was going to do with you to the whole nation. I suggest that you re-think about what is going to happen to you," Matt was now shouting at the couple.

Matt looked Edward straight in his eyes and he could see that he was beginning to get anxious about what Matt was saying.

"You have been down here for a month and I can see that it will probably be another couple of months before you will be taken to a prison. I can do one of two things. I can arrange for a cage to be made with a bucket in the corner for you to pee and shit into and of course you will be forced to empty it and you both will be put in it and there you will stay until the Allies retake this area. You will then have no freedom to roam around like you can now," Matt told them.

"I will not do my business in a bucket or clean one out, Edward I will not," exclaimed Wallace.

Matt ignored that comment and continued, "Or we can make some rules up that will allow you to look after yourselves, but essentially you will have the freedom of the bunker. I am going to ask what you want to do."

Edward looked at Wallace who was nearly in tears and then turned to Matt, "We don't want to be caged up."

"In that case I will agree for the time being for it to remain the same, but I will write down the rules and if they are not stuck to then the cage will be built."

"What are the rules?" asked Wallace.

"First there is going to be a routine. You will rise at 0800 hours and retire at 2100 hours. You will not talk to my men unless they speak to you first. When you are spoken to by my men you will stand up and that includes you Madam. You will clean up both yourselves and this place. It needs cleaning and you will do it. You will clean up after you have cooked and eaten and you will do all this before you go to bed. You will do your washing daily and if you don't you will be stripped naked and you will wear nothing and then you will have nothing to wash so that would resolve that problem but that is, of course, your choice. None of my men or women will do anything for you in future and as I have a report daily about your behaviour I will assess if you are sticking to these rules. If you are not, then I will put in place the cage and the bucket. Do I make myself clear?" Matt said.

"I will not go naked," was all that Wallace could say but Edward, trying to act as if he was above all these threats said, "I have never washed my clothes before."

"Well I suggest you learn. Wallace was an ordinary housewife before you two got together so

I suggest that you get her to show you how to do it. I will be back down in 2 days and if the situation hasn't changed by then, well, I will ensure that it will be changed. Oh yes one final thing. I have given the men the ok to instil punishments on you if you do not do as they say, so I suspect that you could be in for a more brutal time," Matt said.

Matt had not issued any such order and never would, but he needed to have some sort of threat hanging over them. Matt left with Sergeant Green and told him to ignore the last comment and he hoped that this would do the trick.

Two days later he returned to the bunker and was amazed at the difference. When Matt arrived, Edward was on his feet immediately and offered him the one seat that was left. Matt declined but Edward stayed on his feet. He looked clean and his clothing looked immaculate. Someone had certainly been busy. He surveyed the bunker and found that it was also in great shape. It was clean and tidy. The bunks were made up and the kitchen was gleaming. They must have spent hours doing this. Sergeant Green had told him that Wallace had spent most of her time over the last 48 hours cleaning and making sure that Edward did his bit too. They also do not speak until they are spoken to and they stand up whenever any of the men or women approached them. They were obviously scared that they would get punished and now, hopefully, things would stay like this.

"I am glad you have come to your senses. It had better stay like this or I can assure you, you will be punished," Matt said.

Matt was about to leave when Edward asked, "Sir, I was wondering if you could provide us with some books. We need something to do when we are not cleaning, cooking and the likes. Reading is a good way to pass the time."

Matt thought about this and deciding that this may help this situation in the bunker said, "I will see what I can do. I am afraid that we are not able to go to the library for you, but I will see if any of my men feel they can lend you any of their books."

"Thank you Sir," Edward said.

Matt left, and Edward and Wallace behaved themselves from then on.

CHAPTER 24

It was the beginning of May and well over seven months since the invasion. It had been a long and tiring time, both mentally and physically, for the Auxiliaries and the men who were now working with them. They had continued throughout this time, with dangerous missions involving destroying property and killing as many Germans as possible. The Germans in the area were becoming very tense and had retaliated viciously on the civilian population. Although the civilians were angry at the Germans, it was becoming apparent that they were also angry about the acts of sabotage that was causing these reprisals. This was worrying to Matt and his men. The Allies forward line was not moving forward as quickly as the British, left behind in Southern England, had hoped. One piece of good news was that the front had not been pushed back. All the people in southern England were becoming impatient. They wanted their revenge on the Germans and they wanted to take up arms against them. The men in charge, such as Matt, were having trouble keeping them in check.

Matt had been very busy with plans for sabotaging certain targets. He had been informed that the salvage operation of the ship that George had sunk was now nearly completed by the Germans and he was looking at other ways to keep the port closed but was coming up short of an appropriate way to do it. The heavy wires were still draped across the port, but engineers had been brought into England from Germany and were seen assessing exactly what could be done about these wires. Pip had been cultivating an informant who used to work at the port and he felt that this man may be able to come up with a way to help Matt with this problem. Pip had left the previous day to go to Fishersgate to meet up with this man. This, was not unusual, as sometimes the men had to go into hiding for a while to prevent being captured by the Germans. Matt was only partially concerned at this stage, but come the night, if Pip had not returned, he would try and find out where he was. He had informed the men to be careful, just in case Pip had been captured.

Matt needed to go down to the Cement Works to speak to Jake about some explosives for a prospective target. Jake was the man who knew everything about the effects of explosives and seemed to know instinctively how much to use for the result that Matt required. He also had the ability to think of other methods of achieving Matt's aim usually whilst he was putting together the explosives. Matt climbed out of the bunker and was just starting to make his way through the wooded area towards the Cement Works when he heard a noise. He could hear men's voices and he could hear them making their way through the wood. Matt immediately sensed danger and he back-tracked to an area near the entrance to the bunker. He hid himself using shrubs and natural vegetation, especially the foliage on the ground. He was in such a position, about 10 yards from the entrance, where he could see who these men were, that were walking through the wood. He lay still and waited. Suddenly the men came into his sight. They were Germans and there were seven of them. Matt was worried, they seemed to be searching for something. A man was pushed forward and initially Matt didn't recognise him. This man had swelling and cuts to his face and he was hunched over as if he was in severe pain. Matt then identified him as Pip. It looked like he had been badly beaten. Pip reluctantly moved towards the tree where the notches were. This tree was still showing the marks, although they had weathered slightly. Pip then moved forward a few paces and indicated where the hatch was. The German said something to Pip and although Matt couldn't quite hear what was said, he assumed Pip was told to open it. Pip was aware of the alarm system and Matt was desperately hoping that he wouldn't disconnect it and the men inside would be warned.

Pip opened the hatch and he got up and stepped back. The German beside him then pushed him away into the arms of another German. The German who was in charge indicated for three Germans to go down the ladder. They entered and after a while Matt could hear some shouting coming from the bunker, then there were a couple of explosions and smoke appeared from the bunker entrance. The Germans at the entrance started to shout down to their comrades but as there was no reply they sent 2 more men down the ladder. Just after they went down, there was the sound of another explosion. Matt was shaking with fear. He didn't know what had happened and had no way of finding out yet.

In the bunker the men had heard the alarm go off and after the initial shock they realised they may have been compromised. They quickly headed for the escape tunnel, collecting some papers and Doug collected his code books as they went. Jack and Sid told Johnny and Doug to go first and they immediately went to the detonator in the tunnel. They heard the Germans break down the door from the entrance shaft. Jack hit the detonator and at the same time Sid, who had a grenade ready, threw it into the arsenal of arms. They then ran down the length of the escape tunnel after the other men. They felt the explosion in the main body of the bunker as they ran and then as he caught up with the other men he heard the grenade explode, which in turn, exploded incendiaries in the room where the arms were, so there were further explosions. The bunker end of the escape tunnel was now blocked because of the explosives and weapons that were in the arsenal. There was a timed delay on one of the explosives in the entrance shaft and after 4 minutes they heard that explode. The men felt they were now safe. All they had to do was to make sure that their exit was clear. They had never used this exit before. They climbed the ladder, climbed out in to a derelict barn and hid. They watched the area for a minute and realising they that there was no one in the vicinity and they were safe, they then made their way to the Cement Works.

Matt, still hidden in the shrubs and foliage, watched what was occurring outside the bunker entrance. There were now only 2 Germans with Pip and they were looking down the bunker entrance shaft and shouting to the men who had gone down. They didn't know if the explosions were caused by them or it was done by others down in the bunker. Pip was standing back and appeared to be in a daze. Matt was under no doubt that the beating he had sustained had slowed him down. Matt reached down to his pocket and pulled out his pistol as quietly as possible. He carefully stood up and he took aim. One of the Germans was bent over the entrance and the other was standing back from him, but still looking towards the entrance. Both these men had their backs to Matt. He fired at the man standing back from the entrance and then fired at the man who was bent over the entrance shaft. The first man fell to the ground and the second man fell into the bunker. Matt got up and checking that the man lying on the floor was dead he went up to Pip. Pip seemed so dazed that he didn't even recognise Matt. Both his eyes were so swollen Matt wondered if he could see him properly. Matt took hold of Pip and said in a very soft voice, "You are safe now, Pip. Come on we need to get going."

Pip responded to Matt's voice and he was led through the wood away from the normal route and then down to the Cement Works. Matt spoke softly to Pip. Occasionally Pip stumbled and at one time he fell badly. He screamed out in pain and Matt could see from this that his body was badly bruised, if not broken in places. Matt carefully helped him up, put his arm around him and took his weight which seemed to ease Pip's pain. Matt eventually arrived at the Cement Works and Pip was laid down on one of the makeshift beds and he was then cared for by Trudy and her nurses. Matt was relieved to find all his team there and they all stood vigil over Pip to discover what exactly had happened to him. No one condemned him for giving the bunker away. They had all been told to hold out for 24 hours before giving any information, which Pip had. Pip was in and out of consciousness and Trudy told them that apart from the severe beating he had also been electrocuted. The Germans had put electrodes on his testicles. He was in considerable pain and Matt, hearing the treatment that he had received, asked if they should get a doctor to him. Trudy told Matt that there is nothing that a doctor could do that they weren't doing for him. They had given him pain killers and he would be kept on them until the pain subsided. Matt needed to speak to him because he needed to know if he had told them anything else. Trudy told him to wait until the current pain killers wore off a little and he came too. The pain killers made the patient sleepy, but Trudy was adamant that Matt should keep the conversation short as he needed to have more medication quickly to prevent him becoming too distressed with the pain. Matt waited over an hour for Pip to come too and when Matt spoke to him it was obvious that he was in agony.

"Pip, I know you are in pain, but I need to know what happened," Matt said softly.

"That informant told them about me. They were waiting for me when I arrived. I was taken to the Police Station where they interrogated me. I kept quiet for 24 hours. I honestly did, but I had to speak, I just couldn't bear it any more. I thought if I went with them and showed them I could set the alarm off. Did all the men get out?" he talked stopping every so often trying to get his breath back and control his pain and when he moved, at one point, Matt could see tears appear in his eyes.

"They all got out and they are safe, thanks to you. Pip did you tell them anything else," Matt asked gently.

"No. I kept quiet. It was only at the end that I told them about the bunker. I also told them that it was the only bunker in the area, so I hope they will not be looking for any more. You know the man who interrogated me and was at the bunker with me…. well… I am not quite sure how much he reported. I got the feeling that he wanted all the praise and we made our way to it nearly as soon as I told him. What happened to the Germans?" Pip asked.

"All the ones that were with you were killed. The ones that went into the bunker were killed when it was blown up and the ones outside, I killed," Matt told him.

"Good. I hope they rot in hell," Pip said.

"Thank God you are alive, but you will take a while to mend, so I suggest you do what Trudy tells you and get better soon. Just one other thing, I need to know the name and address of your informant," Matt asked.

Pip managed to give Matt that information and then he appeared to crumble up in pain and Trudy shoved Matt out of the way and administered some really strong medication and Pip went to sleep.

Matt and the other men set up a base in the corner of the storage area in the Cement Works. They were now without a radio for immediate use. Doug would have to go to Lancing Ring to use theirs. The Radio, along with the wireless, from Coombehead Wood had been removed when it was taken over by Edward and Wallace and had been kept in storage. Matt and his men were in a dilemma because the radio couldn't be set up in the Cement Works as it could lead detector vans to the area. There was no other place that it could be put that was secure. Matt pondered over this for the next couple of days. Eventually it was Nellie that came up with a solution. She had wanted this radio functioning for her use as well and had been thinking about a solution for a long time, longer than the team.

"Matt, I know that we need this radio urgently and I think that I may have come up with a possible way to do it. You know the sheds that house the canoes? Well couldn't we convert one of them to accommodate the radio and the operator? The detector vans will think that the signal will be coming from the river and if the transmissions are kept to 20 minutes they wouldn't have a clue. The aerial can be put in the shrubs around the shed and the operator would be safely concealed. When they leave the shed they would be covered by the vegetation around them. We can get it hooked up to a local electricity supply and hide the wires in the undergrowth. One other thing I have thought about, is the wireless that you took from the other bunker, well couldn't we have it here. We can connect it to the electricity in here and that way we can all be in contact with the outside world."

Matt sat there thinking about everything she had said and agreed that putting the radio so close to the river could work. He spoke with Doug and he thought it was a brilliant idea and immediately started to organise it. It was agreed that they would not use any of the sheds near to the Cement Works but one that were nearer to Bramber and Steyning. Matt also wondered why he hadn't thought about the wireless being put in the Cement Works before. Sometimes you need other people to also think about problems with a fresh view.

Over the next couple of weeks, work was carried out on a shed. The work had to be done mainly at night. The canoes were moved to other sheds and they built a platform over the river where they could put the radio. The operator would have to sit cross legged to send and receive messages. The aerial was attached around the door of the shed and then continued into the vegetation beside it. It was agreed that when Doug or Nellie used the radio they would have a look out near to the road and they had a rope that would be tugged to warn the operator that a German patrol was in the area. They built a Hide using the local vegetation, for the look out to stay in. This Hide was completely invisible from the road or the river. Having built the accommodation for the radio they needed to find out if it worked so two weeks later they did their first transmission to HQ from it. The radio worked brilliantly and although it was a bit uncomfortable for the operator, Doug and Nellie were happy with these arrangements.

Ever since Pip had been tortured and electrocuted, Matt had wanted to deal with the man who had informed the Germans about Pip. He had already sent Jack down to Fishersgate to find out this man's routine, so that they could grab him and 'interview' him. Sid understood Matt's anger, but it was apparent to him that revenge on civilian people may make it worse. He spoke to Matt about this, but Matt had made his mind up, if nothing else he needed to speak to him to find out why he did it. The man involved was called Alan Carter. He used to work in the port but when the Germans arrived he was made redundant. He was 27years old, and had a club foot, which meant he was unable to join the army. He lived in a house with his parents. He worked part time for a local grocer and, from what Matt's team could learn, he was popular with the people in the neighbourhood. Jack had even managed to speak casually to him and he appeared to be very anti-German. Matt listened to the reports given to him by Jack and decided that he wanted to speak to him urgently. He arranged for him to be taken the following night when he was making his way home. They had found a derelict house in the road where they would pick him up and which they would use to speak to him. The following night, Johnny and Jack went up to him in the street. It was deserted so they pointed a gun at him and told him to come with them. He followed, and they took him to the house where Matt, Sid and Doug were waiting. Matt ordered Doug and Jack to go outside to stand guard and he told Alan to sit on a chair in the middle of the only room that was habitable, and it looked safe from debris. Alan again did as he was told.

"I have been expecting you," said Alan before anyone else spoke.

Matt did not expect that comment, "What did you just say?"

"I said I was expecting you and I suppose you have come to deal with me," Alan repeated.

"Perhaps, it depends on what you have to say. A couple of weeks ago you arranged to meet up with a colleague of mine and when he arrived Germans were waiting for him. Why was that?" asked Matt.

"You are right I did arrange to meet him, and the Germans were waiting there, but it wasn't him that they were after, it was me," Alan said.

Matt was taken aback about this. What did this man mean? What had he done to be wanted by the Germans?

"Alright Alan, let's start at the beginning. You arranged to meet my colleague, that is correct, so how come you did not appear and why were the Germans here at that time and place?" Matt asked.

"I did appear. I was out of sight waiting for Pip. When Pip arrived, I was just about to reveal myself when the Germans barged in, they must have followed me. I managed to get away, but I saw them take Pip. I was concerned. I decided to continue as before and see if either the Germans or Pip's colleagues came first," he said.

"Are you still being followed?" asked Matt.

"I haven't seen anyone since then. I was worried for Pip. Is he alright?" Alan asked.

"Yes, but you could have warned him you were being followed," Matt said.

"You are right of course, but I wasn't certain. There was this one German who seemed to have a problem with me. I saw him the day before Pip was taken and, on the day, that I was due to meet Pip. I couldn't warn Pip because I didn't know how to," he said.

"Why were the Hun following you, anyway?" asked Sid.

"I thought you knew. I'm not a very nice person. I steal, rob and do anything for money. I thought Pip would have told you. Well I have been stealing things from the Germans and I suppose they don't like it. I also damage things especially if they belong to them. They must have been annoyed with me," Alan said.

Alan looked shifty but at least he was honest about it.

"When I was approached by Pip I thought I may be able to help get rid of the Krauts by helping you. You know I really hate them and I want them gone. I may be a shit, but I am a patriotic shit. I was upset about Pip," he said.

"Not as upset as Pip was. He was really hurt but we managed to get him back to us," said Matt who was starting to like this man and felt that he was sincere. He then asked, "Alan, what were you going to tell Pip?"

"He wanted to know about the Port and how we could block it. I am afraid that I don't know of a way other than to destroy the lock gates then although the front part of the port would still be accessible to boats the inner harbour wouldn't be."

"How could they be destroyed?" Matt asked.

"That's the interesting thing, isn't it? My uncle is the lock keeper and he is the only man who is permitted to work the damn things. He may do the deed if we ask him," Alan said.

"But surely if he did damage them, the Germans would know about it," Matt said.

"Not necessarily, if the workings got damaged he could say that they had rusted up or just broken and as the replacement parts come from Northern

England then they would become unusable," Alan said.

"I see what you mean," said Matt looking at Johnny and Sid. "But if you did work for us, how do we know you are not setting us up?"

"I wouldn't do that. I hate the Krauts. I want them to go and I would do anything to help. I am sorry about Pip, but it wasn't my fault, well it was but… you know what I mean," Alan said.

Matt liked him more the longer he spoke to him and he believed him, so he was going to risk it. He did say though, "Alan I am going to give you the benefit of the doubt. However, if you ever cross us, I will make sure that your parents will be violently harmed. Do I make myself clear?"

"What, hurt Mum and Dad? You wouldn't do that. Would you?" Alan said. This last comment of Matts put a frown on his face.

"Let's put it like this. You will find out if you double cross me or any of my men. We are just a small group; the rest of our team will know about you, and you and your parents will come to an untimely death," Matt reiterated.

"Look you don't have to threaten me, I will not double cross you, I promise," Alan said.

Now Matt believed him.

"As we have got that straight, will you speak to your uncle and see if he can help?" Matt asked.

"I have already spoken to him and he has agreed, so long as it looks like it is damaged naturally, he will help," he said.

"Good so tell him to get on with it and if he needs anything then let us know," Matt said.

"Ok."

Matt had finished with Alan, other than arranging a time to meet up with him again, but Alan had not finished with him.

"Look before you go, I need to speak to you about another matter," he said.

"Yes," said Matt.

"Well the locals here in Fishersgate had heard of a meeting that took place, a while back, with the local resistance about helping out when the army got closer. We want to be involved as well. There are about 75 of us, young and old and even some women that would like to fight, but we haven't got access to many arms and we need to be organised. I was hoping to speak to Pip about it. Are you the ones to speak to?"

Matt nodded.

"Well I can get them together. We meet up in the local primary school every other week. We first started when the Germans invaded to give support to people who needed it, mainly because people started to go missing and the community got concerned. Then, as the time went on we started to organise little acts of sabotage and now as the Allies are advancing back we started to worry about the women and children getting hurt. These meetings are obviously done in secret and dangerous, but the locals wanted to continue. It was like a lifeline to them," Alan said.

"When's the next meeting?" asked Matt.

"This coming Wednesday at 8.30," Alan said.

"We'll try and make it," Matt replied.

"Good and thanks. We know what you are doing and although some of the people have been killed we want you to continue," he said.

"Thank you, Alan for your support. If you think that you are being followed, we need you to warn us. Can you think how it can be done?" Matt asked.

"Well do you know where I live?" he enquired.

"Of course," Matt replied.

"Yes, that was a silly question. In the front window, Mum has a couple of vases, if something is wrong I will remove one of the vases," said Alan.

"Good."

Matt and his team left Alan and agreed that they should meet the locals at the meeting on Wednesday.

When they arrived back at the Cement Works, Matt went over to Pip first to check up on his condition. He was making a quick recovery. He was still badly bruised, and Trudy thought that his confidence had had a kicking, but he was healing well. His testicles were still very swollen and bruised and although he was walking around now he found it hard to sit down. Trudy had told Matt that it would probably only take a couple of weeks for the injuries to be healed, but she wondered about his mental health. He had found it difficult to speak about exactly what had happened. She had asked Sid and Johnny to try and get him to talk to him, but they found it difficult to get him chatting about the incident. He thought that he was weak giving in to the Germans and he feels guilty about giving up the bunker and putting the men at risk. Matt had even told him that he had obeyed all the standing orders about lasting out for 24 hours, and the alarm had warned the men. As far as Matt and the men were concerned he was a hero. Pip thought that Matt was only just saying that and found it difficult to accept he had been tortured and he thought that the other men would have lasted longer than he did. Matt, as well as Sid and Johnny had tried to tell him that because of the extent of the torture done to him they suspected that few men would have lasted as long as he did. Again, Pip thought they were only being kind.

Matt found him lying on his bed chatting with one of the nurses. He was actually 'chatting' her up. When Matt approached, the nurse hurried away, but her face had reddened as she did so.

"What is going on here?" asked Matt jokingly.

"Gillian is such a fantastic nurse. She is so gently and really caring," Pip said.

"Do I feel a relationship occurring?"

Pip looked at Matt and realising that he was joking said, "It wouldn't hurt, now would it."

"No, it wouldn't. Look Pip, we have spoken with Alan," Matt told him, and he then told him what Alan had said. Pip agreed that it could have happened as he said. Matt also told Pip that he thought Alan was a likeable chap and believed him. Pip agreed and that is why he was so surprised to see the Germans there. He thought that Alan had betrayed him, but now hearing what Matt had said he realised that his first thoughts about Alan were correct. Pip felt better about things. It appeared that it was sheer bad luck that had got Pip caught.

Wednesday arrived and they decided that Matt, Sid and Jack would go down to the meeting in Fishersgate. That way Johnny would still be around with Jake and Doug if anything did go wrong. Although Johnny was the same rank as Matt, it had never been an issue about who was the Officer in Command. It had always been Matt, but if anything did go wrong and Matt got injured or killed then Johnny would take over.

They arrived at the school at 2015 hours. They didn't go straight into the school; they watched it for 10 minutes. Before arriving at the school Jack had gone past Alan's house and found that 2 vases were in the window, so it appeared that everything was in order. Matt, Sid and Jack were not complacent, and they waited outside the school to see people arriving, but to their surprise they saw no one enter the school. Sid wanted to leave, but Matt said that he and Jack would enter and see if there was anybody inside. Sid would stay outside to watch for trouble. Sid had his pistol ready as he thought there was going to be trouble. Matt and Jack, very slowly and carefully, entered the entrance to the school at 2030 hours. They followed the hallway to an assembly hall. The door to this hall had a small window which allowed them to be able to look inside and they could see about 50 people sitting on chairs. No one could be heard speaking. Matt looked through the window and could see Alan standing to one side and there was someone sitting in front of the people. It appeared to be a civilian. He was talking in a very low voice, which made it impossible for Matt to hear him. He could see that there was another door at the rear of the hall, so he and Jack followed the hallway round to that door. This door also had a window in it and could see the people better from here. They were sitting listening to the man at the front. Alan was looking at the first door that Matt and Jack had looked through and he had a frown on his face. Matt wondered if it was safe and how did all these people get into the hall without him seeing them. He could see that the hall overlooked a playground and some fields, perhaps they had come across those. Matt told Jack in a whisper "I'm going in, stay here and wait, just in case. I will use the other door"

Jack nodded, and he had his pistol drawn and ready. Matt went around to the other door and very slowly opened it. He entered. Alan immediately went up to him and said in a whisper, "We have to keep fairly quiet, but we have lookouts and as far as we know we are safe."

The man who was sitting in front of the people came up to him and said, "I am Cyril Campbell, a local councillor, and I have been trying to keep these people safe from the Germans. You are very welcome here. Is there only one of you?"

"For the moment yes," said Matt.

This man was in his 60's. He was large and tall. He had an imposing manner and it was obviously that if he spoke, people listened to him.

"Now I hear you have come to speak to the people about helping when the Allies arrive," he said.

"Yes, amongst other things," Matt said.

"In that case we need to keep it quiet and brief. Can I introduce you?" Cyril asked.

"No names please. I will just state my rank to them," Matt said.

Very quietly Cyril turned to the people and said, "This man will speak to you but will not give his name," he turned to Matt and Matt stepped forward.

"Ladies and gentlemen, I am a Major in the Auxiliary Home Guards. My men and I are responsible for much of the sabotage occurring in the area."

A murmur of approval went around the hall, he continued, "The other day I was asked about what will happen when the Allies get near to this location and that is the reason I am here today to ask you for help and to tell you how woman, children and any vulnerable people will be able to get to a safe place. We have got over 3,000 men ready and armed to take the Germans from the rear when they retreat. We are going to fight them. Other areas are also planning for the Germans retreat. We have many local men from the Shoreham, Southwick, Bramber, Steyning and Upper Beeding areas who will also take up arms to fight with us when the time comes. The person I spoke to from your area confirmed that people from Fishersgate also want to assist," again a murmur went around the people in the hall.

"Please put your hand up if you want to help."

Most of men and even some women put up their hands.

"Just to let you know, if you cannot or don't want to fight there are other things that can be done. We need medics to help with the wounded." With that every man and even a couple more of women put their hands in the air.

"Thank you," said Matt. He continued, "Now there is a plan already in existence to get the women and children to safety and when the time comes you will be approached by a woman and told where to go to. You are the furthest away from the safe area, so I suggest that you have a bag packed ready to go at a moment's notice."

A woman put her hand up. "Yes," said Matt.

"Are you saying that woman cannot fight?" she asked. "I have lost my husband, my child and my mother because of the Germans. I want to kill them just as much as any man here and I know I can."

"It is not right for a woman to be on the front line. I am sorry for your loss, but would it help if you were killed as well. You need to tell the world what happened to you when the time comes. The Germans have done some dreadful and barbaric acts against the civilian population and we need that to be told, especially for the people who cannot speak for themselves because they are either dead or missing. You and other women could do that. You can help, of course, a hospital is being set up and people will be required to keep that safe. Women will be employed to do that as well as working with a number of nurses that we have," Matt said.

The women in the hall all seemed to nod in unison.

A man then put his hand up. "How will we know when and where to report?"

Matt explained the system he had set up with the other men and it was agreed that they would use that system. Just as Matt was finishing, Sid came through the door of the hall saying, "There is a German patrol in the area and they are showing a lot of interest in the school."

At the same time two people entered the hall from the playground saying the same thing.

Everyone in the hall seemed to move together. They got up and all headed towards the doors to the playground. Suddenly there was a volley of bullets sprayed through the doors from the hall way. Jack who was in the hallway moved to a position where he could see who was firing. It was a German Patrol of 6 men. He threw a grenade down the hallway at the men and he then backtracked and went into the hall through the door he was guarding. The people in the hall were panicking and some had fallen. Jack was unsure if the fallen people had been shot or had fallen in the stampede that occurred when the shots were fired. The people were helping with the ones that had fallen and soon the hall was nearly empty. Jack saw Matt and Sid had taken cover by some Gym equipment and he could see Matt's arm was covered in blood. Sid had opened fire at the door where the Germans had been. There were some other shots coming from the hallway into the hall, but the Germans had dead or injured troops from the grenade and were obviously wary of coming straight into the hall so were peppering the hall with shots. Jack opened fire, as well, at the door to allow the remaining civilians to leave the hall. Within minutes all the civilians had left.

Matt, Sid, Jack, Alan and Cyril plus two other men, who had firearms, were eventually all that were left in the hall. The Germans had a couple of men left in the hallway. Matt thought that they may call for back up and he wanted to leave the hall as quickly as possible. Sid was trying to look at Matt's wound, but Matt told him to leave it as it did not hurt. Matt knew that the adrenalin was running around his body which took all the pain of the injury away. Matt told Sid and Jack to open fire and told Alan, Cyril and the other men to head for the door to the playground, which they did. Matt went with them and then stood behind the door way and fired at the door giving cover to Sid and Jack. Once Sid and Jack were with them, Matt closed the door and lodged a grenade carefully behind it. Within seconds all of them were across the playground and making their way over a field, when they heard an explosion. In the distance behind them Matt could see that another group of Germans were running towards them. They were a fair distance away but were gaining on them. Alan and Cyril led the way through some burnt out and derelict houses, which bordered the field. The Germans also entered these houses. The two other armed men decided to split up from Matt's group and headed in another direction. This effectively split the Germans up. Alan then led them down a couple of alley's and into a house where they waited. If the Germans approached, Matt and his men would deal with them. They had a couple of grenades ready and they had their firearms cocked and ready to use. They waited for a while, but the Germans did not come into the house. Matt, Sid, Jack, Alan and Cyril waited for half an hour just to make sure, and then, with Alan leading, they made their way through some more alley ways and into an undamaged house using the back door. Matt and Alan watched the road at the front through the curtained lounge windows and it seemed to be clear. Sid, Jack and Cyril watched the rear for any movements. A woman in the house, who appeared to be Cyril's wife, offered the men some tea which they refused, and they then waited to make sure they were safe. The woman had seen that Matt had been hurt and started to fuss over his arm. Matt allowed her to put on a makeshift bandage, but that was all. He would get Trudy to look at it when he got back. Everyone was tense and concerned, but Matt and his men decided that they would wait for a while before they left. Cyril, Sid and Jack were chatting in the kitchen keeping an eye on the rear of the premises and Alan and Matt were in the lounge.

Alan said to Matt in a low voice, "Can I have a word with you?"

"What's the problem?" Matt asked.

"Don't you think this attack is odd? This is the second time I have been nearly caught or killed. We have been having these meetings since the invasion and the Germans have never got wind of them, but the day you come they know exactly where to come. Also, the day I was supposed to meet Pip they were there. I suspect that there is someone who is snitching me up or you lot up," Alan said in a whisper.

Matt completely trusted his men, so he said, "Do you have any ideas about who it can be? I can assure you that my men are completely trustworthy."

"I know. There are a couple and one of them is Cyril. He and two others were aware I was speaking with Pip. The other two were my uncle and father and I really don't think they would grass me up. Cyril was the only one who knew the actual location. Do you think it could be him?" asked Alan.

"What would his motive be?" asked Matt in a low voice.

"I have no idea, although because of his position as councillor he has had to deal with the Germans on a number of occasions. It's all to do with the running of the area. Do you think he has done a deal with them?" Alan asked.

"I don't know. We need to find out sooner than later, because of what was said tonight," Matt said. "That's why I thought I had better tell you," he said.

Matt thought about what Alan had said and decided that he needed to deal with it tonight. As he and Alan were standing at the window, Cyril and Sid entered the lounge.

"I think we have the all clear to get going," said Sid.

"Not... so... quickly" Matt said slowly. He then turned to Cyril and said, "Cyril, I hear that you have been having meetings with the Germans. May I ask what they have been about?"

Cyril looked at Matt and seemed to stand upright and in a commanding sort of way. It was as if he was trying to tell Matt how important he was.

He said, "Why do you need to know that?"

"I was just wondering. Can you enlighten me?" Matt asked politely.

"If you must know, it was to do with the running of the area," Cyril said.

"Yes, but what exactly did they want from you. You see, in Shoreham, which is bigger than Fishersgate there are no such meetings with council officials and neither does that occur in Southwick or Steyning. The running of the areas is strictly under the control of the Germans and they do not want any influence from any local people, leastways not until they had conquered us. I just wondered why Fishersgate area is so different to the others," Matt asked.

Cyril looked round at Alan and then Sid.

"Alan you know how easy the transition was here, with the Germans being in charge, and that was due to me dealing with the Germans," he said.

Alan responded, "Actually Cyril I often wondered why there were so few incidents, when other areas were so harshly hit by them, in retaliation to the sabotage incidents. What did you offer them not to hurt our people? I presume that's what you did."

"I did no such thing. I am not prepared to stand in my house and listen to this. I look after my constituency and its people. I will not be spoken to like this," he said.

Cyril looked horrified at the accusation.

"Just a minute. I think we need to speak to you somewhere else, as I do not feel safe here now. I think we should all leave, including you Cyril. Once I am satisfied that you are genuine then you will be released. Tell your wife that you will be coming with us. If you don't do as you are told I will shoot you where you stand." Matt removed his pistol as he was speaking, and it was pointing at Cyril's stomach as he finished.

Cyril began to shake as he knew that Matt meant what he said. They all went into the kitchen and Cyril told his wife he would be back soon. Matt had put his gun in his pocket as he left the lounge, but it was still aimed at Cyril's back as he spoke to his wife. They all left. Alan told Matt he knew a place, so they followed him. Jack had not heard what had been said and could feel the tension between everyone, but he did not say anything. About 5 minutes later they entered the rear door of another house which was empty.

"This is the house of a Jewish couple that went missing. I thought it would be safe to speak in here. Just don't turn any lights on," said Alan.

"Thank you Alan, Jack can you keep watch at the rear, just in case anyone saw us entering." Jack left, and Matt went up to Cyril and Sid went behind him.

"Right now, let's find out exactly what you have said and what you have done," said Matt. "Now you can do this the easy way or the hard way. Just to let you know how serious I am I will tell you how the Germans dealt with my colleague when he was taken whilst he was here in Fishersgate."

Matt then explained in graphic detail what had happened to Pip. As he was speaking he could see, even though it was dark, Cyril visibly pale. When he spoke of the electrodes being put on Pip's testicles Cyril's legs seemed to buckle. He just managed to stay standing.

"So now I shall ask you again, what did you tell them?" Matt asked.

"I was trying to protect my people. They promised them safety if I told them about any approach by you or your people. When Alan told me how he was approached by someone wanting information about the port I just told the Germans about it. They wanted to know where the meeting would take place and who would be there. I made them promise not to take Alan, which they didn't," he said.

"What else did you tell them?"

"They… they first wanted all the names of the Jews in the area. I gave them that and suddenly all the people I had told them about went missing. I realised then that they were acting on my information," said Cyril and then added as if to justify his actions, "But I did protect the locals."

"But weren't the Jewish people local people?" Sid asked.

"Yes, but they are different," Cyril said.

"How?" asked Sid.

Cyril was at a loss as what to say in response.

"Now about tonight, what did you tell them about it?" Matt asked.

"I told them you would be there, but I told them that none of the locals were to be injured or killed. I thought I was going to inform them about what you said. I didn't think they would come in firing guns indiscriminately. They told me that the meetings could go ahead if I obeyed them and gave them other information," Cyril said. Matt realised how naive Cyril was.

"You are a German informant," said Alan, who had been listening intently to what was said. "But why? We were all willing to fight against them and you were aware of that. We were happy to hear about the sabotage acts and even if there were repercussions, so what, that's life. Surely it wasn't up to you to decide for us. You shouldn't have done that. Pip was British, and you gave him up to the Krauts. That is so wrong. What is wrong with you?"

Alan was really upset about this and pushed forward with his fists raised ready to strike him. Sid reacted first and restrained Alan before he could hit Cyril.

"Alan, go outside with Jack," Matt said. He could see that Alan losing his temper would not help matters and Matt still thought there was more information to get out of Cyril. Alan started to protest, but Sid took hold of Alan's arm gently and said, "Come on lad, leave this to us." Alan reluctantly left.

Once they were alone Matt nodded at Sid and Sid hit Cyril in the kidneys. It was very painful. Cyril fell to his knees and cried out in pain.

"Stand up," said Matt, and after a couple of minutes Cyril managed to. He then said, "Now what else did you tell them, and I want to know everything or else you will be as badly beaten as Pip."

"I told them that Pip was here to gather information about the Port and I told them that you were here to arrange for when the Germans retreat to the area. I didn't give specifics as I didn't know them then. I also told them of real dissenters that would cause them trouble. Those people have gone missing as well. That is it really," Cyril said but Matt felt that he couldn't see that he had done any wrong.

"Who knew you were telling the Germans this, your wife, your family?" Matt asked.

"No, they know nothing about it. I worked alone," he said.

Sid looked at Matt and again Matt nodded. Sid hit Cyril again in the kidney area. Cyril again cried out in pain and again fell to the floor. Matt said, "Get some wire Sid."

Although Cyril was hurting, he heard that last order and said, "What are you going to do?"

"Electrocute you, like they did to Pip," Matt said with no emotion.

"Why, I have told you everything. I won't tell them about you," exclaimed Cyril.

"I want to know if you have told me everything. I will torture you until I am convinced," Matt told him.

Sid had found some wire which he got from a lamp that was standing on a table and Matt said,

"Remove his trousers." Matt knew that he could never do this, but he needed to know if that was all Cyril had told the Germans. Sid stepped forward to undo his trousers.

Cyril said almost crying, "I didn't tell them anything else. I didn't, honestly. If I did I would tell you."

Sid stepped closer to him and Cyril continued, now crying, "I didn't, please, don't do that to me. I didn't say anything else. I am sorry, I am so sorry."

Matt stopped Sid from continuing and said, "I think we have the full story now." Matt left Sid with Cyril and went out to Alan.

"Alan, he has not only turned in all the Jewish people in the area but some he called dissenters. I take it from that he got the Germans to get rid of all the people who would cause trouble. He was responsible for Pip and for tonight."

"My God, what a bastard. One of my mates went missing and we assumed that he must have got caught doing a job, you know nicking or damaging something. So perhaps it was Cyril that gave him up and all those Jews, that is just not right. What are you going to do with him now?" asked Alan.

"We cannot let him go, can we? He will go straight to the Germans and tell them what exactly was said at the meeting tonight and he has seen our faces as well as heard our names spoken. I want to execute him," Matt said.

"I think that is the right thing to do. We don't want anyone else killed or mysteriously disappearing. It could cause trouble in the area though, as he is well liked," Alan said.

"Can you pass it around that the Germans got him and killed him. Apparently, he worked alone so we don't want any reprisals on his wife or his family. She would probably be as horrified as you and I are," said Matt.

"I agree, yes I can do that. Fortunately, we were the last to leave the hall, so I will say that they were waiting for us near his house and that they caught him, although all of us managed to get away. I will say it was because he couldn't run as fast as us because of his age. It will make the locals angry with the Germans," Alan said.

Matt and Jack entered the lounge area where Sid and Cyril were. Matt said to Cyril, "You are a very stupid man and it has been decided that you will be killed."

"No... Oh please no. I am sorry, I will not do it again," Cyril pleaded.

"Cyril, you cannot be trusted. You are a traitor and if we kept you alive then when the Allies do come you would be tried as one. I would make sure of it and you would be hung, but this way we can say you were killed by the Germans and your wife and family will be safe from reprisals," Matt said.

Matt already had his gun in his hand. He raised it and shot Cyril in the head.

It was dark outside, so Sid and Jack quietly dug a hole in the ground using some shovels they found in the garden shed and then put Cyril in it.

Before Matt and his men left, Alan told them that his uncle had already started to sabotage the lock at the port. He was not oiling some of the lock mechanisms and hopefully they will seize up, but it may take a couple of days for this to happen. Matt was pleased. He told Alan that he would be in touch with him soon and once Sid and Jack had finished burying Cyril they left and returned to the Cement Works.

Matt's arm was really hurting by the time they arrived back, so he submitted himself to the care of Trudy and her nurses to administer to it. The wound was just a scratch. A bullet had grazed his upper arm and although there seemed to be a lot of blood, it didn't even need to be stitched, just bandaged. Nellie who had seen the blood on his jacket when he returned fussed over him and insisted that he rest for a while until he was fully recovered.

CHAPTER 25

The next couple of weeks allowed the unit along with the men at the Lancing Ring bunker to continue with missions. The port had reopened, and ships had been coming in regularly. They had obtained information from an informer who ran a pub in Southwick about a munitions convoy going to the German Front and they were able to hijack it. The Germans used his pub and once they had a few beers they became talkative. This had started to be a good source of information for Matt and his team. Henry at the Waterside Club also gave Matt a lot of information, but because of the German's retreat, his Club was being used less and less. He still, however, heard a few snippets of information which assisted Matt. Jo's pub was being used more and more by the Germans, probably because it was near the station and in the centre of the town. He reported information when he heard it. The port remained open for some time, but suddenly there were a fleet of ships moored up in the open sea outside the port. Enquiries revealed that the lock had eventually broken, and the Germans were unable to repair it. This caused a problem as there were ships in the port that could not get out and the ships moored outside that had to wait to be unloaded because there was only limited space in the outer part of the port. Matt was happy with this and went over to Fishersgate to speak to Alan and tell him what a good job his uncle had done. Alan stated that his uncle had a part that could replace the broken one when the port was retaken by the British and the Germans had gone.

The Cement Works were getting crowded, not with people but with trucks of munitions, so it was decided to remove some of the arms over to the camp and dump the trucks. They would also unload the other trucks and get rid of all of them except two. This happened without a hitch. Everything was going so well for Matt and his people and the Germans, who were supposed to be disciplined and well ordered, appeared to be in disarray. The German troops in the area were obviously not the disciplined ones that were fighting on the front line and they were becoming lax and careless. They had now heard that their forces were retreating as they were told to arrange shipping for withdrawing the forces back across the channel. Their morale was low, and they were resigned to the fact that they were losing the battle for Britain.

Matt went over to the camp to speak to Colonel Grant about plans for the taking of the port. It was decided that more troops needed to be taken out of the camp before that time. Matt agreed and when the Allies were 10 miles from Shoreham, he would get 500 men out of the camp and leave the remainder to take over the camp. Once the camp was taken they would then join up with Matt at the port. Matt had enough equipment to give to those men but the men in the camp would have to be armed, with the weapons in the cellars. Matt also told Colonel Grant that the nurses under the command of Major Dave Briggs were going to collect as many civilians as possible and get them to come to the Camp. Again, under Major Briggs they would then keep the camp safe. It would allow the men to be released for the main objective of the port and the subsequent battle with the retreating army. Colonel Grant had questioned the use of the women and Matt had to explain that this had been put through to HQ and they had agreed with these arrangements. He did say that because Major Briggs oversaw them, they would come under control of the army. Matt also wanted Colonel Grant to stay at the camp to oversee everything. Colonel Grant objected but diplomatically Matt pointed out to him that because of his age and because of the treatment he had had in the camp he was not fit enough to take command of hit and run operations. That should be left to the younger Officers. After a while Colonel Grant agreed that it was probably wiser if he did stay at the camp. They also talked at length about the taking of other key objectives such as the Railway Station, the Police Station, the Adur Bridge, the port and the goods yards. There was one further objective and that was Lancing College. HQ wanted the Officers in Command of all the areas to be taken so it was essential to have a company of men, about 100 in all, to take the College and hopefully secure the senior officers in the area. Matt knew that all the huts that the PoWs had built now enabled most of the men in the camp to leave their tents and live in them, so it was decided that any prisoners taken should be bought to the camp and kept in a number of these huts. They would leave 50 men along with the women to keep the camp and especially the prisoners secure. The hospital would be run by the doctors and the nurses and the security would be provided by the nurses and the other civilian women bought in from the neighbouring towns. There are also people like Father Andrew and Bert who would help along with men who did not want to fight alongside the army lads, although Bert would be required to assist regarding the control of the station when the time came. They wanted to block the station with trains so that other trains would not be able to get through. Colonel Grant was pleased with the arrangements and he told Matt that he would get his officers in the camp onto organising the men into various companies with objectives.

The Allies' front was moving slowly south. Over the past couple of weeks, it had moved 10 miles towards the English Channel and sometimes, if you stood on the Downs you could distinctly hear explosions and guns. HQ and the wireless were keeping all the auxiliaries, resistance fighters and the general population up to date with the advance. The line was now about 15 to 20 miles north of the coast. The Allies wanted to get Portsmouth back into their hands, so they would have a base for the British ships, which was of strategic importance to them. They had put reinforcements in the west of their line and that part of the front was moving forward quicker than elsewhere. It would only be a matter of days before Portsmouth would be taken. The Cement Works were glued to the wireless for news and a couple of days later Nellie who had been sending a message over the radio came running back to the Cement Works screaming and clutching a piece of paper in her hands. Everyone thought she was warning them to get out and the Germans were coming, but once she calmed down a little she told them what the message had said:

Portsmouth in British hands.
You will be next.
Good luck

Everyone was jubilant. All the women were hugging and kissing each other, and the men dropped their British reserved and joined in. Dave who had been absent from the Cement Works came into the celebrations clutching a large box. He started to scream out, "I have news."

Everyone said almost at the same time, "So have we."

Dave had picked up a message at a drop point to discover a box secreted in the bushes. There was a note on it in code. He didn't want to open the box there so after hiding it again he went into a secluded area nearby and encoded the message. It read:

As Portsmouth is now in the hands of the British it will only be a matter of time before your area will be liberated. In the box are field radios for the forces in your area to use. We will try and arrange more in the next couple of days.

When Dave looked into the box he saw that there were 3 back packs which contained 3 field radios each. He excitedly but carefully bought them back to the Cement Works. The news therefore was the same. He joined in the celebrations after handing them over to Doug.

All along the South Coast the auxiliaries and resistance groups were put on standby. They suspected that it would only be a matter of days before they would be called to fight. Matt had noticed that the local towns were getting full up with injured Germans and men who looked like they had battle fatigue. They were wandering around and Matt had heard that they were having a problem getting ships into the port to get the wounded or tired men back to Europe. Matt also realised that now was the time to start putting his plans into action. He was monitoring all the radio messages and he would go up on the Downs at night to listen to the sound of the guns and from these sounds he knew that they were now very close. He was concerned for the women in the area especially Nellie and one night he had asked her if she wanted to come up on to the Downs with him. They stood at an area near to Truleigh Hill and could even see the sky light up occasionally. This they assumed were the guns being fired.

"Nellie, I know that you will do your bit when the Allies arrive, but I still want to make sure that you are safe. Please stay in the camp regardless of what you hear. I know that you will have to monitor the radio and send messages as and when required, but as soon as you can I want you in the camp. I have already informed HQ about the airport being a safe haven, a hospital and where the local women and children will be, so please, for once, please do as I ask," Matt pleaded.

"Darling, I will. I had no plans to take up arms and fight beside you, but please will you be careful as well. I have plans after this," Nellie looked at Matt lovingly.

"I will be careful, but you know that I will probably be in the thick of it. Look I also have plans after this battle and I would like to be around to deal with them," he said.

"Matt, I know that, and I do hope that your plans are the same as mine, but nevertheless I hope you will be careful," Nellie said.

"Of course."

Matt bent over and kissed Nellie.

They sat down on the ground and they stared up at the skyline watching what looked like a firework display. They cuddled each other like a couple of teenagers every so often stealing a kiss. They stayed up on the Downs for a couple of hours and when they returned to the Cement Works Doug approached Matt to tell him to read the last message that he had received from HQ.

Allies are going to have a large reinforcement of men and arms tomorrow. Huge push anticipated within the next 24 hours. Start your preparations to take the strategic places in your areas. Hopefully will be at your position within 3 days. Good luck to your team.
Colonel Armstrong.

CHAPTER 26

Matt sat down on a chair. He was relieved that it was beginning. All the planning had been done and now he would see if his plans would be productive. Doug said, "Its beginning isn't it? When do we start?"

Matt looked at Doug and then as if a renewed energy surged through his body he got up and said, "Get the men together in 15 minutes and include Dave, Father Andrew, Trudie, Nellie and Bert."

Doug went off and all the men and the two women were sitting on the floor in front of Matt within 10 minutes. Johnny was sitting next to Matt and he had a huge smile on his face.

"Men, Ladies, I have here a message from Colonel Armstrong. For those of you here who do not know who he is, he is the man in charge of the Auxiliaries. He is my boss," Matt said smiling. He then read the message to them. When he had finished everyone chatted excitedly for a couple of minutes. Matt indicated that he wanted quiet and continued, "I have been busy making plans over the last couple of months regarding what we will have to do. I have spoken at length with Colonel Grant and he agrees with the plans. First Father Andrew and Trudie, I presume that you have arranged the women into areas to get the locals evacuated." Father Andrew nodded. "Good, but that cannot be done until the camp and the Adur Bridge which includes the railway bridge are taken, so I want to ask you to curb the women's enthusiasm and keep them here until that is done. Dave and Trudie I need you to make sure that all the women are co-ordinated especially when they get to the camp." Dave said it would be done and Trudie nodded in agreement. Matt continued, "We have radios now, and I was hoping for more, but they need to be monitored and Father Andrew and Pip I would like you to have one here so that you can do that, that is until you, Father Andrew, leave with the women. Pip you will stay here with all the plans of where the men are deployed. You may have to allocate or reallocate men to places so you will need to have a map and plot our progress." Father Andrew and Pip both acknowledge their roles. "Nellie, I need you to monitor the radio transmissions from HQ. You will need to inform Pip and he will pass on anything that is urgent over the field radios."

Nellie said that she would.

"Dave, any chance of any more radios?" Matt asked.

"Yes, I was hoping they would be here today. I will find out after this meeting."

"Good, now for the rest of you. Sid, Jack and Doug I need you to go to the camp and arrange for the 500 men to leave straight away and to tell

Colonel Grant that he needs to take the camp immediately. Bring the men here and we will arm them. Then we will make our way to the port with 450 of them. Sid and Johnny, you will take 50 of them and take the Bridge. Once the Bridge and the Camp are taken, Father Andrew and your women can leave here and inform the locals to make their way to the airport, but I want you to keep clear of the port. Jake you need to get the local men informed and I suggest you start with Fishersgate area as it is the furthest away. The cascade system that we devised should have them informed very quickly and I believe that they are expecting the call so there won't be any unnecessary delay. They are to come here, and you will stay here to arm them and then bring them down to the town. I want you, with these men, to take the Railway Station. Once it is taken Bert you will be needed." Bert had recovered from his beating at the hands of the Germans and had since remained at the Cement Works. He was still a little shaky on his legs, but he was excited to get his town back in the hands of the British and wanted to help in any way that he could.

"I want the station to be blocked. Can you arrange for any trains coming into the station to stay there? If we block the tracks with trains, then no trains can pass through," Matt said.

Bert nodded and said, "It can be done although it may take a while waiting for the trains to come in."

"Thank you but stay here until you are called to do it. You can help Jake arm the men." Bert nodded. "Doug you will be with me at the port and Sid and Jack, after you have taken the Bridge, you will make your way to the port with some of your men that are not needed to keep the Bridge secure. This is just in case we need reinforcements. All of you will be involved in fighting the Germans and if you must deal with them then you can either capture them or kill them. Just remember that we are not like the Germans so capturing them is the best option. You will then have to allocate men to escort them over to the airport where they will be held. The airport will have men and women there who will look after the prisoners. We will start as soon as this meeting is over. Now has anyone got any questions?"

Sid put his hand up. "Yes Sid," said Matt.

"I thought we were going to be taking their HQ at Lancing College and the Police Station?"

"You are right, but the College will be taken by a company of men from the camp. They have orders to capture Oberst Baumhauer and his hench men, if it is possible. The Police Station will be taken once every other objective is taken. There will be a lot of Germans heading for the Station once they realise that they are under attack I believe that it will take a full-scale assault to secure those premises. I suggest that until we do that the civilian population should be told to keep clear of that area when making their way to the airport. Once we have taken all our objectives we will then set up points on the Downs, which will be heavily armed and wait for the retreating army. Hopefully they will realise that their retreat is hopeless, and they will surrender, but we must be prepared for the worse. I have a plan here that shows all the points where I will need lookouts along the Downs as well as other places to let us know when the army is coming. I will arrange those later. Nellie, you will probably hear first when the Allies will be approaching this area. Any more questions?" Matt asked.

No one put their hands up and Matt was just about to dismiss the men when Father Andrew stood and said, "I know that what we are planning to do will take its toll on all of us both mentally and physically. I know that you are all capable, but I would like to offer up a prayer, giving us strength for what we, or should I say you, are about to do." All the men nodded in agreement and with that Father Andrew bowed his head, all the men did too, and he said a prayer asking God to give them strength, to keep them safe and to be strong enough to do what is required of them. At the end everyone said Amen and Matt then dismissed them after wishing them good luck.

Sid, Jack and Doug left immediately for the camp, Jake left to start the cascade system of the local men and Dave went out to see if more radios had been left. Whilst they were gone Matt went over with Pip what he had to do regarding keeping tabs on the men and where they were. If any objective was having problems and more men were needed, he would allocate more to aid them. That would be up to Pip's judgement and if he was unsure then to discuss it with Dave, if he was about. Within an hour the first of the 500 men started to arrive. Sid, Jack and Doug were using Sergeant Green's men to help getting them across the river on rafts. It was daylight, so they had to have lookouts on the road, but ironically, they hadn't seen any German patrols in the area. The men from the camp were given a Mauser Karabiner 98K bolt action rifle and ammunition. They were German rifles and they were told that if they ran out of ammunition then they can use any they find on the German troops. The British ammunition for rifles was not compatible with the Germans weapons. Sid had returned, informing Matt, that Colonel Grant was now in the process of securing the camp. Once they had 50 men from the camp armed, Sid and Johnny left with them to secure the Adur Bridge. This was a vital point that needed to be taken urgently. They took one of the radios.

Over in the camp Major Russell led his men over to the wire. They had armed themselves from the weapons in the cellars and they had about their person either a Luger P08 pistol or a Mauser Karabiner 98K rifle. They first took the guards that were patrolling the wire at the perimeter of the camp. They then called for the guards in the towers to come down. A couple of his men spoke perfect German and speaking German told them to come down as the Commandant needed to speak to them. Once they were on the ground they were taken prisoner. Once all of them were removed from their posts, which was done without firing one shot, Colonel Grant and Lieutenant Lewis along with 20 men, headed for the airport building where the Commandant and the Officers were. They entered the outer offices, to the surprise of the men working there. Colonel Grant produced a pistol and within minutes, had all the Germans up against a wall with the prisoners removing their weapons. The Colonel then entered the Commandant's office.

"Why didn't you knock," shouted the Commandant who was at his desk looking at some papers. He assumed it was one of his officers. Colonel Grant walked up to his desk and said, "Because this camp is now in my hands and you are my prisoner. Don't move and leave your hands on your desk Hauptmann Mencken."

Mencken looked up and said, "Don't be ridiculous, Meyer come here," he shouted to his clerk. No one came. Colonel Grant was getting pretty fed up with all this and having no patience with this man who he held in complete contempt said, "Get up Mencken. You will be held here until the Allies arrive and you can then answer for all the ill treatment of my men. Now get up and move."

Hauptmann Mencken was stunned by the way Colonel Grant spoke to him, but he did not say anything. He slowly rose, and a couple of Colonel Grant's men took hold of him, roughly, searched him for weapons and then marched him out of his office and on to the huts where they were keeping the prisoners. Colonel Grant then got hold of one of the men in his command that was fluent in German and ordered him to go through the papers in the office and see if there was anything of interest. Colonel Grant then left the office with Lieutenant Lewis and made their way to the men who were waiting for deployment. He had previously arranged for the men left in the camp to create a holding area for the prisoners once the German camp personnel had started to be taken. They knew that there was some barbed wire kept in one of the stores by the airport building. That would do the trick. They surrounded 5 huts with it and left a small opening for access which would be guarded. The actual taking over of the camp had taken less than half an hour. The guards on the gate had been replaced by men from the camp and they had set up a Maschinengewehr 34 machine gun mounted on a tripod there in case any Germans tried to retake the camp. They had also set up a similar machine gun suitably manned outside the huts where they were keeping the German prisoners.

Colonel Grant now needed to wait for orders for the men to leave. He knew that the Bridge would need to be taken first.

At the Adur Bridge there were 5 Germans guarding the east side and 4 guards on the west side. Sid approached the bridge from the east and Johnny approached it from the west having gone across the river upstream using the canoes. They had a machine gun mounted on one side of the bridge which was manned by two men on the east side. Sid with 6 men approached the guards who they knew would stop them. And Johnny, with another 6 men approached the other side of the bridge. The Germans were blasé about stopping people thinking that they were unbeatable. Even though they knew that their troops were retreating they were arrogant enough to believe that they would still win. As soon as Sid's men were adjacent with the machine gun placement and the guards they produced their weapons and opened fire. On the west side Johnny and his men did the same. The men who were manning the machine gun were killed instantly and the 4 guards were killed. The remainder of the guards who were uninjured surrendered immediately. They had taken the Adur Bridge and the railway bridge in 5 minutes. They radioed the Cement Works that the Bridge was secured. Johnny sent a couple of his men to the camp to tell them that the Bridge had been taken and it was now safe for his men to leave the camp and make their way to the town. Johnny and Sid arranged for their men to man the machine gun which was on the east side of the river and they set up another machine gun placement on the west side. Some of the men were also put onto the banks of the river to the north and south of the bridges and on both sides of the river. Their position overlooked the road and these positions were to ensure that any counter attack would be repelled.

Matt was really surprised that the bridge had been so easy to take, and he was also surprised that the camp was taken so quickly. Once he heard he sent out Father Andrew and the women to deal with the locals. The men from the camp had now all arrived at the Cement Works and they were all now armed with weapons. Matt left with them, making their way to the port. This was not going to be as easy as the camp and the bridges. Jake had arrived back at the Cement Works as Matt was just about to leave telling him that the cascade system was now in progress. Dave also returned just as Matt was leaving and with him he had another big box. Inside were 4 more field radios. Matt ordered him to ensure that the camp had a radio, as well as the men who were going to take Lancing College and he wanted Jake to have one when he went to the station. Finally he wanted one with the men at the bridge.

Matt decided to approach the port through the back streets and as they were going along they came across civilians making their way to the airport. Because he had such a large force of men it was impossible to keep them a secret. The men dealt with a couple of patrols, which they killed as they needed all the men for the attack on the port. He did not want them tied up with transporting prisoners to the camp. It was now getting dark as the men approached the port gates. Sid, Jack and Doug with their men met up with the main body of the attacking force. Matt had sent 50 men to the east side of the port and the same amount to the west side. They would have to scale a wall to get in on the east side, but on the west side they could just walk in. It was hoped they would be able to secure their part of the port as the armed men at the port seemed to be located at the entrance area. The time to attack was allocated and Matt waited, watching his watch. The wait was excruciating. He could feel his stomach being tied up in knots.

He looked at his men and from the expressions on their faces he could see that they were feeling the same. The time appeared to be going very slowly, and he watched each second go by. Then the allotted time was upon him, he took a deep breath and he ordered the advance. The Germans were surprised by the attack, but they tried to defend their positions. Matt saw a couple of his men fall but they managed to reach the gates and they succeeded in killing a few of the Germans. There was a massive gun fight just behind the gates and Matt lost a dozen men. The men who had entered from the east and the west had done so successfully, and they had secured their areas. They realised that the men at the gate were under a deadly attack, so they edged towards the gate area and they attacked the Germans from the rear. This allowed Matt to get a foothold at the gate. The Germans retreated into the office building and Matt ordered his men into the office block. There was some heavy fighting in there and Matt's men decided that the only way to clear the place was to use grenades. They went down the first corridor and upon reaching each office they threw in a grenade. Once they had killed or captured all the Germans there, they proceeded onto the next office. This took time, but they managed to clear the whole place of Germans. Some of the Germans tried to escape down a fire escape but fortunately they were seen by some of the men outside and they were gunned down. Soon it was evident to the Germans that they were losing this battle and the Germans surrendered. Matt then proceeded into the docks and although there were pockets of resistance it was minor compared to the fight they had had at the gates and in the office block. The Captain of one of the ships that was in port had obviously seen what was happening and was hastily trying to leave the dock. Matt wanted to prevent this from happening, so he ordered some of his men to board the ship and secure it. They needed to get to the wheel house. There was some fierce fighting on the ship, but after losing 3 men they managed to secure it. The Captain and his crew were removed and held in a warehouse with all the other men they had captured. Matt and his men went from ship to ship and from warehouse to warehouse, but the port was massive. After 5 hours Matt was satisfied that they had taken the port area. Now it had to be held. Matt had just walked up to the gates when he was met by Lieutenant Lewis who told Matt that all appeared to be secure on the roads coming to the port. Matt was pleased and reported to Pip that the port was in their hands. Lieutenant Lewis had also told Matt that the civilians were arriving at the airport and the hospital was ready to take the injured. Matt allocated officers to commandeer a truck and take the injured and dead to the hospital at the airport. Matt had lost 26 men and he had 39 injured, which was bad, but it was predictable. Apart from that everything had gone as expected. Now they were to march on the Police Station.

Colonel Grant had ordered one of his officers, Major Walsh, with a company of 300 men to go to Lancing College. His orders were to take the College and to take the commander of the area, Oberst Baumhauer, alive, if possible along with as many Officers he could find there. He had arrived at the College and his men were secreted in the tree line to the south of it. He could see that there was a lot of coming and going and the Major was aware that they weren't expecting an assault. Fifty of Major Walsh's men were sent to the rear of the College, 15 minutes later, at the agreed time, they attacked. The attack at the front did not go as expected. The Germans had mounted machine guns at windows on the first floor of the College and once the first of the Major's men advanced forward the windows were flung opened and they were gunned down. This was disastrous. They needed to get a foothold in the college, but they couldn't get near to it. In the first attack Major Walsh lost nearly 20 men. He decided that it was necessary to change tactics. He could hear shooting coming from the rear, but not machine guns so he decided to split his men in two, with 20 men remaining at the front of the building to shoot anyone who tried to leave. They had bought with them a machine gun and they set this up in the tree line at the front of the building. It was about 20 yards away from the building. As soon as the other groups attempted to enter they would open fire on the vehicles at the front and hopefully destroy them as well as firing on the machine guns in the windows. The rest made their way to the sides of the building, half on one side and the other half on the other. Major Russell then ordered the attack on the building from the sides. This was successful and both groups managed to gain entry to the building one using a fire escape door, which they blew off its hinges and the other group smashing a ground floor window.

Inside Oberst Baumhauer, hearing the attack, was shouting orders for papers to be burnt and for the few men inside to repel the attack. Just prior to hearing the attack on his building he had just had a report that there was an attack on the port and had ordered the man who had bought the news to inform the man in charge of the port to hold it. He also wanted to know who the men were that were attacking his HQ. As far as he was aware the British army was still 10 miles away.

Oberleutnant Schafer ran into Oberst Baumhauer's office saying, "They are in the College. We do not have sufficient men to hold it. What do you want to do?"

"Get the car, we are leaving. Tell the men to hold them in the corridors on the ground and first floor and we will escape down the fire escape from the outer office."

Oberleutnant Schafer immediately went to the outer office and shouted orders to his officers, who immediately scuttled away to do his bidding. Oberst Baumhauer put on a plain coat which concealed his uniform and he left with Oberleutnant Schafer and two armed men. They reached the window with the fire escape outside, but this was facing the front. As they opened the window and attempted to make their way onto the fire escape stairs they were immediately fired upon by the machine gun outside. They retreated into the office and decided that they were going to have to risk making their way through the college to where their car was parked. They went down the staircase but before they reached the bottom they had to retreat again because Major Walsh and his men had also just reached the bottom of the stairs and were starting to make their way up them. Oberst Baumhauer was effectively cornered. He took out his pistol and started to fire it over the balustrade of the stairs. He didn't manage to hit any of the British men. Oberleutnant Schafer grabbed hold of his senior officer's arm, and said, "This way, we'll try the servants entrance and the kitchens."

They headed along a long corridor and reached a second set of stairs at the rear of the building. They carefully descended them, and this time managed to reach the bottom. It was very quiet in this area of the College, but they could still hear gun fire coming from other parts of the college. They crept along the corridor and entered a door that was marked kitchen. Very carefully they edged their way through the kitchen and reached a door that led to a laundry room, but just as they were going to open the door a very soft voice said, "No further. Throw your guns down, put your hands up and turn around."

Oberst Baumhauer and Oberleutnant Schafer stood still. Both had their guns in their hands.

"I would suggest that you do not try anything. If you do I will not hesitate," the person said.

Schafer was the first to move. He turned around and saw that there were 4 men all with their rifles aimed at them. He threw his gun down on to the floor. Oberst Baumhauer then turned and realised immediately that he was outnumbered and outgunned.

"How dare you. Do you know who I am? I am in charge of this area and you will do as I say," he demanded.

"No, we are in charge, now drop that gun or else I will shoot you," one of the British men said.

Then the soft voiced man shouted, "DROP IT."

Oberst Baumhauer dropped his gun.

"Stand against that wall," indicating a wall beside them, which they did, and both men were very unceremoniously searched for weapons. During the search Oberleutnant Schafer suddenly turned and from his sleeve he produced a large knife. He swung out and caught one of the men searching him cutting him badly on his arm. The man jumped back clutching his arm and Oberleutnant Schafer swung his knife out again at another man who was standing near to them. The man who was giving the orders fired at him and shot him in the chest. Oberleutnant Schafer fell to the floor and after a deep breath died. Oberst Baumhauer was stunned that his man was killed and was going to say something until he looked at the man who had shot Oberleutnant Schafer. His face was fierce, and he knew that if he said anything or did anything then he would be shot as well. He submitted to what these men wanted and eventually his hands were tied behind his back with some wire from the lamps in the hallway and he was made to sit down on the floor. They could all hear sporadic firing in the College but very soon it went quiet. After about 10 minutes the kitchen door opened and in walked Major Walsh. He had blood on his face, which seemed to come from a small wound on his forehead, but otherwise he was unharmed. He said, "I presume you are Oberst Baumhauer."

"You are correct, and I would like to know who you are?" Oberst Baumhauer asked.

"I am Major Walsh."

"Major are you from the front? I thought they were some way off," he said.

"No, we are from the PoW camp on the airfield," Major Walsh informed him.

"What!" exclaimed Oberst Baumhauer.

"Yes, we were recruited by the men who were left behind and, from what I can gather, have been giving you a real headache. They and Colonel Grant planned these attacks and we have taken over the area, completely. You are now our prisoner," Major Walsh said with a large smile on his face.

"How did they get in the camp?" asked Oberst Baumhauer.

"Wouldn't you like to know, well one day you may find out? I, however, need to get going as we must deal with other orders. You and your men will be marched to the camp and you will be held there until the Allies' arrive," said Major Walsh.

Oberst Baumhauer who was still full of his own importance said, "Walk to the camp. I have a car outside."

"You will be marched over and I will be using your car, if it is still intact, for my duties. You are not important enough to have a car for your transport. If you do not walk, then I have ordered my men to shoot those who refuse. I do hope I am making myself clear," said Major Walsh.

Oberst Baumhauer's face was redder than a beetroot. He was seething but was unable to do anything about the situation.

The injured and the dead were loaded up into a troop carrier and conveyed over to the airfield hospital and the soldiers then marched all the captured Germans there too. Major Walsh left a couple of his men at the location to guard the building as there was paperwork that may be of interest to someone, but they did not have anyone with them that spoke German to go through it. They also acquired a German radio, along with a machine that looked like a typewriter, but from what one of the German Officers said, it was the way they coded their messages. This was obviously important, so they needed to keep it safe. There were also some code books which would be of use. Major Walsh then made his way, with the remainder of his men, to the Cement Works to report that the mission had been successful.

Jake, who was leading the civilian men, who numbered about 250, approached the Railway Station. He could see that because of the noise of the fighting at the port, the Germans at the station were uneasy and didn't know exactly what was happening. Since the raid on the goods yard, the station now had 10 Germans there and they also had a machine gun manned by 2 Germans on one of the platforms. Jake arranged his men to hit the station from the front, from the car park and from the rear. At the arranged time they all charged forward. They managed to kill 3 Germans immediately and they got into the ticket office. There was a gun battle for a while with the Germans relying on the machine gun to prevent the British men from moving forward. The men who came from the car park could see that the machine gun was facing away from them, so they crept up and they threw a couple of grenades in the general direction of it. It exploded wiping out the gun and the operators. The other Germans seeing this, realised that they were beaten as there were so many British attacking, so they surrendered. The civilians were worked up with the fighting and after being under the control of Germans for the last 8 months and having seen atrocities done to their family and friends by Germans, they were unable to forgive them so instead of taking them prisoner they opened fire on them and killed all of them. Jake was horrified but could understand the reasoning behind their actions. Anyway, the station was taken. Jake contacted Pip to arrange for Bert to be bought to the station immediately. Bert arrived 15 minutes later, and it took no time for him to work out that a train was due in from the west in 10 minutes and 5 minutes later another one was due in from the east. Jake ordered the men to set up machine guns at both ends of the platform, on both sides, so immediately the train arrived, they would empty it of anybody on board and the driver and then Bert would keep the trains there to prevent the rail network from being used. The trains arrived on time and there was no one on the first other than a driver and a guard who were removed from the train very quietly. The second train had people travelling from Brighton, so they were asked politely to leave the train and again this happened quietly. All the Germans on board were detained and they were taken over to the airport. Jake then radioed Pip stating that he had secured the station and the railways were inoperable. Jake left 30 of his men at the station with Bert and radioed in to ask where they wanted him next.

Matt had decided that taking the Police Station was going to need a serious effort. As predicted the remaining German troops in the area that had not been taken prisoner, killed or injured were holed up in the station and it was now important that this was dealt with. He had 100 of his men from the port, the rest were needed to hold the port and he had nearly 500 men from the camp, along with some of Major Walsh's men and Jake's men. They met up in the church which was about a five minute walk to the Police Station. Amongst the civilian men were a couple who had been special Police officers before the war and they had worked out of this station. He had listened to their description of the building and of the layout inside. Matt decided that it would be suicidal for them to approach the building from the front, so they decided to use Jakes knowledge of explosives to blow up part of the building. There was a back entrance with a large area of land behind it. This space of land had German troops camped out there and they were all ready for the British. The side of the building abutted onto an alley. The alley way had a machine gun at one end, but a mortar would take that out. Matt ordered for the M19 Maschinengranatwefer mortar to be set up at the entrance to the alley. This was a heavy and complicated piece of weaponry, but Matt was lucky that he had some army lads who were proficient in this type of equipment. It fired 50mm mortars and had a maximum range of 750 metres. One mortar was fired in the direction of the machine gun. It was a direct hit, which showed the expertise of the men, and they wiped out the machine gun and the men operating it, along with any Germans that were nearby. Jake moved in and attached explosives to the side wall of the Police Station. The destruction of the wall would be a signal for the men to attack the rear of the Police Station. The front was watched by about 50 men and any Germans trying to leave by that means would be gunned down. Jake had placed explosives at the base of the wall as well as up high, that way he was convinced that the whole wall would collapse. He positioned himself with the detonator box further down the alley and well out of the way of the side of the building and he waited for the order to detonate them. Matt gave the signal and Jake pressed the plunger on the detonator box. Not only did it do exactly what he thought would happen it also took away most of the building. There were quite a few Germans inside and they were all killed. The Germans at the rear of the station heard the explosion and started to open fired even though there was no one yet in view. The area at the rear of the station was pounded with mortars from the M19 Maschinengranatwerfer mortars by Matt's men and the uninjured Germans made a hasty retreat into what was left of the building. The mortars also pounded the rear of the building and it was apparent that soon the rear of the building would collapse as well. Suddenly the front door burst open. Initially the Germans inside sent out the guard dogs alone and they had obviously been ordered to attack. These dogs were German and Belgium Shepherd dogs and they were vicious. They had been trained to attack and if they had attacked any man they would have inflicted serious injury to them. It was obviously a ploy thought up by the Officers inside the building. The British men were forced to shoot each dog as they appeared. Six dogs were released. After about 10 minutes the German troops started to try and leave, but they were shot as they attempted it. There was no escape for them. The building was unsafe due to the mortars that were being fired at the rear and if the Germans did not leave it would soon fall around them. The Germans that were left soon recognised that they were surrounded and in danger and if they did not surrender they would be killed. They produced a white flag and waved it about through the front door. Matt, who had made his way to the front of the building, ordered his men to stop firing and he shouted at the Germans to throw their weapons out through the door, which they did. He then told them to come out 5 at a time and to walk straight ahead. Each group of men were searched and made to sit in an adjoining street until the building was empty. They had captured over 75 Germans, who were then escorted over to the airfield.

Matt radioed to Pip to tell him that the Police Station had been taken. All Matt's objectives had now been taken. He wanted to know if anything had been heard from HQ. Pip informed him that Nellie had just heard that the front line was now just 5 miles from Shoreham town and they anticipated that the Germans should be on their doorsteps within 12 hours. If all went according to plan, then the British army should be with them within the next 24 hours.

Thirty men were then told to patrol the streets of Shoreham and Southwick to make sure that they had all the Germans in the area. This took over 2 hours and they now confirmed that the town was back in British hands.

In the meantime, Matt, Johnny, Major Walsh, Sid and Jake went into the church with a map of the Downs and the area and it was pointed out where men were needed to be placed so that they could attack the Germans from the rear when they came into sight. Matt arranged for Major Walsh and Johnny with Sid and Jake as their advisors to take all the men that were not needed at the port, bridge, station or airfield to go to their positions on their Downs. Matt would join them there just as soon as he made sure that everything was in hand at the airport, and at the Cement Works. He also wanted to check up on the injured and the women.

CHAPTER 27

The South Downs from the river Adur to Mile Oak had over 2,000 men, with Johnny and Sid in charge, waiting for the German retreat. They were dug in and they had all the weaponry that Matt and his team had managed to procure. They not only had rifles, grenades, and pistols, they also had machine guns and mortars. They would never be able to fight against tanks, but they would do their best with the equipment they had. There were also 1,000 men on the Downs on the West side of the river, with Major Walsh and Jake in charge. Matt had put 250 men on the road between Shoreham and Bramber. They anticipated that this is where the tanks may try to get through. The men in this area were armed with the M19 mortars, which Matt hoped would damage the tanks if they came. They would certainly give the retreating Germans a surprise. This was happening all the way along the coast with other Auxiliaries and resistance, although not with such large numbers of men. Matt's area was fortunate because of the camp and his ability to have been able to get in contact with them and then to use them. The German retreat was not going to be easy.

Matt had commandeered one of the German's Kubelwagens. He headed first to the airfield where he was joined by a jubilant Colonel Grant and Dave. They had been monitoring the radio and were aware that all the objectives had been taken. They took Matt to the hospital. The local people had bought with them medical supplies which were welcome as the medics had been low on medication. They had also managed to secure all the medical stores at the camp from the Germans. Matt had seen a container which contained medical equipment and stores in the port and he had ordered a couple of his men to load them onto a truck and take it to the airfield. This had arrived and now the medics had a fully functioning and fully equipped hospital. Matt was glad to see all the nurses from the Cement Works, especially Trudy. She welcomed him, but she was busy with the injured men. Matt wanted to know how many had died and how many had been wounded. To date 89 had died and they had nearly 187 wounded. Colonel Grant was pleased with those numbers "It could have been worse," he said. Matt was horrified that so many had been killed but didn't say anything. He spoke to a couple of soldiers and then he recognised a man lying on one of the stretchers in a hallway waiting to be seen by the doctors. It was Jack. He had a bandage round his head and his arm was a real mess.

He went over to where he was laying, "Jack, what the hell happened to you? Are you alright?"

Jack replied, "Sorry about this, but got in the way of a bullet. It bloody hurts."

"Well at least you are alive and in the best place. Trudy will make sure you are looked after. How did it happen?" Matt asked.

"At the port, I went on board that bloody ship and copped a bullet there," he said.

"Haven't you been taught to duck when the shooting begins? Still you look as if you will live. I have to go now, but I'll look in later if I can," Matt said pleased that although his injuries were serious he would live.

"Before you go, are the rest of the team alright?" Jack asked.

"Yes, although I haven't seen Doug for a while. Sid, Jake and Johnny are up on the Downs. Don't worry about them, they will be fine." Although Matt said that, he was not quite sure that he believed it himself. Still Jack would be safe enough here. He said his goodbyes to Jack, had a quick word with Trudy about Jack and she immediately took him in to see the doctors. He then left, and he and Colonel Grant made their way across the camp to the prisoners. He could see that the people in the camp had been busy. They had used the white tents and put them in a cross to indicate a hospital. (They were unable to find any red cloth, so they had to make do with white). This was great as aircraft passing over would realise what it is. He made a mental note for Nellie to radio the change in colour, just in case. The prisoners were mainly sitting outside the huts. The British PoWs had put barbed wire around the area to keep them in and at each corner was a guard suitably armed. In front of the huts and behind the huts were machine guns manned and ready to open fire. There were women walking round the perimeter with rifles slung over their shoulders. When the German prisoners made any comments to them, these women would remove their rifles and aim them at the offender. This shut them up. As Matt was chatting to Colonel Grant about the prisoners, Oberst Baumhauer, who was lording it over his men, went up to the barbed wire fence and spoke to Matt and Colonel Grant. "Are we going to get any food today?"

Matt looked this man up and down. This was the man who had shot Harry and he wanted very much to take out his gun and shoot him in the head. Matt had never felt hate like this before. He just said one word, "NO."

"What do you mean no?" demanded Oberst Baumhauer. "What about the Geneva Convention. We should be fed at least once a day."

At this comment Matt did pulled his gun out of his holster and pointed it at Oberst Baumhauer and said, "If I shoot you then I wouldn't be in breach of any convention, now would I?"

This shut him up, but he said in defiance, "You wouldn't, you are a soldier."

"Can you see my uniform?" Matt asked.

Oberst Baumhauer realised for the first time that the man was dressed as a farm worker. Then he addressed himself to Colonel Grant, "I thought you were the one in charge."

"I am due to my rank, but this man is in charge of what has happened in the area. He is the one that has been a thorn in your side since you came here... uninvited," Colonel Grant said grinning and laughing at the German.

"You!" he said.

"Yes, me, and I must admit I am, at this moment, having trouble controlling my instincts to shoot you in the stomach and let you die a revolting and painful death. You will answer for killing harmless civilians, including women and children, and when they try you for your crimes I am going to bear witness against you. These women you see walking around with rifles have all lost someone because of you and your goons so I suggest that you do as little as you can to annoy them or else you may not live for very long. I do hope I am clear on that point. You will not be fed until all of my men are fed and as we have over 3,000 of them waiting for your retreating army it will be a long wait," Matt said. He was disgusted by this German.

Oberst Baumhauer was speechless. He had no reply for Matt. He just looked at him as if he wanted to etch Matt's face on his mind for a later time. Matt turned around and walked away.

Matt got back in his vehicle and he headed across the Adur Bridge and up to the Cement Works. When he entered the building, he found it empty except for Pip, who was monitoring the field radio and doing a wonderful job, and Nellie, who had been at the shed sending and receiving messages over the radio. This radio needed to be moved to the camp and both Pip and Nellie needed to get over there as well. This place may not be safe once the action on the Downs started. Using the vehicle Matt took Nellie to the radio where he helped her dismantle the aerial and the lead from the electrical supply and put it in the vehicle. He then returned to the Cement Works picked up Pip and took them to the airfield. Colonel Grant gave them the office next to Hauptmann Mencken's office, where they set up the radio and Matt left relieved that Nellie would be relatively safe here. Hauptmann Mencken's office had been sealed for someone to go through the paperwork properly in case there was anything that the intelligence people needed.

Up on the Downs all the men had dug in. When Matt arrived, he was surprised at how many men there were. They seemed to go on forever. He found Johnny and he was told that they could now hear gun fire coming closer, so it wouldn't be too long. Matt had to inform them that a message that Nellie had received from HQ estimated that the Germans should be here within the next 12 hours. Johnny said that he would be pleased to see them as it was really nerve racking just waiting. Matt agreed. Johnny and Matt walked the lines of men, chatting with some of them and having a cigarette with others. They seemed to be excited about the forthcoming battle and as they said, 'kicking the German's arses into the Channel'. Sid came up to him and he asked them if they had seen Doug. They hadn't. Matt wondered where he could be.

Matt realised that the men had not eaten for a long time and as they had a long wait they needed to get some food and drinks for them. He ordered 4 men to go to the port and bring back as much food and drink as they could find in the containers there. They left using the vehicle that Matt had been using.

The waiting was unbearable and even though Matt and the Officers tried to boost the morale of the men, which wasn't really that hard, they were feeling concerned about the forthcoming battle that they knew was coming.

About an hour later 3 trucks and 2 other vehicles arrived on the Downs. In two of the trucks were food and drinks for the men which were immediately distributed. There were chocolate bars, German sausages, biscuits, and fruit. The drinks were mainly water but there were some fizzy drinks on the trucks as well. In the other truck was weaponry that the men had discovered in another container and they bought it up in case it may be needed. There was more ammunition for the rifles and extra mortars. They also found a few flame throwers, Flammenwerfer 35. These were distributed to the men who were proficient in using such weaponry. Behind this truck and the other vehicles were 33.7cm Pak 36 anti-tank guns which they had also found in the port. The men thought that these may be useful if the Germans used tanks against them. In the trucks they had the shells for the guns. They told Matt that there were another six at the port. Matt immediately dispatched the men and two others to collect those guns. He told them to deliver two to Major Walsh on the west side of the Downs and two to the road by the Cement Works. The other two were to be bought to Matt.

Four hours had passed. The Pak 36 anti-tank guns were now all in place with appropriately qualified men to operate them and every one of his men had had something to eat and drink. Some of the men fell asleep whilst others kept watch. Time passed very slowly. Matt and his Officers all tried to speak and pass time with the men. The civilian men were eager to go against the Germans and found it harder than the military men. The military men had been through this before when the invasion had occurred.

Nine hours had passed, and they could now hear firing much closer to their position. Time and time again they saw aircraft fly over them, some headed out over the English Channel and Matt and the men suspected that they were attempting to keep the German shipping at bay. Some of the planes were heading northwards and they were attacking the German lines. They could hear bombs being dropped although they did not see anything yet. This was a dangerous situation. Matt was concerned that they may make a mistake and drop bombs on the British lines, so he radioed Pip on a field radio to tell Nellie to inform HQ who would inform the RAF where exactly Matt's men were and to be careful when dropping bombs. It was apparent that the RAF seemed to know this as a couple of times when they went over they dipped their wings as if to say, 'It's alright lads, we know you are there,' then they went up to the Germans lines and dropped their bombs or strafed the German troops. As each bomb was dropped the men in the line had started to cheer and although they couldn't see the Germans fall they all wished them dead.

Two hours later the men were really getting fidgety when suddenly they saw men on the horizon. Matt shouted, "Here we go lads, do not open fire on them until you get the order, pass it down the line."

Matt then grabbed a man who had a field radio and he spoke to all the men with the radios on the line and told them the same. 'To wait for the order to fire'.

As the men on the horizon got nearer they could see that they were firing at something to the north. Suddenly they could see an aircraft go over and they dropped a bomb onto the line of men coming towards them, then another one strafing the lines of troops. When the aircraft appeared, the men fell to the ground. Matt radioed Pip to inform them that the German line was less than half a mile from them and to inform the RAF of their position again.

The line of German soldiers was getting closer. Matt, Johnny, and Sid, in the east, and Major Walsh and Jake, in the west, got into one of the dugout holes and Matt, using his binoculars, could see now that they had many Germans in front of them and beyond them was a line of British soldiers, but the British soldiers were well over a mile away. Matt was holding his breath. These Germans needed to be a little closer, just a little bit more and then he shouted out "Fire" and all the men in his line started firing. The noise was earth shattering. The smell of cordite was foul, but the Germans fell to the ground. They had no cover and it was like shooting ducks at a fairground. The Officers were stunned, they did not know where the shooting had come from and they did not know which way their troops should fire. The British army was north of them but who was behind them, to the south. They did not know. Matt ordered them to continue firing. The machine guns were red hot and the operators were burning their hands firing them. The M19 mortars were achieving their goals and they were landing right in the middle of the lines. During the height of the battle Johnny who was manning the radio reported that German tanks were coming at them from the right flank. Matt ordered that the Pak 36 anti-tank guns fire in the direction they were coming from. This they did and after a couple of misses they started hitting their target, not every time, but they were improving with each shell. Matt didn't know if it was beginners luck, he really didn't care, so long as they were taking out those bastard machines. Suddenly an aircraft went over, it was a Spitfire. They were firing on the tanks and they managed to disable another one. The odds were in the British favour. The battle raged, and the Germans fought like devils possessed. The German soldiers were now close enough for flamethrowers to be used and this forced many of the German soldiers back towards the British army that was just behind them. Three hours it continued. The smell of the battle was intoxicating. There had been a few injured men, but Matt was surprised at how few there were. He was greatly relieved by this. He did see a couple of his men had been hit by bullets and he was astounded by how much blood could be lost from a wound. Matt felt all the hurt of his injured men, but he had to continue. All his men were bravely doing their 'bit'. The medics were getting the wounded to safety using anything, from their own coats as make shift stretchers, to physically pulling the injured away from the action. Matt was proud of them all.

At one stage during the battle the road by the River Adur came under fire from a Panzer division of tanks that were trying to get through. They had many Germans on foot walking behind the tanks. The anti-tank guns which were situated on high ground above the road started and relentlessly pounded the tanks. The tanks retaliated and took out one of the guns, but the damage that the other anti-tank guns were doing was horrendous. Matt was informed that the road area was being badly attacked and he instructed one of his anti-tank guns on the Downs to be moved so it was able to fire onto the tanks on the road. This was a success and they were able to destroy 5 tanks and the M19 mortars were being fired at these Germans on the road helped to immobilise others. The overhead aircraft also assisted and eventually the whole road was blocked with disabled tanks. The troops walking behind them were mowed down by machine gun fire and they were also forced to retreat towards the British army.

The battle continued, and Matt could see that many Germans were injured or killed but still they fought on. Although they were being attacked by the British army and from the rear by Matt's men, this did not seem to make any difference to them. They fought gallantly. What surprised Matt was the amount of men the Germans had, and they knew that they were not just fighting in this area, but all along the coast. Nellie had been informed by HQ that the battle was as fierce in other parts of Southern England. Matt's men were firing at targets that were moving and were hitting a good majority of them. The mortars were being fired towards the centre of their lines and the machine guns were not allowing the forward men to stand up or move in any direction. This continued for ages and Matt was certain that they were winning.

Matt, along with his officers, noticed that there was silence from the German ranks and it was apparent that they were not firing at the English any more. Matt was uncertain if this was a ruse or whether they had given up. Because of his, he did not order his men to cease fire. The firing from his ranks was sporadic as if the men were uncertain about what they should do. Suddenly they saw that Germans were walking towards them with their arms in the air.

"They are surrendering," shouted Sid.

And down the radio Matt heard Jakes voice shout, "Bloody hell, we have done it, they're giving up."

"Cease fire," Matt shouted and then shouted it again. He told Johnny to radio all positions to do the same. The silence after all that noise was deafening. The Germans came towards them, some of them throwing their rifles, ammunition and grenades on to the ground as they came. The British cautiously moved to meet them with their rifles at the ready, but it was apparent that the Germans were tired of fighting. The Germans were made to sit in front of them whilst the British men removed all their remaining weaponry from them. There seemed to be hundreds of them. They all looked dirty and were exhausted. Matt believed that they were relieved to stop fighting. From behind the Germans, Matt could see another line of men on the horizon. He began to get worried. He was just about to order all his men back in their dug outs when Sid, who was using a pair of binocular said, "They are ours. They are the British army."

And with that a great cheer went up from all the men. The British troops arrived and were surprised to see the army they had been fighting for so long sitting cross legged on the ground. A man in a General's uniform approached a couple of them and asked them who their commanding officer was. They pointed at Matt. He approached Matt and said in a very military way, "Whom am I addressing?"

Matt stood up straight, tried to do an acceptable salute, and said, "Sir, I am Major Fletcher from the Auxiliary Home Guard."

"The Auxiliaries. You are the ones that have been behind enemy lines since the beginning of the invasion?" he asked.

"Yes sir," replied Matt.

"Good show and this is spectacular. You will get a medal for this," the General said.

"Thank you Sir, but it was both the PoW's and the civilian men that helped to achieve this," indicating the sitting Germans. "We have taken the port and the town, and we have in custody the bastard who ran the area. They are at present being held at the airport which is also our makeshift hospital. Oh yes and we have Edward and Wallace in custody," Matt said.

"It was you that did that. My god that's absolutely bloody marvellous," the General enthused. "Who is your commanding officer?"

"Colonel Armstrong. I have been in touch with him and he is fully aware of everything. I suspect that as soon as the whole of this area is secure he will be down to see me," Matt said.

"Good show, good show," said the General. He then hit Matt on the back and headed back to his men who were chatting with Matt's men.

The Germans were told to get up and they were marched over to the airport. It was becoming full up because of the number of prisoners they now had, but Matt had no doubt that Colonel Grant would manage, and he had help from the General who Matt had taken over to the airport. Afterwards Matt met up with Johnny and Sid who had previously met up with Major Walsh and Jake and they dismissed the civilian men after congratulating them on a wonderful job that they did. They then told all the military men to report to Colonel Grant at the airport. They would then be dismissed by him, but before they went he managed to tell them how proud he had been to fight alongside them.

The British Army immediately took over the port and the RAF, although had been continually patrolling the English Channel, immediately headed there en mass to locate any German shipping that had been sent to try and get their army back to Europe. Spitfires and Bombers were seen over the English Channel over the next couple of weeks to ensure that there was no further threat from German shipping. The Royal Navy managed to get a foothold in the Channel as well and although there was still a threat from the U-boats, their sonar was able to detect their presence and the ships used depth charges to destroy them.

The British civilians were in vibrant form the night after the battle. They had opened nearly all the local pubs and Clubs and they were all full, not only with locals but with the army lads. Doug had still not been located and Matt had arranged with the hospital and with the mortuary people to look out for him. There was nothing he could do about him as it was still a bit of a muddle in the area. Matt and his team except Jack decided to celebrate their victory and they went down to the Crabtree Pub. When they entered, they not only found Jo working behind the bar, but Bert sitting in his normal place, but the whole place was full of locals and army alike. The beer was flowing, and the place was in a jubilant mood. When Matt and his team arrived, a massive cheer went up. Drinks were bought for them and they joined Bert in his corner. They had a brilliant evening and they all got very drunk. That night Bert invited them to stay at his house and this was the first time in nearly 8 months that they all slept in a house and in a bed.

CHAPTER 28

The next week was hectic. The British army liberated the whole of the South Coast and towns like Shoreham became home to thousands of men. The civilians that had moved to the airport returned to their homes, opened their business and started to resume their lives. One thing that the locals did was to round up the known collaborators. The majority were held and would be put on trial for their actions, but occasionally a group of locals would find a particular person who had informed and caused death to civilians and would wreak vengeance on them. If these collaborators were women, they shaved their hair and if they were men they were killed. It was a very volatile period. The army was forced to put out patrols to prevent revenge attacks from occurring.

The airport was transferred from being a PoW camp for British soldiers into being a PoW camp for the Germans. The tunnel that Matt and his men used to get in was locked up and there was no chance of any of the Germans getting out. The German Officers were going to be moved to prisons in London as there were going to be inquiries into their actions during the occupation. Some of the non-commissioned men were going to stay at Shoreham Airport for the time being, but some were going to be moved immediately to other camps that had been set up further north. Shoreham Airport was going to be needed as the war in Europe was continuing but the relocation of the Germans would take some time. This was because new camps had to be set up. Once this happened then the remainder of the Germans would go to them. The injured in the camp were moved to the hospital in Shoreham, which was re-opened to accommodate them.

Doug had been located. He had been killed during the taking of the port. Matt was sad as he loved that man. He decided that he would visit his parents when things died down and tell them what a wonderful and brave man Doug was. Sid and Jake came out of the battle unharmed and Jack recovered very quickly. His wounded arm was in a sling and he had a bandage over his head, but he was fine. Johnny was also unharmed, and Pip was recovering from the beating, especially now that Britain had been liberated. He did have the help of the lovely Gillian who had nursed him when he was in the Cement Works. Father Andrew had done a wonderful job getting many people to the airport with the aid of the nurses but now he had returned to his church and helped not only the locals but the British soldiers who were far from home and in need of spiritual guidance. He also went over to the camp regularly to administer to the Germans and said that he would continue until they moved away. He was aware that the German men in the camp had lost many of their fellow troops during the battles that they had been in, over the last 8 months and some were really traumatised by it.

Trudy went to the hospital in Shoreham with her nurses and continued to work there until they were reassigned. Nellie went home to her boys. She found Cora in good voice and full of stories about the German retreat. Apparently, Cora and Howard had to hide in a cellar on Frank's farm and she had heard much of the fighting that had happened above them. Howard, however, was quite sad, as he had enjoyed looking after the boys so much that now he would miss the work, so Nellie offered him a job as a stable hand, which he jumped at. Matt visited Nellie only once in that week, but she was aware that he was busy and would be round as soon as he could make it. Bert, who was still quite traumatised from the beating he had from the Germans and the death of his beloved wife, took up his old job at the station, but decided that he would only work part time and only until they had the trains running properly and the tracks rebuilt. Jo continued looking after his bar.

Colonel Armstrong and Major Taylor appeared at the airport looking for Matt the day after the Germans surrendered. They found him helping to move the injured. They went into an office in the terminal building and they sat him down.

"Well my lad, what a fantastic job you have done here. We have already had reports from General Aimes about you and your men forcing the surrender. We have also had a report from Colonel Grant on your superb leadership abilities and the work that you did for the men in the camp, you know keeping up moral and keeping them informed about what was happening in the outside world. We hear that you lost 2 of your original men and one of the men who you recruited from the camp, I am sorry, but then none of you should have survived. Other areas lost all their men and their Officer in Charge, so you did exceptionally well. Look Matt, I can call you that?" Matt nodded, "You have done a fantastic job and you have been put up for a medal as well as your men. Private Harry Smith, Private Doug Harris and Private Steve Crane will be awarded it posthumously. You by the way have also been given a field promotion to Colonel," Colonel Armstrong said proudly.

"Pardon, did you say Colonel?" Matt asked. Matt was astonished by this and did not know what to say so said, "Thank you sir."

"Well you deserve it. You and your men need to be debriefed and I will need you to come to Tottington Manor for that to happen. I will need all your team to come with you," said the Colonel.

"Sir, I have some things to deal with. I need to hand over Edward and Wallace and then I can release the people who are looking after them," he said.

"My God, I nearly forgot about them. Yes, Winnie wants them in London and he wants to meet you and your team. I will arrange transport. Can you and your team be ready tomorrow? You will have to act as guards for them on the way to London," the Colonel said.

"Of course, do you want my present team Sergeant Sid Carpenter, Corporal Jack Wilson, Private Jake Jolly, Private Pip Crumpton and Major Johnny Jackson or just the original ones?" asked Matt

"No all of them should come with you," he said.

"I will round them up and we will be ready tomorrow," Matt said.

"Shall we say 1000 hours, here and then you can pick up their Royal Highnesses and the debriefing will take place in 3 days, shall we say 1100 hours at the Manor?"

"That will be fine sir," Matt said.

"Good show Colonel Fletcher. By the way, I need all of you in uniform tomorrow. I have some in the car. They are of various sizes and ranks. I hope they fit."

Matt nodded, and he followed Colonel Armstrong and Major Taylor to the car, where he took hold of a packing case full of clothes. He shook hands with them both and they got back into the car and left.

The following morning at exactly 1000 hours, 2 cars arrived. They were Bentleys and they were the height of luxury. All the men were suitably dressed in uniforms and Matt, in his one showing the insignia of a Colonel, much to the delight of his men, got into them and they showed the drivers the way to Coombehead Woods. The team looking after Edward and Wallace were expecting them. They had informed Edward and Wallace that the Germans had been defeated and that they were going to be transported to London. When Matt arrived, he saw two defeated people. They were quiet and withdrawn. If he hadn't disliked them so much he would have felt sorry for them. Edward and Wallace left the bunker for the first time in over 3 months and they had their hands tied up in front of them. They were escorted down to the Bentleys where Matt put Sid and Jake in with Edward and Wallace. Matt did not want to be stuck with them all the way to London. The rest of the team travelled in the second Bentley with him. They set off. It took them nearly 2 hours to get to London. They were all astonished at the damage that had been done to many of the historical buildings and to houses in ordinary streets. The fighting must have been fierce. They passed the Houses of Parliament and saw that part of the building had been destroyed. They were very surprised to see Westminster Abbey completely intact. Not even so much as a bullet hole. Matt thought this reminded him of the church in Shoreham. How can there be so much damage to surrounding buildings and yet the church was not touched. Perhaps God kept it safe! They passed statues that had been toppled and they saw areas that had many tents in them. They were told these were for the civilians that had lost their homes. It was going to take a lot to get this town back into some semblance of order again.

They were to meet with Winston Churchill at the War Office in Whitehall. They arrived there at 1230 hours and were surprised to discover that the media were there. They were there because Winston was in the building and apparently, they follow him wherever he went in London. They were very shocked to discover the occupants of the Bentleys were Edward and Wallace and the atmosphere became very hostile. Matt was concerned that not only Edward and Wallace, but his men, could be hurt. They rushed the royal couple inside, pushing the media men and women to one side as they passed and once inside they were greeted by someone who called himself a secretary to the Prime Minister. They were led up some very grand looking stairs and they were showed into a room which had a very impressive fire place. The furniture and curtains were stunning. They were told to wait, and the secretary left. The men stood in the middle of the room not knowing if they should sit down to wait or whether they should stand in case they ruined the fantastic surroundings. Edward and Wallace went over to a couch and sat on it. They looked wretched. The door to the room opened and in walked Winston Churchill accompanied by 4 men. He ignored the men and went over to Edward and Wallace and without any formality said, "You two should be ashamed of yourselves. You are a disgrace and you should thank God that you are still alive. I can assure you that it will not be for long. You are to be tried at a public trial and I will make sure that you both hang as traitors. Your family do not want to speak or hear from you and you have both been stripped of your titles." He then turned to a couple of men who came in the room with him and he nodded at them. These men went up to Edward and Wallace and roughly took hold of their arms and led them out of the room. The door closed, and Winston Churchill then turned to Matt and said, "Colonel Fletcher. How nice to meet you? I do hope that you and your men will join me and the King and Queen, as well as the Princesses for lunch." Matt was taken back with this invitation.

"Of course Sir, we will be delighted," Matt said completely bemused by this.

"Good, now come on, we are going to the Palace. His Majesty George VI and Queen Elizabeth, oh and let's not forget his lovely daughters are looking forward to speaking with you all. What a marvellous job you all did," Winston said.

For a large man he moved very quickly. He left the room, followed by Matt and his men and they went back down to the Bentleys. The press people were still there, and their numbers had grown. News that Edward and Wallace were in the building had obviously got around. As Winston passed them he was bombarded with questions. He completely ignored them all and got into one of the Bentleys. Matt and his men got into them and they went to Buckingham Palace. The Palace had been damaged in places, but it was liveable. They lunched with the King, Queen and Princesses and of course the Prime Minister.

The King was particularly interested in the bunkers and how they managed for such a long time in those conditions. He also wanted to know how they managed being behind enemy lines. He commented about how many of the Auxiliaries had died. Matt and his men answered all his questions as best as they could. He also wanted to know about the battle that ended the occupation.

The King and Winston were truly interested in what everyone had to say. The King and Queen talked about the day they had to leave London and how distressing it was for them. They wanted to know how the people in Southern England faired under the Nazi rule and discussed about visiting the various areas as soon as they could. Matt, during the meal, asked Winston Churchill, what would happen to Edward and Wallace and where would they be kept. He told him that they would be kept at a special house that had been set up in Hertfordshire. They would be guarded day and night until they were bought to trial. The trial would take place at the Old Bailey and they would be charged with Treason. This did carry the death penalty, especially as it occurred at a time of war. The King was listening to this and he said, "I hope they rot in hell. He abdicated for that woman and he made me take over. I didn't want that. I was not bought up to it, he was. I personally think that hanging is too good for them; still, we will see what the good people of the country will do with them. One thing is for sure, they will never step inside any of our palaces again and no one will ever hear a word from them again."

Matt was surprised at the anger and contempt in the Kings voice when he spoke of them. Edward was, after all, his brother, but he supposed that they had been very hurt by what Edward and Wallace had done, not only with the abdication but with siding with the enemy. The King had gone very red in the face and The Queen who had sat very quietly when they spoke of Edward and Wallace said in a very dignified manner, as if she was trying to calm her husband down, "Bertie, I think that we shouldn't be so angry now. I believe, as you rightly said, that the people will do the right thing and we will never have to see them again. I think that we should just forget about them. We have our whole country back and the people are wonderful." The King nodded and said, "Yes, quite right my dear, quite right"

At the end of the meal all the men were taken into another room where they were all lined up. Standing in front of them was The King and Queen and Winston and to one side were the Princesses. The King presented each of them with the Military Medal for bravery. They also had three medals for Harry, Steve and Doug and they were told that they would be given to their families posthumously later. Matt was speechless, but his men made up for this, as they were so excited that they wouldn't keep quiet. The whole day was amazing and on the return to the south coast, still in a Bentley, they talked incessantly about the it.

Two days later they all reported to Tottington Manor. They were let in by Mrs Johns and were shown into the lounge. There, waiting for them, was Colonel Armstrong, Major Taylor and 4 other men who were introduced as men from Army intelligence. They were all taken individually into different rooms and they were interviewed regarding what had occurred during their time behind enemy lines. These interviews continued for the next 24 hours. They were allowed to have an 8 hour break to sleep and meal breaks but the interviews were intensive and needed as evidence for when various Germans were bought to trial. At the end of these interviews, the 4 men from army intelligence, who were conducting the interviews, left, and Colonel Armstrong and Major Taylor hosted a meal for the men.

They were a jovial crowd and they had a jolly good time. Matt needed to go to the toilet so left the table. When he was returning he bumped into Mrs Johns in the hallway.

"Can I have a word," said Mrs Johns.

"Of course," replied Matt.

"In the kitchen," said Mrs Johns. Matt looked puzzled but followed her into the kitchen.

In the kitchen Matt asked, "What is the matter, Mrs Johns?"

"Nothing, it's just that yesterday I went over to Nellie's to make sure that she was getting on alright and she told me about what had happened during the last 8 months. She is a lovely girl and I am very fond of her. In fact, since her mother died, I have tried to look out for her, you know what I mean?" said Mrs Johns.

"Yes, but…," Matt started.

"No don't interrupt me. Let me finish. She told me how you looked after her and how you have a sort of relationship growing. Well I want to thank you for looking after her and keeping her safe. She can be a bit enthusiastic and I must admit when I asked her to be a courier and radio operator I did think twice about it, but from the reports that I got from her trainers she was a natural. I worried about her constantly and when I heard that her radio room had been found I was frantic. Anyway, what I am trying to say is that because of you and your men making sure that she came to no harm, I am truly thankful. You have my blessing as the closest thing Nellie has to a mother, if you want to continue with a relationship with her, yes… you have my consent. And just a final thing, I believe that if Nellie's mother was alive today, she would have approved of you," Mrs Johns said.

"I don't know what to say, but Mrs Johns…," Matt was interrupted again.

"Call me Mavis."

"Right, Mavis I do hope to see Nellie again. I will always treat her with respect. She is a fantastic person with depths to her personality I think you know about. She is wonderful, brave, witty and intelligent. I could not wish for anyone better, so I do hope that we will see each other again and soon," Matt told her.

"Thank you for saying that. I do hope that you will both come over for supper soon. I will get in touch with her and arrange it," Mrs Johns said.

"Thank you, now I must get back to lunch or else they may think that I got lost going to the toilet," Matt laughed.

He went back into the dining room and continued his lunch.

After lunch, Johnny asked Colonel Armstrong, "Sir, do you know what we will be assigned to now?"

"Johnny this is something that we need to discuss with you and Matt, but we want to speak with the Prime Minister first to confirm what he wants, so you will all be asked back here later. But in the meantime, I think that you all deserve some rest and relaxation. How about 2 weeks off and then report back here," he said.

Everyone left happy and looking forward to the time off. They all had their plans. Sid, Jake and Jack were all going to go home and see their parents. Johnny wanted to go back to his regiment to make sure that his men were well, and he wanted to see his girlfriend who was in London. He hadn't heard from her and he wanted to find out if she was safe after having the Germans camped out on her doorstep, as he called it. Pip was going to see his parents and then he wanted to return to Shoreham to see Gillian. Matt was going to see his parents for a couple of days and then he was going to see Doug, Harry and Steve's parents to tell them what had happened to their sons and to tell them how brave they all were. He then wanted to return and spend as much time as he could with Nellie.

Matt walked up to Nellie's house. He had not seen her for over a week and he was nervous about seeing her. It was mid-morning and the sun was shining. He could see behind the house the paddocks and fields bathing in the sunlight and in the distance, he could see the Downs in all their glory. There were still signs of scorching on the Downs, but with the sun shining on them they still looked wondrous to him. It was a fabulous setting. He knocked on the door but there was no reply. He knocked again. He turned and went to the stable yard. He entered the gate and he could see a man with one of Nellies horses, not Madison, her other one called Barnaby.
"Hello," shouted Matt.
The man turned around and said, "Hi there."
"Where's Nellie?"
"She is in the office," he said.
"Thank you."
Matt walked past the man and the horse and entered the stables. He could see Madison in one of the stalls. He turned towards the office but

couldn't see anyone inside. He entered, and he stood there looking around. No one was in there. The wall of the office had been rebuilt and he wondered if Nellie had kept the secret room. He went over to the peg on the wall and he turned it. The door in the wall clicked open. He opened the door fully and entered. There sitting at the desk was Nellie. She looked radiant. The fresh air of the last couple of weeks had put colour in her face and her hair was hanging loose down her back.

"You took your time," said Nellie.

"What do you mean?" asked Matt.

"To get from the house to here. Look my light is on and you have kept me waiting for 5 minutes," Nellie laughed.

"Oh, I thought…," Nellie stood up and kissed Matt passionately. They stood kissing for ages and when they eventually released each other Matt said, "What are you doing in here anyway?"

"I had the wall rebuilt and I thought that it would be a good place to keep. I come in here occasionally and think about what we have been through. Only you, your men and the nurses know exactly what we did and how we did it. It was amazing really and now I just sit in here and think of the close shave I had and how you were my knight in shining armour," she said.

"You are silly, amazing, but silly. Come on, let's go to the house," Matt said heading for the door.

They left the room and the stable. As they went through the stable yard they passed the man grooming the horse.

"Howard, is Barnaby doing alright?" she asked.

"Absolutely now you are back. They both missed you," he said.

"I know," Nellie replied.

Nellie and Matt went into the house and they stayed there for 2 days. They made love and they ate beautiful fresh meals and then they made love again. They were both falling head over heels in love with each other. On the third day they emerged from the house and they took Madison and Barnaby out for a ride. They went up their bridle path and then up onto the South Downs. There was a lot of evidence of the battle that had taken place up there. There were large craters in the landscape and there was scorching to the ground, which was quite severe in places. The farmers had put some of their livestock up on the Downs to encourage the ravaged earth to be restored back to its original state. Rural Britain was starting to get back to normal. They went down to South Downs Farm and spoke to Bill Bolt who was now getting his farm up and running properly now the Germans had gone and was even beginning to prepare his fields, so he could start growing crops again. He offered them a drink, which they refused. They then went into the woods and Matt showed Nellie the entrance to the bunker. Amazingly after all the time she had been a courier and then all the time she had spent in the Cement Works she did not know exactly where Matt had been living. Of course, it had been demolished so she couldn't go down it. They then went to the Cement Works and they went in. There was nothing left inside other than the make shift beds, but they bumped into a man who worked for the Cement Works who told them the company were returning and resuming their operations. He wanted to know if Matt and Nellie knew who all the stuff in the storage area belonged to. Matt and Nellie looked at each other and said they didn't have a clue who it belonged to and then started to laugh. The man looked at each of them and then shrugged his shoulders, turned and left.

Matt and Nellie went into Shoreham that night and they found a little restaurant that was open, and they eat there. The food was not brilliant, in fact it was really a workman's café, but during the evening the owner put table clothes on the tables and they were able to have a beer or wine with their meal.

Half way through the meal Matt said, "Nellie, when we were holed up in the Cement Works I vowed to myself that when the Germans left I would take you out for a slap-up meal. Well this is it, but I am sorry it is not better."

"It is lovely. Look I have been living off army rations for so long that any meal out is a luxury," Nellie said.

"Thank you for that. I also promised myself that when the Germans left I wanted to say something," Matt was having a problem finding the right words but continued, "Nellie, would you do me the honour of becoming my wife?"

Nellie was beaming with love and happiness. She reached over, and she kissed Matt.

"Well say something," said Matt.

"Yes, yes of course I will. I love you so much," said Nellie.

Matt reached into his pocket and he pulled out a small leather case. He opened it and removed a beautiful gold ring with a single small diamond. He held Nellie's hand and he placed the ring on her third finger of her left hand. It fitted perfectly. Nellie looked at the ring and smiled

"It is beautiful."

"Just like you" said Matt?

He had managed to find a jeweller that was open near to his mother and father's home when he last visited, and he bought the ring there, and had had it on him since then.

They finished the meal and then they went to the Crabtree Pub. Jo and Bert were there and when they told them that they had just got engaged, Jo went down into his cellar and he came up with a large bottle of Champagne, which he had had hidden since the war began, and they all drank Nellie and Matt's health.

The following day Cora came over to the house and was told of the engagement and she was thrilled about the news. Mavis was informed by phone and she appeared later in the day with another bottle of Champagne. Cora and Howard came over and they had a spur-of-the-moment party, where they all got rather drunk.

Matt stayed with Nellie until he had to report at Tottington Manor. It was a bit of a reunion as his team were all there. Matt told them that he had asked Nellie to marry him and she had agreed. They all congratulated him and they all wanted to have a celebration drink at the Crabtree Pub that evening. Before any celebration drink they were to be told what their new assignments were to be.

Colonel Armstrong was in the lounge with Major Taylor and another man who was introduced to them as Mr Carnegie. They were not told who he was or why he was there. They were all invited to sit down, and Colonel Armstrong stood by the fire and started to speak.

"Men, Winston Churchill was so impressed with you and what you achieved, and the debriefing team were astounded by your work and how you managed to last for the amount of time that you did. Everyone was impressed with your planning and the execution of your missions, especially you Matt, with the plans that you devised for the final battle. We do not have many people with your abilities and therefore we want to use them to the full. We have just had authorisation from Winston that a new department will be created for operatives to work behind enemy lines. We need people like you to go to France and other invaded countries and to work with resistance groups and liaise between them and us here in England. We also need other operatives to be trained. So, your new assignment is the training of operatives to work behind enemy lines and even to go yourselves if need be. The new department will be called the 'Special Operations Executive' and you will be the people to make it work. Matt you will be working with Mr Carnegie, who is in direct contact with Winston and we will be setting up a training centre at Beaulieu House in Hampshire. There will be other training centres set up around the country, but Beaulieu will be the first. You will devise training programs that will cover use of firearms, unarmed combat, communications, planning of missions, stealth, and any other things that you can think of to cover. You are the experts now and I trust that you will succeed as this is how we are going to win this war."

Matt and his men were surprised with being offered this assignment. They thought that they would be assigned to a regiment and would be going over to France when the time came, fighting the Germans head on. They all agreed, and they were told to report to Beaulieu House in five days. This would be the start of a new chapter in their lives. The old one where they didn't anticipate living past 14 days was now over.

THE END

EPILOGUE

This story is made up and of course the Germans never invaded this country. It was mainly due to the work of the Royal Air Force. They won the battle of Britain and even though they lost many pilots, they fought an amazing war. The British people put up with a lot during the war years, but they never had to tolerate an invading force, unlike the civilian people in Europe. No doubt, if they had been invaded, they would have done as much as possible to repel the invaders.

This story is a fictional story about a group of men called the Auxiliary Home Guards who stayed behind enemy lines and fought them, but in reality, men had been picked and trained to do just that. These units really existed but they, of course, were not needed, but were there just in case. They knew that their life expectancy was going to be 14 days because that was how much food, that the bunkers where they were going to be holed up in, had, and the commanding Officers anticipated that once they had to go out to get more food they would be captured and killed. These men were brave although they never had to do what they were trained to do. They were there in case an invasion occurred.

The characters in this story are not based on any person living or dead apart from the Duke and Duchess of Windsor. They were known to have German sympathies but there is no evidence that they would have collaborated with the Germans in the way described in this novel. William Joyce, Lord Haw Haw, did exist and was tried and executed for treason after the war. The town and port of Shoreham are on the south coast of England, but the author has made a few changes to the layout of the town and its bridges to fit in with the story. Coleshill House has a website which may be of interest the readers.

In other countries resistance groups were set up to fight the Germans and they had a modicum of success. They were ordinary people who wanted to fight the Germans and help remove them for their country. They had to have assistance from people who were co-ordinating the war and people from Britain were sent to assist them. They would have to have knowledge of how to work behind enemy lines. The Auxiliaries were only given the basic of training, they had no direct knowledge of military tactics on how Germans thought or reasoned. They were like the resistance groups all over Europe. The main difference between the resistance groups and the Auxiliaries were that they were set up in advance. If Britain had been invaded they would have been deployed. These men were as brave as any fighting soldier even though they were never used in these circumstances.

This novel was inspired by a book called 'The Secret Sussex Resistance' by Stewart Angell published by Middleton Press 1996.

OTHER BOOKS BY

JENNIFER M. CARR

RANK CONSPIRACY

NOBLESS OBLIGE

AIM AT THE TARGET

ELIMINATION

OBADIAS – SERVANT OF GOD

THE BRITISH AGENT

UNTIL WAR ENDS

WHEN THE BUBBLE BURST

WHO CAN THEY TRUST

THE LEGACY

Printed in Great Britain
by Amazon